Sister

Rosamund Lupton

piatkus

PIATKUS

First published in Great Britain as a paperback original in 2010 by Piatkus

A CIP catalogue record for this book
is available from the British Library.

ISBN 978-0-7499-4201-4

Typeset in Goudy by Palimpsest Book Production Limited,
Falkirk, Stirlingshire
Printed and bound in Great Britain by
Clays Ltd, St Ives plc

Papers used by Piatkus are natural, renewable and recyclable
products sourced from well-managed forests and certified
in accordance with the rules of the Forest Stewardship Council.

Mixed Sources
Product group from well-managed
forests and other controlled sources
www.fsc.org Cert no. SGS-COC-004081
© 1996 Forest Stewardship Council

Piatkus
An imprint of
Little, Brown Book Group
100 Victoria Embankment
London EC4Y 0DY

An Hachette UK Company
www.hachette.co.uk

www.piatkus.co.uk

To my parents, Kit and Jane Orde-Powlett, for their life-long gift of encouragement.

And to Martin, my husband, with my love.

Rosamund Lupton has worked for many years as a scriptwriter. She lives with her husband and two sons in London. This is her first novel.

'Where shall we see a better daughter or a kinder sister or a truer friend?'

Jane Austen, *Emma*

'But flowers distill'd, though they with winter meet
Leese but their show, their substance still lives sweet.'

Shakespeare, *Sonnet 5*

1

Sunday evening

Dearest Tess,

I'd do anything to be with you, right now, right this moment, so I could hold your hand, look at your face, listen to your voice. How can touching and seeing and hearing – all those sensory receptors and optic nerves and vibrating eardrums – be substituted by a letter? But we've managed to use words as go-betweens before, haven't we? When I went off to boarding school and we had to replace games and laughter and low-voiced confidences for letters to each other. I can't remember what I said in my first letter, just that I used a jigsaw, broken up, to avoid the prying eyes of my house-mistress. (I guessed correctly that her jigsaw-making inner child had left years ago.) But I remember word for word your seven-year-old reply to my fragmented homesickness and that your writing was invisible until I shone a torch onto the paper. Ever since kindness has smelled of lemons.

The journalists would like that little story, marking me out as a kind of lemon-juice detective even as a child and showing how close we have always been as sisters. They're outside your flat now, actually, with their camera crews and sound technicians (faces sweaty, jackets grimy, cables trailing down the steps and getting tangled up in the railings). Yes, that was a little throwaway, but how else to tell you? I'm not sure what you'll make of becoming a celebrity, of sorts, but suspect you'll find it a little funny. Ha-ha funny and weird funny. I can only find it weird funny, but then I've never shared your sense of humour, have I?

'But you've been gated, it's serious,' I said. 'Next time you'll be expelled for definite and Mum's got enough on her plate.'

You'd been caught smuggling your rabbit into school. I was so very much the older sister.

'But it's a little funny too, isn't it, Bee?' you asked, your lips pursed trying not to let the laughter out, reminding me of a bottle of Lucozade with giggle bubbles rising, bound to escape with fizzing and popping on the surface.

Just thinking of your laughter gives me courage and I go to the window.

Outside, I recognise a reporter from a satellite news channel. I am used to seeing his face flattened into 2D on a plasma screen in the privacy of my New York apartment, but here he is large as life and in 3D flesh standing in Chepstow Road and looking straight back at me through your basement window. My finger itches for the off button on the remote; instead I pull the curtains.

But it's worse now than when I could see them. Their lights glare through the curtains, their sounds pound against the windows and walls. Their presence feels like a weight that could bulldoze its way into your sitting room. No wonder the press are called the press, if this goes on much longer I could suffocate. Yes, OK, that was a little dramatic, you'd probably be out there offering them coffee. But as you know, I am easily annoyed and too precious about my personal space. I shall go into the kitchen and try to get on top of the situation.

It's more peaceful in here, giving me the quiet to think. It's funny what surprises me now; often it's the smallest things. For instance, yesterday a paper had a story on how close we have always been as sisters and didn't even mention the difference in our age. Maybe it doesn't matter any more now that we're grown up but as children it seemed so glaring. 'Five years is a big gap . . . ?' people would say who didn't know, a slight rise at the end of their sentence to frame it as a question. And we'd both think of Leo and the gap he left, though maybe gaping void would be more accurate, but we didn't ever say, did we?

The other side of the back door I can just hear a journalist on her mobile. She must be dictating to someone down the phone, my own name jumps out at me, 'Arabella Beatrice Hemming'. Mum said no one has ever called me by my first name so I've always assumed that even as a baby they could tell I wasn't an Arabella, a name with loops and flourishes in black-inked calligraphy; a name that contains within it girls called Bella or Bells or Belle – so many beautiful possibilities. No, from the start I was clearly a Beatrice, sensible and unembellished in Times New Roman, with no one hiding inside. Dad chose the name Arabella before I was born. The reality must have been a disappointment.

The journalist comes within earshot again, on a new call I think, apologising for working late. It takes me a moment before I realise that I, Arabella Beatrice Hemming, am the reason for it. My impulse is to go out and say sorry, but then you know me, always the first to hurry to the kitchen the moment Mum started her tom-tom anger signal by clattering pans. The journalist moves away. I can't hear her words but I listen to her tone, appeasing, a little defensive, treading delicately. Her voice suddenly changes. She must be talking to her child. Her tone seeps through the door and windows, warming your flat.

Maybe I should be considerate and tell her to go home. Your case is subjudice so I'm not allowed to tell them anything till after the trial. But she, like the others, already knows this. They're not trying to get facts about you but emotions. They want me to clench my hands together, giving them a close-up of white knuckles. They want to see a few tears escaping and gliding snail-like down my cheek leaving black mascara trails. So I stay inside.

The reporters and their entourage of technicians have all finally left, leaving a high tide mark of cigarette ash on the steps down to your flat, the butts stubbed out in your pots of daffodils. Tomorrow I'll put out ashtrays. Actually, I misjudged some of them. Three apologised for intruding and a cameraman even gave me some chrysanthemums from the corner shop. I know you've never liked them.

'But they're school-uniform maroon or autumnal browns, even in spring,' you said, smiling, teasing me for valuing a flower for its neatness and longevity.

'Often they're really bright colours,' I said, not smiling.

'Garish. Bred to be spotted over acres of concrete in garage forecourts.'

But these wilting examples are stems of unexpected thoughtfulness, a bunch of compassion as surprising as cowslips on the verge of a motorway.

4

The chrysanthemum cameraman told me that this evening the *News at 10* is running a 'special' on your story. I just phoned Mum to tell her. I think in a strange mum-like way she's actually proud of how much attention you're getting. And there's going to be more. According to one of the sound technicians there'll be foreign media here tomorrow. It's funny, though – weird funny – that when I tried to tell people a few months ago, no one wanted to listen.

Monday afternoon

It seems that everyone wants to listen now – the press; the police; solicitors – pens scribble, heads crane forwards, tape recorders whirr. This afternoon I am giving my witness statement to a lawyer at the Criminal Prosecution Service in preparation for the trial in four months' time. I've been told that my statement is *vitally important* to the prosecution case, as I am the only person to *know the whole story*.

Mr Wright, the CPS lawyer who is taking my statement, sits opposite me. I think he's in his late thirties but maybe he is younger and his face has just been exposed to too many stories like mine. His expression is alert and he leans a fraction towards me, encouraging confidences. A good listener, I think, but what type of man?

'If it's OK with you,' he says, 'I'd like you to tell me everything, from the beginning, and let me sort out later what is relevant.'

I nod. 'I'm not absolutely sure what the beginning is.'

'Maybe when you first realised something was wrong?'

I notice he's wearing a nice Italian linen shirt and an ugly printed polyester tie – the same person couldn't have chosen both. One of them must have been a present. If the tie was a present he must be a nice man to wear it. I'm not sure if

5

I've told you this, but my mind has a new habit of doodling when it doesn't want to think about the matter in hand.

I look up at him and meet his eye.

'It was the phone call from my mother saying she'd gone missing.'

⁂

When Mum phoned we were hosting a Sunday lunch party. The food, catered by our local deli, was very New York – stylish and impersonal; same said for our apartment, our furniture and our relationship – nothing home-made. The Big Apple with no core. You are startled by volte-face I know, but our conversation about my life in New York can wait.

We'd got back that morning from a 'snowy romantic break' in a Maine cabin, where we'd been celebrating my promotion to Account Director. Todd was enjoying regaling the lunch party with our big mistake:

'It's not as though we expected a Jacuzzi, but a hot shower wouldn't hurt, and a landline would be helpful. It wasn't even as if we could use our mobiles, our provider doesn't have a mast out there.'

'And this trip was spontaneous?' asked Sarah incredulously.

As you know, Todd and I were never noted for our spontaneity. Sarah's husband Mark glared across the table at her. 'Darling.'

She met his gaze. 'I hate "darling". It's code for "shut the fuck up", isn't it?'

You'd like Sarah. Maybe that's why we're friends, from the start she reminded me of you. She turned to Todd. 'When was the last time you and Beatrice had a row?' she asked.

'Neither of us is into histrionics,' Todd replied, self-righteously trying to puncture her conversation.

But Sarah's not easily deflated. 'So you can't be bothered either.'

There followed an awkward silence, which I politely broke, 'Coffee or herbal tea anyone?'

In the kitchen I put coffee beans into the grinder, the only cooking I was doing for the meal. Sarah followed me in, contrite. 'Sorry, Beatrice.'

'No problem.' I was the perfect hostess, smiling, smoothing, grinding. 'Does Mark take it black or white?'

'White. We don't laugh any more, either,' she said, levering herself up onto the counter, swinging her legs. 'And as for sex . . .'

I turned on the grinder, hoping the noise would silence her. She shouted above it, 'What about you and Todd?'

'We're fine thanks,' I replied, putting the ground beans into our seven-hundred-dollar espresso maker.

'Still laughing and shagging?' she asked.

I opened a case of 1930s coffee spoons, each one a differently coloured enamel, like melted sweets. 'We bought these at an antiques fair last Sunday morning.'

'You're changing the subject, Beatrice.'

But you've picked up that I wasn't; that on a Sunday morning, when other couples stay in bed and make love, Todd and I were out and about antique shopping. We were always better shopping partners than lovers. I thought that filling our apartment with things we'd chosen was creating a future together. I can hear you tease me that even a Clarice Cliff teapot isn't a substitute for sex, but for me it felt a good deal more secure.

The phone rang. Sarah ignored it. 'Sex and laughter. The heart and lungs of a relationship.'

'I'd better get the phone.'

7

'When do you think it's time to turn off the life-support machine?'

'I'd really better answer that.'

'When should you disconnect the shared mortgage and bank account and mutual friends?'

I picked up the phone, glad of an excuse to interrupt this conversation. 'Hello?'

'Beatrice, it's Mummy.'

You'd been missing for four days.

I don't remember packing, but I remember Todd coming in as I closed the case. I turned to him. 'What flight am I on?'

'There's nothing available till tomorrow.'

'But I have to go now.'

You hadn't shown up to work since the previous Sunday. The manageress had tried to ring you but only got your answerphone. She'd been round to your flat but you weren't there. No one knew where you were. The police were now looking for you.

'Can you drive me to the airport? I'll take whatever they've got.'

'I'll phone a cab,' he replied. He'd had two glasses of wine. I used to value his carefulness.

❧

Of course I don't tell Mr Wright any of this. I just tell him Mum phoned me on the 26th of January at 3.30 p.m. New York time and told me you'd gone missing. Like you, he's interested in the big picture, not tiny details. Even as a child

8

your paintings were large, spilling off the edge of the page, while I did my careful drawings using pencil and ruler and eraser. Later, you painted abstract canvasses, expressing large truths in bold splashes of vivid colour, while I was perfectly suited to my job in corporate design, matching every colour in the world to a pantone number. Lacking your ability with broad brushstrokes, I will tell you this story in accurate dots of detail. I'm hoping that like a pointillist painting the dots will form a picture and when it is completed we will understand what happened and why.

'So until your mother phoned, you had no inkling of any problem?' asks Mr Wright.

I feel the familiar, nauseating, wave of guilt. 'No. Nothing I took any notice of.'

☙

I went first class, it was the only seat they had left. As we flew through cloud limbo land I imagined telling you off for putting me through this. I made you promise not to pull a stunt like this again. I reminded you that you were going to be a mother soon and it was about time you started behaving like an adult.

'"Older sister" doesn't need to be a job title, Bee.'

What had I been lecturing you about at the time? It could have been one of so many things; the point is that I've always viewed being an older sister as a job, one that I am ideally suited for. And as I flew to find you, because I would find you (looking after you is an essential part of my job description), I was comforted by the familiar scenario of being the superior, mature, older sister telling off the flighty, irresponsible young girl who should know better by now.

The plane started to descend towards Heathrow. West

London sprawled beneath us, thinly disguised with snow. The seat-belt light came on and I made deals with God: I'd do anything if you were found safe. I'd have made a deal with the devil if he'd been offering.

As the plane bumped clumsily onto the tarmac, my fantasy annoyance crumbled into sickening anxiety. God became the hero in a children's fairy story. My powers as an older sister dwindled to still impotency. I remembered viscerally Leo's death. Grief like swallowed offal made me wretch. I couldn't lose you too.

꩜

The window is surprisingly huge for an office and spring sunshine floods through it.

'So you made a connection between Tess's disappearance and Leo's death?' Mr Wright asks.

'No.'

'You said you thought about Leo?'

'I think about Leo all the time. He was my brother.' I'm tired of going through this. 'Leo died of cystic fibrosis when he was eight. Tess and I didn't inherit it, we were born perfectly healthy.'

Mr Wright tries to turn off the glaring overhead light, but for some reason it won't switch off. He shrugs at me apologetically and sits down again.

'And then what happened?' he asks.

'Mum met me and I went to the police station.'

'Can you tell me about that?'

꩜

Mum was waiting at the arrivals gate wearing her Jaeger camel coat. As I got closer, I saw that she hadn't brushed

10

her hair and her make-up was clumsily applied. I know; I hadn't seen her that way since Leo's funeral.

'I got a taxi all the way from Little Hadston. Your plane was late.'

'Only ten minutes, Mum.'

All around us lovers and relatives and friends were hugging each other, reunited. We were physically awkward with each other. I don't think we even kissed.

'She might have been trying to phone while I've been gone,' Mum said.

'She'll try again.'

But I'd checked my mobile countless times since the plane had landed.

'Ridiculous of me,' continued Mum. 'I don't know why I should expect her to phone. She's virtually given up calling me. Too much bother, I suppose.' I recognised the crust of annoyance. 'And when was the last time she made the effort to visit?'

I wondered when she'd move on to pacts with God.

I rented a car. It was only six in the morning but the traffic was already heavy on the M4 into London; the frustrated, angry crawl of the absurdly named rush hour, made even slower because of the snow. We were going straight to the police station. I couldn't make the heater work and our words were spoken puffs hanging briefly in the cold air between us. 'Have you already talked to the police?' I asked.

Mum's words seemed to pucker in the air with annoyance. 'Yes, for all the good it did. What would I know about her life?'

'Do you know who told them she was missing?'

'Her landlord. Amias something or other,' Mum replied.

Neither of us could remember his surname. It struck me as strange that it was your elderly landlord who reported you missing to the police.

11

'He told them that she'd been getting nuisance calls,' said Mum.

Despite the freezing car, I felt clammy with sweat. 'What kind of nuisance calls?'

'They didn't say,' said Mum. I looked at her. Her pale anxious face showed around the edge of her foundation, a middle-aged geisha in Clinique bisque.

It was seven thirty but still winter-dark when we arrived at the Notting Hill police station. The roads were jammed but the newly gritted pavements were almost empty. The only time I'd been in a police station before was to report the loss of my mobile phone; it hadn't even been stolen. I never went past the reception area. This time I was escorted behind reception into an alien world of interview rooms and cells and police wearing belts loaded with truncheons and handcuffs. It had no connection to you.

⁂

'And you met Detective Sergeant Finborough?' Mr Wright asks.

'Yes.'

'What did you think of him?'

I choose my words carefully. 'Thoughtful. Thorough. Decent.'

Mr Wright is surprised, but quickly hides it. 'Can you remember any of that initial interview?'

'Yes.'

⁂

To start with I was dazed by your disappearance, but then my senses became overly acute; I saw too many details and

12

too many colours, as if the world was animated by Pixar. Other senses were also on heightened alert; I heard the clank of the clock's hand, a chair leg scraping on linoleum. I could smell a cigarette clinging to a jacket on the door. It was white noise turned up full volume, as if my brain could no longer tune out what didn't matter. Everything mattered.

Mum had been taken off by a WPC for a cup of tea and I was alone with DS Finborough. His manner was courteous, old-fashioned even. He seemed more Oxbridge don than policeman. Outside the window I could see it was sleeting.

'Is there any reason you can think of why your sister may have gone away?' he asked.

'No. None.'

'Would she have told you?'

'Yes.'

'You live in America?'

'We phone and email each other all the time.'

'So you're close.'

'Very.'

Of course we are close. Different yes, but close. The age gap has never meant distance between us.

'When did you last speak to her?' he asked.

'Last Monday, I think. On Wednesday we went away to the mountains, just for a few days. I did try phoning her from a restaurant a few times but her landline was always engaged; she can chat to her friends for hours.' I tried to feel irritated – after all, it's me that pays your phone bill; trying to feel an old familiar emotion.

'What about her mobile?'

'She lost it about two months ago, or it was stolen. She's very scatty like that.' Again trying to feel irritated.

DS Finborough paused a moment, thinking of the right

way to phrase it. His manner was considerate. 'So you think her disappearance is not voluntary?' he asked.

'Not voluntary.' Gentle words for something violent. In that first meeting no one said the word 'abduction', or 'murder'. A silent understanding had been reached between DS Finborough and me. I appreciated his tact; it was too soon to name it. I forced out my question. 'My mother told me she'd been getting nuisance calls?'

'According to her landlord, yes, she has. Unfortunately she hadn't given him any details. Has Tess told you anything about them?'

'No.'

'And she didn't say anything to you about feeling frightened or threatened?' he asked.

'No. Nothing like that. She was normal; happy.' I had my own question. 'Have you checked all the hospitals?' As I asked it, I heard the rudeness and implicit criticism. 'I just thought she might have gone into labour early.'

DS Finborough put his coffee down, the sound made me jump.

'We didn't know she was pregnant.'

Suddenly there was a lifebuoy and I swam for it. 'If she'd gone into labour early, she could be in hospital. You wouldn't have checked the maternity wards, would you?'

'We ask hospitals to check all their in-patients, which would include maternity,' he replied and the lifebuoy slipped away.

'When's the baby due?' he asked.

'In just under three weeks.'

'Do you know who the father is?'

'Yes. Emilio Codi. He's a tutor at her art college.'

I didn't pause, not for a heartbeat. The time for discretion was over. DS Finborough didn't show any surprise, but then maybe that's part of police training.

14

'I went to the art college—' he began, but I interrupted. The smell of coffee in his Styrofoam cup had become nauseatingly strong.

'You must be very worried about her.'

'I like to be thorough.'

'Yes, of course.'

I didn't want DS Finborough to think me hysterical, but reasonable and intelligent. I remember thinking it shouldn't matter what he thought of me. Later I would discover that it mattered a great deal.

'I met Mr Codi,' said DS Finborough. 'He didn't say anything about his relationship with Tess, other than as a former student.'

Emilio still disowned you, even when you were missing. I'm sorry. But that's what his 'discretion' always was – disownership hiding behind a more acceptable noun.

'Do you know why Mr Codi wouldn't want us to know about their relationship?' he asked.

I knew it all too well. 'The college doesn't allow tutors to have sex with their students. He's also married. He made Tess take a "sabbatical" when the bump started to show.'

DS Finborough stood up; his manner had shifted up a gear, more policeman now than Oxbridge don. 'There's a local news programme we sometimes use for missing people. I want to do a televised reconstruction of her last known movements.'

Outside the metal-framed window a bird sang. I remembered your voice, so vividly that it was like you were in the room with me:

'In some cities birds can't hear each other any more above the noise. After a while they forget the complexity and beauty of each other's song.'

15

'What on earth's that got to do with me and Todd?' I asked.

'Some have given up birdsong altogether, and faultlessly imitate car alarms.'

My voice was annoyed and impatient. 'Tess.'

'Can Todd hear your song?'

At the time I dismissed your student intensity of emotion as something I'd grown out of years before. But in that police room I remembered our conversation again, because thoughts about birdsong, about Todd, about anything, was an escape from the implications of what was happening. DS Finborough sensed my distress. 'I think it's better to err on the side of caution. Especially now I know she's pregnant.'

He issued instructions to junior policemen. There was a discussion about the camera crew and of who would play you. I didn't want a stranger imitating you so I offered to do it. As we left the room, DS Finborough turned to me. 'Mr Codi is a great deal older than your sister?'

Fifteen years older and your tutor. He should have been a father figure, not a lover. Yes, I know I've told you that before, many times, building to a critical mass which forced you to tell me in so many words to butt out, only you would have used the English equivalent and told me to stop putting my nose in. DS Finborough was still waiting for my reply.

'You asked me if I am close to her, not if I understand her.'

Now, I think I do, but not then.

DS Finborough told me more about the reconstruction.

'A lady working at the post office on Exhibition Road remembers Tess buying a card and also air-mail stamps, some time before two p.m. She didn't say Tess was pregnant, but

I suppose there was a counter between them so she wouldn't have seen.'

I saw Mum coming along the corridor towards us as DS Finborough continued.

'Tess posted the card from the same post office some time before two fifteen.'

Mum's voice snapped with exhausted patience. 'The card was my birthday card. She hasn't been to see me for months. Hardly ever phones. But sends me a card as if that makes it all right.'

A couple of weeks before, I'd reminded you that it was her birthday coming up, hadn't I?

Before we go on, as I want to be honest in the telling of this story, I have to admit that you were right about Todd. He didn't hear my song. Because I'd never once sung to him. Or to anyone else for that matter. Perhaps I am like one of those birds that can only imitate car alarms.

❦

Mr Wright gets up to close a Venetian blind against the bright spring sunshine.

'And later that day you did the reconstruction?' he asks.
'Yes.'

Mr Wright has the reconstruction on tape and doesn't need additional details of my extraordinary game of dress-up, but I know you do. You'd love to know what kind of you I made. I didn't do badly, actually. I'll tell you about it without hindsight's glaring clarity.

❦

A middle-aged woman police officer, WPC Vernon, took me to a room to change. She was pink-cheeked and healthy, as

17

if she'd just come in from milking cows rather than policing London streets. I felt conscious of my pallor, the red-eye flight taking its toll.

'Do you think it'll do any good?' I asked.

She smiled at me and gave me a quick hug, which I was taken aback by but liked. 'Yes, I do. Reconstructions are too much of a palaver if there isn't a good chance of jogging someone's memory. And now we know that Tess is pregnant it's more likely that someone will have noticed her. Right then, let's get your clothes sorted out, shall we?'

I found out later that although forty, WPC Vernon had only been a policewoman for a few months. Her policing style reflected the warm and capable mother in her.

'We've fetched some clothes from her flat,' she continued. 'Do you know what kind of thing she might have been wearing?'

'A dress. She'd got to the point where nothing else would fit over the bump and she couldn't afford maternity clothes. Luckily most of her clothes are baggy and shapeless.'

'*Comfortable* Bee.'

WPC Vernon unzipped a suitcase. She had neatly folded each tatty old garment and wrapped them in tissue paper. I was touched by the care that she had shown. I still am.

I chose the least scruffy dress; your purple voluminous Whistles one with the embroidery on the hem.

'She got this in a sale five years ago,' I said.

'A good make lasts, doesn't it?'

We could have been in a Selfridges' changing room.

'Yes, it does.'

'Always worth it if you can.'

I was grateful to WPC Vernon for her ability to make small talk, a verbal bridge between two people in the most unlikely of situations.

'Let's go with that one then,' she said and tactfully turned away while I took off my uncomfortable tailored suit.

'So do you look like Tess?' she asked.

'No, not any more.'

'You used to?'

Again I appreciated her small talk, but suspected it would get bigger.

'Superficially I did.'

'Oh?'

'My mother always tried to dress us the same.'

Despite the difference in age, we'd be in kilts and Fair Isle sweaters, or striped cotton dresses depending on the season. Nothing fussy or frilly remember? Nothing nylon.

'And we had our hair the same, too.'

'A *decent trim*,' Mum would command and our hair would fall to the floor.

'People said Tess would look just like me when she was older. But they were being kind.'

I was startled that I had said that out loud. It wasn't a path I had gone down with anyone else before, but it's well worn with my footsteps. I've always known that you would grow up to be far more beautiful than me. I've never told you that, have I?

'That must have been hard on her,' said WPC Vernon. I hesitated before correcting her, and by then she had moved on, 'Is her hair the same colour as yours?'

'No.'

'Not fair the way some people get to stay blonde.'

'Actually, this isn't natural.'

'You'd never guess.'

This time there was a point bedded down in the small talk that spiked through. 'Probably best if you wear a wig then.'

I flinched, but tried to hide it. 'Yes.'

As she got out a box of wigs, I put your dress over my head and felt the much-washed, soft cotton slip down over my body. Then suddenly you were hugging me. A fraction of a moment later I realised it was just the smell of you; a smell I hadn't noticed before: a mix of your shampoo and your soap and something else that has no label. I must have only smelt you like that when we hugged. I drew in my breath, unprepared for the emotional vertigo of you being close and not there.

'Are you OK?'

'It smells of her.'

WPC Vernon's maternal face showed her compassion. 'Smell is a really powerful sense. Doctors use it to try to wake up people in a coma. Apparently newly cut grass is a favourite evocative smell.'

She wanted me to know that I wasn't overreacting. She was sympathetic and intuitive and I was grateful that she was there with me.

The wig box had every type of hair, and I presumed they were used not only for reconstructions of missing people but also for the victims of violent crimes. They made me think of a collection of scalps and I felt nauseous as I rummaged through them. WPC Vernon noticed.

'Here, let me try. What's Tess's hair like?'

'Long, she hardly ever cuts it, so it's ragged round the edges. And it's very shiny.'

'And the colour?'

Pantone number PMS 167, I thought immediately, but other people don't know the colours of the world by their pantone numbers, so instead I replied, 'Caramel.' And actually your hair has always made me think of caramel. The inside of a Rolo, to be precise, liquidly gleaming. WPC Vernon found a wig that was reasonably similar and nylon-shiny. I forced myself to put it on over my own neatly cut hair, my fingers recoiling. I thought we were finished. But WPC Vernon was a perfectionist. 'Does she wear make-up?' she asked.

'No.'

'Would you mind taking yours off?'

Did I hesitate? 'Of course not,' I replied. But I did mind. Even when I woke up, I would have pink lip and cheek stain applied from the previous night. At the small institutional sink, with dirty coffee cups balanced on the rim, I washed off my make-up. I turned and caught sight of you. I was stabbed by love. Moments later I saw that it was just my own reflection caught in a full-length mirror. I went closer and saw myself, scruffy and exhausted. I needed make-up, properly cut clothes and a decent haircut. You don't need any of those to look beautiful.

'I'm afraid we'll have to improvise the bump,' said WPC Vernon. As she handed me a cushion I voiced a question that had been itching at the back of my mind, 'Do you know why Tess's landlord didn't tell you she was pregnant when he reported her missing?'

'No, I'm afraid I don't. You could ask Detective Sergeant Finborough.'

I stuffed a second cushion under the dress and tried to plump them into a convincing-looking bump. For a moment the whole thing turned into an absurd farce and I laughed. WPC Vernon laughed too, spontaneously, and I saw that a smile was her natural expression. It must be a facial effort for her to be genuinely serious and sympathetic so much of the time.

Mum came in. 'I've got you some food, darling,' she said. 'You need to eat properly.' I turned to see her holding a bag full of food and her mothering touched me. But as she looked at me, her face turned rigid. Poor Mum. The farce I found blackly comic had turned cruel.

21

'*But you have to tell her. It'll just get worse the longer you leave it.*'

'*I saw a tea towel the other day with that printed on it. Underneath was "never put off till tomorrow what you can do today".*'

'*Tess . . .*' (Or did I just give an eloquent older-sister sigh?)

You laughed, warmly teasing me. 'Do you still have knickers with days of the week embroidered on them?'

'*You're changing the subject. And I was given those when I was nine.*'

'*Did you really wear them on the right day?*'

'*She's going to be so hurt if you don't tell her.*'

I looked back at Mum acknowledging and answering her question without a word being spoken. Yes, you were pregnant; yes, you hadn't told her and yes, now the whole world, at least the TV-watching world, would know about it.

'Who's the father?'

I didn't reply; one shock at a time.

'That's why she hasn't been to see me for months, isn't it? Too ashamed.'

It was a statement rather than a question. I tried to appease her but she brushed my words aside, using her hands in a rare physical gesture. 'I see he's going to marry her at least.'

She was looking at my engagement ring, which I hadn't thought to take off. 'It's mine, Mum.' I was absurdly hurt that she hadn't noticed it before. I took the large solitaire diamond off my finger and gave it to her. She zipped it into her handbag without even looking at it.

'Does he have any intention of marrying her, Beatrice?'

Maybe I should have been kind and told her that Emilio Codi was already married. It would have fuelled her anger with you and kept icy terror away a while longer.

'Let's find her first, Mum, before worrying about her future.'

22

2

The police film unit was set up near South Kensington tube station. I – the star of this little film – was given my instructions by a young policeman in a cap, rather than a helmet. The trendy director-policeman said 'OK, go.' And I began to walk away from the post office and along Exhibition Road.

You've never needed the confidence boost of high heels so I had reluctantly traded mine for your flat ballet pumps. They were too large for me and I'd stuffed the toes with tissues. Remember doing that with Mum's shoes? Her high heels used to clatter excitingly, the sound of being grown up. Your soft ballet shoes moved silently, discreetly, their soft indoor leather sinking into ice-cracked puddles and soaking up the sharply cold water. Outside the Natural History Museum there was a long fractious queue of impatient children and harassed parents. The children watched the police and the camera crew, the parents watched me. I was free entertainment until they could get in to see the animatronic *Tyrannosaurus rex* and the great white whale. But I didn't care. I was just hoping that one of them had been there the previous Thursday and had noticed you leaving the post office. And then what? What would they have noticed then? I wondered how anything sinister could have happened with so many witnesses.

It started to sleet again, the iced water hammering down onto the pavement. A policeman told me to keep going; although it was snowing the day you disappeared sleet was near enough. I glanced at the queue outside the Natural History Museum. The buggies and prams had sprouted plastic carapaces. Hoods and umbrellas were covering the parents. The sleet forced them into myopia. No one was looking at me. No one would have been watching you. No one would have noticed anything.

The sleet soaked the wig of long hair and ran in a rivulet down my back. Beneath my open jacket your fine cotton dress, heavy with icy water, clung to my body. Every curve showed. You would have found this funny, a police recon-struction turning into a soft porn movie. A car slowed as it passed me. The middle-aged male driver, warm and dry, looked at me through the windscreen. I wondered if someone had stopped and offered you a lift, was that what happened? But I couldn't allow myself to think about what had happened to you. Wondering would lead me into a maze of horrific scenarios where I would lose my mind and I had to stay sane, or I would be of no help to you.

Back at the police station, Mum met me in the changing room. I was soaked through, shivering uncontrollably from cold and exhaustion. I hadn't slept for over twenty-four hours. I started to take off your dress. 'Did you know that smell is made up of minute fragments that have broken away?' I asked her. 'We learned about it at school once.' Mum, uninterested, shook her head. But as I'd walked in the sleet I'd remembered and realised that the smell of your dress was because tiny particles of you were trapped in the fine cotton fibres. It hadn't been irrational to think you close to me after all. OK, yes, in a macabre sort of way.

I handed Mum your dress and started putting on my designer suit.

'Did you have to make her look so shabby?' she asked.

'It's what she looks like, Mum. It's no good if nobody recognises her.'

Mum used to neaten us up whenever our photo was taken. Even during other children's birthday parties she'd do a quick wipe of a chocolaty mouth, a painful tug with a handbag-sized brush over our hair as soon as she spotted a camera. Even then she told you how much better you would look if 'you made an effort like Beatrice'. But I was shamefully glad, because if you did 'make an effort' the glaring difference between us would be clear for everyone to see, and because Mum's criticism of you was a backhanded compliment to me – and her compliments were always sparse on the ground.

Mum handed me back my engagement ring and I slipped it on. I found the weight of it around my finger comforting, as if Todd was holding my hand.

WPC Vernon came in, her skin damp with sleet and her pink cheeks even pinker.

'Thank you, Beatrice. You did a fantastic job.' I felt oddly flattered. 'It's going to be broadcast tonight on the local London news,' she continued. 'DS Finborough will let you know immediately if there's any information.'

I was worried a friend of Dad's would see it on TV and phone him. WPC Vernon, emotionally astute, suggested the police in France told Dad you were missing 'face to face', as if that was better than us phoning and I accepted her offer.

❦

Mr Wright loosens his polyester tie; the first spring sunshine taking centrally heated offices unawares. But I'm grateful for the warmth.

'Did you speak any more to DS Finborough that day?' he asks.

'Just to confirm the number he could reach me on.'

'What time did you leave the police station?'

'Six thirty. Mum had left an hour earlier.'

No one at the police station had realised that Mum can't drive, let alone owns a car. WPC Vernon apologised to me, saying that she'd have driven her home herself if she'd known. Looking back on it, I think WPC Vernon had the compassion to see the fragile person under the shell of navy pleated skirt and middle-class outrage.

۞

The police station doors swung shut behind me. The dark, ice-hardened air slapped my face. Headlights and streetlights were disorientating, the crowded pavement intimidating. For a moment, amongst the crowd, I saw you. I've since found out it's common for people separated from someone they love to keep seeing that loved one amongst strangers; something to do with recognition units in our brain being too heated and too easily triggered. This cruel trick of the mind lasted only a few moments, but was long enough to feel with physical force how much I needed you.

I parked by the top of the steps to your flat. Alongside its tall pristine neighbours your building looked a poor relative that hadn't been able to afford a new coat of white paint for years. Carrying the case of your clothes, I went down the steep icy steps to the basement. An orange street lamp gave barely enough light to see by. How did you manage not to break an ankle in the last three years?

I pressed your doorbell, my fingers numb with cold. For a few seconds I actually hoped that you might answer. Then I started looking under your flowerpots. I knew you hid your front door key under one of the pots and had told me the name of the occupying plant, but I couldn't remember it. You and Mum have always been the gardeners. Besides I was too focused on lecturing you on your lack of security. How could anyone leave their front door key under a flower-pot *right by their door*? And in London. It was *ridiculously irresponsible. Just inviting burglars right on in.*

'What do you think you're doing?' asked a voice above me. I looked up to see your landlord. The last time I'd seen him he was a storybook grandpa – stick a white beard on him and he'd be a regular Father Christmas. Now, his mouth was drawn into a hard scowl, he was unshaven, his eyes glared with the ferocity of a younger man.

'I'm Beatrice Hemming, Tess's sister. We met once before.'

His mouth softened, his eyes become old. 'Amias Thornton. I'm sorry. Memory not what it was.'

He carefully came down the slippery basement steps. 'Tess stopped hiding her spare key under the pink cyclamen. Gave it to me.' He unzipped the coin compartment of his wallet and took out a key. You had completely ignored my lecture in the past, so what had made you suddenly so security conscious?

'I let the police in two days ago,' continued Amias. 'So they could look for some clue. Is there any news?' He was near to tears.

'I'm afraid not, no.'

My mobile phone rang. Both of us started, I answered it hurriedly. He watched me, so hopeful.

'Hello?'

'Hi, darling.' Todd's voice.

I shook my head at Amias.

'No one's seen her and she's been getting weird calls,' I said, startled by the judder in my own voice. 'There's going to be a police reconstruction on TV this evening. I had to pretend to be her.'

'But you look nothing like her,' Todd replied. I found his pragmatism comforting. He was more interested in the casting decision than the film itself. He obviously thought the reconstruction an absurd overreaction.

'I can look like her. Kind of.'

Amias was carefully going back up the steps towards his own front door.

'Is there a letter from her? The police say she bought airmail stamps just before she went missing.'

'No, there was nothing in the mail.'

But a letter might not have had time to reach New York.

'Can I call you back? I want to keep this phone free in case she tries to ring.'

'OK, if that's what you'd prefer.' He sounded annoyed and I was glad you still irritated him. He clearly thought you'd turn up safe and sound and he'd be first in line to lecture you.

I unlocked the door to your flat and went in. I'd only been to your flat, what, two or three times before, and I'd never actually stayed. We were all relieved, I think, that there wasn't room for Todd and me so the only option was a hotel. I'd never appreciated how badly fitting your windows are. Squalls of sleet-cold air were coming through the gaps. Your walls were impregnated with damp, moist and cold to touch. Your eco-friendly light bulbs took ages to throw off any decent light. I

28

turned your central heating up to maximum, but only the top two inches of the radiators gave off any heat. Do you simply not notice such things or are you just more stoical than me?

I saw that your phone was disconnected. Was that why your phone had been engaged when I'd tried to ring you over the last few days? But surely you wouldn't have left it unplugged all that time. I tried to cool my prickling anxiety – you often disconnect the phone when you're painting or listening to music, resenting its hectoring demand for undeserved attention; so the last time you were here you must have just forgotten to plug it in again.

I started putting your suitcase of clothes away in your wardrobe, welcoming my customary surge of irritation.

'But why on earth can't you put your wardrobe in the bedroom, where it's designed to go? It looks ridiculous in here.'

My first visit, wondering why on earth your tiny sitting room was full of a large wardrobe.

'I've made my bedroom into a studio,' you replied, laughing before you'd finished your sentence. 'Studio' was such a grand name for your tiny basement bedroom.

One of the things I love about you is that you find yourself ridiculous faster than anyone else and laugh at yourself first. You're the only person I know who finds their own absurdities genuinely funny. Unfortunately it's not a family trait.

As I hung up your clothes I saw a drawer at the bottom of the wardrobe and pulled it out. Inside were your baby things. Everything in your flat was just so shabby. Your clothes were from charity shops, your furniture from skips, and these baby clothes were brand new and expensive. I took out a pale-blue cashmere baby blanket and tiny hat; so soft my hands felt coarse. They were beautiful. It was like finding an Eames chair

29

in a bus stop. You couldn't possibly have afforded them, so who'd given you the money? I thought Emilio Codi tried to force you to have an abortion. What was going on, Tess?

The doorbell rang and I ran to answer it. I had 'Tess' in my mouth, almost out, as I opened the door. A young woman was on the doorstep. I swallowed 'Tess'. Some words have a taste. I realised I was shaking from the adrenaline rush.

She was over six months pregnant but despite the cold her Lycra top was cropped showing her distended belly and pierced tummy button. I found her overt pregnancy as cheap as her yellow hair colour.

'Is Tess here?' she asked.

'Are you a friend of hers?'

'Yes. Friend. I am Kasia.'

I remembered you telling me about Kasia, your Polish friend, but your description didn't tally with the reality on the doorstep. You'd been flattering to the point of distortion, lending her a gloss that she simply didn't have. Standing there in her absurd miniskirt, her legs textured by goose-bumps and the raised veins of pregnancy, I thought her far from a 'Donatello drawing'.

'Me and Tess met at clinic. No boyfriend too.'

I noted her poor English rather than what she was saying. She looked up at a Ford Escort, parked by the top of the steps, 'He came back. Three weeks.'

I hoped my face showed its complete lack of interest in the state of her personal life.

'When will Tess home?'

'I don't know. Nobody knows where she is.' My voice started to wobble, but I'd be damned if I'd show emotion to this girl. The snob in Mum has been healthily passed on to me. I continued briskly, 'She hasn't been seen since last Thursday. Do you know where she might be?'

Kasia shook her head. 'We've been holiday. Majorca. Making up.'

The man in the Ford Escort was leaning on the horn. Kasia waved up at him and I saw she looked nervous. She asked me to tell you she'd been, in her broken fractured English, and then hurried up the steps.

Yes, Miss Freud, I was angry she wasn't you. Not her fault.

I went up the basement steps and rang on Amias's doorbell. He answered it, fiddling with the chain.

'Do you know how Tess got all those expensive baby clothes?' I asked.

'She had a spree in the Brompton Road,' he replied. 'She was really chuffed with—'

I impatiently interrupted him, 'I meant how did she afford it?'

'I didn't like to ask.'

It was a reprimand; he had good manners, but I did not.

'Why did you report her missing?' I asked.

'She didn't come and have supper with me. She'd promised she would and she never broke her promise, even to an old man like me.'

He unhooked the chain. Despite his age he was still tall and un-stooped, a good few inches taller than me.

'Maybe you should give the baby things away,' he said.

I was repelled by him and furious. 'It's a little premature to give up on her, isn't it?'

I turned away from him and walked hurriedly down the steps. He called something after me, but I couldn't be bothered to try and make it out. I went into your flat.

'Just another ten minutes, and we'll call it a day,' Mr Wright says and I'm grateful. I hadn't known how physically draining this would be.

'Did you go into her bathroom?' he asks.

'Yes.'

'Did you look in her bathroom cabinet?'

I shake my head.

'So you didn't see anything untoward?'

'Yes, I did.'

⁂

I felt exhausted, grimy and bone cold. I longed for a hot shower. It was still two hours till the reconstruction was on TV, so I had plenty of time but I was worried that I wouldn't hear you if you phoned. So that made me think it was a good idea – following that logic which says your crush is bound to turn up on the doorstep the minute you've put on a face mask and your grungiest pyjamas. OK, I agree, logic is hardly the name for it but I hoped having a shower would make you phone. Besides, I also knew my mobile took messages.

I went into your bathroom. Of course, there wasn't a shower just your bath with its chipped enamel and mould around the taps. I was struck by the contrast to my bathroom in New York – a homage to modernist chic in chrome and lime-stone. I wondered how you could possibly feel clean after being in here. I had a familiar moment of feeling superior and then I saw it: a shelf with your toothbrush, toothpaste, contact lens solutions and a hairbrush with long hairs trapped among the bristles.

I realised I'd been harbouring the hope that you'd done something silly and student-like and gone off to whatever festival or protest was on at the moment; that you'd been your usual irresponsible self and hang the consequences of being over eight months pregnant and camping in a snowy field. I'd fantasised about lecturing you for your crass thoughtlessness. Your shelf of toiletries crashed my fantasy. There was no harbour for hope. Wherever you were, you didn't intend to go there.

⁂

Mr Wright switches off the tape machine. 'Let's end it there.' I nod, trying to blink away the image of your long hairs in the bristles of your hairbrush.

A matronly secretary comes in and tells us that the press outside your flat has become alarming in number. Mr Wright is solicitous, asking me if I'd like him to find me somewhere else to stay.

'No. Thank you. I want to be at home.'

I call your flat home now, if that's OK with you. I have been living there for two months now and it feels that way.

'Would you like me to give you a lift?' he asks. He must see my surprise because he smiles. 'It's no trouble. And I'm sure today has been an ordeal.'

The printed polyester tie was a present. He is a nice man.

I politely turn down his offer and he escorts me to the lift. 'Your statement will take several days. I hope that's all right?'

'Yes. Of course.'

'It's because you were the principal investigator as well as being our principal witness.'

'Investigator' sounds too professional for what I did. The lift arrives and Mr Wright holds the door open for me, making sure I get safely inside.

'Your testimony is going to seal our case,' he tells me, and as I go down in the crowded lift, I imagine my words being like tar, coating the hull of the prosecution boat, making it watertight.

Outside, the spring sunshine has warmed the early evening air and by cafés white mushroom parasols sprout from hard grey pavements. The CPS offices are only a couple of streets away from St James's Park and I think that I will walk some of the way home.

I try to take a short cut towards the park but my hoped-for cut-through is a dead end. I retrace my footsteps and hear footsteps behind me, not the reassuring click-clack of high heels, but the quietly threatening tread of a man. Even as I feel afraid, I am aware of the cliché of the woman being stalked by evil and try to banish it, but the footsteps continue, closer now, their heavy tread louder. Surely he will overtake me, walking on the other side, showing he means no harm. Instead he comes closer. I can feel the chill of his breath on the back of my neck. I run, my movements jerky with fear. I reach the end of the cul-de-sac and see people walking along a crowded pavement. I join them and head for the tube, not looking round.

I tell myself that it is *just not possible*. He's on remand, locked up in prison, refused bail. After the trial he's going to go to prison for the rest of his life. I must have imagined it.

I get into a tube and risk a look around the carriage. Immediately I see a photo of you. It's on the front page of the *Evening Standard*, the one I took in Vermont when you visited two summers ago, the wind whirling your hair out behind you like a shining sail, your face glowing. You are arrestingly beautiful. No wonder they chose it for their front page. Inside there's the one I took when you were six, hugging Leo. I know you had just been crying but there's no sign of it. Your

34

face had pinged back to normal as soon as you smiled for me. Next to your picture is one of me that they took yesterday. My face doesn't ping back. Fortunately I no longer mind what I look like in photographs.

I get out at Ladbroke Grove tube station, noticing how deftly Londoners move – up stairways and through ticket barriers – without touching another person. As I reach the exit I again feel someone too close behind me, his cold breath on my neck, the prickle of menace. I hurry away, bumping into other people in my haste, trying to tell myself that it was a draught made by the trains below.

Maybe terror and dread, once experienced, embed themselves into you even when the cause has gone, leaving behind a sleeping horror, which is too easily awakened.

I reach Chepstow Road, and am stunned by the mass of people and vehicles. There are news crews from every UK station and from the looks of it from most of the ones abroad too. Yesterday's collection of press now seems a village fete that's morphed into a frenetic adventure theme park.

I am ten doors away from your flat when the chrysanthemums technician spots me. I brace myself, but he turns away; again his kindness takes me aback. Two doors later a reporter sees me. He starts to come towards me and then they all do. I run down the steps, make it inside, and slam the door.

Outside, sound booms fill the space like triffids; lenses of obscene length are shoved up to the glass. I pull the curtains across, but their lights are still blinding through the flimsy material. Like yesterday I retreat to the kitchen, but there's no sanctuary in here. Someone is hammering on the back door and the front doorbell is buzzing. The phone stops for a second at most, then rings again. My mobile joins in the cacophony. How did they get that number? The sounds are insistent and hectoring, demanding a response. I think back to the first evening I spent in your flat. I thought then that there was nothing as lonely as a phone that didn't ring.

> ⁊⁊

At 10.20 p.m. I watched the TV reconstruction on your sofa, pulling your Indian throw over me in a futile effort to keep warm. From a distance, I really was quite a convincing you. At the end there was an appeal for information and a number to ring.

At 11.30 p.m. I picked up the phone to check it was working. Then I panicked that in that moment of checking someone had been trying to ring: you, or the police to tell me you'd been found.

12.30 a.m. Nothing.

1.00 a.m. I felt the surrounding quietness suffocating me.

1.30 a.m. I heard myself shout your name. Or was your name buried in the silence?

2.00 a.m. I heard something by the door. I hurried to open it but it was just a cat, the stray you'd adopted months before. The milk in the fridge was over a week old and sour. I had nothing to stop its cries.

At 4.30 a.m. I went into your bedroom, squeezing past your easel and stacks of canvasses. I cut my foot and bent down to find shards of glass. I drew back the bedroom curtains and saw a sheet of polythene taped over the broken windowpane. No wonder it was freezing in the flat.

I got into your bed. The polythene was flapping in the icy wind, the irregular inhuman noise as disturbing as the cold. Under your pillow were your pyjamas. They had the same smell as your dress. I hugged them, too cold and anxious to sleep. Somehow I must have done.

I dreamed of the colour red: pantone numbers PMS 1788 to PMS 1807; the colour of cardinals and harlots; of passion and pomp; cochineal dye from the crushed bodies of insects; crimson; scarlet; the colour of life; the colour of blood.

The doorbell woke me.

⁂

Tuesday

I arrive at the CPS office where spring has officially arrived. The faint scent of freshly mown grass from the park wafts in with each turn of the revolving door; the receptionists on the front desk are in summer dresses with brown faces and limbs that must have been self-tanned last night. Despite the warm weather I am in thick clothes, overdressed and pale, a winter leftover.

As I go towards Mr Wright's office, I want to confide in him about my imagined stalker of yesterday. I just need to hear, again, that he is locked away in prison and after the trial will stay there for life. But when I go in, the spring sunshine floods the room, the electric light glares down, and in their brightness my ghost of fear left over from yesterday is blanched into nothing.

Mr Wright turns on the tape recorder and we begin.

'I'd like to start today with Tess's pregnancy,' he says and I feel subtly reprimanded. Yesterday he asked me to start when I first 'realised something was wrong' and I began with Mum's phone call during our lunch party. But I know now that wasn't the real beginning. And I also know that if I had taken more time to be with you, if I had been less preoccupied with myself and listened harder, I might have realised something was very wrong months earlier.

'Tess became pregnant six weeks into her affair with Emilio Codi,' I say, editing out all the emotion that went with that piece of news.

'How did she feel about that?' he asks.

'She said she'd discovered that her body was a miracle.'

I think back to our phone call.

'Almost seven billion miracles walking around on this earth, Bee, and we don't even believe in them.'

'Did she tell Emilio Codi?' asks Mr Wright.

'Yes.'

'How did he react?'

'He wanted her to have the pregnancy terminated. Tess told him the baby wasn't a train.'

Mr Wright smiles and quickly tries to hide it, but I like him for the smile.

'When she wouldn't, he told her she'd have to leave the college before the pregnancy started to show.'

'And did she?'

'Yes. Emilio told the authorities she'd been offered a sabbatical somewhere. I think he even came up with an actual college.'

'So who knew about it?'

'Her close friends, including other art students. But Tess asked them not to tell the college.'

38

I just couldn't understand why you protected Emilio. He hadn't earned that from you. He'd done nothing to deserve it.

'Did he offer Tess any help?' asks Mr Wright.

'No. He accused her of tricking him into pregnancy and said that he wouldn't be pressurised into helping her or the baby in any way.'

'Had she "tricked" him?' asks Mr Wright.

I'm surprised at the amount of detail he wants from me, but then remember that he wants me to tell him everything and let him decide later what is relevant.

'No. The pregnancy wasn't intentional.'

I remember the rest of our phone call. I was in my office overseeing a new corporate identity for a restaurant chain, multitasking with my job as older sister.

༄

'But how can it possibly be an accident, Tess?'

The design team had chosen Bernard MT condensed type-face, which looked old-fashioned rather than the retro look I'd briefed.

'Accident sounds a little negative, Bee. Surprise is better.'

'OK, how can you get a "surprise" when there's a Boots in every high street selling condoms?'

You laughed affectionately, teasing me as I chastised you. 'Some people just get carried away in the moment.'

I felt the implied criticism. 'But what are you going to do?'

'Get larger and larger and then have a baby.'

You sounded so childish; you were acting so childishly, how could you possibly become a mother?

'It's happy news, don't be cross.'

༄

'Did she ever consider an abortion?' Mr Wright asks.

'No.'

'You were brought up as Catholics?'

'Yes, but that wasn't why she wouldn't have an abortion. The only Catholic sacrament Tess ever believed in is the sacrament of the present moment.'

'I'm sorry, I'm afraid I don't know . . .'

I know that it's of no use to the trial, but I'd like him to know more about you than hard-edged facts in lever-arch files.

'It means living in the here and now,' I explain. 'Experiencing the present without worrying about the future or cluttering it with the past.'

I've never bought that sacrament; it's too irresponsible, too hedonistic. It was probably tacked on by the Greeks; Dionysus gatecrashing Catholicism and making sure they at least had a party.

There's something else I want him to know. 'Even at the beginning, when the baby was little more than a collection of cells, she loved him. That's why she thought her body was a miracle. That's why she would never have had an abortion.'

He nods, and gives your love for your baby a decently respectful pause.

'When was the baby diagnosed with cystic fibrosis?' he asks.

I am glad he called him a baby not a foetus. You and your baby are starting to become more human to him now.

'At twelve weeks,' I reply. 'Because of our family history of CF she had a genetic screen.'

'It's me.' I could tell that at the other end of the phone you were struggling not to cry. 'He's a boy.' I knew what was coming, 'He has cystic fibrosis.' You sounded so young. I didn't know what to say to you. You and I knew too much about CF for me to offer platitudes. 'He's going to go through all of that, Bee, just like Leo.'

⚜

'So that was in August?' asks Mr Wright.

'Yes. The tenth. Four weeks later she phoned to tell me that she'd been offered a new genetic therapy for her baby.'

'What did she know about it?' asks Mr Wright.

'She said that the baby would be injected with a healthy gene to replace the cystic fibrosis gene. And it would be done while he was still in the womb. As he developed and grew the new gene would continue to replace the faulty cystic fibrosis gene.'

'What was your reaction?'

'I was frightened of the risks she'd be taking. Firstly with the vector and—'

Mr Wright interrupts. 'Vector? I'm sorry I don't . . .'

'It's the way a new gene gets into the body. A taxi if you like. Viruses are often used as vectors because they are good at infecting cells in the body and so they carry in the new gene at the same time.'

'You're quite an expert.'

'In our family we're all amateur experts in the genetics field, because of Leo.'

⚜

'But people have died in these gene therapy trials, Tess. All their organs failing.'

41

'Just let me finish, please? They're not using a _virus_ as a vector. That's the brilliant thing about it. Someone's managed to make an _artificial chromosome_ to get the gene into the baby's cells. So there's no risk to the baby. It's incredible, isn't it?'

It was incredible. But it didn't stop me from worrying. I remember the rest of our phone call. I was wearing my full older-sister uniform.

'OK, so there won't be a problem with the vector. But what about the modified gene itself? What if it doesn't just cure the CF but does something else that hasn't been predicted?'

'Could you please stop worrying?'

'It might have some appalling side-effect. It might mess up something else in the body that isn't even known about.'

'Bee—'

'OK, so it might seem like a small risk—'

You interrupted, elbowing me off my soapbox. 'Without this therapy, he has cystic fibrosis. A big fat one-hundred-per-cent definite on that. So a small risk is something I have to take.'

'You said they're going to inject it into your tummy?'

I could hear the smile in your voice. 'How else will it get into the baby?'

'So this gene therapy could well affect you too.'

You sighed. It was your 'please get off my back' sigh, the sigh of a younger sister to an older one.

'I'm your sister. I have a right to be concerned about you.'

'And I'm my baby's mother.'

Your response took me aback.

'I'll write to you, Bee.'

You hung up.

༄

'Did she often write to you?' asks Mr Wright.

I wonder if he's interested or if there's a point to the question.

'Yes. Usually when she knew I'd disapprove of something. Sometimes when she just needed to sort out her thoughts and wanted me as a silent sounding board.'

I'm not sure if you know this, but I've always enjoyed your one-way conversations. Although they often exasperate me, it's also liberating to be freed from my role as critic.

'The police gave me a copy of her letter,' says Mr Wright.

I'm sorry. I had to hand all your letters to the police.

He smiles. 'The human angels letter.'

I'm glad that he's highlighted what mattered to you, not what's important for his investigation. And I don't need the letter to remember that part of it:

'All these people, people I don't know, didn't even know about, have been working hour after hour, day after day, for years and years to find a cure. To start with the research was funded by charitable donations. There really are angels, human angels in white lab coats and tweed skirts organising fun runs and cake sales and shaking buckets so that one day, someone they've never even met, has her baby cured.'

'Was it her letter that allayed your fears about the therapy?' asks Mr Wright.

'No. The day before I got it, the gene therapy trial hit the US press. Chrom-Med's genetic cure for cystic fibrosis was all over the papers and wall-to-wall on TV. But there were just endless pictures of cured babies and very little science. Even the broadsheets used the words "miracle baby" far more than "genetic cure".'

Mr Wright nods. 'Yes. It was the same here.'

43

'But it was also all over the net, which meant I could research it thoroughly. I found out that the trial had met all the statutory checks, more than the statutory checks, actually. Twenty babies in the UK had so far been born free of CF and perfectly healthy. The mothers had suffered no ill effects. Pregnant women in America who had foetuses with cystic fibrosis were begging for the treatment. I realised how lucky Tess was to be offered it.'

'What did you know about Chrom-Med?'

'That they were well established and had been doing genetic research for years. And that they had paid Professor Rosen for his chromosome and then employed him to continue his research.'

Allowing your ladies in tweed skirts to stop shaking buckets.

'I'd also watched half a dozen or so TV interviews with Professor Rosen, the man who'd invented the new cure.'

I know it shouldn't have made a difference but it was Professor Rosen who changed my mind about the therapy, or at least opened it. I remember the first time I saw him on TV.

༡༕

The morning TV presenter purred her question at him. 'So how does it feel, Professor Rosen, to be the "man behind the miracle", as some people are dubbing you?'

Opposite her Professor Rosen looked absurdly clichéd with his wire glasses and narrow shoulders and furrowed brow, a white coat no doubt hanging up somewhere off camera. 'It's hardly a miracle. It's taken decades of research and—'

She interrupted. 'Really.'

It was a full stop but he misinterpreted her and took it as an invitation to carry on. 'The CF gene is on chromosome seven. It makes a protein called cystic fibrosis transmembrane conductance regulator, CFTR for short.'

She smoothed her tight pencil skirt over her streamlined legs, smiling at him. 'If we could have the simple version, Professor Rosen.'

'This is the simple version. I created an artificial microchromosome—'

'I really don't think out viewers,' she said, waving her hands as if this was beyond mortal understanding. I was irritated by her and was glad when Professor Rosen was too.

'Your viewers are blessed with brains are they not? My artificial chromosome can safely transport a new healthy gene into the cells with no risks.'

I thought that someone probably had had to coach him in how to present his science in Noddy language. It was as if Professor Rosen himself was dismayed by it and could do it no longer. 'The human artificial chromosome can not only introduce but stably maintain therapeutic genes. Synthetic centromeres were—'

She hurriedly interrupted him. 'I'm afraid we'll have to skip our science lesson today, Professor, because I've got someone who wants to say a special thank you.'

She turned to a large TV screen, which had a live feed from a hospital. A teary-eyed mother and proud new father, cuddling their healthy newborn, thanked Professor Rosen for curing their beautiful baby boy. Professor Rosen clearly found it distasteful and was embarrassed by it. He wasn't revelling in his success and I liked him for it.

༄

'So you trusted Professor Rosen?' asks Mr Wright, without volunteering his own impression, but he must have seen him on TV during the media saturation of the story.

'Yes. In all the TV interviews I watched of him he came across as a committed scientist, with no media savvy. He seemed modest, embarrassed by praise, and clearly not enjoying his moment of TV fame.'

I don't tell Mr Wright this, but he also reminded me of Mr Normans (did you have him for maths?), a kindly man but one who had no truck with the silliness of adolescent girls and used to bark out equations like firing rounds. Lack of media savvy, wire-rimmed glasses and a resemblance to an old teacher weren't logical reasons to finally accept the trial was safe, but the personal nudge I'd needed to overcome my reservations.

'Did Tess describe what happened when she was given the therapy?' asks Mr Wright.

'Not in any detail, no. She just said that she'd had the injection and now she'd have to wait.'

⁂

You phoned me in the middle of the night, forgetting or not caring about the time difference. Todd woke up and took the call. Annoyed, he passed the phone to me, mouthing, 'It's four thirty in the morning for chrissakes.'

'It's worked, Bee. He's cured.'

I cried; sobbing, big-wet-tears crying. I had been so worried, not about your baby, but about what it would be like for you looking after and loving a child with CF. Todd thought something terrible had happened.

'That's bloody wonderful.'

I don't know what surprised him more, the fact I was crying over something wonderful, or that I swore.

'I'd like to call him Xavier. If Mum doesn't mind.'

46

I remembered Leo being so proud of his second name; how he'd wished it were what he was called.

'Leo would think that really cool,' I said, and thought how sad it is that someone dies when they're still young enough to say 'really cool'.

'Yeah, he would, wouldn't he?'

❧

Mr Wright's middle-aged secretary interrupts with mineral water and I am suddenly overwhelmed by thirst. I drink my flimsy paper cupful straight down and she looks a little disapproving. As she takes the empty cup I notice that the inside of her hands are stained orange. Last night she must have done a self-tan. I find it moving that this large heavy-set woman has tried to make herself spring pretty. I smile at her but she doesn't see. She's looking at Mr Wright. I see in that look that she's in love with him, that it was for him she made her arms and face go brown last night, that the dress she's wearing was bought with him in mind.

Mr Wright interrupts my mental gossip. 'So as far as you were concerned there weren't any problems with the baby or the pregnancy?'

'I thought everything was fine. My only worry was how she would cope as a single mother. At the time it seemed like a big worry.'

Miss Crush Secretary leaves, barely noticed by Mr Wright who's looking across the table at me. I glance at his hand, on her behalf: it's bare of a wedding ring. Yes, my mind is doodling again, reluctant to move on. You know what's coming. I'm sorry.

3

For a moment the doorbell ringing was part of my colour red dream. Then I ran to the door, certain it was you. DS Finborough knew he was the wrong person. He had the grace to look both embarrassed and sympathetic. And he knew my next emotion. 'It's all right, Beatrice. We haven't found her.'

He came into your sitting room. Behind him was WPC Vernon.

'Emilio Codi saw the reconstruction,' he said, sitting down on your sofa. 'Tess has already had the baby.'

But you would have told me. 'There must be a mistake.'

'St Anne's Hospital has confirmed that Tess gave birth there last Tuesday and discharged herself the same day.' He waited a moment, his manner compassionate as he lobbed the next hand grenade. 'Her baby was stillborn.'

I used to think 'stillborn' sounded peaceful. Still waters. Be still my beating heart. Still small voice of calm. Now I think it's desperate in its lack of life; a cruel euphemism packing nails around the fact it's trying to cloak. But then I didn't even think about your baby. I'm sorry. All I could think about was that this had happened a week ago and I hadn't heard from you.

'We spoke to the psychiatry department at St Anne's,' DS Finborough continued. 'Tess was automatically referred because of the death of her baby. A Dr Nichols is looking after her. I spoke to him at home and he told me that Tess is suffering from post-natal depression.'

Facts of exploding shrapnel were ripping our relationship apart. You didn't tell me when your baby died. You were depressed but you hadn't turned to me. I knew every painting you were working on, every friend, even the book you were reading and the name of your cat. (Pudding, I'd remembered it the next day.) I knew the minutiae of your life. But I didn't know the big stuff. I didn't know you.

So the devil had finally offered me a deal after all. Accept that I wasn't close to you and, in return, you had not been abducted. You had not been murdered. You were still alive. I grabbed the deal.

'We're obviously still concerned about her welfare,' said DS Finborough. 'But there's no reason to think anybody else is involved.'

I briefly paused, for formality's sake, to check the small print of the deal. 'What about the nuisance phone calls?'

'Dr Nichols thinks Tess most probably overreacted because of her fragile emotional state.'

'And her broken window? There was glass on the floor of her bedroom when I arrived.'

'We investigated that when she was first reported missing. Five cars in the road had their windscreens smashed by a hooligan on Tuesday night. A brick must have also gone through Tess's window.'

Relief washed the tension from my body making space for overwhelming tiredness.

After they'd left I went to see Amias. 'You knew her baby had died, didn't you?' I asked him. 'That's why you said I may as well give away all her baby things.'

He looked at me, distressed. 'I'm sorry. I thought you knew that too.'

I didn't want to go down that track, not yet.

'Why didn't you tell the police anything about the baby?'

'She's not married.' He saw the lack of comprehension on my face. 'I was worried that they'd think she was loose. That they wouldn't bother looking for her.'

Maybe he had a point, though not exactly as he meant. Once the police knew you were suffering from post-natal depression the search for you stopped being urgent. But at the time this fact hardly registered.

'Tess told me her baby had been cured?' I asked.

'Yes, of cystic fibrosis. But there was something else they didn't know about. His kidneys, I think.'

I drove to Mum's to tell her the good news. Yes, good news, because you were alive. I didn't think about your baby, I'm sorry. As I said, a devil's deal.

And a false one. As I drove, I thought I'd been a fool to have been so easily conned. I'd wanted so much to accept the deal that I'd blinkered myself from the truth. I've known you since you were born. I was with you when Dad left. When Leo died. I know the big stuff. You would have told me about your baby. And you would have told me if you

50

were going away. So something – someone – must have prevented you.

Mum felt the same relief as I had. I felt cruel as I punctured it. 'I don't think they're right, Mum. She wouldn't just take off somewhere, not without telling me.'

But Mum was holding the good news tightly and wasn't going to let me take it away from her without a fight. 'Darling, you've never had a baby. You can't begin to imagine what she must be feeling. And the baby blues are bad enough without all of the rest of it.' Mum's always been deft with a euphemism. 'I'm not saying I'm glad her baby died,' Mum continued. 'But at least she has a second chance. Not many men are prepared to take on another man's child.' Finding a bright future for you, Mum-style.

'I really don't think she's gone missing voluntarily.'

But Mum didn't want to listen to me. 'She'll have another baby one day in far happier circumstances.' But her voice wavered as she tried to put you into a safe and secure future.

'Mum—'

She interrupted me, refusing to listen. 'You knew that she was pregnant, didn't you?'

Now, instead of projecting you into the future, Mum was going backwards into the past. Anywhere but what was happening to you now.

'Did you think it was *all right* for her to be a single mother?'

'You managed on your own. You showed us it's possible.'

I'd meant it to be kind, but it infuriated her further.

'There's no comparison between Tess's behaviour and mine. None. I was married before I was pregnant. And my

51

husband may have left the marriage, but that was never my choice.'

I'd never heard her call him 'my husband' before, have you? He's always been 'your father'.

'And I have some concept of shame,' continued Mum. 'It wouldn't hurt Tess to learn a little about it.'

As I said, anger can take the chill from terror, at least for a while.

It started blizzarding as I drove from Little Hadston back to London, transplanting the M11 into a violently shaken snow globe. Millions of flakes were falling frenziedly towards the ground, hitting the windscreen, too many and too fast for the wipers to clear them. Signs on the motorway flashed up warnings of dangerous driving conditions and issued slower speed limits, keeping motorists safe. An ambulance sped past, siren blaring.

'It's not a din, Bee.'

'OK, racket then.'

'A siren is the sound of the twenty-first-century cavalry on its way.'

You'd just started art college and were full of thoughts no-one-but-you-had-ever-had-before. And you had that other annoying student trait of thinking non-students incapable of understanding.

'I mean a cavalry of a fire engine, or a police car or an ambulance racing to the rescue.'

'I'd got the point first time, thanks, Tess.'

'But you thought it too silly to comment on?'

'Yup.'

You giggled. 'Seriously though, to me a siren's the sound of a society taking care of its citizens.'

The ambulance had gone from sight now, the siren no longer audible. Was there any cavalry for you? I stopped myself thinking like this. I couldn't let myself wonder what was happening to you. But my body felt cold and frightened and alone.

The roads near your flat hadn't been gritted and were treacherously icy. I skidded when I parked, almost knocking over a motorbike by your flat. A man in his early twenties was sitting at the bottom of the steps, holding an absurdly large bouquet, snowflakes melting as they landed on the cellophane wrapping. I recognised him from your description – Simon the MP's son. You're right; his pierced lips do make his childish face seem tortured. His biker clothes were soaked and his fingers were white with cold. Despite the freezing air, I could smell aftershave. I remembered you telling me about his clumsy advances and your response. You must be one of very few people who actually deliver the promised consolation prize of being friends.

I told him you were missing and he hugged the bouquet to his chest, crushing the flowers inside. His Eton-educated voice was quiet. 'How long?'

'Last Thursday.'

I thought his face went white. 'I was with her on Thursday.'

'Where?'

'Hyde Park. We were together till around four.'

That was two hours after you were seen in the post office. He must have been the last person to see you.

'She'd phoned me that morning, asked to meet me,' continued Simon. 'She suggested the Serpentine Gallery in Kensington Gardens. We'd meet there for a coffee, see how things went.'

His accent had changed to North London. I wondered which accent was genuine.

'Afterwards I asked her if I could walk her home,' continued Simon. 'But she turned me down.' His voice was filled with self-pity. 'Since then I haven't phoned her, haven't been to see her. And yes, that's not supportive of me, but I wanted her to know what the cold-shoulder treatment felt like.'

His ego must be monstrous to believe his hurt feelings could matter to you after your baby had died, or to me now that you were missing.

'Whereabouts did you leave her?' I asked.

'She left me, OK? I walked with her across Hyde Park. Then she left. I didn't leave her anywhere.'

I was sure he was lying. The North London accent was the fake.

'Where?'

He didn't reply.

I yelled my question at him again. '*Where*?!'

'By the lido.'

I'd never yelled at someone before.

I phoned DS Finborough and left an urgent message for him. Simon was in your bathroom, warming his numb white hands under the hot tap. Later your bathroom would smell of his aftershave and I would be angry with him for masking the smell of your soap and shampoo.

'What did the police say?' he asked when he came in.

'They said they will check it out.'

'How American of them.'

Only you are allowed to tease me like that. What the policeman had actually said was, 'I'll look into it straight away.'

'So they're going to search Hyde Park?' Simon asked.

But I was trying not to think about what the policeman

54

had meant by 'looking into it'. I'd replaced his English euphemism with an American euphemism, bubble-wrapping the sharp reality of what his words contained.

'And they'll ring us?' he asked.

I am your sister. DS Finborough would ring me.

'DS Finborough will let me know if there's anything, yes,' I replied.

Simon sprawled on your sofa, his snow-caked boots marking your Indian throw. But I needed to ask him some questions so I hid my annoyance.

'The police think she has post-natal depression. How did she seem to you?'

He didn't answer for a few moments and I wondered if he was trying to remember or constructing a lie. 'She was desperate,' he said. 'She had to take these special pills, to stop her breast milk. She told me that was one of the worst things, still making all this food for her baby and not being able to give it to him.'

The death of your baby started to penetrate, a little way. I'm sorry that it was taking so long. My only defence is that there wasn't space for your baby in my worry for you.

Something was niggling me about Simon. I pinned it down, 'You said *was*.'

He looked taken aback.

'You said she *was* desperate?'

For a moment I thought he looked cornered, then he recovered his composure. His voice was back to fake North London. 'I meant when I saw her on Thursday afternoon she was desperate. How am I meant to know how she's doing now?'

His face no longer looked childish to me but cruel; the piercings not marks of an adolescent rebellion but of an enjoyed masochism. I had another question to ask him.

55

'Tess told me the baby had been cured?'

'Yeah, it wasn't anything to do with the cystic fibrosis.'

'Was it because he was three weeks early?'

'No. She told me it was something that would have killed him even if he'd been born at the right time. Something to do with his kidneys.'

I steeled myself. 'Do you know why she didn't tell me when her baby died?'

'I thought she had.' There was something triumphant in his look. 'Did you know I was going to be godfather?'

He left with bad grace after my polite hints had turned uncharacteristically into an outright demand.

I waited two and a half hours for DS Finborough to phone me back, and then I phoned the police station. A police-woman told me DS Finborough was unavailable. I decided to go to Hyde Park. I was hoping that DS Finborough would be nowhere to be seen; I was hoping that he was unavailable because he was now investigating a more urgent case, yours having been relegated to a missing person who'd turn up in her own good time. I was hoping that I was wrong and he was right; that you had just taken off somewhere after the death of your baby. I locked the door and put your key under the flowerpot with the pink cyclamen in case you came home while I was out.

As I neared Hyde Park a police car, siren wailing, over-took. The sound panicked me. I drove faster. When I got to the Lancaster Gate entrance the police car, which had overtaken me, was joining others already parked, their sirens electronic howls.

I went into the park, soft snow falling around me. I wish I'd waited a little longer and had an hour or so more of my life first. To most people that would sound selfish, but you've lived with grief or, more accurately, a part of you has died with grief so you, I know, will understand.

A distance into the park I could see police, a dozen of them or more. Police vehicles were coming towards them, driving into the park itself. Onlookers were starting to come towards the site of the activity – reality TV unboxed.

So many footprints and tyre tracks in the snow.

I walked slowly towards them. My mind was oddly calm, noticing at a remove that my heart was beating irregularly against my ribs, that I was short of breath, that I was shivering violently. Somehow my mind kept its distance, not yet a part of my body's reaction.

I passed a park ranger, in his brown uniform, talking to a man with a Labrador. 'We were asked about the lido and the lake, and I thought that they were going to dredge them but the chief officer fellow decided to search our disused buildings first. Since the cuts we've got a lot of those.' Other dog walkers and joggers were joining his audience. 'The building over there used to be the gents toilets years ago, but it was cheaper to put in new ones than renovate.'

I passed him and his audience, walking on towards the police. They were setting up a cordon around a small derelict Victorian building half-hidden by bushes.

A little way from the cordon was WPC Vernon. Her normally rosy cheeks were pale, her eyes puffy from crying; she was shaking. A policeman had his arm around her. They didn't see me. WPC Vernon's voice was quick and uneven. 'Yes, I have, but only in hospital, and never someone so young. Or so alone.'

Later, I would love her for her physical compassion. At

the time, her words burned into my consciousness, forcing my mind to engage with what was happening.

I reached the police cordon. DS Finborough saw me. For a moment he was bewildered by what I was doing there and then his expression became one of sympathy. He walked towards me.

'Beatrice, I'm so sorry—'

I interrupted him. If I could stop him saying the words then it wouldn't be true. 'You're wrong.'

I wanted to run away from him. He took hold of my hand. I thought he was restraining me. Now I think he was offering a gentle gesture of kindness.

'It's Tess we've found.'

I tried to pull my hand away from his. 'You can't know that for sure.'

He looked at me, properly, making eye contact; even then I realised that this took courage.

'Tess had her student ID card with her. I'm afraid there isn't any mistake. I'm so sorry, Beatrice. Your sister is dead.'

He released my hand. I walked away from him. WPC Vernon came after me. 'Beatrice . . .'

I heard DS Finborough call her back. 'She wants to be alone.'

I was grateful to him.

I sat under a copse of black-limbed trees, leafless and lifeless in the silencing snow.

At what point did I know you were dead? Was it when DS Finborough told me? When I saw WC Vernon's pale tearful face? When I saw your toiletries still in your bathroom? Or when Mum phoned to say you'd gone missing? When did I know?

I saw a stretcher being taken out of the derelict toilet building. On the stretcher was a body bag. I went towards it.

A strand of your hair had caught in the zip.

And then I knew.

4

Why am I writing this to you? I deflected that question last time, talked about my need to make sense of it all, my dots of detail revealing a pointillist painting. I ducked the real part of the question – why to you? Is this a make-believe game of the almost insane? Sheets and blankets make a tent, a pirate ship or a castle. You are the fearless knight, Leo is the swashbuckling prince and I am the princess and narrator – telling the story, as I want it. I was always the storyteller, wasn't I?

Do I think you can hear me? Absolutely yes / Definitely not. Take your pick; I do hourly.

Put simply, I need to talk to you. Mum told me I didn't say very much till you were born, then I had a sister to talk to and I didn't stop. I don't want to stop now. If I did, I'd lose a part of me. It's a part of me I'd miss. I know you can't criticise or comment on my letter to you, but that doesn't mean I don't know your criticisms or guess at your comments just as you used to know and guess at mine. It's a one-way conversation, but one that I could only have with you.

And it's to tell you why you were murdered. I could start at the end, give you the answer, the final page, but you'd ask a question which would lead back a few pages, then another, all the way to where we are now. So I'll tell you one step at a time, as I found out myself, with no reflecting hindsight.

꿎

'A policeman I hadn't met before asked me to identify her.'

I have told Mr Wright what I have told you, minus deals with the devil and the other non-essential detours from my statement.

'What time was this?' he asks and his voice is kind, as it has been throughout this interview, but I can't answer him. The day you were found time went demented; a minute lasted half a day, an hour went past in seconds. Like a children's storybook, I flew in and out of weeks and through the years; second star to the right and straight on to a morning that would never arrive. I was in a Dali painting of drooping clocks, a Mad Hatter's tea-party time. No wonder Auden said, 'Stop all the clocks'; it was a desperate grab for sanity.

'I don't know what time it was,' I reply. I decide to chance a little of my truth. 'Time didn't mean anything to me any more. Usually time alters and affects everything, but when someone you love dies time cannot change that, no amount of time will ever change that, so time stops having any meaning.'

When I saw your strand of hair I knew that grief is love turned into an eternal missing. A little too much for Mr Wright, I agree, but I want him to know more about the

61

reality of your death. It can't be contained in hours or days or minutes. Remember those 1930s coffee spoons, each one like a melted sweet? That's how I'd been living my life, in tiny measured doses. But your death was a vast sea and I was sinking. Did you know that an ocean can be seven miles deep? No sun can penetrate that far down. In the total darkness only misshapen, unrecognisable creatures survive; mutant emotions that I never even knew existed until you died.

'Shall we break there?' Mr Wright asks and for a moment I wonder if I've voiced my thoughts out loud and he's worried I'm a crazy woman. I'm pretty sure I managed to keep my thoughts under wraps and he's being considerate. But I don't want to have to revisit this day again. 'I'd rather finish.' He stiffens, almost imperceptibly, and I sense he is bracing himself. I hadn't considered this would be difficult for him. It was hard for the Ancient Mariner to tell his tale, but hard too for the poor wedding guest forced to listen. He nods and I continue.

'The police had brought Mum to London but she couldn't face identifying Tess, so I went to the police morgue on my own. A police sergeant was with me. He was in his late fifties. I can't remember his name. He was very kind to me.'

❦

As we went into the morgue the police sergeant held my hand and he kept holding it. We went past a room where they do post-mortems. The shiny metal surfaces, white tiles and sharp lighting made it look like a high-tech designer kitchen taken to an extreme. He led me to a room where you were. The smell of antiseptic was overwhelming. The

62

sergeant asked me if I was ready. I never would be. I nodded. He pulled back the blanket.

You were wearing your thick winter coat, my Christmas present to you. I'd wanted to make sure you were warm. I was stupidly glad that you were wearing it. There is no description of the colour of death, no pantone number to match your face. It was the opposite of colour; the opposite of life. I touched your still satin-shiny hair. 'She was so beautiful.'

The sergeant tightened his fingers around mine. 'Yes. She is beautiful.'

He used the present tense and I thought he hadn't heard me properly. But I think now that he was trying to make it a little better; death hadn't robbed you of everything yet. He was right; you were beautiful in the way that Shakespeare's tragic heroines are beautiful. You'd become a Desdemona, an Ophelia, a Cordelia; pale and stiff with death; a wronged heroine; a passive victim. But you were never tragic or passive or a victim. You were joyful, passionate and independent.

I saw that the thick sleeves of your coat were soaked through in blood, now dried, making the wool stiff. There were cuts to the insides of your arms, where your life had bled from you.

I don't remember what he said or if I replied. I can only remember his hand holding mine.

As we left the building the sergeant asked if I wanted the police in France to tell Dad for us, and I thanked him.

Mum was waiting for me outside. 'I'm sorry. I just couldn't bear to see her like that.' I wondered if she thought I could bear it. 'You shouldn't have to do that sort of thing,' she continued. 'They should use DNA or something. It's barbaric.' I didn't agree. However appalling, I had needed to see the brutal reality of your no-colour face to believe you were dead.

'Were you all right on your own?' Mum asked.

'There was a policeman with me. He was very kind.'

'They've all been very kind.' She needed to find something good in this. 'Not fair the way the press go on at them, is it? I mean, they really couldn't have been nicer or . . .' She trailed off; there was no good in this. 'Was her face . . . ? I mean, was it . . . ?'

'It was unmarked. Perfect.'

'Such a pretty face.'

'Yes.'

'It always has been. But you couldn't see it for all that hair. I kept telling her to put her hair up or have it properly cut. I meant so that everyone could see what a pretty face she had, not because I didn't like her hair.'

She broke down and I held her. As she clung to me, we had the physical closeness both of us had needed since I got off the plane. I hadn't cried yet and I envied Mum, as if a little of the agony could be shed through tears.

I drove Mum home and helped her to bed. I sat with her till she finally slept.

In the middle of the night I drove back to London. On the M11 I opened the windows and screamed above the noise of the engine, above the roar of the motorway; screaming into the darkness until my throat hurt and my voice was hoarse. When I reached London the roads were quiet and empty and the silent pavements deserted. It was unimaginable that the dark, abandoned city would have

64

light and people again in the morning. I hadn't thought about who had killed you; your death had shattered thought. I just wanted to be back in your flat, as if I'd be nearer to you there.

The car clock showed 3.40 a.m. when I arrived. I remember because it was no longer the day you were found, it was the day after. Already you were going into the past. People think it's reassuring to say 'life carries on', don't they understand that it's the fact your life carries on, while the person you love's does not, that is one of the acute anguishes of grief? There would be day after day that wasn't the day you were found; that hope, and my life with my sister in it, had ended.

In the darkness, I slipped on the steps down to your flat and grabbed hold of the icy railing. The jolt of adrenaline and cold forced the realisation of your death harder into me. I fumbled for the key under the pink cyclamen pot, scraping my knuckles on frozen concrete. The key wasn't there. I saw that your front door was ajar. I went in.

Someone was in your bedroom. Grief had suffocated all other emotions and I felt no fear as I opened the door. A man was inside rummaging through your things. Anger cut through the grief.

'What the fuck are you doing?'

In the new mindscape of deep-sea mourning, even my words were unrecognisable to me. The man turned.

※

'Shall we end it there?' asks Mr Wright. I glance at the clock; it's nearly seven. I am grateful to him for letting me finish the day you were found.

'I'm sorry, I didn't know how late it was.'

'As you said, time stops making any sense when someone you love has died.'

I wonder if he'll follow this up. I feel the inequality of our respective situations. He's had my feelings stripped naked for the last five hours. There's a silence between us and I half-think about asking him to strip off too.

'My wife died two years ago, a car crash.'

Our eyes meet and there's comradeship between us; two veterans of the same war, battle-weary and emotionally bloody. Dylan Thomas was wrong; death does have dominion. Death wins the war and the collateral damage is grief. I never thought when I was an English literature student that I'd be arguing with poets, rather than learning their words.

Mr Wright escorts me down a corridor towards the lift. A cleaner is vacuuming; other offices are in darkness. He presses the lift button and waits with me for it to arrive. Alone, I get inside.

As the lift goes down, I taste the bile in my throat. My body has been playing a physical memory alongside the spoken one and I have again felt the rising nausea as if I were physically trying to expel what I knew. Again, my heart has been pummelling my ribs, sucking the breath from my lungs. I leave the lift, my head still viciously painful as it was the day you were found. Then the fact of your death detonated inside my brain, exploding again and again and again. As I talked to Mr Wright, I was again blindfolded in a minefield. Your death will never be disarmed to a memory, but I have learned on some days, good days, how to edge around it. But not today.

I leave the building and the evening is warm, but I am still shivering and the hairs on my arms are standing upright trying to conserve body heat. I don't know if it was the bitter cold or the shock that made me shiver so violently that day.

Unlike yesterday, I don't feel a menacing presence behind me, maybe because after describing the day you were found I have no emotional energy left for fear. I decide to walk rather than take the tube. My body needs to take cues from the real outside world, not the climate of memory. My shift at the Coyote starts in just over an hour, so I should have time to walk it.

You're astonished, and yes, I am a hypocrite. I can still remember my patronising tone.

'But barmaiding? Couldn't you find something just a little less . . . ?'
I trailed off but you knew what to fill in: 'brain-numbing'; 'beneath you', 'dead end'.
  'It's just to pay the bills, it's not a career choice.'
  'But why not find a day job that may lead on to something?'
  'It's not a day job, it's an evening job.'
  There was something brittle behind your humour. You had seen the hidden jibe; my lack of faith in your future as an artist.

Well it's more than a day or evening job for me, it's the only job I have. After three weeks of compassionate leave my boss's sympathy ran out. I had to tell him *one way or the other, Beatrice* what I was going to do, so by staying in London I resigned. That makes it sound like I'm an easy-going person who can respond to situations in a flexible way, trading in senior manager of a corporate identity design company for part-time barmaid with barely a break in my stride. But you know that I am nothing like that. And my New York job with its regular salary and pension scheme and orderly hours was my last foothold on a life that was predictable and safe. Surprisingly, I enjoy working at the Coyote.

The walking helps and after forty minutes my breathing slows; my heartbeat returns to a recognisable rhythm. I finally take notice of you telling me I should at least have phoned Dad. But I thought his new bride would comfort him far better than me. Yes, they'd been married eight years, but I still thought of her as a new bride – fresh and white and sparkling with her youth and fake diamond tiara, untainted by loss. Little wonder Dad chose her over us.

I reach the Coyote and see Bettina has put up the green awning and is laying the old wooden tables outside. She welcomes me by opening her arms, a hug waiting for me to walk into. A few months ago, I would have been repelled. Fortunately, I have become a little less bigot-touchy. We hug tightly and I am grateful for her physicality. I finally stop shivering.

She looks at me with concern. 'Are you feeling up to working?'

'I'm fine, really.'

'We watched it on the news. They said the trial would be in the summer?'

'Yes.'

'When do you reckon I'll get my computer back?' she asks, smiling. 'My writing's illegible, no one can read their menus.'

The police took her computer, knowing that you often used it, to see if there was anything on it that could help with their investigation. She does have a truly beautiful smile and it always overwhelms me. She puts her arm around me to escort me inside and I realise she was deliberately waiting for me.

I do my shift, still feeling nauseous and headachy, but if anyone notices my quietness no one comments. I was always good at mental maths so that side of barmaiding comes easily, but the banter with the customers does not. Fortunately, Bettina can talk for two and I rely on her this evening, as I often used to on you. The customers are all regulars and have the same courtesy towards me as the staff, not asking me questions or commenting on what is happening. Tact is catching.

By the time I get home it's late and, physically wrung out by the day, I long to sleep. Fortunately, only three stalwart reporters remain. Maybe they're freelancers in need of cash. No longer part of a pack, they don't shout out questions or force lenses in my face. Instead it's more of a cocktail party type of scenario, where they are at least conscious that I may not want to talk to them.

'Miss Hemming?'

Yesterday it was 'Beatrice' and I resented the false intimacy. (Or 'Arabella' from those who'd been too sloppy to do their homework.) The woman reporter continues, at a polite distance. 'Can I ask you some questions?' It's the reporter I heard outside the kitchen window on Sunday evening talking on her mobile.

'Wouldn't you rather be at home reading bedtime stories?'

She is visibly startled.

'I was eavesdropping.'

'My son's with his aunt tonight. And unfortunately I don't get paid for reading bedtime stories. Is there anything you'd like people to know about your sister?'

'She'd bought her baby finger-paints.'

I'm not sure what made me say that. Maybe because for the first time you weren't just living in the present, but planning for the future. Understandably the reporter wants something else. She waits.

I try to summarise you into a sentence. I think of your

69

qualities but in my head it starts turning into a personal ad: 'Beautiful, talented, 21-year-old, popular and fun-loving seeks . . .' I hear you laugh. I left out good sense of humour but in your case that's entirely true. I think of why people love you. But as I list those reasons I wobble perilously close to an obituary and you're too young for that. An older male reporter, silent until now, barges in. 'Is it true she was expelled from school?'

'Yes. She hated rules, especially ridiculous ones.'

He scribbles and I continue my quest for an encapsulating sentence about you. How many sub-clauses can a single sentence hold?

'Miss Hemming?'

I meet her eye. 'She should be here. Now. Alive.'

My six-word summary of you.

I go inside the flat, close the door, and hear you telling me that I was too harsh on Dad earlier. You're right, but I was still so angry with him then. You were too young to take in what Mum and Leo went through when he left, just three months before Leo died. I knew, rationally, that it was the cystic fibrosis that made him leave; made Leo so ill that he couldn't bear to look at him; made Mum so tense that her heart knotted into a tight little ball that could barely pump the blood around her body let alone beat for anyone else. So I knew that rationally Dad had his reasons. But he had children and so I thought there were no reasons. (Yes, *had*, because two of his children were dead and the third was no longer a child.)

You believed him when he said he'd be back. I was five years older but no wiser and for years I had a fantasy of a happy-ever-after ending. The first night I spent at university my fantasy ended, because I thought a happy-ever-after was pointless. Because with my father I didn't want to hope for a happy ending but to have had a happy beginning. I wanted to have been looked after by Daddy in childhood, not finding resolution with my father as an adult. But I'm not so sure of that now.

Outside your window, I see the reporters have all gone. Pudding bends her purring body around my ankles, blackmailing me into giving her more food. When I've fed her, I fill a watering can and go out of the kitchen door.

'This is your backyard?' I asked on my first visit to your flat, astonished that you hadn't meant 'backyard' in the American sense of a garden, but in the literal one of a few feet of rubble-strewn earth and a couple of wheelie bins. You smiled. 'It'll be beautiful, Bee, just wait.'

You must have worked like a Trojan. All the stones cleared, the earth dug through and planted. You've always been passionate about gardening, haven't you? I remember when you were tiny you'd trail Mum around the garden with your child-sized, brightly painted trowel and your special gardening apron. But I never liked it. It wasn't the long wait between seed and resulting plant that I minded about (you did, hotly impatient), it was that when a plant finally flowered it was over too quickly. Plants were too ephemeral and transient. I preferred collecting china ornaments, solid and dependable inanimate objects that wouldn't change or die the following day.

But since staying in your flat I have really tried, I promise, to look after this little patch of garden outside the back door. (Fortunately, Amias is in charge of your flowerpot garden of Babylon down the steps to your flat at the front.) I've watered the plants out here every day, even adding flower food. No,

71

I'm not absolutely sure why – maybe because I think it matters to you; maybe because I want to nurture your garden because I didn't nurture you? Well, whatever the motivation, I'm afraid I have failed abysmally. All the plants out here are dead. Their stalks are brown and the few remaining leaves desiccated and crumbling. Nothing is growing out of the bare patches of earth. I empty the last drops from the watering can. Why do I carry on this pointless task of watering dead plants and bare earth?

'It'll be beautiful, Bee, just wait.'

I'll refill the watering can and wait a while longer.

5

I arrive at the Criminal Prosecution Service offices and notice Miss Crush Secretary staring at me. Actually, scrutinising seems more accurate. I sense that she is assessing me as a rival. Mr Wright hurries in, briefcase in one hand, newspaper in the other. He smiles at me openly and warmly; he hasn't yet made the switch from home life to office. Now I know that Miss Crush Secretary is definitely assessing me as a rival because when Mr Wright smiles at me her look becomes openly hostile. Mr Wright is oblivious. 'Sorry to keep you waiting. Come through.' Mentally he's still knotting his tie. I follow him into his office and he closes the door. I feel his secretary's eyes the other side, still watching him.

'Were you all right last night?' he asks. 'I know this must be harrowing.'

Before you died the adjectives about my life were second league: 'stressful'; 'upsetting'; 'distressing'; at the worst 'deeply sad'. Now I have the big gun words –

73

'harrowing', 'traumatic', 'devastating' – as part of my thesaurus of self.

'We'd got to you finding someone in Tess's bedroom?'

'Yes.'

His mental tie is knotted now, and we resume business. He reads me back my own words, '"What the fuck are you doing?"'

༄

The man turned. Despite the freezing flat, his forehead had a film of sweat. There was a moment before he spoke. His Italian accent was, intentionally or not, flirtatious. 'My name is Emilio Codi. I'm sorry if I startled you.' But I'd known immediately who he was. Did I sense threat because of the circumstances, because I suspected him of killing you – or would I have found him threatening even if that wasn't the case? Because unlike you, I find Latinate sexuality – that brash masculinity of hard jawline and swarthy physique – menacing rather than attractive.

'Do you know that she's dead?' I asked, and the words sounded ridiculous; an over-the-top stagy piece of dialogue that I didn't know how to deliver. Then I remembered your colourless face.

'Yes. I saw it on the local news. A terrible, terrible tragedy.' His default voice mode was charm, however inappropriate, and I thought that to charm can also mean to entrap. 'I just came to get my things. I know it seems like indecent haste—'

I interrupted him, 'Do you know who I am?'

'A friend, I presume.'

'Her sister.'

'I'm sorry. I'm intruding.'

74

He couldn't hide the adrenaline in his voice. He started to walk towards the door but I blocked his path.

'Did you kill her?'

I know, pretty blunt, but then this wasn't a carefully crafted Agatha Christie moment.

'You're obviously very upset—' he replied, but I cut him off.

'You tried to make her have an abortion. Did you want her out of the way too?'

He put down what he was carrying and I saw they were canvasses. 'You're not being rational, and that's understandable, but—'

'Get out! Get the fuck out!'

I yelled my ugly grief at him, yelling over and over, still yelling when he'd gone. Amias came hurrying in through the open front door, bleary from sleep. 'I heard shouting.' In the silence he looked at my face. He knew without me saying anything. His body caved and then he turned away, not wanting me to witness his grief.

The phone rang and I let the answerphone get it. 'Hi, it's Tess.'

For a moment the rules of reality had been broken, you were alive. I grabbed the receiver.

'Darling? Are you there?' asked Todd. What I had heard earlier was, of course, just your answerphone greeting. 'Beatrice? Have you picked up?'

'She was found in a public lavatory. She'd been there for five days. All alone.'

There was a pause; the information not squaring with his predicted scenario. 'I'll be there as soon as I can.'

Todd was my safety rope. That was why I'd chosen him. Whatever happened I'd have him to hold on to.

I looked at the pile of canvasses Emilio had left behind. They were all nudes of you. You've never had my shyness

75

that way. He must have painted them. In each of the paintings your face was turned away.

❦

'The next morning you went to DS Finborough with your concerns?' Mr Wright asks.

'Yes. He said that Emilio collecting his paintings was extremely insensitive, but not necessarily anything more than that. He told me the coroner would be asking for a post-mortem and we should wait for the results before making any accusations or reaching any conclusions.'

His language was so measured, so controlled. It infuriated me. Maybe in my volatile state I was jealous of his balance.

'I thought that DS Finborough would at least ask Emilio what he was doing the day she was killed. He told me that until the results of the post-mortem they wouldn't know when Tess had died.'

Miss Crush Secretary comes in with mineral water and I am glad of the interruption. Oddly dehydrated, I gulp down the water and notice first her pearly pink nail varnish and then a wedding ring on her finger. Why was it that I only checked Mr Wright's left hand yesterday? I feel sad for Mr Crush Secretary who, while not in any danger of imminent sexual betrayal, is emotionally cuckolded 9.00 to 5.30 on a daily basis. Mr Wright smiles at her. 'Thanks, Stephanie.' His smile is innocent of any overtone, but its very openness is alluring and can be misinterpreted. I wait for her to leave.

'So I went to see Emilio Codi myself.'

I go back into that precipitous past; my grip a little firmer because of nail varnish and wedding rings.

❦

76

I left the police station, anger sparking through exhaustion. DS Finborough had said that they didn't yet know when you had died, but I knew. It was Thursday. You left Simon by the lido in Hyde Park on that day as he'd said, but you never got out of the park. Nothing else made any sense.

I phoned your art college and a secretary with a German accent tartly told me Emilio was sorting out coursework at home. But when I told her I was your sister, she sweetened and gave me his address.

As I drove there I remembered our conversation about where Emilio lives.

'I've no idea. We only ever meet at the college or at my flat.'

'So what's he trying to hide?'

'It just doesn't crop up, that's all.'

'I expect he lives somewhere like Hoxton. Trendily middle class, but with the chic edge of poor people around.'

'You really loathe him, don't you?'

'With just enough graffiti to keep the urban jungle look. I reckon people like him go out at night with spray paints just so that the area stays trendily tagged and doesn't degenerate into middle-class middle-income nappy valley.'

'What's he done to deserve this?'

'Oh I don't know. Perhaps having sex with my little sister, getting her pregnant and then abnegating all responsibility.'

'You make me sound like I'm completely incompetent at running my own life.'

I let your words hang in the wire between our two phones. I could hear the chuckle in your voice. 'You left out him being my tutor and abusing his position of authority.'

You never could take my seriousness seriously.

Well I found out where he lives, and it isn't Hoxton or

77

Brixton or any of those places where the trendy middle classes arrive once there's a café with skinny lattes. It's Richmond; beautiful, sensible Richmond. And his house is not a Richard Rogers type of building but a Queen Anne gem whose large front garden alone must be worth a street or two in Peckham. I walked through his impressively long front garden and knocked on his original period doorknocker.

You can't believe I went through with it, can you? My actions seem extreme, but new raw grief strips away logic and moderation. Emilio opened the door and I thought the adjectives which apply to him are stock phrases in romantic fiction: he is devilishly handsome; he has animal magnetism; adjectives that have threat embedded in them.

'Did you kill her?' I asked. 'You didn't answer my question last time.'

He tried to close the door on me, but I held it open. I had never used physical force against a man before and I was surprisingly strong. All those meticulously kept meetings with a personal trainer had had a purpose after all.

'She told her landlord she was getting frightening phone calls. Was that you?' I asked.

Then I heard a woman's voice in the hallway behind him, 'Emilio?' His wife joined him at the doorway. I still have our emails about her.

From: tesshemming@hotmail.co.uk
To: Beatrice Hemming's iPhone

Hi Bee, I asked him about her, before any of this started, and he told me that they married in haste and are at leisure together but not repenting. They enjoy each other's company but the physical relationship between them stopped years ago. Neither of them is jealous of the other. Happy now?
T XXXX

Dearest T,

How convenient for him. I imagine she's also
forty-something and as nature's far more cruel to women
than men what other choice is she left with? Not happy.
lol
Bee
PS Why are you using 'Coreyshand' as a
typeface for emails? It's not easy to read.

Dearest Bee, You walk down your straight and narrow
moral tightrope, not even teetering, while I fall off at
the first small wobble. But I do believe him. There's no
reason why anyone should get hurt.
T XXXX
PS I thought it was a friendly kind of typeface.
PPS Did you know lol means laughing out loud?

Dear Tess
You're surely not that naïve? Wise up.
Lol
Bee
(From me it means lots of love)

'Wise up'? You'll be telling me next to seek closure.
You need to leave the states and come home. Have a
nice day hon, T. X

I had imagined a forty-something woman whose looks had unfairly faded while her husband's had not. I had imagined parity at twenty-five, but a marriage of unequals fifteen years later. But the woman in the hall was no more than thirty. She has unnervingly pale-blue eyes.

'Emilio? What's going on?'

Her voice was cut-lead-glass aristocratic; the house must be hers. I didn't look at her, directing my question at Emilio. 'Where were you last Thursday, the twenty-third of January, the day my sister was murdered?'

Emilio turned to his wife. 'One of my students, Tess Hemming. She was on the local news last night, remember?'

Where was I when the news was on? Still in the morgue with you? Putting Mum to bed? Emilio put his arm around his wife, his voice measured. 'This is Tess's older sister. She's going through a terribly traumatic time and is . . . lashing out.' He was explaining me away. Explaining you away.

'For God's sake, Tess was your lover. And you know me because I interrupted you getting your paintings out of her flat last night.'

His wife stared at him, her face suddenly looked fragile. He tightened his arm around her.

'Tess had a crush on me. That's all. It was just a fantasy. The fantasy got out of control. I wanted to make sure there was nothing in her flat that she'd fabricated about me.'

I knew what you wanted me to say. 'Was the baby a fantasy too?'

His arm was still around his wife who was still and mute. 'There is no baby.'

I'm sorry. And I'm sorry for this next bit too.

'Mummy?'

A little girl was coming down the stairs. His wife took the child's hand. 'Bedtime, sweetie.'

I asked you once if he had children and you sounded astonished I'd even asked the question. '*Of course he doesn't, Bee.*' It was an '*Of course he doesn't because if he did I wouldn't be having sex with him, what do you take me for?*' Your moral tightrope might be a lot wider than mine, but that's your boundary and you wouldn't have crossed it. Not after Dad. So that was what he'd been trying to hide at home.

Emilio slammed the door shut in my face, this time my strength was no match for his. I heard him pulling the chain across. 'Leave me and my family alone.' I was left on the doorstep shouting through the door. Somehow I'd become the obsessed madwoman on the doorstep, while he was part of a persecuted little family besieged in their beautiful period home. I know, the previous day I had used lines from a TV cop show, now I was going Hollywood. But real life, at least my real life, hadn't given me any kind of model for what was happening.

I waited in their front garden. It grew dark and icily cold. In this stranger's snowy garden, with nothing familiar around me, I had Christmas carols playing silently in my head. You always liked the jolly ones, 'Ding Dong Merrily on High'; 'We Three Kings from Orient Far'; 'God Rest ye Merry Gentlemen'; singing about parties and presents and having a good time. I've always gone for the quiet reflective ones, 'Silent Night'; 'It Came Upon a Midnight Clear'. This time it was 'In the deep midwinter/Frosty wind made moan/ Earth stood hard as iron/Water like a stone.' I'd never realised that it was a song of the bereaved.

Emilio's wife came out of the house, interrupting my silent solo. A security light switched on illuminating her path towards me. I imagined she was coming to appease the madwoman in the garden before I started boiling up the bunnies.

'We weren't introduced earlier. I'm Cynthia.'

Maybe sang-froid is in the genes of the aristocracy. I found myself responding to this strange formal politeness, holding out my hand to take hers. 'Beatrice Hemming.'

She squeezed my hand, rather than shake it. Her politeness was something warmer. 'I'm so sorry about your sister. I have a younger sister too.' Her sympathy seemed genuine. 'Last night,' she continued, 'just after the news, he said he'd left his laptop at the college. It's an expensive one, important for his work, and he's a convincing liar. But I'd seen it in his study before dinner. I thought he was going off for sex.' She was talking quickly, as if she needed to get this over and done with. 'I'd known about it, you see, just hadn't confronted him with it. And I'd thought it had stopped. Months ago. But it serves me right. I know that. I did the same to his first wife. I'd never properly realised before what she must have gone through.'

I didn't reply, but found myself warming to her in this most unlikely of situations. The security light from the house flipped off, and we were in almost darkness together. It felt strangely intimate.

'What happened to their baby?' she asked. I'd never thought of him as anything other than your baby before. 'He died,' I said and in the darkness I thought her eyes had tears in them. I wondered if they were for your baby or for her failed marriage.

'How old was he?' she asked.

'He died while he was being born so I don't think he gets an age.'

It adds to the stillness in stillborn. I saw her hand move unconsciously to her tummy. I hadn't noticed before that it was a little distended, maybe five months pregnant. She brusquely wiped her tears away. 'This probably isn't what you

82

want to hear, but Emilio was working from home last Thursday, he usually does that one day a week. I was with him all day and then we went to a drinks party. Emilio's weak, with no moral fibre to speak of, but he wouldn't hurt anyone. Physically, at least.'

She turned to go, but I had a bomb to drop on her life first.

'Tess's baby had cystic fibrosis. It means Emilio must be a carrier.'

I might as well have punched her. 'But our little girl, she's fine.'

You and I have grown up with genetics, as other children grow up knowing about their dad's football team. This wasn't a great time for a crash course, but I tried.

'The CF gene is recessive. That means that even if you and Emilio both carry it, you both also carry a healthy gene. So your baby would have a fifty-per-cent chance of having CF.'

'And if I'm not a carrier of the CF gene?'

'Then there's no way your baby can have it. *Both* parents have to carry it.'

She nodded, still reeling.

'It's probably best to get checked out.'

'Yes.'

I wanted to steady the shakiness in her voice. 'Even in the worst case scenario, there's a new therapy now.'

I felt her warmth in the snowy garden. 'You're very generous to be concerned.'

Emilio came out onto the doorstep and called her name. She didn't move or acknowledge him in any way, looking intently at me. 'I hope they find the person who killed your sister.'

She turned and walked slowly back to the house, triggering the security light. In its glare I could see Emilio putting an arm around her, but she shrugged him off, hugging her arms tightly around herself. He caught sight of me watching then turned away.

I waited in the wintry darkness till the lights in the house were switched off.

6

As I drove back to your flat along precariously icy roads, Todd phoned to say he was getting a flight to Heathrow, landing in the morning and the thought of him made the road feel a little more secure somehow.

The next morning, standing at the arrivals barrier, I didn't recognise him when he walked through, my eyes still scanning for someone else – an idealised Todd? You? When I did see him he seemed slighter than I remembered him, a little smaller. The first thing I asked was if a letter from you had arrived, but there was nothing.

He had brought a case of clothes for me with everything he thought I'd need, including an appropriate outfit for your funeral and a prescription of sleeping pills from my US doctor. That first morning, and from then on, he made sure I ate properly. The description of him, of us, feels a little disconnected I know, but that's how it felt.

He was my safety rope. But he wasn't – yet – breaking my fall.

I have left out Todd's arrival but told Mr Wright about my confrontation on Emilio's doorstep and my time in the garden with his wife.

'I knew Emilio had a motive for killing Tess – losing his job and possibly his marriage. Now I also knew that he was capable of living with a lie. And of twisting the truth into the shape he wanted. Even in front of me, her sister, he had claimed Xavier was no more than the fantasy of an obsessed student.'

'And Mrs Codi, did you believe her alibi for him?'

'At the time I did. I liked her. But later, I thought she might have chosen to lie for him to protect her little girl and unborn baby. I thought that her children came first with her and for their sake she wouldn't want him in prison; and that her little girl was the reason she hadn't left Emilio when she'd discovered he'd been unfaithful.'

Mr Wright looks down at a file in front of him. 'You didn't tell the police about this encounter?'

The file must be the police log of my calls.

'No. Two days later, DS Finborough told me that Emilio Codi had made a formal complaint about me to his boss, Detective Inspector Haines.'

'What did you think his reason was?' asks Mr Wright.

'I wasn't sure, and I didn't think about it at the time because in that same phone call DS Finborough said that they'd got the post-mortem results back. I was surprised they'd done it so quickly but he told me that they always try to, so that the family can have a funeral.'

I'm sorry that your body had to be cut again. The Coroner requested it and we had no say in it. But I don't think you mind. You've always been a pragmatist about death, having no sentiment for the body left behind. When Leo died Mum and I hugged his dead body to us, cheating ourselves with the illusion that we were still hugging Leo. At just six years old you walked away. I pitied you for your courage.

I, on the other hand, have always been reverential. When we found Thumbelina dead in her hutch, you prodded her with slender five-year-old fingers to discover what death felt like, even as you wept; while I wrapped her in a silk scarf believing with all the solemnity of a ten-year-old that a dead body is precious. I can hear you laughing at me for talking about a rabbit – the point is I've always thought a body is more than a vessel for the soul.

But the night you were found I had a powerful sense of you leaving your body and vortex-like sucking up all that you are with you. You were trailing clouds of glory in the opposite direction. Maybe the image was prompted by your Chagall print in the kitchen, those ethereal people rising heavenwards, but whatever caused it, I knew that your body no longer held any part of you.

Mr Wright is looking at me and I wonder how long I have been silent.

'What was your reaction to the post-mortem?' he asks.

'Strangely, I didn't mind about what happened to her body,' I say, deciding to keep Chagall and trailing clouds of glory in reverse to myself. But I will confide in him a little. 'A child's body is so much a part of who they are; maybe because we can hold a little boy in our arms. We can hold the whole of him. But when we grow too large to be held our body no longer defines us.'

'When I asked you what your reaction was to the post-mortem, I meant whether you believed its findings.'

I am hotly embarrassed but thankful that I at least kept Chagall to myself. His face softens as he looks at me. 'I'm glad I wasn't clear.'

I still feel heatedly ridiculous but smile back at him, a

tentative first step to laughing at myself. And I think I knew, really, that he wanted me to talk about its findings. But just as I'd chosen to ask DS Finborough why the post-mortem had been done so quickly, with Mr Wright I was again putting off its results. Now I must address it.

'Later that day DS Finborough came round to the flat with the post-mortem report, to give me the results.'

He'd said he'd rather do it in person and I thought it kind of him.

⸙

From your sitting-room window I watched DS Finborough coming down the steep basement steps, and I wondered if he was walking slowly because they were slippery with ice or because he was reluctant to have this meeting. Behind him was WPC Vernon, her sensible shoes giving her a good grip, her gloved hand holding the railing just in case; a sensible woman who had children at home to look after that evening.

DS Finborough came into your sitting room but didn't sit down or take off his coat. I'd tried to bleed your radiators but your flat was still uncomfortably cold.

'I'm sure you'll be relieved to know that Tess's body showed no evidence of any sexual assault.'

That you had been raped had been an unarticulated anxiety, corrosively hideous at the edge of my imagining. I felt relief as a physical force.

DS Finborough continued, 'We know for definite now that she died on Thursday twenty-third of January.'

It confirmed what I already knew, that you had never made it out of the park after seeing Simon.

'The post-mortem shows that Tess died because of bleeding from the lacerations to her arms,' continued DS Finborough.

'There are no signs of any struggle. There's no reason to believe that anyone else is involved.'

It took a moment for the meaning of his words to make sense, as if I was translating a foreign language into my own.

'The Coroner has returned a verdict of suicide,' he said.

'No. Tess wouldn't kill herself.'

DS Finborough's face was kind. 'Under normal circumstances I'm sure you're right, but these weren't normal circumstances, were they? Tess was suffering not only grief but also post-natal—'

I interrupted him, angry that he dared tell me about you when he didn't know you. 'Have you ever watched someone die from cystic fibrosis?' I asked. He shook his head, and was going to say something, but I headed him off. 'We watched our brother struggling to breathe and we couldn't help him. He tried so hard to live, but he drowned in his own fluid and there was nothing we could do. When you've watched someone you love fight for life, that hard, you value it too highly to ever throw it away.'

'As I said, in normal circumstances, I'm sure—'

'In *any* circumstances.'

My emotional assault had not dented his certainty. I would have to convince him with logic; muscular, masculine argument. 'Surely there must be a connection to the threatening phone calls she was getting?'

'Her psychiatrist told us that they were most likely all in her head.'

I was astonished. 'What?'

'He's told us that she was suffering from post-natal psychosis.'

'The phone calls were delusional and my sister was mad? Is that it now?'

'Beatrice . . .'

89

'You told me before she was suffering from post-natal depression. Why has that suddenly changed to psychosis?'

Against my hectoring anger, his tone was so measured. 'From the evidence that seems now to be the most probable.'

'But Amias said the phone calls were real, when he reported her missing, didn't he?'

'But he was never actually there when she got one of the phone calls.'

I thought about telling him that your phone was unplugged when I arrived. But that didn't prove anything. The calls could still have been delusional.

'Tess's psychiatrist has told us that symptoms of post-natal psychosis include delusions and paranoia,' DS Finborough continued. 'Sadly, many of those women suffering also have thoughts of harming themselves and tragically some actually do.'

'But Tess didn't.'

'A knife was found next to her body, Beatrice.'

'You think she carried a knife now?'

'It was a kitchen one. And it had her fingerprints on it.'

'What kind of kitchen knife?'

I'm not sure why I asked, maybe some dimly remembered seminar on the questioner taking authority. There was a moment of hesitation before he replied, 'A Sabatier five-inch boning knife.'

But I only heard the word 'Sabatier', maybe because it distracted me from the ugly violence of the rest of the description. Or maybe the word 'Sabatier' struck me because it was so absurd to think you would own one.

'Tess couldn't possibly have afforded a Sabatier knife.'

Was this conversation degenerating into farce? Bathos?

'Maybe she got it from a friend,' suggested DS Finborough. 'Or it was a gift from someone.'

'She would have told me.'

Sympathy tempered his look of disbelief. I wanted to make him understand that we shared the details of our lives, because they were the threads that braided us so closely together. And you would have been certain to tell me about a Sabatier knife, because it would have had the rare value of being a detail in your life which tied directly into mine – our lives sharing top-end kitchenware.

'We told each other the little things, that's what made us so close I think, all the small things and she'd have known I'd want to hear about a Sabatier knife.'

No, I know, it didn't sound convincing.

DS Finborough's voice was sympathetic but firm, and I briefly wondered if, like parents, the police believed in setting parameters. 'I understand how hard this must be for you to accept. And I understand why you need to blame someone for her death, but—'

I interrupted with my certainty about you. 'I've known her since she was born. I know her better than anyone else possibly could. And she would never have killed herself.'

He looked at me with compassion; he didn't like doing this. 'You didn't know when her baby died, did you?'

I couldn't answer him, winded by his punch to a part of me already bruised and fragile. He'd told me once before, indirectly, that we weren't close, but then it came with the upside that you had run off somewhere without telling me. Not being close had meant you were still alive. But this time there was no huge pay-off.

'She bought airmail stamps, just before she died, didn't she? From the post office on Exhibition Road. So she must have written to me.'

'Has a letter from her arrived?'

I'd asked a neighbour to go in and check the apartment

daily. I'd phoned our local post office in New York and demanded they search. But there was nothing; and it would surely have arrived by now.

'Maybe she meant to write to me, but was prevented.'

I heard how weak it sounded. DS Finborough was looking at me with sympathy.

'I think Tess was going through hell after her baby died,' he said. 'And it isn't a place anyone could join her. Even you.'

I went through to the kitchen, 'stropping off' as Mum used to call it, but it wasn't a strop, more of an absolute physical denial of what he was saying. A few minutes later I heard the front door shut. They didn't know that words could seep through your badly fitting windows.

WPC Vernon's voice was quiet. 'Wasn't that a little . . . ?' She trailed off, or maybe I just couldn't hear.

Then DS Finborough's voice, sounding sad, I thought. 'The sooner she accepts the truth, the sooner she'll realise she's not to blame.'

But I knew the truth, as I know it now: we love each other; we are close; you would never have ended your own life.

A minute or so later, WPC Vernon came back down the steps, carrying your knapsack.

'I'm sorry, Beatrice. I meant to give you this.'

I opened the knapsack. Inside was just your wallet with your library card, your travel card and your student ID card – membership badges of a society with libraries and public transport and colleges for studying art; not a society in which a twenty-one-year-old can be murdered in a derelict toilets building and left for five days before being dismissed as a suicide case.

I tore open the lining, but there was no letter to me trapped inside.

WPC Vernon sat on the sofa next to me. 'There's this, too.' She took a photograph out of a board-backed envelope, sandwiched between more cardboard. I was touched by her care, as I had been by the way she'd packed your clothes for the reconstruction. 'It's a photo of her baby. We found it in her coat pocket.'

I took the Polaroid from her, uncomprehending. 'But her baby died.'

WPC Vernon nodded – as a mother she had more understanding. 'Then maybe a photo was even more important to her.'

To start with all I looked at in the photo were your arms as you held the baby, your uncut wrists. The photo didn't show your face, and I didn't dare imagine it. I still don't.

I looked at him. His eyes were closed, as if asleep. His eyebrows were just a pencil line of down, barely formed and impossibly perfect; nothing crude or cruel or ugly in the world had ever been seen by his face. He was beautiful, Tess. Faultless.

I have the photo with me now. I carry it all the time.

WPC Vernon wiped her tears so that they wouldn't drop onto the photo. She had no edge around her compassion. I wondered if someone as open would be able to stay as a policewoman. I was trying to think of something other than your baby; other than you as you held him.

❧

As soon as I've told Mr Wright about the Polaroid I abruptly stand up and say I need to go to the loo. I get to the Ladies', tears running as soon as the door closes behind me. There's a woman at the basins, maybe a secretary, or lawyer. Whoever she is, she's discreet enough not to comment on my tears, but gives a little half-smile as she leaves, a gesture of some kind of solidarity. There's more for me to tell you, but not Mr Wright, so as I sit in here and have a weep for Xavier, I'll tell you the next part.

❧

An hour or so after WPC Vernon had gone, Mum and Todd arrived at the flat. He'd driven all the way to Little Hadston to pick her up in my hire car, showing himself to be, as I knew he would, a chivalrous son-in-law. I told Mum and Todd what DS Finborough had said and Mum's face seemed to crumple into relief. 'But I think the police are wrong, Mum,' I said and saw her flinch. I saw her willing me not to carry on, but I did. 'I don't think she committed suicide.'

Mum pulled her coat more tightly around her. 'You'd rather she'd been murdered?'

'I need to know what really happened. Don't you—'

She interrupted me. 'We all know what happened. She wasn't in her right mind. The Inspector's told us that.' She'd promoted DS Finborough to Inspector, reinforcing her side of the argument. I caught the note of desperation in her voice. 'She probably didn't even know what she was doing.'

'Your mother's right, darling,' Todd chimed in. 'The police know what they're talking about.'

He sat down next to Mum on the sofa and did that man thing of spreading his legs wide; taking up twice as much room as was necessary; being masculine and large. His smile skidded over my closed-in face to Mum's receptive one. He sounded almost hearty.

'The good thing is that now the post-mortem is over and done with we can organise her funeral.'

Mum nodded, looking gratefully at him, like a little girl. She clearly bought his big-man thing.

'Do you know where you'd like her laid to rest?' he asked.

'Laid to rest', like you would be put to bed and in the morning it would all be better. Poor Todd, not his fault that his euphemisms infuriated me. Mum clearly didn't mind. 'I'd like her buried in the churchyard in the village. Next to Leo.' In case you don't know already, that's where your body is. In my more vulnerable moments I fantasise about you and Leo being together somewhere, wherever that somewhere is. The thought of the two of you having each other makes me feel a little less desperate. But of course if there is a somewhere, a third person would be with you too.

I want to warn you that what's coming will be painful. I took the photo out of the cardboard casing and handed it to Mum. 'It's a photo of Tess's baby.'

Mum wouldn't take the picture from me; she didn't even look at it. 'But it was dead.'

I'm sorry.

'The baby was a boy.'

'Why have a picture? It's macabre.'

Todd tried to come to the rescue. 'I think they let people have photos when their babies die now as part of the grieving process.' Mum gave Todd one of her looks that she normally only reserves for family. He shrugged as if to distance himself from such an outlandish and distasteful notion.

I carried on, alone. 'Tess would want her baby buried with her.'

Mum's voice was suddenly loud in the flat. 'No. I won't have it.'

'It's what she'd want.'

'She'd want everyone to know about her illegitimate baby? That's what she'd want? To have her shame made public?'

'She would never have found him shameful.'

'Well she should have done.'

It was Mum on autopilot; forty years of being infected with Middle England's prejudices.

'Do you want to stick an "A" on her coffin for good measure?' I asked.

Todd butted in. 'Darling, that's uncalled for.'

I stood up. 'I'm going out for a walk.'

'In the snow?'

The words were more critical than concerned. It was Todd who said it, but it could just have easily been Mum. I'd never spent time with both of them together before and was only just realising their similarities. I wondered if that was the real reason I was going to marry him; maybe familiarity, even negative familiarity, breeds feelings of security rather than contempt. I looked at Todd, was he coming?

'I'll stay here with your mother then.'

I'd always thought that whatever worst-case scenario happened in my life I'd have Todd to cling to. But now I realised why no one could be my safety rope. I'd been falling since you were found – plummeting – too fast and too far for anyone to break my fall. And what I needed was someone who would risk joining me now seven miles down in the dark.

☙

Mr Wright must see my puffy face as I walk in. 'Are you all right to carry on?'

'Absolutely fine.' My voice sounds brisk. He senses that this is the style that I want and continues, 'Did you ask DS Finborough for a copy of the post-mortem?'

'Not then, no. I accepted DS Finborough's word that nothing else had been found in the post-mortem apart from the cuts to her arms.'

'And then you went to the park?'

'Yes. On my own.'

I'm not sure why I added that. My feeling of being let down by Todd must still survive, even now, in all its irrelevancy.

I glance at the clock, almost one.

'Would it be OK if we break for lunch?' I ask. I'm meeting Mum at ten past in a restaurant round the corner.

'Of course.'

I said I'd tell you the story as I found out myself – no jumping forwards – but it's not fair on you or Mum to keep back what she feels now. And as I set the rules, I'm allowed to curve them a little now and then.

I arrive at the restaurant a few minutes early and through a window see Mum already sitting at a table. She no longer has her hair 'done' and without the scaffolding of a perm it hangs straight and limp around her face.

When she sees me her taut face relaxes. She hugs me in the middle of the restaurant, only mildly concerned that she is holding up a waiter en route to the kitchen. She strokes my hair (now longer) away from my face. I know, not Mum at all. But grief has pressed out of her all that we thought of as Mum-ish, leaving exposed someone who felt deeply familiar, connected to the rustle of a dressing gown in the dark and a feeling of warm arms before I could talk.

I order a half-bottle of Rioja and Mum looks at me with concern. 'Are you sure you should be drinking?'

'It's only half a bottle, Mum. Between two of us.'

'But even a little alcohol can be a depressive. I read about it somewhere.'

There's a moment of silence and then we both laugh, almost a real laugh, because being depressed would be so welcome compared with the pain of bereavement.

'It must be hard going through everything, having to remember it all,' she says.

'It's not so bad actually. The CPS solicitor, Mr Wright, is very kind.'

'Where have you got to?'

'The park. Just after the post-mortem result.'

She moves her hand to cover mine, so that we hold hands as lovers do, openly on the tablecloth. 'I should have stopped you going. It was freezing.' Her warm hand over mine makes tears start behind my eyes. Fortunately, Mum and I travel everywhere now with at least two packets of Handy-Andy tissues in pockets and handbags, and little polythene bags to put the sodden ones into. I also carry Vaseline and lipsalve and the futile-hopeful Rescue Remedy for when tears overwhelm me somewhere inappropriate like the motorway or the supermarket. There's a whole range of handbag accessories that go with grief.

'Todd should have gone with you,' she says and her criticism of Todd is somehow an affirmation of me.

I wipe my nose with a handkerchief she gave me last week, a little-girl cotton one with embroidered flowers. She says cotton stings less than a tissue, besides it's a little more eco and I know you'd appreciate that.

She squeezes my hand. 'You deserve to be loved. Properly loved.'

From anyone other than Mum it would be a cliché, but as Mum has never said any of this stuff before it feels newly minted.

'You too,' I reply.

'I'm not all that sure that I'm worth having.'

You must find this conversation strange in its directness. I have got used to it but you won't have done yet. There were always spectres at our family feasts, taboo subjects that no one dared acknowledge, that our conversations tiptoed around, going into cul-de-sacs of not talking to each other at all. Well, now we strip these unwanted guests bare, Mum and I: Betrayal; Loneliness; Loss; Rage. We talk them into invisibility so that they're no longer sitting between us.

There's a question I've never asked her, partly because I'm pretty sure I know the answer and because, deliberately I think, we'd never created the opportunity.

'Why did you call me by my second name not my first?' I ask. I presume that she and Dad, especially Dad, thought Arabella, a beautiful romantic name, inapplicable to me from the very beginning, so they opted instead for starchy Beatrice. But I'd like the detail.

'A few weeks before you were born we'd been to the National Theatre to see *Much Ado about Nothing*,' Mum replies. She must see my surprise because she adds, 'Your father and I used to do things like that, before children came along, we'd go to London for the evening and get the last train home. Beatrice is the heroine. She's so plucky. And outspoken. Her own person. Even as a baby, it suited you. Your father said Arabella was too wishy-washy for you.'

Mum's answer is so unexpected, and I am a little stunned actually. I wonder if I'd known the reason for my name as a child whether I'd have tried to live up to it, instead of being a failed Arabella I might have become a plucky Beatrice. But, although I'd like to, I can't linger on this. I only asked the question as a lead up to the real one.

99

You're upset that she could believe you committed suicide – after Leo – and knowing the suffering it would cause. I tried to tell you, as I reported it, that she was grabbing at a safety rail, that it was a self-protection reflex, but you need to hear it from her.

'Why did you think Tess had committed suicide?' I ask.

If she's surprised by the question she doesn't show it, not hesitating for a moment in her reply. 'Because I'd rather feel guilty for the rest of my life than for her to have felt a second's fear.'

Her tears fall onto the white damask tablecloth but she doesn't mind the waiter's stare, not caring any more about 'form' and socially correct behaviour. She's the mother in the rustling dressing gown sitting at the end of our beds smelling of face cream in the dark. The glimpse I had as she first shed her old Mum-ness is now fully exposed.

I never knew so much love could exist for someone until I saw Mum grieving for you. With Leo, I was away at boarding school and didn't witness it. I find her grief both shocking and beautiful. And it makes me afraid of being a mother, of risking what she feels now – what you must have felt for Xavier.

There's a short silence, a hangover from a previous time of silences, but then Mum talks into it. 'You know I don't mind much about the trial. Not at all if I'm being totally honest.' She looks at me, checking for a reaction, but I say nothing. I've heard her say this before in a myriad of different ways. She doesn't care about justice or revenge, just you.

'She's been in the headlines for days,' Mum announces with pride. (I think I already told you that she's proud of all the media attention?) She thinks you deserve to be on everybody's front page and topping the bill on the news, not because of your story but because everyone should know all about you. They should be told about your kindness, your warmth, your talent, your beauty. For Mum it's not 'Stop the clocks', but 'Run the presses!', 'Turn on the TV!', 'Look at my wonderful daughter!'

'Beatrice?'

My vision is blurring. I can just hear Mum's voice. 'Are you all right . . . ? Poppet . . . ?'

The anxiety in her voice jolts me back into full consciousness. I see the worry on her face and hate to be the cause of it, but the waiter is still clearing the next table, so it can't have been for long.

'I'm fine. Shouldn't have had wine, that's all, it makes me woozy at lunch time.'

Outside the restaurant I promise to come and see her at the weekend and reassure her that I'll phone her this evening, as I do every evening. In the bright spring sunshine we hug goodbye and I watch her walk away. Amongst the shining hair and brisk walk of office workers returning from lunch breaks, Mum's non-reflective grey hair stands out for its dullness, her walk uncertain. She seems weighted down by her grief, physically stooping as if not strong enough to bear it. As I watch her amongst the crowd she reminds me of a tiny dingy in an enormous sea, impossibly still afloat.

There's a limit to how much I can ask her in one wallop. But you want to know if Xavier is buried with you. Of course he is, Tess. Of course he is. In your arms.

7

I arrive back for the afternoon session with Mr Wright, a few minutes late. My head still feels strange, not quite in focus. I ask Mrs Crush Secretary for a strong coffee. I need to tell your story with sharp reflexes, a memory with neurons firing, not half-asleep. I want to say what I have to and go home and phone Mum to make sure she's OK.

Mr Wright reminds me where we'd got to.

'Then you went to Hyde Park?'

❧

I left Mum and Todd, walking hurriedly up your icy basement steps, pulling on my coat. I'd thought that my gloves were in my pocket, but only one remained. It was mid-afternoon and the pavements were almost deserted; it was too cold to be out for no reason. I walked hurriedly towards Hyde Park, as if there was a deadline to keep, as if I was late. When I got to the Lancaster Gate entrance I stopped. What was I doing here? Was this just a strop that had needed to find a focus? 'I'm *not* sulking! I'm going to find my tea set!' I remember my six-year-old outrage as I ran up the stairs. There was a real purpose this time, even if it had been prompted by wanting to get away from Mum and Todd. I needed to see where your life had ended.

I went through the open wrought-iron gates. The cold and the snow was so like the day you were found that I felt time pulling me back through the previous six days to that afternoon. I started walking towards the derelict toilets building, pushing my gloveless hand deep into the pocket of my coat. I saw young children building a snowman with energetic earnestness, a mother watching and stamping her feet to keep warm. She called to them to finish now. The children and their snowman were the only things to be different, perhaps that was why I focused on them, or maybe it was their ignorance and innocence of what had happened here that meant I wanted to watch them. I walked on towards the place you were found, my gloveless hand stinging with cold. I could feel the packed snow beneath the thin soles of my shoes. They were not meant for a snowy park but a New York lunch party in a different life.

I reached the derelict toilets building, totally unprepared for the bouquets. There were hundreds of them. We're not talking a Princess Diana ocean of floral grief, but masses, nonetheless. Some were half-buried in snow, they must have been there for a few days, others were newer, still pristine in their bouquet cellophane. There were teddy bears too, and for a moment I was perplexed before realising they were for Xavier. There was a police cordon around the small building, making a neat parcel of the scene of your death with a yellow and black plastic ribbon. I thought it odd that the police should make their presence felt here so long after you'd needed their help. The ribbon and flowers were the only colours in the white-out park.

103

I checked there was no one around, then climbed over the yellow and black ribbon. I didn't think it strange then that there was no police officer. WPC Vernon has since told me that a police officer always has to be present at a crime scene. They have to stand by that cordon, come what may, in all weathers. She says she gets desperate for the loo. It's this, she's told me, that will end her career as a policewoman rather than being too empathetic. Yes, I'm prevaricating.

I went inside. I don't need to describe to you what it looked like. Whatever state you were in, you'd have noticed your surroundings in detail. Your eyes are an artist's eyes and I wish that the last place you'd seen hadn't been stained and vile and ugly. I went into a cubicle and saw bloodstains on the concrete floor and splatters of blood on the peeling walls. I vomited into a basin, before realising it wasn't attached to any drain. I knew that no one would willingly choose to go into that place. No one would choose to die there.

I tried not to think of you being there for five nights, all alone. I tried to cling on to my Chagall image of you leaving your body, but I couldn't be sure of the time scale. Did you leave your body, as I so fervently hoped, the moment you died? Or maybe it was later, when you were found, when your body was seen by someone other than your murderer. Or was it in the morgue when the police sergeant pulled back the blanket and I identified you – did grief release you?

I walked out of the foul-smelling, vile building and breathed in the cold till it hurt my lungs, grateful for the white iced air. The bouquets made sense to me now. Decent people were trying to fight evil with flowers; the good fighting under the pennants of bouquets. I remembered the road to Dunblane lined with soft toys. I had never understood before why anyone would think a family whose child had been shot would want a teddy. But now I did; against the sound of gunshots a thousand compassionate soft toys muffled a little their reverberating horror. 'Mankind isn't like this,' the offerings say, 'we are not like this. The world isn't only this way.'

I started reading the cards. Some of them were illegible, soaked with snow, the ink melting into the sodden paper. I recognised Kasia's name, she'd left a teddy with 'Xavier' in large childish writing, the dot of the 'i' a heart, crosses to show kisses, circles for hugs. The snob in me flinched at her bad taste, but I was also touched and felt guilty for my snobbishness. I resolved to look up her phone number when I got home and thank her for her thoughtfulness.

I gathered up the legible cards to take away with me – no one else would want to read them but Mum and I. As I put them into my pockets I saw a middle-aged man with a Labrador a little distance away, his dog on a tight leash. He was carrying a bunch of chrysanthemums. I remembered him from the afternoon you were found, watching the police activity; the dog was straining to get away then, too. He was hesitating, maybe waiting for me to go before he laid his flowers. I went up to him. He was wearing a tweed hat and Barbour jacket, a country squire who should be out in his estate not a London park.

'Were you a friend of Tess's?' I asked.

'No. I didn't even know her name till it was on the television,' he replied. 'We just used to wave, that's all. When you pass someone quite frequently, you start to form some kind of connection. Just a small one of course, more like recognition.' He blew his nose. 'I've really no right to be upset, absurd I know. How about you, did you know her?'

'Yes.'

Whatever DS Finborough said, I knew you. The Country Squire hesitated, unsure of the etiquette of keeping up a conversation by floral tributes. 'That policeman's gone then? He said the cordon will be going down soon, now that it's not a crime scene.'

Of course it wasn't a crime scene, not when the police had decided you'd committed suicide. The Country Squire seemed to be hoping for a reaction; he prodded a little further.

'Well you knew her, so you probably know what's going on better than me.'

Perhaps he was enjoying having a chat about this. The sensation of tears pricking isn't unpleasant. Terror and tragedy at enough removes is titillating, exciting even, to have a little connection to grief and tragedy that isn't yours. He could tell people, and no doubt did, that he was involved a little in all this, a bit player in the drama.

'I am her sister.'

Yes, I used the present tense. You being dead didn't stop me being your sister, our relationship didn't go into the past, otherwise I wouldn't be grieving now, present tense. The squire looked appalled. I think he hoped I was at a decent emotional remove too.

I walked away.

The snow, which had been falling randomly in soft flakes, became denser and angrier. I saw that the children's snowman was disappearing, engorged by new snow. I decided to go out of a different park exit, the memory of how I felt leaving the previous time too raw to be walked over again.

As I neared the Serpentine Gallery it started blizzarding fiercely, suffocating trees and grass with white. Soon, your flowers and Xavier's bears would be covered, turned invisible. My feet were numb, my gloveless hand aching with cold. The vomiting had left me with a foul taste in my mouth. I thought I'd go into the Serpentine Gallery and see if they had a café with water. But as I approached the building I saw it was in darkness, the doors chained. A notice on the window said the gallery was not opening again until April. Simon could not have met you there. He was the last person to see you alive and he'd lied. His lie played over in my head, like tinnitus, the only sound not muffled by the falling snow.

I walked along Chepstow Road back to your flat, holding on my mobile for DS Finborough, my pockets stuffed with the cards from teddies and bouquets. From a distance, I saw Todd outside, pacing in short anxious strides. Mum had already taken the train home. He followed me into the flat, relief mutating his anxiety into annoyance. 'I tried to phone you, but you've been engaged.'

'Simon lied about meeting Tess at the Serpentine Gallery. I have to tell DS Finborough.'

Todd's reaction, or rather lack of it, should have prepared me for DS Finborough's. But just then DS Finborough came onto the line. I told him about Simon.

He sounded patient, gentle even. 'Maybe Simon was just trying to look good.'

'By lying?'

'By saying they met at a gallery.' I could hardly believe DS Finborough was making excuses for him. 'We did talk to Simon, when we knew he'd been with her that day,' he continued. 'And there's no reason to think that he had any involvement in her death.'

'But he lied about where they were.'

'Beatrice, I think you should try to—'

I flipped through the clichés I imagined he was about to use; I should try to 'move on', 'put it behind me', even with a little flourish of clauses 'accept the truth and get on with my life'. I interrupted before any of these clichés took verbal form.

'You've seen the place where she died, haven't you?'

'Yes I have.'

107

'Do you think anyone would choose to die there?'

'I don't think it was a matter of choice.'

For a moment I thought he had started to believe me, then realised he was blaming mental illness for your murder. Like an obsessive compulsive who has no choice but to repeat the same task a hundred times, a woman with post-natal psychosis gets swept along by her mental tide of madness to inevitable self-destruction. A young woman with friends, family, talent and beauty who is found dead arouses suspicion. Even if her baby has died there's still a question mark about the end of her life. But throw psychosis into the list of life-affirming adjectives and you take away the question mark; you give a mental alibi to the killer, framing the victim for her own murder.

'Somebody forced her into that terrible place and killed her there.'

DS Finborough was still patient with me. 'But there was no reason any one would want to kill her. It wasn't a sexual crime, thank God, and there was no theft involved. And when we were investigating her disappearance, we couldn't find anyone who wished her harm, in fact quite the reverse.'

'Will you at least talk to Simon again?'

'I really don't believe there's anything to be gained by that.'

'Is it because Simon is the son of a cabinet minister?'

I threw that at him in an attempt to make him change his mind, to shame him into it.

'My decision not to talk to Simon Greenly again is because there is no purpose to be served by it.'

Now I know him better I know that he uses formal language when he feels emotionally pressurised.

'But you're aware that Simon's father is Richard Greenly MP?'

'I don't think this phone call is getting us very far. Perhaps—'

'Tess isn't worth the risk to you, is she?'

❧

Mr Wright has poured me a glass of water. Describing the toilets building made me retch. I have told him about Simon's lie and my phone call to DS Finborough. But I have left out that as I spoke to DS Finborough Todd hung up my coat; that he took the cards out of the pockets and neatly laid each one out to dry; and that instead of feeling that he was being considerate, each damp card smoothed out felt a criticism; that I knew he was taking DS Finborough's side, even though he could only hear mine.

'So after DS Finborough said he wouldn't interview Simon you decided to do it yourself?' asks Mr Wright. I think I detect a hint of amusement in his voice; it wouldn't be surprising.

'Yes, it was getting to be something of a habit.'

And just eight days earlier, flying into London, I'd been someone who always avoided confrontation. But in comparison to the murderous brutality of your death, confrontation with words seemed harmless and a little trivial. Why had I ever been daunted by it before, afraid even? That seemed so cowardly – ludicrous – now.

❧

Todd was going off to buy a toaster. ('*I can't believe your sister had to grill her toast.*') Our toaster in New York had a defrost function and a croissant warming mode that we actually used. At the door he turned to me.

'You look exhausted.'

109

Was he being concerned or critical?

'I told you last night you should take one of Dr Broadbent's sleeping pills I got for you.'

Critical.

He left to go and get the toaster.

I hadn't explained to him why I couldn't take a sleeping pill – that it would have felt cowardly blotting you out, even for a few hours. Nor would I tell him now that I was going to see Simon, because he would have felt duty-bound to stop me being 'so rash and ridiculous'.

I drove to Simon's address, which I'd found on a Post-it in your address book, and parked outside a three-storey mansion in Kensington. Simon buzzed me in and I made my way up to the top flat. When he opened the door I barely recognised him. His soft baby face was ridged with tiredness; his designer stubble grown into the beginnings of a sparse beard.

'I'd like to talk to you about Tess.'

'Why? I thought you knew her best.' His voice was snide with jealousy.

'You were close to her too, weren't you?' I asked.

'Yeah.'

'So can I come in?'

He left the door open and I followed him into a large opulent drawing room. It must be his father's London pad when he isn't in his constituency. On one wall, running along the length of the double drawing room, was a vast painting of a prison. Looking closer, I saw that it was actually a collage; the prison made from thousands of passport-sized photos of babies' faces. It was engrossing and repelling.

'The Serpentine Gallery is closed until April, you couldn't have met Tess there.'

He just shrugged, apparently unconcerned.

'Why did you lie?' I asked.

110

'I just liked the idea, that's all,' he replied. 'It made our meeting sound like a date. The Serpentine Gallery is the kind of place Tess would choose for a date.'

'But it wasn't a date, was it?'

'Does it really matter now if I rewrite our history a little? Make it something I want it to be? Put a little fantasy in? There's no harm in that.'

I wanted to yell at him, but nothing would be served but the brief instant gratification of expressed rage.

'So why did you meet her in the park? It must have been freezing out.'

'It was Tess who wanted to go to the park. Said she needed to be outside. Told me she was going crazy stuck indoors.'

'"Crazy"? She used that word?'

I've never heard you say it. Although you talk nineteen to the dozen you choose words carefully, and you're patriotically English about vocabulary, berating me for my Americanisms.

Simon picked up a velvet bag from a mirrored glass cabinet. 'Maybe she said she was claustrophobic. I don't remember.' That sounded more likely.

'Did she give a reason for wanting to see you?' I asked.

He fussed around with Rizla papers not replying.

'Simon . . . ?'

'She just wanted to spend time with me. Jesus, is that so hard for you to understand?'

'How did you find out she was dead?' I asked. 'Did a friend tell you? Did they tell you about the slashes to the insides of her arms?'

I wanted to tip him into tears, because I know that tears dissolve into wet saltiness the defences around what we want to keep private.

'Did they tell you she'd been there for five nights, all alone, in a stinking foul toilets building?'

111

Tears were welling up in his eyes, his voice quieter than usual. 'That day you found me outside her flat. I waited, just round the corner, till you left. Then followed you on my bike.'

I dimly remembered the sound of a motorbike revving as I left for Hyde Park. I hadn't taken any notice of it after that.

'I waited, for hours, outside the park gates. It was snowing,' continued Simon. 'I was already frozen, remember? I saw you come out with that policewoman. I saw a blacked-out van. No one would tell me anything. I wasn't family.'

His tears were flowing now; he made no effort to stop them. Like his art, I found him repellent.

'Later that evening it was on the local news,' he continued. 'Just a short item, barely two minutes, about a young woman who had been found dead in a Hyde Park toilet. They showed the student picture of her. That's how I discovered she was dead.'

He had to blow his nose and wipe his eyes and I judged it the right time to confront him.

'So why did she really want to meet you?'

'She said she was frightened and wanted me to help her.'

The tears had worked, as I knew they would; since that first night at boarding school when I broke down and admitted to my house mistress that it wasn't home and Mum I missed, but Dad.

'Did she tell you why she was frightened?' I asked.

'She said she'd been getting weird phone calls.'

'Did she tell you who it was?'

He shook his head. And I suddenly wondered if his tears were genuine or like the proverbial crocodile's, ruthless and without remorse.

'Why do you think she chose you, Simon? Why not one of her other friends?' I asked.

He had dried his tears now, closing up. 'We were very close.'

Maybe he saw my scepticism because his tone became angrily wounded. 'It's easier for you, you're her sister, you have a right to mourn her. People expect you to be in pieces. But I can't even say she was my girlfriend.'

'She didn't phone you, did she?' I asked.

He was silent.

'She would never have exploited your feelings for her.'

He tried to light his joint but his fingers were trembling and he couldn't get his lighter to work.

'What really happened?'

'I'd called her loads of times, but the answerphone was always on, or the line was engaged. But this time she answered it. She said she needed to get out of the flat. I suggested the park and she agreed. I didn't know that the Serpentine Gallery was shut. I'd hoped we could go there. When we met up in the park she asked me if she could stay at my flat. Said she needed to be with someone twenty-four/seven.' He paused, angry. 'She said I'm the only person at the college who doesn't have a part-time job.'

' "Twenty-four/seven?" '

'Round the clock. I can't remember her exact expression. Jesus, does it matter?' It did matter because it authenticated what he was telling me. 'She was frightened and she asked for my help, because I was convenient for her.'

'So why did you leave her?'

He seemed jolted by the question. 'What?'

'You said she wanted to stay with you, so why didn't you let her?'

He finally managed to light the joint and took a drag. 'OK, I told her what I felt for her. How much I loved her. Everything.'

113

'You came on to her?'

'It wasn't like that.'

'And she rejected you?'

'Straight out. No wrapping the bullet. She said this time she didn't think she could offer "with credibility" to be friends.'

His monstrous ego had sucked any pity for you, for your grief, into turning himself into the victim. But my anger was bigger than his ego.

'She turned to you and you tried exploit her need for protection.'

'She wanted to exploit me, it was that way round.'

'So she still wanted to stay with you?'

He didn't answer, but I could guess the next bit. 'But with no strings attached?'

Still he was silent.

'But you wouldn't allow that, would you?' I asked.

'And be emasculated?'

For a moment I think I just stared at him, too astonished by his gross selfishness to respond. He thought I didn't understand.

'The only reason she wanted to be with me was because she was terrified witless. How do you think that made me feel?'

'Terrified witless?'

'I exaggerated, I meant—'

'You said "frightened" before, now it's "terrified witless"?'

'OK. She said she thought a man had followed her into the park.'

I forced my voice into neutral. 'Did she tell you who the man was?'

'No. I searched for him. Even went scrapping around in the bushes, getting covered in snow and frozen dog turds. No one.'

'You have to go to the police. Talk to an officer called DS Finborough. He's at the Notting Hill police station, I'll give you the number.'

'There's no point. She committed suicide. It was on the local news.'

'But you were there. You know more than the TV, don't you?' I was talking as I would to a child, trying to coax, trying to hide my desperation. 'She told you about the man following her. You *know* she was frightened.'

'He was probably just a paranoid delusion. They said post-natal psychosis makes women go completely crazy.'

'Who said that?'

'Must have been the TV.'

He heard how lame that sounded. He met my eye, casually unconcerned. 'OK. Dad found out for me. I hardly ever ask anything of him, so when I do . . .'

He trailed off, as if he couldn't be bothered to complete the sentence. He took a step closer towards me and I smelled his aftershave, pungent in the overly warm flat. It brought into sharp sensory focus the first sight I'd had of him, sitting in the snow outside your flat, holding a bouquet, smelling of the same aftershave despite the cold air. I hadn't taken it in then, but why the flowers and the aftershave when you'd only ever offered him the consolation prize of friendship? And now, when I knew you'd turned him down outright?

'You had a bouquet when I found you waiting for her. You smelled of aftershave.'

'So?'

'You thought you'd try it again, didn't you? Maybe she'd be desperate enough by then to accept your conditions.'

He shrugged, not finding fault with himself. Spoilt since the time he was born; spoiling him so that he'd turned into

115

this man rather than the person he may once have had the potential to become.

I turned away from him, to see his enormous collage of babies' faces making up a picture of a prison.

I flinched from it and went to the door.

As I opened it, I felt tears on my face before realising I was crying.

'How could you have just left her there?'

'It wasn't my fault she killed herself.'

'Is anything ever your fault?'

❦

I am back with Mr Wright, the smell of Simon and his flat still pungent in my memory. I am grateful for the open window, the faint scent of newly mown grass reaching us from the park.

'Did you tell the police what Simon had told you?' Mr Wright asks.

'Yes, a junior of DS Finborough's. He was polite but I knew it would do no good. The man following her was her murderer but he could also have been a product of her supposed paranoia. The facts which pointed to murder also backed up the diagnosis of psychosis.'

Mr Wright looks at his watch, five fifteen. 'Shall we call it a day?'

I nod. Somewhere at the back of my nose and throat linger the remembered particles of dope and aftershave and I am grateful that I can go outside and breathe the fresh air first hand.

I walk across St James's Park then get a bus to the Coyote. I know you're curious about how I've come to be working

116

there. Initially I went to question the people you worked with, hoping someone could give me a clue about your death. But no one could help, they hadn't seen you since the Sunday before you'd had Xavier and they didn't know much about your life outside the Coyote. Meanwhile, my boss in the States had, *with great reluctance, Beatrice*, 'let me go' and I had no idea when I'd get another job. I knew my share of the mortgage for the New York apartment would soon eat up all my savings. I needed to earn something to live on, so I went back to ask Bettina for a job.

꽃

I was wearing my only clean clothes, which were a MaxMara trouser suit, and Bettina thought I was joking to start with but then realised I was genuine.

'OK. I could do with an extra pair of hands, two shifts at weekends and three during the week. You can start this evening. Six pounds per hour plus free dinner cooked by me if you're doing a shift longer than three hours.'

I must have looked a little startled that she had offered me such immediate work.

'The truth is,' said Bettina, 'I just really fancy you.' She giggled at my horror-struck face. 'Sorry, I couldn't resist.' Her laughter at my shockability reminded me of you; there was no cruelty in it.

As I did my shift that evening, I thought that as you had died there was, of course, a part-time position that had needed filling. But recently I discovered someone else had already taken the job so she'd hired me out of loyalty to you and sympathy for me.

꽃

I get home from the Coyote at almost midnight and don't expect many, if any, press. It's too late and in any case after the frenzy of the last few days they must have got all the pictures and footage they need. But I was wrong; as I get near I see there's a gang of them, their huge lights shining, and illuminated in the middle is Kasia. She's been at a friend's house for the last two days, until I thought the press attack would have died down enough for her to return. She's living with me now, which I think you're pleased about but curious about how we fit. Well, she has your bed and I have a futon in the sitting room, which I unroll out each night, and we somehow squash in.

As I get closer I see how shy she looks, anxious about the attention, and exhausted. Feeling furiously protective, I shoo photographers and journalists out of the way.

'How long have you been waiting?' I ask her.

'Hours.'

For Kasia that could mean ten minutes upwards.

'What happened to your key?'

She shrugs, embarrassed. 'Sorry.' She's always losing something and this reminds me of you. Sometimes I find her scattiness endearing. This evening, I have to admit to being a little irritated. (Old habits die hard and to be fair I'm exhausted after a long stint at the CPS, a shift as a barmaid, and now I've got the press shoving cameras into my face for what I imagine to be a poignant moment shot.)

'Come on, you need something to eat.'

She's only a week away from her due date now and she shouldn't go too long without food. She gets faint and I'm sure it can't be good for the baby.

I put my arm around her to usher her inside and the cameras click in synch.

Tomorrow, next to the picture of me with my arm around Kasia, will be articles as there were today about me 'saving' Kasia. They actually use words like that, 'saving' and 'owing her life to'; comic-book words that are in danger of turning me into someone who wears pants on the outside of her tights, switches outfits and personas in a telephone box and has web coming out of my wrists. They will write that I was too late to save you (that telephone box change just not quite quick enough), but how because of me Kasia and her baby will live. Like all of us, their readers want a happy ending to the story. It's just not my story. And my ending was a strand of hair caught in a zip.

8

Thursday

I am walking across St James's park towards the CPS offices.
The sky is blue again today, pantone PMS 635 to be precise,
a hopeful sky. This morning Mr Wright is going to ask me
about the next instalment in your story, which is my meeting
with your psychiatrist. But still half-asleep, my mind lacks
the necessary clarity so I will run through it out here first,
a mental dress rehearsal before I tell Mr Wright.

❦

Dr Nichols' NHS waiting list was four months, so I paid to
see him. His private patients' waiting room looked more
upmarket hairdressing salon than anything remotely medical:
vases of lilies; glossy magazines; a mineral water dispenser.
The young receptionist had the same de rigueur disdainful
look, lording her keeper-to-the-gate power over the clients
waiting. As I waited, I flicked through a magazine (I've
inherited Mum's anxiety about looking 'at a loose end'). It
had the next month's date on the cover and I remembered

you laughing at time-travelling fashion mags, saying the date on the cover should alert people to their absurdity inside. Nervous mental chatter because there was so much riding on this meeting. It was because of Dr Nichols that the police were convinced you had post-natal psychosis; because of him that they were sure you committed suicide. It was because of Dr Nichols that no one was looking for your murderer.

The receptionist glanced at me. 'What time did you say your appointment was?'

'Two thirty.'

'You were fortunate Dr Nichols made a space to see you.'

'I'm sure I'll be charged accordingly.'

I was limbering up for a little more confrontation. She sounded irritated. 'Have you completed the form?'

I gave her back the form, blank apart from my credit card details. She took it from me, voice snide, eyes scornful. 'You haven't filled in any of your medical history.'

I thought of people coming here who were depressed, or anxious, or losing their grip on reality and falling into the void of madness; fragile, vulnerable people who were owed at least a little civility by the first person they would have to talk to.

'I'm not here for a medical consultation.'

She didn't want to show me she was interested. Or maybe she thought I was just another barmy patient, not worth the bother.

'I'm here because my sister was murdered and Dr Nichols was her psychiatrist.'

For a moment I had her attention. She took in my greasy hair (hair washing is one of the first corner cuttings of grief), my lack of make-up and the bags under my eyes. She saw the markers of grief but interpreted them as signs of madness. I wondered if, in a larger way, this was what happened to you – your signals of fear being interpreted as insanity. She took the form back from me without another word.

121

As I waited, I remembered our emails when I told you once that I was thinking of seeing a therapist.

From: tesshemming@hotmail.co.uk
To: Beatrice Hemming's iPhone
A shrink?! Why on earth do you want one of them, Bee? If you want to talk about something, why not talk to me or to one of your friends?
T xox

From: Beatrice Hemming's iPhone
To: tesshemming@hotmail.co.uk
I just thought it would be interesting, valuable even, to see a psychiatrist. It's completely different to talking to a friend.
lol
Bee XX
PS They're not called shrinks any more.

From: tesshemming@hotmail.co.uk
To: Beatrice Hemming's iPhone
But talking to me comes free and I'd have your best interests at heart, and I wouldn't limit you to an hour time slot. T x o x o
PS They're a hot cycle for the personality, shrinking you down to something that fits a category in a textbook.

From: Beatrice Hemming's iPhone
To: tesshemming@hotmail.co.uk
They're highly trained. A psychiatrist (rather than a psychologist) is a fully qualified medical doctor who then specialises. You wouldn't say they were washing machines if you were bipolar or demented or schizophrenic would you?
Lol
Bee

Fair point. But you're not.
T X
Ps I'll shout that a bit louder in case it didn't reach you up on that podium

I wasn't just talking about the severely mentally ill needing a psychiatrist; the walking wounded sometimes need professional help too.
Lol Bee x

Bee, I'm sorry. Can you tell me about it?
T X XXXX

I have to go to a v. important meeting, talk later.
Bee x

And I'm meant to be waitressing not emailing you from Bettina's computer and table four's still waiting for their cheese but I'm not budging till you reply.
T Xxxx

From: tesshemming@hotmail.co.uk
To: Beatrice Hemming's iPhone

Table four's gone home cheese-less.
Give me a break here will you? I'm even using
Americanisms, so you can see how desperate I am for
you to forgive me.
T XOX

From: tesshemming@hotmail.co.uk
To: Beatrice Hemming's iPhone

My shift's over now Bee-bean, and I'm still at Bettina's
computer, so email back as soon as you get this will
you? Please?
T XXXOOOO

From: Beatrice Hemming's iPhone
To: tesshemming@hotmail.co.uk

I wasn't avoiding you, I was just in a meeting that ran on.
Don't read anything into this shrink business. It's just a
case of when in New York, do as New Yorkers ... It must
be past midnight in London so go home and get some
sleep.
lol
Bee X

From: tesshemming@hotmail.co.uk
To: Beatrice Hemming's iPhone

If you don't want to tell me, that's OK. I'm guessing
that your wound is to do with Leo? Or Dad?
lol
T X

The receptionist looked up at me from her desk. 'Dr Nichols
can see you now.'

124

As I walked to his room I remembered our phone call that evening (my time; two in the morning your time). I still didn't tell you why I wanted to see a psychiatrist but you explained why you didn't think it was useful.

'Our mind is who we are; it's where we feel and think and believe. It's where we have love and hate and faith and passion.'

I was getting a little embarrassed by your earnestness but you continued, 'How can someone hope to treat another person's mind unless they are also a theologian and a philosopher and a poet?'

I opened the door to Dr Nichols consulting room and went in.

When you saw Dr Nichols in his NHS clinic he would have worn a white coat, but in his private consulting room he was in faded corduroys and old lambswool sweater, looking scruffy against the regency striped wallpaper. I put him in his late thirties, do you think that's about right?

He got up from his chair and I thought I saw compassion in his rumpled face.

'Miss Hemming? I am so very sorry about your sister.'

I heard the sound of thumping from beneath his desk and saw an ancient Labrador dozily chasing rabbits in her sleep, tail wagging onto the floor. I realised that his office smelled slightly of dog, which I liked more than the lilies of the waiting room. I imagined the receptionist dashing in between patients with air-freshener.

He gestured to a chair near his own. 'Please take a seat.'

As I sat down I saw a photo of a little girl in a wheel-chair prominently displayed and I liked Dr Nichols for being unconditionally proud.

'How can I help you?' he asked.

'Did Tess tell you who was frightening her?'

Clearly taken aback by my question, he shook his head.

'But she did tell you that she was getting threatening phone calls?' I asked.

'Distressing phone calls, yes.'

'Did she tell you who made them? Or what the person said to her?'

'No. She was reluctant to tell me about them and I didn't think it helpful to pursue it. At the time, I assumed they were most likely a cold caller or someone phoning a wrong number and it was because of her depressed state of mind that she felt victimised by them.'

'Did you tell Tess that?'

'I suggested to her that might be the case, yes.'

'And she cried?'

He looked surprised that I knew. But I've known you all your life. At four years old you could have grazes on your knees, a bloody nose but you never cried – unless someone didn't believe you when you were telling the truth and then your streaming tears would express your outraged indignation.

'You said *at the time* you assumed them to be a cold caller or wrong number?' I asked.

'Yes. Later I realised that Tess wasn't depressed as I'd first thought, but was suffering from puerperal psychosis, more commonly called post-natal psychosis.'

I nodded. I'd done my homework. I knew that puerperal psychosis simply means the six weeks after the birth.

'Anyhow,' continued Dr Nichols, 'once I realised that she was suffering from puerperal psychosis I realised that the phone calls were, most likely, auditory hallucinations. In lay terms, "hearing voices" or in Tess's case the sound of the phone too.'

'You changed your diagnosis after she was found dead, didn't you?' I asked and saw a flash of emotion over his crumpled face, momentarily hardening it. There was a moment before he spoke.

'Yes. I think it may be helpful if I tell you a little more about puerperal psychosis. The symptoms can include paranoia, delusions and hallucinations. And the consequences, tragically, are a highly increased risk of suicide.'

From my own research, I already knew that.

'I'd like to get this clear,' I said. 'It was *after* she died that you changed your diagnosis from depression to psychosis. And it was only then that the phone calls became "auditory hallucinations"?'

'Yes, because auditory hallucinations are a symptom of psychosis.'

'She didn't have psychosis. Puerperal, or post-natal, or any other kind.' He ineffectually tried to interrupt me but I continued, 'How many times did you meet my sister?'

'Psychiatry isn't about intimate knowledge of a specific person, as you get in close friendships or with family members, nor in acute cases is it anything like the long-term relationship a psychiatrist has with a patient as a therapist. When a patient has mental illness the psychiatrist is trained to recognise certain symptoms that the patient demonstrates.'

For some reason I imagined him practising all this in the mirror beforehand. I repeated my question, 'How many times?'

He glanced away from me. 'Just once. She was automatically referred to me, because of her baby's death, but she discharged herself from hospital almost immediately after the birth, so I couldn't visit her on the ward. She was given an emergency out-patient appointment two days later.'

'Was she an NHS patient?'

'Yes.'

'On the NHS your waiting list is four months. That's why I am paying to see you.'

'Tess was an emergency. All potential puerperal depression and psychosis cases are dealt with immediately.'

'Dealt with?'

'I'm sorry. What I meant was in terms of jumping any waiting list.'

'How long is an NHS appointment?'

'I'd rather have more time with each patient but—'

'With a waiting list of four months you must be under a great deal of pressure to get through them.'

'I spend as much time as I possibly can with each patient.'

'But it's not enough, is it?'

He paused a moment. 'No. It's not.'

'Puerperal psychosis is an acute psychiatric emergency, isn't it?'

I thought I saw him flinch that I knew this, but I'd done my research beforehand.

'Yes, it is.'

'Requiring hospitalisation?'

His body language was rigidly controlled, arms held determinedly at his sides, his corduroyed legs a little splayed, but I knew that he wanted to cross his arms over his chest, and put one leg over the other, to give physical expression to his mental defensiveness.

'Many psychiatrists would have interpreted Tess's symptoms, as I did, as indicators of depression rather than psychosis.' He absent-mindedly reached down and stroked his dog's silky ears as if he needed comfort and continued, 'Diagnosis in psychiatry is far harder than in other branches of medicine. There aren't any X-rays or blood tests to help us. And I didn't have access to her notes so I didn't know if there was a history of mental illness.'

'There isn't any history. When was her appointment with you?'

'The twenty-third of January. At nine a.m.'

He hadn't consulted his diary or looked at his computer.

He had come prepared for this meeting, of course he had. He'd probably been on the phone all morning to his medical defence union. I saw in his face a beat of some genuine emotion. I wondered if it was fearfulness for himself, or genuine upset about you.

'So you saw her the day that she died?' I asked.

'Yes.'

'And you thought *the morning she died* that she was suffering from depression not psychosis?'

He could no longer hide his defensiveness, crossing one leg over the other, huddling into himself. 'At the time I didn't see any indicators of psychosis. And she didn't show any signs that she was considering hurting herself. There was nothing to suggest that she was going to take her life.'

I wanted to scream at him that of course there were no signs because you didn't take your life; you had it violently cut from you. I heard my voice sounding distantly quiet against the shouting in my head. 'So it was her death that rewrote your diagnosis?'

He didn't reply. I no longer found his rumpled face and corduroys endearingly scruffy, but hopelessly negligent.

'Your mistake wasn't that you diagnosed her with depression when she was actually psychotic.' He tried to interrupt me but I continued, 'Your mistake is that you didn't once think that she might be telling the truth.' Again he tried to interrupt me. Did he interrupt you too as you tried to tell him what was happening to you? I thought psychiatrists were meant to listen. I suppose in an emergency NHS appointment probably shoe-horned into a full clinic there's not much time for listening.

'Did you ever even consider that the phone calls threatening her were real just as the man who followed her to the park that day and murdered her was real?' I asked.

'Tess wasn't murdered.'

I thought it strange he was so adamant. After all, murder would have let him off the misdiagnosis hook. He paused, then forced the words out as if they physically pained him.

'Tess was having auditory hallucinations, which I've told you about, and we can disagree about the interpretation if you wish. But she was also having visual hallucinations. At the time I interpreted them as vivid nightmares, not uncommon for a patient who's depressed and bereaved,' continued Dr Nichols. 'But I've reread her notes and it's clear they were hallucinations, which I missed.' The beat of upset in his face I'd seen earlier seemed to spread across his features. 'Visual hallucinations are a clear signifier of acute psychosis.'

'What were the "hallucinations"?'

'I have to respect patient confidentiality.'

I thought it strange he suddenly thought of doctor/patient confidentiality when it hadn't hindered him up until now. I wondered if there was a reason for it, or if it was just another incidence of his incompetence.

'I asked her to paint what she saw,' he continued and his face looked kind. 'I thought it would be helpful to her. Maybe you could find a painting?'

The secretary came in. Time was up, but I didn't leave.

'You must go to the police and tell them you have doubts she had puerperal psychosis.'

'But I don't have any doubts. The signs were there, as I said, but I missed them.'

'You're not the reason she died, but you could be why her murderer gets away with it. Because of your diagnosis no one is even looking for him.'

'Beatrice . . .'

It was the first time he'd used my Christian name. The

130

bell had been rung; it was after school, so now he could be intimate. I didn't stand up, but he did.

'I'm sorry, but I can't help you any more. I can't change my professional judgement because you want me to, because it fits with a construct that you have put onto her death. I made a mistake, a terrible misjudgement. And I have to face up to that.'

His guilt was seeping out around the edges of his words; a trickle to start with before becoming the mainstream subject. It looked as if it was a relief to finally give way to it.

'The harsh facts are that a young woman with puerperal psychosis went undiagnosed and I must take my share of blame for her death.'

I thought it ironic that decency can be harder to argue with than it's self-serving reprehensible opposite. The moral high ground is just too certain, however uncomfortable.

Outside the open office window it's raining, spring rain, collecting the scent of grass and trees before falling onto the concrete pavements below. I feel the slight drop in temperature and smell it before I see it. I have almost finished telling Mr Wright about my meeting with Dr Nichols.

'I thought he believed he'd made a terrible mistake and was genuinely appalled with himself.'

'Did you ask him to go to the police?' asks Mr Wright.

'Yes, but he maintained he was certain she had puerperal psychosis.'

'Even though it reflected badly on him professionally?'

'Yes. I found it surprising too. But I put his motive down to misplaced moral courage; agreeing with me that Tess didn't have psychosis but was murdered would be a cowardly

131

option. By the end of our meeting I thought he was a hopeless psychiatrist but a decent man.'

We break for lunch, Mr Wright has a lunch meeting scheduled and I leave on my own. Outside it is still raining.

I never did answer your email and tell you the real reason I saw a therapist. Because I did go in the end. It was six weeks after Todd and I had become engaged. I'd thought getting married would stop me feeling so insecure. But an engagement ring around my finger wasn't the new hold on life I'd thought it would be. I saw Dr Wong, a highly intelligent and empathetic woman, who helped me understand that with Dad leaving and Leo dying within the space of a few months it was hardly surprising I felt abandoned and consequently insecure. You were right about those two wounds. But it was being sent to boarding school, the same year, that felt the final abandonment.

During my therapy sessions, I realised that Mum wasn't rejecting me but was trying to protect me. You were so much younger and she could shield you from her grief, but it would have been far harder to hide it from me. Ironically, she sent me to boarding school because she thought it would be emotionally more secure.

So with Dr Wong's help, I came to understand not only myself better but also Mum, and quick facile blame transmuted into harder-won understanding.

The problem was, knowing the reason I was insecure didn't help me to undo the damage that had been done. Something in me had been broken, and I now knew it was well intentioned – a duster knocking the ornament onto the tiled floor rather than it being smashed deliberately – but broken just the same.

So you'll understand, I think, why I don't share your

scepticism about psychiatrists. Although I do agree that they need an artistic sensibility as well as scientific knowledge (Dr Wong majored in comparative literature before going into medicine), and that a good psychiatrist is the modern version of a renaissance man. As I tell you that, I wonder if my respect and gratitude towards my own psychiatrist coloured my opinion of Dr Nichols; if that's the real reason I felt that he was fundamentally decent.

I get back to the CPS offices earlier than Mr Wright, who hurries in five minutes later, looking hassled. Maybe the lunch meeting hasn't gone well. I presume it's about you. Your case is huge – headline news, MPs calling for a public inquiry. It must be a big responsibility for Mr Wright but not only is he adept at hiding the strain he must be under, he doesn't load any pressure onto me, which I appreciate. He turns on the tape recorder and we continue.

'How soon after your meeting with Dr Nichols did you find the paintings?'

He doesn't need to specify, we both know which paintings he means.

'As soon as I got back to the flat I looked for them in her bedroom. She'd moved all her furniture out apart from her bed. Even the wardrobe was in the sitting room where it looked ridiculous.'

I'm not sure why I told him that. Maybe because if you have to be a victim I want him to know that you're a victim with quirks, some of which used to irritate your older sister.

'There must have been forty to fifty canvasses propped up around the walls,' I continue. 'Most of them were oils, some on thick board, a few collages. They were all large, a minimum of a foot across. It took me a while to look through them. I didn't want to damage any of them.'

Your paintings are staggeringly beautiful. Did I ever tell you that, or was I just too concerned that you weren't going to earn a living? I know the answer. I was anxious about no one buying enormous canvasses with colours that wouldn't go with their decor, wasn't I? I worried that the paint was so thickly applied that it might snap off and ruin someone's carpet rather than realising you'd made colour itself tactile.

'It took me about half an hour to find the ones Dr Nichols had told me about.'

Mr Wright has only seen the four 'hallucination' pictures, not the ones you did before. But I think it was the contrast that shocked me the most.

'Her other pictures were all so . . .' What the hell, I might as well go for it. 'Joyous. Beautiful. Explosions on canvas of life and light and colour.'

But you painted these four paintings in the palette of the nihilists, pantone numbers PMS 4625 to PMS 4715, the blacks and browns spectrum, and in their subject matter you forced the viewer to recoil. I don't need to explain this to Mr Wright, he has photos of them in the file and I can just glimpse them. Made smaller, and even upside down, they still disturb me and I look hurriedly away.

'They were at the back of a big stack. Paint from the front of one had smeared the back of the next. I thought that she must have hidden them quickly, before they'd had time to dry properly.'

Did you have to hide the woman's face, her gash of a mouth as she screamed so that you could sleep? Or was it the masked man, dark with menace in the shadows, who disturbed you as violently as he did me?

'Todd thought they were proof that she had psychosis.'

'Todd?'

'My fiancé at the time.'

134

We are interrupted by Mrs Crush Secretary who gives Mr Wright a sandwich; clearly his lunchtime meeting didn't include any lunch and she has thought about this, looked after him. She barely glances at me as she gives me mineral water. He smiles at her, his open, winning smile. 'Thanks, Stephanie.' His smile is going out of focus. The office is dimming. I can hear his concerned voice.

'Are you all right?'

'Yes.'

But the office is in darkness. I can hear but not see. It happened at lunch with Mum yesterday and I blamed the wine, but today there's no scapegoat. I know that I must keep calm and the darkness will clear. So I continue, forcing myself to remember back – and in the darkness your dull-toned paintings are vivid.

⁂

I was crying when Todd came in, my tears falling onto the paintings and becoming drops of inky black and mud brown sliding down the canvas. Todd put his arm around me. 'It wasn't Tess who did these, darling.' For a moment I was hopeful; someone put them here, someone other than you had felt like this. 'She wasn't herself,' continued Todd. 'She wasn't the sister you knew. Madness does that, it takes away someone's identity.' I was angry he thought he knew about mental illness; that a few sessions with a therapist when he was thirteen after his parents divorce made him some sort of expert.

I turned back to the paintings. Why had you painted them, Tess? As a message? And why had you hidden them? Todd didn't realise my silence had been filled with urgent mental chatter.

'Someone has to tell it as it is, darling.'

He'd got so redneck all of a sudden; as if being resolutely wrong was being masculine; as if he could turn the aftermath of your death into an Iron John weekend. This time he sensed my anger. 'I'm sorry, mad is maybe too blunt to describe it.'

At the time I silently and furiously disagreed with him. 'Psychotic' sounded far worse to me than 'mad'. I thought that you can't be psychotic as a hatter or a march hare. No playful light-hearted storybook images for psychotic. Nor was King Lear psychotic when he discovered great truths in the midst of his ravings. I thought that we can relate to madness as emotion experienced at an intense and troubling level, even respect it for its honourable literary pedigree, but psychosis is way out there, to be feared and shunned.

But now I fear madness rather than look at its literary pedigree. And I realise my earlier viewpoint was that of onlooker rather than the sufferer. 'Not mad sweet heaven' – because loss of sanity, of self, generates despairing terror whatever label you want to use for it.

I came up with some excuse to leave the flat, and Todd looked disappointed. He must have thought the paintings would put an end to my 'refusal to face the truth'. I'd heard that phrase in his quiet concerned chats on the phone to mutual friends in New York, when he thought I couldn't hear; even to my boss. From his perspective, your paintings would force me to confront reality. It was there in front of me, four times, a screaming woman and a monster-man. Psychotic, frightening, hellish pictures. What more did I need? Surely, I would now accept the fact that you committed suicide and move on. We could put things behind us. Get on with our lives. The hackneyed life-coach phrases could become reality.

Outside it was dark, the air raw with cold. Early February is not a good time to be constantly stropping off. Again, I felt in my coat pocket for the non-existent glove. If I'd been a lab rat I'd have been a pretty poor specimen at learning patterns and punishment. I wondered if slipping on the steps would be worse than gripping a snow-covered iron railing with a naked hand. I decided to grip, wincing as I held the biting cold metal.

I knew I really had no right to be angry with Todd, because if it was the other way around I'd want him to return to being the person I thought I knew too – someone sensible and level-headed, who respected authority and didn't cause unnecessary embarrassment. But I think you're pleased that I argued with policemen and accosted grown men on their doorsteps and in their flats and took no notice of authority and that it's all down to you.

As I walked alone through the streets, slippery with frozen-over slush, I realised that Todd didn't really know me at all. Nor me him. Ours was a relationship of small talk. We'd never stayed awake long into the night hoping to find in that nocturnal physical conversation a connection of minds. We hadn't stared into each other's eyes because if eyes are the window to the soul it would be a little rude and embarrassing to look in. We'd created a ring-road relationship, circumventing raw emotions and complex feelings, so that our central selves were strangers.

Too cold to walk any further, I returned to the flat. As I reached the top of the steps I collided with someone in the dark and jolted with fear, before realising it was Amias. I think he was equally startled to see me.

'Amias?'

'I'm so sorry. Did I give you a fright? Here . . .' He held a torch for me to see my footing. I saw that he was carrying a bag of earth.

'Thanks.'

It suddenly struck me that I was living in his flat. 'I should pay you something while we stay here.'

'Absolutely not. Anyway, Tess had already paid next month's rent.'

He must have guessed I didn't believe him. 'I asked her to pay me with her paintings,' he continued. 'Like Picasso with his restaurant bills. And she'd painted ones for February and March in advance.'

I used to think you spent time with him because he was another of your waifs and strays, but he's got a rare kind of charm, hasn't he? Something masculine and upper class, without being sexist or snobbish, making me think in black and white of steam trains and trilbies and women in floral frocks.

'I'm afraid it's not the most salubrious of dwellings,' he continued. 'I did offer to modernise it but Tess said it had character.'

I felt ashamed of myself for being irritated by the lack of mod cons in the kitchen, the state of the bathroom, the draughty windows.

My eyes were further accustomed to the darkness and I could see that he had been planting up your pots outside your door, his bare hands stained with earth.

'She used to come and see me every Thursday,' continued Amias. 'Sometime just for a drink, sometimes for supper. She must have had so many other things she'd rather be doing.'

'She liked you.'

I'd realised that was true. You've always had friends, proper friends, in different generations. I'd imagined you'd do it in reverse as you got older. One day you'd be an octogenarian chatting to people decades your junior. Amias was totally at ease with my silence and with consideration seemed to sense when my train of thought had finished before speaking.

'The police didn't take a great deal of notice of me when

I reported her missing. Until I told them about the nuisance phone calls. They made a big song and dance about that.'

He turned his face back to his planting and I tried to have the courtesy for him too to finish his train of thought in peace before I butted in.

'Did Tess tell you anything about the phone calls?'

'She just said she'd been getting vicious calls. She only told me because she said she'd unplugged her phone and was worried I might need to phone her. She used to have a mobile, but I think she lost it.'

'"Vicious"? That was the word she used?'

'Yes. At least I think so. The ghastly thing about old age is you can't rely on yourself to be accurate any more. She cried though. She tried not to, but she did.' He broke off, for just a moment, struggling to keep his composure. 'I told her she ought to go to the police.'

'Tess's psychiatrist told the police the phone calls were in her head.'

'Did he tell Tess that too?'

'Yes.'

'Poor Tessie.' I hadn't heard anyone call you that since Dad left. 'Awful not to be believed.'

'Yes.'

He turned to me. 'I heard the phone ring. I told the police but I couldn't swear that it was one of the nuisance calls. But it was immediately afterwards that Tess asked me to look after the key. It was just two day before she died.'

I could see the anguish in his face, illuminated by the orange glow of the street light.

'I should have insisted she went to the police.'

'It's not your fault.'

'Thank you, you're very kind. Like your sister.'

I wondered whether to tell the police about the key, but

it would make no difference. It was just another instance of your supposed paranoia.

'A psychiatrist thinks that she was mad. Do you think that she was, after the baby, I mean?' I asked.

'No. She was very upset, and very frightened I think. But she wasn't mad.'

'The police think she was mad too.'

'And did anyone in the police ever meet her?'

He carried on planting bulbs and his old hands, the skin paper thin and misshapen by arthritis, must have been aching in the cold. I thought that this must be the way he was coping with grief: planting dead-looking bulbs that would miraculously flower in spring time. I remembered how after Leo died you and Mum seemed to spend so much time gardening. I'd only just seen the connection.

'These are King Alfreds,' said Amias. 'Her favourite variety of daffodils because they're such a strong yellow. You're meant to plant them in autumn but they come up in about six weeks, so they should have time to flower this spring.' But even I knew that you shouldn't plant things in frozen earth. For some reason thinking that Amias's bulbs would never flower made me furious.

Just in case you're wondering, yes I even suspected Amias at the start of all this. I suspected everyone. But as he planted bulbs for you any residual suspicion withered into absurdity. I'm sorry it was ever there.

He smiled at me. 'She told me that scientists have put a daffodil gene into a rice plant and made rice with vitamin A. Imagine that.'

You'd told me that too.

'The vitamin A in daffodils is what makes it yellow. Isn't that amazing, Bee?'

140

'Yes, I suppose it is.'

I was trying to concentrate on my design team's roughs for a new corporate logo for an oil distribution company, noting with annoyance that they'd used PMS 683, which was already used in a competitor's logo. You didn't know there was any other chatter in my head.

'Thousands of children used to go blind because of a lack of vitamin A in their diet. But now with the new rice they're going to be fine.'

For a moment I stopped thinking about the logo.

'Children are going to see, because of the yellow in a daffodil.'

I think it was the fact a colour could save sight that you found so miraculously appropriate. I smiled back at Amias and I think in that moment we both remembered you in exactly the same way: your enthusiasm for life, for its myriad possibilities, for its daily miracles.

༄

My vision is returning to normal again, the darkness transmuting into light. I am glad for the faulty electric light that can't be turned off and the spring sunshine pouring in through the overly large window. I see Mr Wright looking at me with concern.

'You're very pale.'

'I'm fine, really.'

'We're going to have to stop there. I have a meeting to get to.'

Maybe he does, but it's more likely he's being considerate.

Mr Wright knows that I am ill and I think it must be on his orders that his secretary makes sure I always have mineral water, and why he is drawing our session to an early close

141

today. He is sensitive enough to understand that I don't want to talk about my physical problems, not yet, not till I have to.

You'd already picked up that I'm unwell, hadn't you? And you wondered why I didn't tell you more. You must have thought it ludicrous yesterday when I said a glass of wine at lunch time could make me black out. I wasn't trying to trick you, I just didn't want to admit, to myself, my body's frailties. Because I need to be strong to get through this statement. And I must get through it.

You want to know what's made me ill, I know, and I will tell you, when we get to that point in the story – the point when your story becomes mine too. Until then I will try not to think about the cause because my thoughts, cowards that they are, turn tail and flee from it.

Music blaring interrupts our one-way conversation. I am near our flat and through the un-curtained window I see Kasia dancing to her *Golden Hits of the 70s* CD. She spots me and appears moments later at the front door. She takes hold of my arm and doesn't even let me take my coat off before trying to make me dance too. She always does this, actually, '*Dancing very good for body*.' But today, incapable of dancing, I make up an excuse then sit on the sofa and watch. As she dances, face beaming and sweating, laughing that the baby loves it, she seems so blithely unaware of the problems that she will face being an unemployed, Polish, single mother.

Upstairs, Amias is banging his foot on our ceiling in time to the music. The first time he did it I thought he was asking us to keep the noise down. But he enjoys it. He says it was so quiet before Kasia came to stay. I finally persuade a breathless Kasia to stop dancing and eat something with me.

While Kasia watches TV, I give Pudding a bowl of milk then take a watering can into your back garden, leaving the door slightly ajar so I can see. It's starting to get dark and cold, the spring sunshine not strong enough to heat the air for long into evening. Over the fence, I see that next door your neighbours use the same outside area to house three wheelie bins. As I water the dead plants and bare earth I wonder as usual why I'm doing this. Your wheelie-bin neighbours must think I'm absurd. I think I'm absurd. Suddenly, like a magician's slight of hand, I see tiny green shoots in the dead twigs. I feel a surge of excitement and astonishment. I open the kitchen door wide, lighting the tiny garden. All the plants that were dead have the same tiny bright green shoots growing out of them. Further away, in the grey soil are a cluster of dark-red leaves, a peony that will flower in all its exuberant beauty again this summer.

I finally understand your and Mum's passion for gardening. It is seasonally miraculous. All that health and growth and new life and renewal. No wonder politicians and religions hijack green shoots and imagery of spring for themselves. This evening I too exploit the image for my own ends and allow myself to hope that death may not be final after all; that somewhere, as in Leo's beloved Narnia books, there is a heaven where the white witch is dead and the statues have life breathed back into them. Tonight it doesn't seem quite so inconceivable.

9

Although late, I am walking slowly to the CPS offices. There are three things that I find particularly hard in the telling of this story. I've done the first, finding your body and what's coming up is next. It sounds trivial, a bill, that's all, but its effect was devastating. As I dawdle, I hear Mum's voice telling me that it's already ten to nine, we're going to be late, *come on*, Beatrice. Then you whiz past on your bike, book bag looped over a handlebar, eyes exhilarated, with pedestrians smiling at you as you whirred past them, literally creating a breath of fresh air. *We haven't got all day, Beatrice.* But you knew that we had and were seizing it moment by moment.

I reach Mr Wright's office and, not commenting on my late arrival, he hands me a Styrofoam cup of coffee, which he must have bought from the dispenser by the lift. I am grateful for his thoughtfulness, and know that a tiny part of my reluctance to tell him the next episode in the story is because I don't want him to think badly of me.

❧

144

Todd and I sat at your Formica table, a pile of your post in front of us. I found the task of sorting out your admin oddly soothing. I've always made lists and your pile of post represented an easily achievable line of ticks. We started with the red urgent reminders, then worked our way down to the less urgent bills. Like me, Todd is adept at the bureaucracy of life and, as we worked companionably together, I felt connected to him for the first time since he'd arrived in London. I remembered why we were together and how the small everyday things formed a bridge between us. It was a quotidian relationship based on practical details rather than passion but I still valued its small-scale connections. Todd went to talk to Amias about the 'tenancy agreement' despite me saying that I doubted there was such a thing. He pointed out, sensibly I thought, that we wouldn't know unless we asked him.

The door closed behind him and I opened the next bill. I was feeling the most relaxed since you'd died. I could almost imagine making a cup of coffee as I worked, switching on Radio 4. I had a flicker of normality and in that brief moment could envisage a time without bereavement.

༄

'I got out my credit card to pay her phone bill. Since she'd lost her mobile, I'd paid the landline one every month. It was my birthday present to her and she said it was too generous, but it was for my benefit too.'

I told you I wanted to make sure that you could phone me, and talk to me as long as you wanted to, without worrying about the bill. What I didn't tell you is that I needed to make sure that if I wanted to ring you, your phone wouldn't have been disconnected.

'This bill was larger than previous months. It was itemised

so I decided to check it.' My words are slower, dawdling. 'I saw that she'd phoned my mobile on the twenty-first of January. The call was at one p.m. her time, eight a.m. New York time, so I would have been in the subway getting to work. I don't know why there was even a few seconds connection.' I must do this all in one go, no pausing, or I won't be able to start again. 'It was the day she had Xavier. She must have phoned me when she went into labour.'

I break off for just a moment, not looking at Mr Wright's face, then continue, 'Her next call to me was at nine p.m. her time four p.m. New York time.'

'Eight hours later. Why do you think there was such a long gap?'

'She didn't have a mobile, so once she left her flat to go to the hospital it would have been hard for her to ring me. Besides, it wouldn't have been urgent. I mean, I wouldn't have had time to get to her and be with her for the birth.'

My voice becomes so quiet that Mr Wright has to bend towards me to hear.

'The second call must have been when she got home from the hospital. She was ringing me to tell me about Xavier. The call lasted twelve minutes and twenty seconds.'

'What did she say?' he asks.

My mouth is suddenly dry. I don't have the saliva needed to talk. I take a sip of cold coffee, but my mouth still feels parched.

'I didn't talk to her.'

⁂

'You were probably out of the office, darling. Or stuck in a meeting,' said Todd. He'd come back from Amias's full of

146

incredulity about you paying your rent in paintings to find me sobbing.

'No, I was there.'

I'd got back to my office from a longer than expected briefing to the design department. I vaguely remembered Trish saying that you were holding for me and my boss wanted to see me. I asked her to tell you I'd call you back. I think I made a note on a Post-it and stuck it on my computer as I left. Maybe that's why I forgot, because I'd written it down and didn't need to hold it my head. But there are no excuses. None at all.

'I didn't take her call and I forgot to phone her back.' My voice sounded small with shame.

'The baby was three weeks early, you couldn't possibly have foreseen that.'

But I should have foreseen that.

'And the twenty-first of January, that was the day you were given your promotion,' Todd continued. 'So of course you had your mind on other things.' He sounded almost jocular. He had single-handedly found me an excuse.

'How could I have forgotten?'

'She didn't say it was important. She didn't even leave you a message.'

Exonerating me meant putting the responsibility onto you.

'She shouldn't have had to say it was important. And what message could she have left with a secretary? That her baby was dead?'

I'd snapped at him, trying to shift a little guilt his way. But of course the guilt is mine alone, not for sharing.

❧

'Then you went to Maine?' asks Mr Wright.

'Yes, a last-minute thing, just for a few days. And her baby

147

wasn't due for three weeks.' I despise myself for this pathetic attempt to save face. 'Her bill showed that the day before she died and the morning of her death she phoned my office and apartment fifteen times.'

I saw the column of numbers, all mine, and each was an abandonment of you, indicting me over and over and over.

'Her calls to my apartment lasted for a few seconds.'

Just until your call was put through to voicemail. I should have put on a message saying we were away, but we hadn't, not because we'd been carried away in the spontaneous moment, but because we'd decided it was a security risk. *'Let's not broadcast the fact we're away.'* I can't remember if it was Todd or I who'd said it.

I thought that you must have assumed I'd be back soon, and that's why you didn't leave a message. Or maybe you simply couldn't bear to tell me your ghastly news without hearing my voice first.

'God knows how many times she tried to phone my mobile. I'd switched it off because there wasn't any reception where we were staying.'

'But you did try ringing her?'

I think he's asking this question out of kindness.

'Yes. But the cabin didn't have a landline and my mobile had no reception, so I could only phone her when we went out to a restaurant. I did try, a few times, but her phone was always engaged. I thought she was chatting to her friends, or had unplugged it so she could concentrate on painting.'

But there is no justification. I should have taken your call. And when I didn't do that I should have *immediately* rung you back, and then *kept on* ringing you until I got hold of you. And if I couldn't get hold of you, I should have alerted someone to go and check on you and then got on the next flight to London.

148

My mouth has become too dry to talk.

Mr Wright gets up. 'I'll get you a glass of water.'

As the door closes behind him I get up and pace the room, as if I can leave my guilt behind me. But it tracks me as I walk, an ugly shadow made by myself.

Before this, I'd confidently assumed myself to be a considerate, thoughtful person, vigilant about other people. I scrupulously remembered birthdays (my birthday book being annually transcribed onto the calendar); I sent thank you cards promptly (ready-bought and waiting in the bottom drawer of my desk). But with my numbers on your phone bill I saw that I wasn't considerate at all. I was conscientious about the minutiae of life but in the important things I was selfishly and cruelly neglectful.

I can hear your question, demanding an answer: Why, when DS Finborough told me that you'd had your baby, didn't I realise that you weren't able to phone me and tell me? Why did I focus on you not turning to me rather than realising it was *me* who'd made that impossible? It's because I thought you were still alive then. I didn't know you'd been murdered before I ever reached London. Later, when your body was found, I wasn't capable of logic, of putting dates together.

I can't imagine what you must think of me. (Can't or daren't?) You must be surprised that I didn't start off this whole letter to you with an apology, and then an explanation so that you could understand my negligence. The truth is that, lacking courage, I was putting it off as long as I could, knowing that there are no explanations to be offered.

I'd do anything to have a second chance, Tess. But unlike our storybooks there's no flying back past the second star to the right and through the open window to find you alive in your bed. I can't sail back through the weeks and in and out of the days returning to my bedroom where my supper is warm and waiting for me and I'm forgiven. There is no new beginning. No second chance.

You turned to me and I wasn't there.

You are dead. If I had taken your call you would be alive. It's as blunt as that.

I'm sorry.

10

Mr Wright comes back into the room with a glass of water for me. I remember that his wife died in a car crash. Maybe it was his fault, perhaps he was driving after drinking or momentarily distracted – my guilt shadow would feel better with some company. But I cannot ask him. Instead I drink the glass of water and he switches on the cassette recorder again.

'So you knew Tess had turned to you?'

'Yes.'

'And that you had been right all along?'

'Yes.'

There was a flipside to the guilt. You *had* looked to me for help, we were close, I did know you and therefore I could be absolutely confident in my conviction that you didn't kill yourself. Had my confidence ever wavered? A little. When I thought you hadn't told me about your baby; when I thought you hadn't turned to me for help when you were frightened. Then I questioned our closeness and wondered if I really knew you after all. Then quietly, privately, I also wondered,

Did you really value life too highly to end it? Your phone calls meant that the answer, however painfully obtained, was an unequivocal yes.

⁂

The next morning I woke up so early it was still night. I thought about taking one of the sleeping pills, to escape from guilt now as much as grief, but I couldn't be that cowardly. Careful not to wake Todd, I got out of bed and went outside hoping for escape from my own thoughts or at least some kind of distraction from them.

When I opened the front door, I saw Amias putting carrier bags on your pots, using a torch. He must have seen me illuminated in the doorway.

'Some of them blew off in the night,' he said. 'So I need to get them put back again before too much damage is done.'

I thought about him recently planting daffodil bulbs in the freezing earth. From the beginning the bulbs never stood a chance. Not wanting to upset him, but not wanting to give him false platitudes about the efficacy of his carrier bag greenhouses, I changed the subject.

'It's so quiet at this time in the morning, isn't it?'

'You wait till spring, then it's a racket out here.'

I must have looked confused because he explained, 'The dawn chorus. Not sure why the birds like this street particularly, but for some reason best known to themselves they do.'

'I've never really understood what the dawn chorus was about actually.' Keeping the conversation going to humour him or to avoid my thoughts?

'Their songs are to attract a mate and define territories,'

replied Amias. 'A shame that humans can't take the musical approach to that, isn't it?'

'Yes.'

'Do you know that they have an order?' he asked. 'First blackbirds, then robins, wrens, chaffinches, warblers, song thrushes. There used to be a nightingale too.'

As he told me about the dawn chorus I knew that I would find the person who had murdered you.

'Did you know that a single nightingale can sing up to three hundred love songs?'

That was my single-minded, focused destination; there was no more time for the detour of a guilt trip.

'A musician slowed down the skylark's song and found it's close to Beethoven's Fifth Symphony.'

I owed it to you, even more than before, to win you some kind of justice.

As Amias continued telling me about the musical miracles within the dawn chorus, I wondered if he knew how comforting I found it, and thought that he probably did. He was letting me think, but not on my own, and was giving me a soothing score to bleak emotion. In the darkness I tried to hear a bird singing, but there was nothing. And in the silence and the dark it was hard to imagine a bright spring dawn filled with birdsong.

As soon as it was 9.00 a.m. I picked up the phone and dialled the police station.

'DS Finborough please. It's Beatrice Hemming.'

Todd, still half-asleep, looked at me bemused and irritated. 'What are you doing, darling?'

'I'm entitled to a copy of the post-mortem report. There was a whole load of bumf that WPC Vernon gave me which had a leaflet about it.'

153

I had been too passive; too accepting of information I had been given.

'Darling, you'll just be wasting everyone's time.'

I noted that Todd didn't say 'it's a waste of time', but that *I* was wasting somebody else's time; somebody he didn't even know. Like me, Todd is always conscious of when he's being a nuisance. I used to be, too.

'The day before she died, she called me every hour, and God knows how many more times on my mobile. That same day she asked Amias to look after her spare key because she was too afraid to leave it under the pot.'

'Maybe she'd just started bothering about basic security.'

'No, he told me it was after she'd got one of those calls. The day she was murdered, she phoned me at ten o'clock, which must be when she got home from her psychiatrist. And then every half an hour until one thirty when she must have left to go to the post office and to meet Simon in Hyde Park.'

'Darling—'

'She told her psychiatrist she was afraid. And Simon said she wanted round-the-clock protection; that she was "terrified witless" and that she saw someone following her into the park.'

'So she said, but she was suffering from puerperal—'

DS Finborough came on the line, interrupting us. I told him about your many calls to my office and apartment.

'That must make you feel pretty terrible. Responsible even.'

I was surprised by the kindness in his voice, though I don't know why. He'd always been kind to me. 'I'm sure this isn't much consolation,' he continued, 'but from what her psychiatrist has told us, I think that she would have gone ahead anyway, even if you had been able to talk to her on the phone.'

'Gone ahead?'

'I think that the phone calls were most likely cries for help. But that doesn't mean anyone could have helped her, even her close family.'

'She needed help because she was being threatened.'

'She felt like that, certainly. But in the light of all the other facts, the phone calls don't change our opinion that she committed suicide.'

'I would like to see a copy of the post-mortem report.'

'Are you sure you want to put yourself through that? I have given you the basic findings and—'

'I have every right to read the report.'

'Of course. But I'm worried you're going to find it very distressing.'

'That should be my decision, don't you think?'

Besides, I had seen your body being taken out of a derelict toilets building in a body bag and after that experience I thought I would find 'distressing' a relatively easy adjective to live with. Reluctantly, DS Finborough said he'd ask the coroner's office to send me a copy.

As I put down the phone I saw Todd looking at me. 'What exactly are you hoping to achieve here?' And in the words 'exactly' and 'here' I heard the pettiness of our relationship. We had been united by superficial tendrils of the small and the mundane, but the enormous fact of your death was ripping each fragile connection. I said I had to go to St Anne's, relieved to have an excuse to leave the flat and an argument I wasn't yet ready to have.

༈

Mr Wright turns to a box file in front of him, one of many bulky files, all numbered with some code I have yet to crack, but marked in large scruffy handwriting 'Beatrice Hemming'.

155

I like the personal touch of the scruffy writing alongside the numbers; it makes me think of all the people behind the scenes in the production of justice. Someone wrote my name on the files; maybe it's the same person who will type up the tape that is whirring in the background somewhere like a massive mosquito.

'What did you think of DS Finborough at this point?' asks Mr Wright.

'That he was intelligent and kind. And my frustration was that I could understand why Tess's phone calls to me could be interpreted as "cries for help".'

'You said you then went to St Anne's Hospital?'

'Yes. I wanted to organise her baby to be buried with her.'

I didn't just owe you justice but also the funeral that you would want.

꙰

I'd phoned the hospital at 6.30 a.m. that morning and a sympathetic woman doctor had taken my call, unperturbed by how early it was. She suggested that I came in when they 'opened for business' later that morning.

As I drove to the hospital I put my phone onto hands-free and called Father Peter, Mum's new parish priest, who would be conducting your funeral. I had vague memories from first communion classes of suicide being a sin ('Do not pass Go! Do not collect £200! Go straight to hell!). I started off defensively aggressive. 'Everyone thinks that Tess committed suicide. I don't. But even if she had she shouldn't be judged for that.' I didn't give Father Peter space for a comeback. 'And her baby should be buried with her. There shouldn't be any judgements made about her.'

'We don't bury them at crossroads any more, I promise

you,' replied Father Peter. 'And of course her baby should be with her.' Despite the gentleness in his voice I remained suspicious.

'Did Mum tell you that she wasn't married?' I asked.

'Nor was Mary.'

I was totally thrown, unsure if it was it a joke. 'True,' I replied. 'But she was, well, a virgin. And the mother of God.'

I heard him laughing. It was the first time someone had laughed at me since you'd died.

'My job isn't to go around judging people. Priests are meant to teach love and forgiveness. That to me is the essence of being a Christian. And trying to find that love and forgiveness in ourselves and others every day should be a challenge that we want to achieve.'

Before you died I'd have found his speech in poor taste; the Big Things are embarrassing, best to avoid them. But since your death I prefer a naturist style of conversation. Let's strip it all down to what matters. Let's have emotions and beliefs on show without the modest covering of small talk.

'Do you want to talk through the service?' he asked.

'No. I'm leaving that up to Mum. She said she'd like to.'

Had she? Or had I just wanted to hear that when she said she'd do it?

'Anything you'd like to add?' he asked.

'The truth is I don't really want her buried at all. Tess was a free spirit. I know that's a cliché but I can't think of another way of explaining her to you. I don't mean that she was untrammelled by convention, although that's true, it's that when I think of her now she's up in the sky, soaring. Her element is air not earth. And I can't bear the idea of putting her under the ground.'

It was the first time I'd talked about you like this with someone else. The words came from a strata of thought many

157

layers down from the surface ones that are usually scraped off and spoken. I suppose that's what priests are privy to all the time, accessing the deep thoughts where faith, if it exists, can be found. Father Peter was silent but I knew he was listening, and driving past a Tesco local supermarket I continued our incongruous conversation, 'I hadn't understood funeral pyres before, but now I do. It's ghastly to burn someone you love but watching the smoke going into the sky, I think that's rather beautiful now. And I wish Tess could be up in the sky. Somewhere with colour and light and air.'

'I understand. We can't offer you a pyre I'm afraid. But maybe you and your mother should think about a cremation?' There was lightness in his tone that I liked. I supposed that death and burial were an everyday part of his job and, although not disrespectful, he wasn't going to allow them to edit his conversational flow.

'I thought you weren't allowed a cremation if you're Catholic? Mum said the church thought it was pagan.'

'They did. Once upon a time. But not any more. As long as you still believe in the resurrection of the body.'

'I wish.' I said, hoping to sound light too, but instead I sounded desperate.

'Why don't you think about it further? Ring me when you've decided, or even if you haven't and just want to talk about it.'

'Yes. Thank you.'

As I parked the hire car in the hospital's underground car park I thought about taking your ashes to Scotland, to a mountain with purple heather and yellow gorse, climbing up into the grey skies above the first level of cloud and in the cold clean air scattering you to the winds. But I knew Mum would never allow a cremation.

I'd been to St Anne's before but it had been refurbished beyond recognition with a shiny new foyer and vast art installations and a coffee bar. Unlike any hospital I'd been in, it felt like it was a part of the world outside it. Through the large glass doors I could see shoppers strolling past and the foyer was flooded with natural light. It smelled of roasting coffee beans and brand-new dolls just opened from their boxes on Christmas day (maybe the café's new shiny chairs were made of the same plastic).

I took the lift up to the fourth floor, as instructed, and walked to the maternity wing. The shininess didn't extend up that far and the smell of coffee mixed with brand-new dolls was smothered by the usual hospital smell of disinfectant and fear. (Or is it only we who smell that because of Leo?) There were no windows, just strip lights glaring onto the linoleum beneath; no clocks, even the nurses' watches were upside down; and I was back in a hospital world with its own no-weather and no-time in which the aberrant crises of pain, illness and death were Kafka-like turned ordinary. There was a sign up demanding that I wash my hands using the gel provided and now the hospital smell was on my skin, dulling the diamond on my engagement ring. The buzzer on the locked ward door was answered by a woman in her forties, her frizzy red hair tied back with a bulldog clip, looking competent and exhausted.

'I phoned earlier. Beatrice Hemming.'

'Of course. I'm Cressida, the Senior Midwife. Dr Saunders, one of the obstetricians, is expecting you.'

She escorted me into the post-natal ward. From side wards came the sound of babies crying. I'd never heard hours-old babies cry before and one sounded desperate, as if he or she had been abandoned. The Senior Midwife led me into a relatives' room, her voice was professionally caring. 'I'm so sorry about your nephew.'

For a moment I didn't know who she was referring to. I'd never thought about our own relationship with one another. 'I always call him Tess's baby, not my nephew.'

'When is his funeral?'

'Next Thursday. It's my sister's too.'

The Senior Midwife's voice was no longer professionally caring, but shocked. 'I'm so sorry. I was just told that the baby had died.' I was thankful to the kind doctor I'd spoken to earlier that morning for not turning your death into pass-the-day-away gossip. Though I suppose the subject of death in a hospital is more talking shop than gossip.

'I want her baby to be with her.'

'Yes, of course.'

'And I'd like to talk to whoever was with Tess when she gave birth. I was meant to be with her, you see, but I wasn't. I didn't even take her call.' I started to cry, but tears were completely normal here, even the room with its washable sofa covers was probably designed with weeping relatives in mind. The Senior Midwife put her hand on my shoulder. 'I'll find out who was with her and ask them to come and talk to you. Excuse me a moment.'

She went into the corridor. Through the open doorway I saw a woman on a trolley with a just-born baby in her arms. Next to them a doctor put his arm around a man. 'It's customary for the baby to cry, not the dad.' The man laughed and the doctor smiled at him. 'When you arrived this morning you were a couple and now you're a family. Amazing, isn't it?'

The Senior Midwife shook her head at him. 'As an obstetrician, Dr Saunders, it shouldn't really amaze you any more.'

Dr Saunders wheeled the mother and baby into a side ward and I watched him. Even from a distance I could see that his face was fine-featured with eyes that were lit

160

from the inside, making him beautiful rather than harshly handsome.

He came out with the Senior Midwife. 'Dr Saunders, this is Beatrice Hemming.'

Dr Saunders smiled at me, totally unselfconscious, and reminded me of you in the way he wore his beauty carelessly, as if unacknowledged by the owner.

'Of course, my colleague who spoke to you earlier this morning told me you were coming. Our hospital chaplain has made all the necessary arrangements with the undertakers and they are going to come and get her baby this afternoon.'

His voice was noticeably unhurried in the bustle of the ward; someone who trusted people to listen to him.

'The chaplain had his body brought to the room of rest,' he continued. 'We thought that a morgue is no place for him. I'm only sorry that he had to be there as long as he did.'

I should have thought about this earlier. About him. I shouldn't have left him in the morgue.

'Would you like me to take you there?' he asked.

'Are you sure you have time?'

'Of course.'

Dr Saunders escorted me down the corridor towards the lifts. I heard a woman screaming. The sound came from above, which I guessed to be the labour ward. Like the newborn baby's cries her screams were unlike anything I had ever heard, scraped raw with pain. There were nurses and another doctor in the lift but they didn't appear to notice the screams. I reasoned that they were used to it, working day in, day out in this Kafkaesque hospital world.

The lift doors closed. Dr Saunders and I were pressed lightly against each other. I noticed a thin gold wedding ring hanging on a chain just visible round the neck of his scrubs top. On the second floor everyone else got out and we were alone. He looked at me directly, giving me his full attention. 'I'm so sorry about Tess.'

'You knew her?'

'I may have done, I'm not sure. I'm sorry, that must sound callous but . . .'

I filled in, 'You see hundreds of patients?'

'Yes. Actually we have over five thousand babies delivered here a year. When was her baby born?'

'January the twenty-first.'

He paused for a moment. 'In that case I wouldn't have been here. Sorry. I was at a training course in Manchester that week.'

I wondered if he was lying. Should I ask him for proof that he wasn't around for the birth of your baby and for your murder? I couldn't hear your voice answering me, not even to tease me. Instead I heard Todd telling me not to be so ridiculous. And he'd have a point. Was every male in the land guilty until one by one they could prove their innocence? And who said it had to be a man? Maybe I should be suspicious of women as well, the kind midwife, the doctor I'd spoken to earlier that morning. And they thought *you* were paranoid. But doctors and nurses do have power over life and death and some of them have become addicted to it. Though with a hospital full of vulnerable people what on earth would make a healthcare professional choose a derelict toilets building in Hyde Park to release their psychopathic urge? At this point in my thoughts Dr Saunders smiled at me, making me feel both embarrassed and a little ashamed.

'Our stop next.'

Still not able to hear your voice, I told myself, sternly, that being beautiful does not mean a man is a killer – just someone who would have rejected me in his single days without even being aware that he was doing it. Coming clean, I knew that this was why I was suspicious of him. I

162

was just pegging my customary suspicion onto a different – and far more extreme – hook.

We reached the hospital mortuary, me still thinking about finding your killer rather than about Xavier. Dr Saunders took me to the room they have for relatives to 'view the deceased'. He asked me if I'd like him to come with me but, not really thinking first, I said I'd be fine on my own.

I went in. The room was done out thoughtfully and tastefully like someone's sitting room with printed curtains and a pile carpet and flowers (fake, but the expensive silk kind). I'm trying to make it sound OK, nice even, but I don't want to lie to you and this living room for the dead was ghastly. Part of the carpet, the part nearest to the door, had almost worn through from all the other people who had stood where I was standing, feeling the weight of grief pressing down on them, not wanting to go to the person that they loved, knowing that when they got there they would know for sure that the person they loved was no longer there.

I went towards him.

I picked him up and wrapped him in the blue cashmere blanket you had bought for him.

I held him.

There are no more words.

~

Mr Wright listened with focused compassion when I told him about Xavier, not interrupting or prompting, allowing me my silences. At one point he must have handed me a Kleenex because I now have it, sodden, in my hand.

'And you decided at this point against a cremation?' he asks.

'Yes.'

163

A journalist in one of yesterday's papers suggested that we didn't 'allow a cremation' because I was 'making sure evidence wasn't destroyed'. But that wasn't the reason.

⁂

I must have been with Xavier for about three hours. And as I held him I knew that the cold air above a grey mountain was no place for a baby, and therefore, as his mother, it was no place for you either. When I finally left, I phoned Father Peter.

'Can he be buried in Tess's arms?' I asked, expecting to be told that it was impossible.

'Of course. I think that's the right place for him,' replied Father Peter.

⁂

Mr Wright doesn't press me on the reason I chose a burial and I'm grateful for his tact. I try to carry on, not letting emotion slip out, my words stilted.

'Then I went back to see the Senior Midwife, thinking I'd meet the person who'd been with Tess when she gave birth. But she hadn't been able to find Tess's notes so didn't know who it was. She suggested I come back the following Tuesday when she'd have had time to hunt for them.'

'Beatrice?'

I am running out of the office.

I make it to the Ladies' just in time. I am violently sick. The nausea is uncontrollable. My body is shaking. I see a young secretary look in then dart out again. I lie on the cold tiled floor, willing my body back into my control again.

164

Mr Wright comes in and puts his arms around me, and gently helps me up. As he holds me, I realise that I like being taken care of, not in a patriarchal kind of way, but simply being treated with kindness. I don't understand why I never realised this before, brushing away kindness before it was even offered.

My limbs finally stop shaking.

'Time to go home, Beatrice.'

'But my statement . . .'

'How about we both come in tomorrow morning, if you're up to it?'

'OK.'

He wants to call a taxi for me or at least walk me to the tube, but I politely turn down his offer. I tell him that I just need fresh air and he seems to understand.

I want to be alone with my thoughts and my thoughts are about Xavier. From the moment I picked him up, I loved him for him and not only as your baby.

I get outside and tilt my head up towards the pale-blue sky, to stop the tears from spilling out. I remember the letter you wrote to me about Xavier, the one that in your story I haven't yet read. I think of you walking home from the hospital through the driving rain. I think of you looking up at the black pitiless sky. I think of you yelling 'Give him back to me.' And that no one answered you.

I think of you phoning me.

11

There's hardly anyone up and about at 8.30 on a Saturday morning, the pavements virtually deserted. When I arrive at the CPS building there's only one receptionist at the front desk, informally dressed, and when I get into the lift it's empty. I go up to the third floor. There's no Mrs Crush Secretary here today so I walk straight past the reception and into Mr Wright's office.

I see that he's lined up coffee and mineral water for me.

'You're sure you're up to this?' he asks.

'Absolutely. I feel fine now.'

He sets the tape whirring. But he is looking at me with concern and I think that, since yesterday, he sees me as somebody who is far more fragile than he'd realised.

'Can we start with the post-mortem report? You'd asked for a copy.'

'Yes. Two days later it arrived in the post.'

Mr Wright has a copy of the post-mortem in front of him with lines highlighted in yellow pen. I know which the yellow

166

lines will be and I'll give you them in a moment but first there is a line that won't be yellow but is highlighted in my memory. At the very beginning of your post-mortem report the pathologist makes a promise *'on soul and conscience'* to tell the truth. Your body wasn't treated with cold scientific analysis; it was afforded an archaic and more deeply human approach.

Department of Forensic Medicine, Chelsea & Westminster Hospital, London

I Rosemary Didcott, Bachelor of Medicine, hereby certify on soul and conscience that on the 30th January two thousand and ten at the Chelsea and Westminster hospital Mortuary and at the instance of the Coroner, Mr Paul Lewis-Stevens, I dissected the body of Tess Hemming (21), of 35 Chepstow Road, London, the body being identified to me by Detective Sergeant Finborough of the London Metropolitan Police and the following is a true report.

This was the body of a white Caucasian female of slim build and measuring 5 feet 7 inches in height. There was evidence of having given birth two days before death occurred.

There were old scars, dating from childhood, on the right knee and right elbow.

On the right wrist and forearm was a recent laceration ten centimetres in length and four centimetres in depth bisecting the interosseous muscle and damaging the radial artery. On the left wrist and forearm there was a smaller laceration of five centimetres in length and two centimetres in depth and a larger laceration of six centimetres in length and four centimetres in depth, which severed the ulnar

167

artery. The wounds are consistent with the five-inch boning knife that was found with the body.

I could find no evidence of any other bruising or scars or marks of any kind.

There was no evidence of recent sexual intercourse.

Samples of blood and body tissues were collected and referred to the public analyst.

I estimate that this young woman died six days before the dissection, on the 23rd of January.

From this dissection I am of the opinion that this young woman died of exsanguination from the lacerations of arteries in her wrists and forearms.

London 30 January 2010.

I must have read that document a hundred times but 'boning knife' remains as vicious as it did the first time, no mention of Sabatier to blunt it a little with domesticity.

'Were the results from the public analyst included?' asks Mr Wright. (These are the results of the blood and tissue tests, which were done after the initial post-mortem at a different laboratory.)

'Yes, they were attached at the back and had the previous day's date on them, so they'd only just come through. But I couldn't understand them. They were in scientific jargon, not written to be understood by a layperson. Fortunately, I have a friend who's a doctor.'

'Christina Settle?'

'Yes.'

'I have a witness statement from her.'

I realise there must be scores of people working on your case, taking concurrent statements.

168

I lost contact with my old friends from school and university when I went to the States. But since your death old friends have been phoning and writing; 'rallying round' as Mum calls it. Among the rallyers was Christina Settle, who's a doctor now at Charing Cross Hospital. (She's told me that over half my Nuffield biology A level set are pursuing a scientific career of some sort.) Anyhow, Christina wrote a warm letter of condolence, in exactly the same perfect italic writing that she had at school, ending, as many of the letters did, with 'if there's anything at all I can do to help, please let me know'. I decided to take her up on her offer and phoned her.

Christina listened attentively to my bizarre request. She said she was only a senior house officer and in paediatrics not pathology, so she wasn't qualified to interpret the test results. I thought she didn't want to get involved but at the end of our phone call she asked me to fax her over the report. Two days later she phoned and asked if I'd like to meet her for a drink. She'd got a pathologist friend of a friend to go over the report with her.

When I told Todd I was meeting Christina he was relieved, thinking I was venturing back into normal life by looking up old friends.

I walked into the bistro Christina had chosen and was punched by the normal world at full volume. I hadn't been in a public place since you'd died and the loud voices and laughter made me feel vulnerable. Then I saw Christina waving at me and was reassured partly because she looks almost exactly as she did at school, same pretty dark hair, same unflattering thick glasses, and partly because she'd found a booth for us, closeted away from the rest of the bistro. (Christina is still good at bagging things first.) I thought she wouldn't have remembered you very well – after all, she was in sixth form with me when you started at boarding school – but she was adamant that she did. 'Vividly, actually. Even at eleven she was too cool for school.'

'I'm not sure that "cool" is how I'd—'

'Oh I didn't mean it in a bad way, not cold or aloof or anything. That was the extraordinary thing. Why I remember her so well I think. She smiled all the time; a cool kid who laughed and smiled. I'd never seen that combination in someone before.' She paused, her voice a little hesitant. 'She must have been a hard act to compete with . . . ?'

I didn't know if it was nosiness or concern, but decided to get to the purpose of our meeting. 'Can you tell me what the report means?'

She got the report and a notebook out of her briefcase. As she did so, I saw a sachet of Calpol and a baby's cloth book. Christina's glasses and handwriting might not have changed, but her life clearly had. She looked down at her notebook. 'James, the friend of a friend I told you about on the phone, is a senior pathologist so he knows his stuff. But he's anxious about getting involved, pathologists are being sued all the time and minced by the media. He can't be quoted.'

'Of course.'

'You did English, chemistry and biology didn't you, Hemms?'

That old nickname, dusty with age; it took a moment to connect it to me. 'Yes.'

'Any biochemistry since then?'

'No, I did an English degree, actually.'

'I'll translate into layman's terms then. Putting it very simply, Tess had three drugs in her body when she died.'

She didn't see my reaction, looking down at her notebook. But I was stunned.

'What were the drugs?'

170

'One was Cabergoline, which stops breast milk being produced.'

Simon had told me about that drug and again the fact of it gave me a glimpse into something so painful that I couldn't look any further; I interrupted my own thoughts. 'And the others?'

'One was a sedative. She'd taken a fairly large amount. But because it was a few days before Tess was found and a sample of her blood was taken—' She broke off, upset, and gathered herself before continuing. 'What I mean is, because of the time delay it's hard to be accurate about the actual amount of sedative. James said all he could offer was educated guesswork.'

'And . . . ?'

'She had taken far more than would have been indicated as a normal dose. He thought that it wasn't high enough to kill her, but it would have made her very sleepy.'

So that was why there had been no sign of a struggle, he'd doped you first. Did you realise it too late? Christina read out more of her perfect italic writing, 'The third drug is phenylcyclohexylpiperidine, PCP for short. It's a powerful hallucinogenic, developed in the fifties as an anaesthetic but stopped when patients experienced psychotic reactions.'

I was startled into parrotlike repetition, 'Hallucinogenic?'

Christina thought I didn't understand, her voice patient. 'It means the drug causes hallucinations, in lay terms "trips". It's like LSD but more dangerous. Again James says it's hard to be certain how much she'd taken and how long before she died, because of the delay in finding her. It's also complicated because the body stores this drug in muscle and fatty tissues at full psychoactive potential so it can continue to have an effect, even after the person has stopped taking it.'

For a moment I just heard scientific babble until it settled into something I could understand. 'This drug meant she

171

would have been having hallucinations in the days before she died?' I asked.

'Yes.'

So Dr Nichols had been right after all; but your hallucinations weren't because of puerperal psychosis, but a hallucinogenic drug.

'He planned it all. He sent her out of her mind first.'

'Beatrice . . . ?'

'He made her mad, made everyone think she was mad and then he drugged her before he murdered her.'

Christina's brown eyes looked enormous through the lenses of her pebble glasses, their sympathetic expression magnified. 'When I think about how much I love my own baby, well, I can't imagine what I'd do in Tess's place.'

'Suicide wasn't an option to her, even if she'd wanted to take it. She simply wouldn't have been able to. Not after Leo. And she never touched drugs.'

There was a silence between us and the inappropriate noise of the bar around us broke into the booth.

'You knew her best, Hemms.'

'Yes.'

She smiled at me; a gesture of capitulation to my certainty, which carried a blood-tied weight.

'I really appreciate all your help, Christina.'

She was the first person to have helped me in a practical way. Without her I wouldn't have known about the sedative and the hallucinogenic. But I was grateful to her too for respecting my view enough to withhold her own. Six years of being in the same class as emerging adolescents and I doubt we even touched, but outside the door of the restaurant we hugged tightly goodbye.

❧

'Did she tell you any more about PCP?' Mr Wright asks.

'No, but it was relatively simple to research it on the net. I found out that it causes behavioural toxicity, making the victim paranoid and giving them frightening visions.'

Did you realise you were being mentally tortured? If not, what did you think was happening to you?

'It's especially destructive for people already suffering psychological trauma.'

He used your grief against you, knowing that it would make the effect of the drug even worse.

'There were sites accusing the US military of using PCP at Abu Ghraib and in rendition cases. It was clear that the trips it caused were terrifying.'

What was worse for you: the trips? Or thinking that you were going mad?

'And you told the police?' asks Mr Wright.

'Yes, I left a message for DS Finborough. It was late by then, way past office hours. He phoned back the next morning to say that he'd meet me.'

᠅

'I can't believe you're making the poor man come here again, darling.' Todd was making tea and laying out biscuits as if they could compensate DS Finborough for the inconvenience I'd put him to.

'He needs to know about the drugs.'

'The police will already know about them, darling.'

'They can't do.'

Todd added bourbons to the custard creams on the plate, arranging them in two neat yellow and brown rows, his annoyance expressed through the symmetry of biscuits.

173

'Yes. They can. And they will have reached exactly the same conclusion as me.'

He turned away, taking the boiling pan of water off the hob. Last night he had been silent when I told him about the drugs, asking instead why I hadn't told him the real purpose of meeting Christina.

'I can't believe your sister didn't even own a kettle.'

The doorbell rang.

Todd greeted DS Finborough then left to collect Mum. The plan was for Mum and I to pack up your things together. I think he hoped that packing away your belongings would force me to find closure. Yes, I know, an American word, but I don't know the English equivalent; 'facing facts' Mum would call it I suppose.

DS Finborough sat on your sofa, politely eating a bourbon, as I recounted what Christina had told me.

'We already know about the sedative and PCP.'

I was startled. Todd had been right, after all. 'Why didn't you tell me?'

'I thought you and your mother had enough to deal with. I didn't want to add what I thought would be unnecessary distress. And the drugs simply confirmed our belief that Tess took her own life.'

'You think she *deliberately* took them?'

'There was no evidence of any force. And taking a sedative is frequently used by people intent on committing suicide.'

'But it wasn't enough to kill her, was it?'

'No, but maybe Tess didn't know that. After all she hadn't tried anything like this in the past, had she?'

'No. She hadn't. And she didn't this time either. She must have been tricked into taking it.' I tried to shake the self-possessed compassion on his face. 'Don't you see?

He drugged her with the sedative so that he could kill her without a struggle. That's why her body had no marks.'

But I hadn't dislodged his expression or opinion.

'Or she simply took an overdose that wasn't quite big enough.'

I was nine years old in a comprehension class being guided firmly by a caring teacher to draw the correct answers from the text in front of us.

'What about the PCP?' I asked, thinking there was no answer that DS Finborough could possibly have for that drug being in your body.

'I spoke to an inspector in Narcotics,' replied DS Finborough. 'He told me that dealers have been disguising it and selling it in place of LSD for years. There's a whole list of aliases for it: hog, ozone, wack, angel dust. Tess's dealer probably—'

I interrupted. 'You think Tess had a "dealer"?'

'I'm sorry. I meant the person who gave or sold the PCP to her. He or she would not have told Tess what she was actually getting. I also spoke to Tess's psychiatrist, Dr Nichols and—'

I interrupted. 'Tess wouldn't have touched drugs, whatever they were. She loathed them. Even at school, when her friends were smoking and trying joints, she refused to have anything to do with it. She saw her health as a gift that she'd been given, when Leo hadn't, and she had no right to destroy it.'

DS Finborough paused a moment, as if genuinely considering my point of view.

'But she was hardly a schoolgirl any more, with a schoolgirl's anxieties, was she? I'm not saying she wanted to use drugs, or ever had before, but I do think it would be totally understandable if she wanted to escape from her grief.'

I remembered him saying that after having Xavier you were in hell, a place where no one could join you. Even me. And I thought of my craving for the sleeping pills, for a few hours respite from grief.

But I hadn't taken one.

'Did you know that you can smoke PCP?' I asked. 'Or snort it or inject it or you can just simply swallow it? Someone could have slipped it in her drink without her even realising it.'

'Beatrice—'

'Dr Nichols was wrong about why she was having hallucinations. They weren't from puerperal psychosis at all.'

'No. But as I was trying to tell you, I did speak to Dr Nichols about the PCP. He said that although the cause of the hallucinations has clearly changed, her state of mind would be the same. And sadly the outcome. Apparently it's not at all unusual for people on PCP to self-mutilate or to kill themselves. The inspector in Narcotics said much the same.' I tried to interrupt but he kept going to his logical finale. 'All the factual arrows are still pointing the same way.'

'And the Coroner believed this? That someone with no history whatsoever of taking drugs, had voluntarily taken a powerful hallucinogenic? He didn't even question that?'

'No. In fact he told me that she . . .' DS Finborough broke off, thinking better of it.

'Told you what? What exactly did he say about my sister?' DS Finborough was silent.

'Don't you think I have a right to know?'

'Yes, you do. He said that Tess was a student, an art student, living in London and that he'd have been more surprised if she'd been . . .'

He trailed off and I filled the word in for him, '"Clean"?'

'Something to that effect, yes.'

So you were unclean, with all the dirty baggage the word still carries with it into the twenty-first century. I got the phone bill out of its envelope.

'You were wrong about Tess not telling me when her baby died. She tried to – over and over and over again, but she couldn't. Even if you see these phone calls as 'cries for help', they were cries *to me*. Because we were close. I did know her. And she wouldn't have taken drugs. And she wouldn't have killed herself.'

He was silent.

'She turned to me and I let her down. But *she did turn to me*.'

'Yes, she did.'

I thought I saw a flicker of emotion on his face that wasn't simply compassion.

12

An hour and a half after DS Finborough had left, Todd dropped Mum off at the flat. The heating seemed to have given up completely and she didn't take her coat off.

Her breath was visible in the freezing sitting room. 'Right then, let's make a start on her things. I've brought bubble wrap and packing materials.' Maybe she hoped her brisk sense of purpose could fool us into thinking we could sort out the chaos your death had left in its wake. Though to be fair, death does leave a daunting array of practical tasks; all those possessions that you were forced to leave behind had to be sorted and packed and redistributed in the living world. It made me think of an empty airport and one luggage carousel turning, with your clothes and paintings and books and contact lenses and Granny's clock, round and round, with only me and Mum to claim them.

Mum started cutting lengths of bubble wrap, her voice accusatory. 'Todd said you'd asked DS Finborough to see you again?'

'Yes.' I hesitated before going on. 'There were some drugs found in her body.'

'Todd told me that already. We all knew she wasn't herself, Beatrice. And heaven knows, she had enough she wanted to escape from.'

Not giving me the opportunity to argue with her, she went into the sitting room, to 'make some headway before lunch'.

I got out the nudes Emilio had painted of you and hurriedly wrapped them. Partly because I didn't want Mum to see them, but also because I didn't want to look at them. Yes I am a prude, but that wasn't the reason. I just couldn't bear to see the living colour of your painted body when your face in the morgue was so palely vivid. As I wrapped them, I thought that Emilio had the most obvious motive for murdering you. Because of you he could have lost his career and his wife. Yes, she already knew about your affair, but he didn't know that and might have predicted a different response. But your pregnancy would have given him away so I couldn't understand why – if he killed you to protect his marriage and career – he would have waited until after your baby was born.

I'd finished covering the nudes and begun wrapping one of your own paintings in bubble wrap – not looking at the picture and its singing colours, but remembering your four-year-old glee as you squeezed a bubble of bubble wrap between tiny thumb and finger 'POP!'

Mum came in and looked at the stacks of your canvasses. 'What on earth did she think she was she going to do with all of these?'

'I'm not sure, but the art college wants to exhibit them at their show. It's in three weeks and they want Tess to have a special display.'

They'd phoned me a couple of days earlier and I'd readily agreed.

'They're not going to pay for them though, are they?' asked

Mum. 'I mean, what did she think the point of all of this was, exactly?'

'She wanted to be a painter.'

'You mean like a decorator?' asked Mum, astonished.

'No, it's the word they use for an artist now.'

'It's the PC thing to call it,' you said, teasing me for my outdated vocabulary. 'Pop stars are artists, artists are painters and painters are decorators.'

'Painting pictures all day is what children do at nursery school,' continued Mum. 'I didn't mind so much about the GCSE. I thought it was nice for her to have a break from real subjects, but to call it further education is ridiculous.'

'She was just pursuing her talent.'

Yes, I know. It was a little weak.

'It was infantile,' snapped Mum. 'A waste of all her academic achievements.'

She was so angry with you for dying.

I hadn't told Mum about my arrangements for Xavier to be buried with you, fearful of the confrontation, but I couldn't put it off any longer.

'Mum, I really think that she'd want Xavier—'

Mum interrupted. 'Xavier?'

'Her baby, she would want—'

'She used Leo's name?'

Her voice was horrified; I'm sorry.

She went back into the sitting room and started shoving clothes into a black bin liner.

'Tess wouldn't want it all just thrown away, Mum, she recycled everything.'

'These aren't fit for anyone.'

'She mentioned a textile recycling place once, I'll see—'

But Mum had turned away and was pulling out the drawer at the bottom of the wardrobe. She took a tiny cashmere cardigan out of its tissue paper. She turned to me, her voice soft. 'It's beautiful.'

I remembered my astonishment too when I first arrived at finding such exquisite baby things amongst the poverty of the rest of your flat.

'Who gave them to her?' Mum asked.

'I don't know. Amias just said she had a spree.'

'But with what? Did the father give her money?'

I braced myself; she had a right to this information. 'He's married.'

'I know.'

Mum must have seen my confusion; the softness in her voice had gone. 'You asked me if I wanted to "put an A on her coffin for good measure". Tess wasn't married so "the scarlet letter", the badge of adultery, could only mean that the father was.' Her voice tensed further as she noted my surprise. 'You didn't think I understood the reference, did you?'

'I'm sorry. And it was a cruel thing to say.'

'You girls thought that once you got to A levels you left me behind. That all I ever thought about was the menu for a dull supper party three weeks away.'

'I've just never seen you read, that's all.'

She was still holding Xavier's tiny cardigan, her fingers stroking it as she spoke. 'I used to. I'd stay up with my bedside light on while your father wanted to go to sleep. It irritated him but I couldn't stop. It was like a compulsion. Then Leo was ill. I didn't have the time any more. Anyway, I'd realised that books were full of trivia and tripe. Who cares about someone else's love affair, what a sunrise looks like for page after page? Who cares?'

181

She put down the tiny cardigan and resumed shoving your clothes into a bin liner. She hadn't taken off the wire hangers and the hooks tore the flimsy black plastic. As I watched her clumsily anguished movements I thought of the kiln at school and our trayload of soft clay pots being put inside. They would bake harder and harder until the ones that were imperfectly thrown would break into pieces. Your death had thrown Mum way off centre and I knew, as I watched her tie the bin liner into a knot, that when she finally faced your death grief was a kiln that would shatter her.

An hour later, I drove Mum to the station. When I returned I put your clothes from her frantically crammed bin liners back into your wardrobe; Granny's clock back onto the mantelpiece. Even your toiletries were left untouched in the bathroom cupboard, with mine kept in my washbag on a stool. Who knows, maybe that's the real reason I've stayed in your flat all this time. It's meant I've been able to avoid packing you away.

Then I finished wrapping your paintings. This was just preparing for an exhibition, so I had no problem with it. Finally only four paintings were left. They were the nightmarish canvasses in thick gouache of a masked man bending over a woman, her mouth ripping and bleeding as she screamed. The shape in her arms, the only white in the canvas, I'd realised was a baby. I'd also realised that you'd painted them when you were under the effect of the PCP; that they were a visual record of your tormented trips to hell. I saw the marks my tears had made when I first looked at them, the paint streaking down the canvas. Then, tears were the only response open to me, but now I knew that someone had deliberately tortured you and my tears had dried into hatred. I would find him.

❧

The office is overheated, sunshine pouring in through the window warming it further, making me drowsy. I drain my cup of coffee and try to snap awake.

'And then you went to Simon's flat?' Mr Wright asks.

He must be cross-checking what I am telling him with other witness statements, making sure all our time-lines coincide.

'Yes.'

'To question him about the drugs?'

'Yes.'

※

I rang on Simon's bell and, when a cleaning lady answered, I walked in as if I had every right to be there. I was again struck by the opulence of the place. Having lived in your flat for a while, I had become less dulled to material wealth. Simon was in the kitchen, sitting at a breakfast bar. He looked startled when he saw me and then annoyed. His baby face was still unshaved but I thought that, like the piercings, it was an affectation.

'Did you give Tess money to buy baby things?' I asked. I hadn't even thought of the question until I was inside his flat, but it then seemed so probable.

'What are you doing here, just barging in?'

'Your door was open. I need to ask you some more questions.'

'I didn't give her money. I tried once but she wouldn't take it.' He sounded affronted and therefore credible.

'So do you know who did give her the money?'

'No idea.'

'Was she sleepy that day in the park?'

'Jesus. What is this?'

183

'I just want to know if she was sleepy when you met her?'

'No. If anything she was jumpy.'

So he'd given you the sedative later, after Simon had left you.

'Was she hallucinating?' I asked.

'I thought you didn't believe that she had post-natal psychosis?' he taunted.

'Was she?'

'You mean apart from seeing a non-existent man in the bushes?'

I didn't reply. His voice was ugly with irony. 'No, apart from that she seemed completely normal.'

'They found sedatives and PCP in her blood. It's also called wack, angel dust—'

He interrupted, his response immediate and with conviction. 'No. That's wrong. Tess was a puritan tight arse about drugs.'

'But you take them, don't you?'

'So?'

'So maybe you wanted to give her something to feel better, a drink? With something in it that you thought would help?'

'I didn't spike her drink. I didn't give her money. And I want you to leave now, before this gets out of hand.' He was trying to imitate a man with more authority, his father maybe.

I went into the hall, and passed an open doorway to a bedroom. I caught sight of a photo of you on the wall, your hair loose down your back. I went into the bedroom to look at it. It was clearly Simon's room, his clothes neatly folded, his jackets on wooden coat hangers, an obsessively tidy room.

There was a banner in meticulous calligraphy along one

184

wall, *The Female of The Species*. Underneath it were photos of you, scores of them, Blu-Tacked to the walls. In all of them your back was to the camera. Suddenly Simon was close to me, studying my face.

'You knew I was in love with her.'

But these pictures made me think of Bequia islanders who believe a photograph is the theft of a soul. Simon's tone was boastful. 'They're for my final year portfolio. I chose reportage photography of a single subject. My tutor thinks it's the most original and exciting project of the year group.'

Why hadn't he taken any of your face?

He must have guessed my thoughts. 'I didn't want the project to be about a particular person so I made sure she had no identity. I wanted her to be an every woman.'

Or was it so he could watch you, follow you, unobserved?

Simon's tone was still smug. '"The Female of the Species" is the opening of a poem. The next line is "more deadly than the male".'

My mouth felt tinder dry and my words sparked with anger. 'The poem is about mothers protecting their young. That's why the female is more deadly than the male. She has more courage. It's men that Kipling brands as cowards. "At war with conscience".'

Simon was taken aback that I knew the Kipling poem, probably any poem for that matter, and maybe you are too. But I did read English at Cambridge, remember? I was once an arty kind of person. Though being truthful, it was my scientific analysis of structure that got me through rather than insights into the meaning.

I took a photo of you off the wall, then another and another. Simon tried to stop me, but I carried on until there were no photos of you on his wall; until he couldn't look at you again. Then I left his flat, taking the photographs, with Simon

185

furiously protesting that he needed them for his end of year assessment; that I was a thief and something else that I didn't hear because I'd slammed the door shut behind me.

As I drove home with the photos on my lap I wondered how many times Simon followed you to take photos of you. Did he follow you after you left him in the park that day? I stopped the car and studied the photos. They were all of your back view, with the scenery changing from summer to autumn to winter, and your clothes from T-shirt to jacket to thick coat. He must have been following you for months. But I couldn't find a photo of you in a snowy park.

I remembered that for Bequia islanders a photo can be made part of a voodoo doll and cursed; that a photo is considered as potent as having the victim's hair or blood.

When I arrived home, I saw a new kettle in its box in the kitchen and heard Todd in the bedroom. I went in to see him trying to break one of your 'psychotic paintings', but the canvas was sturdy and not giving way.

'What on earth are you doing?'

'They won't fit in a bin liner and I could hardly leave them at the dump as they are.' He turned to face me. 'There's no point keeping them, not when they upset you so much.'

'But I have to keep them.'

'Why?'

Because . . .' I trailed off.

'Because, what?'

They were proof she was being mentally tortured, I thought, but didn't say. Because I knew it would lead to an argument about how you died; because that argument would inevitably end in our separation. And because I didn't want to be more alone than I already was.

⁂

186

'Did you tell the police about Simon's photos?' Mr Wright asks.

'No. They were already sceptical, more than sceptical, about Tess being murdered and I didn't think the photos would persuade them otherwise.'

I could hardly mention Bequia islanders and voodoo dolls.

'I knew that Simon would argue that they were for his art degree,' I continue. 'He had an excuse for stalking her.'

Mr Wright checks his watch. 'I need to get to a meeting in ten minutes, so let's end it there.'

He doesn't tell me who the meeting is with but it must be important if it's on a Saturday afternoon. Or maybe he's noticed me looking tired. I feel exhausted most of the time, actually, but in comparison to what you went through I know I have no right to complain.

'Would you mind continuing your statement tomorrow?' he asks. 'If you're feeling up to it.'

'Of course,' I say. But surely it's not normal to work on a Sunday.

He must guess my thoughts. 'Your statement is vitally important to secure a conviction. And I want to get as much down as possible while it's fresh in your mind.'

As if my memory is a fridge with pieces of useful information in danger of rotting in the crisper drawer. But that's not fair. The truth is that Mr Wright has discovered that I am more unwell than he originally thought. And he's astute enough to worry that if I am physically declining then my mind, in particularly my memory, may deteriorate too. He's right to want us to continue apace.

I'm now on a crowded bus, squashed up against the window. There's a transparent patch in the misted-up glass and

187

through it I glimpse London's buildings lining our route. I never told you that I wished I'd studied architecture instead of English, did I? Three weeks into the course, I knew I'd made a mistake. My mathematical brain and insecure nature needed something more solid than the structure of similes in metaphysical poetry, but I daren't ask if I could swap in case they threw me off the English course and no place was found for me on the architecture one. It was too great a risk. But each time I see a beautiful building I regret I didn't have the courage to take it.

13

Sunday

This morning there isn't even one receptionist on the front desk and the large foyer area is deserted. I take the empty lift up to the third floor. It must just be Mr Wright and me here today.

He told me that he wants to 'go through the Kasia Lewski part of the statement this morning', which will be strange when I saw Kasia an hour ago in your flat, wearing your old dressing gown.

I go straight into Mr Wright's office and again he has coffee and water waiting for me. He asks me if I'm OK, and I reassure him that I'm fine.

'I'll start by recapping what you've told me so far about Kasia Lewski,' he says, looking down at typed notes, which must be a transcript of an earlier part of my statement. He reads out, '"Kasia Lewski came to Tess's flat on the twenty-seventh of January at about four in the afternoon asking to see her."'

I remember the sound of the doorbell and running to get it; having 'Tess' in my mouth, almost out, as I opened the door and the taste of your name. I remember my resentment when I saw Kasia standing on your doorstep with her high-heeled cheap shoes and the raised veins of pregnancy over goose-pimpled white legs. I shudder at my remembered snobbishness, but am glad my memory is still acute.

'She told you that she was in the same clinic as Tess?' asks Mr Wright.

'Yes.'

'Did she say at which clinic?'

I shake my head and don't tell him that I was too keen to get rid of her to take any interest, let alone ask any questions. He looks down at his notes again.

'She said she'd been single too but now her boyfriend had returned?'

'Yes.'

'Did you meet Michael Flanagan?'

'No, he stayed in the car. He blared the horn and I remember she seemed nervous of him.'

'And the next time you saw her was just after you'd been to Simon Greenly's flat?' he asks.

'Yes. I took some baby clothes round.'

But that's a little disingenuous. I was using my visit to Kasia as an excuse to avoid Todd and the argument I knew would end our relationship.

༄

Despite the snow and slippery pavements, it only took me ten minutes to walk to Kasia's flat. She's since told me that she always came to yours, and I guess that was to avoid Mitch. Her flat is in Trafalgar Crescent – a concrete ugly imposter amongst the crisp symmetrical garden squares and properly shaped crescents of the rest of W11. Alongside and above her street, as if you could reach it as easily as reaching a book on a tall bookshelf, is the Westway, the roar of traffic thundering down the street. In the stairwells, graffiti artists (maybe they're called painters now) have left their tags, like dogs peeing, marking out their patch. Kasia opened the door, keeping it on the chain. 'Yes?'

'I'm Tess Hemming's sister.'

She unhooked the chain and I heard a bolt being pulled back. Even on her own (let alone the fact it was snowing outside and she was pregnant) she was wearing a tight cropped top and high-heeled black patent boots with diamanté studs up the sides. For a moment I worried that she was a prostitute and was expecting a client. I can hear you laughing. Stop.

'Beatrice.' I was taken aback that she remembered my name. 'Come. Please.'

It had been just over two weeks since I'd last seen her – when she came round to the flat, asking for you – and her bump had got noticeably bigger. I guessed she must be around seven months pregnant now.

I went into the flat, which smelled of cheap perfume and air-freshener, which didn't mask the natural smells of mould and damp evident on the walls and carpet. An Indian throw like the one on your sofa (had you given her one of yours?) had been nailed up at the window. I'd thought that I wouldn't try to put down Kasia's exact words or try to get across her accent, but in this meeting her lack of fluency made what she said more striking.

'I'm sorry. You must be . . . How can I say?' She struggled for the word then, giving up, shrugged apologetically. 'Sad, but sad not big enough.'

For some reason her imperfect English sounded more sincere than a perfectly phrased letter of condolence.

191

'You love her very much Beatrice.' Love in the present tense because Kasia had yet to learn the past tense, or because she was more sensitive than anyone else to my bereavement?

'Yes, I do.'

She looked at me, her face warm and compassionate, and she baffled me. Straight off, she had hopped out of the box I'd so neatly stuck her into. She was being kind to me and it was meant to be the other way around. I gave her the small suitcase I'd brought with me. 'I've brought some baby things.' She didn't look nearly as pleased as I'd expected. I thought it must be because the clothes were intended for Xavier; that they were stained with sadness.

'Tess . . . funeral?' she asked.

'Oh yes of course. It's in Little Hadston, near Cambridge on Thursday the fifteenth February at eleven o'clock.'

'Can you write . . . ?'

I wrote down the details for her, and then I virtually pushed the suitcase of baby clothes into her hands.

'Tess would want you to have them.'

'Our priest, he says Mass for her on Sunday.' I wondered why was she changing the subject. She hadn't even opened the suitcase. 'That was OK?'

I nodded. I'm not sure what you'll make of it though.

'Father John. He's very nice man. He's very . . .' She absent-mindedly moved her hand onto her bump.

'Very Christian?' I asked.

She smiled, getting the joke. 'For priest. Yes.'

Was she joking too? Yes, straight back. She was much sharper than I'd thought.

'The Mass. Does Tess mind?' she asked. Again I wondered if the present tense was intentional. Maybe it was – if a Mass is all it's cracked up to be then you're up there in heaven, or in the waiting room of purgatory, present tense. You're in the now, if not in the here and now – and maybe Kasia's Mass reached you and you're now feeling a little foolish about your earthly atheism.

'Would you like to look in the case and decide what you want?'

I'm not sure if I was being kind or trying to get back into a place where I felt superior. I certainly didn't feel comfortable being the recipient of kindness from someone like Kasia. Yes, I was still snobby enough to think 'someone like'.

'I make tea first?'

I followed her into the dingy kitchen. The linoleum on the floor was torn, exposing concrete underneath. But everything was as clean as it could be given the handicap it started with. White chipped china gleamed, old saucepans shone around their rust spots. She filled the kettle and put it on to the hob. I didn't think she'd be able to tell me anything useful but decided to try anyway. 'Do you know if anyone had tried to give Tess drugs?'

She looked aghast. 'Tess never take drugs. With baby, nothing bad. No tea, no coffee.'

'Do you know who Tess was afraid of?'

Kasia shook her head. 'Tess not afraid.'

'But after she had the baby?'

Her eyes filled with tears and she turned away from me, struggling to regain her composure. Of course she'd been away with Mitch in Majorca when you had Xavier. She hadn't come back till after you'd died, when she'd come knocking on your door and found me instead. I felt guilty for upsetting her, for questioning her when she clearly couldn't help me at all. She was now making me tea so I could hardly leave, but I had no idea what to say to her. 'So do you work?'

193

I asked, a rather unsubtle variation on the standard cocktail party line of 'So what do you do?'

'Yes. Cleaning ... Sometime supermarket shelves, but night work, horrible. Sometime I work for magazines.'

I immediately thought of porn mags. My prejudices, based on her wardrobe choices, were too stubbornly entrenched to be shifted without some effort. Though to be a little bit fair to myself I had started to worry about her in the sex trade rather than simply being judgemental. She was astute enough to sense I had reservations about her 'magazine work'.

'The free ones,' she continued. 'I put them in the letter-boxes. The house that have "No Junk Mail" I put in too. I can't read English.'

I smiled at her. She seemed pleased by the first genuine smile I'd given her.

'All the doors in the rich places not want free papers. But we not go to the poor places. Funny, isn't it?'

'Yes.' I searched for another opening conversational gambit. 'So where did you meet Tess?'

'Oh. I not tell you?'

Of course she had, but I'd forgotten – which isn't surprising when you remember how little interest I took in her.

'The clinic. My baby ill too,' she said.

'Your baby has cystic fibrosis?'

'Cystic fibrosis, yes. But now . . .' She touched her stomach. 'Better now. A miracle.' She made a sign of the cross, a gesture as natural to her as pushing her hair away from her face. 'Tess called it the "Mummies with disasters clinic". First time I met her she made me laugh. She asked me to flat.' Her words caught in her throat. She turned away from me. I couldn't see her face but I knew she was trying not to cry. I reached out my hand to put on her shoulder, but just couldn't do it. I find being tactile to a person I don't know as hard

194

as touching a spider if you're arachnophobic. You may find it funny, but it really isn't. It's almost a handicap.

Kasia finished making the tea and put it all on a tray. I noticed how proper she was, with cups and saucers, a jug for milk, a strainer for the tea leaves, the cheap teapot warmed first.

As we went through to the sitting room, I saw a picture on the opposite wall, which hadn't been visible to me before. It was a charcoal drawing of Kasia's face. It was beautiful. And it made me see that Kasia was beautiful too. I knew you'd done it.

'Tess's?' I asked.

'Yes.'

Our eyes met and for a moment something was communicated between us that didn't need language and therefore there was no barrier. If I had to translate that 'something' into words it would be that you and she were clearly close enough for you to want to draw her; that you saw beauty in people that others didn't see. But it wasn't as verbose as that, no language clunked between us; it was a more subtle thing. The sound of a door slamming startled me.

I turned to see a man coming into the room. Large and muscular, about twenty years old, he looked absurdly big in the tiny flat. He was wearing labourers' overalls, no T-shirt underneath, his muscular arms tattooed like sleeves. His hair was matted with plaster dust. His voice was surprisingly quiet for such a large man, but it had the timbre of threat. 'Kash? Why the fuck haven't you bolted the door? I told you—' He stopped as he saw me. 'Health visitor?'

'No,' I replied.

He ignored me, directing his question to Kasia. 'So who the fuck is this then?'

Kasia was nervous and embarrassed. 'Mitch . . .'

He sat down, stating his claim to the room and by implication my lack of one.

Kasia was nervous of him, the same expression I'd seen that day outside your flat when he'd blared the horn. 'This is Beatrice.'

'And what does "Beatrice" want with us?' he asked, mocking.

I suddenly felt conscious of my designer jeans and grey cashmere sweater, de rigueur weekend wardrobe in New York but hardly the kind of outfit to blend in on a Monday morning in Trafalgar Crescent.

'Mitch doing nights. Very hard,' said Kasia, 'He gets very . . .' She struggled to find the word, but you need to have a mother tongue phrase book in your brain to find a euphemism for Mitch's behaviour. 'Out of sorts' was the one that sprung to my mind most quickly; I almost wanted to write it down for her.

'You don't need to fucking apologise for me.'

'My sister, Tess, was a friend of Kasia's.' I said, but my voice had become Mum's; anxiety always accentuates my upper-class accent.

He looked angrily at Kasia. 'The one you were always running off to?' I didn't know if Kasia's English was good enough for her to understand he was being a bully to her. I wondered if he was a physical bully too.

Kasia's voice was quiet. 'Tess my friend.'

It was something I hadn't heard since primary school, standing up for someone simply by saying 'she's my friend'. I was touched by the powerful simplicity of it. I stood up, not wanting to make things more awkward for her. 'I'd better be going.'

Mitch was sprawled in an armchair; I had to step over his legs to get to the door. Kasia came with me. 'Thank you for the clothes. Very kind.'

Mitch looked at her. 'What clothes?'

'I brought some baby things round. That's all.'

'You like playing Lady Bountiful then?'

Kasia didn't understand what he was saying, but could sense it was hostile. I turned to her. 'They're just such lovely things and I didn't want to throw them away or give them to a charity shop where they might have been bought by anybody.'

Mitch leaped in, a pugnacious man intent on a fight, and enjoying it. 'So it's us or a charity shop?'

'When do you get off from your macho posturing?'

Confrontation, which used to seem so alien to me, now felt familiar territory.

'We've got our own fucking baby clothes,' he said going into a bedroom. Moments later he came out with a box and dumped it at my feet. I looked inside. It was filled with expensive baby clothes. Kasia seemed very embarrassed. 'Tess and me, shopping. Together. We . . .'

'But how did you have the money?' I asked. Before Mitch could explode I hurriedly continued, 'Tess had no money either, and I just want to know who gave it to her.'

'The people doing the trial,' said Kasia. 'Three hundred pounds.'

'What trial? The cystic fibrosis trial?' I asked.

'Yes.'

I wondered if it could be a bribe. I'd got into the mental habit of suspecting everyone and everything connected to you – and this trial, which I'd had misgivings about at the very start, was already a soil rich with anxiety for seeds of distrust to take root.

'Can you remember the person's name?'

Kasia shook her head. 'It was in envelope. Just with leaflets, no letter. A surprise.'

Mitch cut across her. 'And you spent the whole fucking lot on baby clothes, which it'll be out of in weeks and Christ knows there's enough else we need.'

Kasia looked away from him. I sensed this argument was old and much worn and had broken any joy she had once felt in buying the clothes.

She accompanied me out of the flat. As we walked down the concrete steps in the graffiti-decorated stairwell she guessed what I would say if we were fluent in each other's languages and replied, 'He is father. Nothing change that now.'

'I'm staying in Tess's flat. Will you come round?'

I was surprised by how much I hoped she would.

Mitch yelled from the top of the stairwell. 'You forgot this.' He threw the suitcase of clothes down the stairwell. As the case hit the concrete landing it opened; tiny cardigans, a hat and baby blanket lay strewn across the damp concrete. Kasia helped me to pick them up.

'Don't come to the funeral, Kasia. Please.'

Yes, because of Xavier. It would have been too hard for her.

I walked home, the sharp wind cutting across my face. With my coat collar pulled up and a scarf around my head, trying to protect myself from the cold, I didn't hear my mobile and it went through to message. It was Mum saying Dad wanted to talk to me and giving me his number. But I knew I wouldn't call him. Instead I became the insecure adolescent who felt her growing body was the wrong shape to fit into his completely formed new life. I felt again the smothering rejection as he blanked me out. Oh, I knew he'd remembered our birthdays, sending us extravagant presents that were too old for us, as if trying to accelerate us into adulthood and away from his responsibility. And the two weeks with him in the summer holidays, when we tarnished the Provence sunshine with our reproachful English faces, bringing our micro climate of sadness. And when we left it was as if we'd never been. I once saw the trunks where 'our' bedroom things were kept – stowed away in the attic for the rest of the year. Even you, in your optimism for life and capacity to see the best in people, felt that too.

As I think about Dad, I suddenly understand why you didn't ask Emilio to take any responsibility for Xavier. Your baby was too precious, too loved, for anyone to turn him into a blemish on their life. He should never feel unvalued or unwanted. You weren't protecting Emilio but your child.

꽃

I haven't told Mr Wright about my non-phone call with Dad, just the money that you and Kasia received for being on the trial.

'The payments weren't large,' I continue. 'But I thought they could have been an inducement to Tess and to Kasia to take part.'

'Tess hadn't told you about the payment?'

'No. She always saw the best in people but she knew I was more sceptical. She probably wanted to avoid the lecture.'

You'd have guessed my bumper sticker warnings: 'There's no such thing as a free lunch'; 'Corporate altruism is a contradiction in terms.'

'Did you think it was the money that persuaded her?' asks Mr Wright.

'No. She believed the trial was her baby's only chance of

199

a cure. She'd have paid them to be on the trial. But I thought that maybe whoever had given her money didn't know that. Like Kasia, Tess looked in need of cash.' I pause while Mr Wright makes a note, then continue. 'I'd researched the medical side of the trial thoroughly when Tess first told me about it, but I'd never looked at the finances. So I started doing that. On the net, I discovered that people are legitimately paid in drugs trials. There are even dedicated websites who advertise for volunteers, promising the money will "pay for your next holiday".'

'And the volunteers on the Chrom-Med trial?'

'There was absolutely nothing about them being paid. Chrom-Med's own website, which had a lot of detail on the trial, had nothing about any payments. I knew that the development of the genetic cure would have cost a fortune, and three hundred pounds was a tiny amount of money in comparison, but it still seemed strange. Chrom-Med's website had email addresses for every member of the company – presumably to look open and approachable – so I emailed Professor Rosen. I was pretty sure it would go to a minion, but thought it was worth a try.'

Mr Wright has a copy of my email in front of him.

From: Beatrice Hemming's iPhone
To: professor.rosen@chrom-med.com
Dear Professor Rosen,
Could you tell me why the mothers on your cystic fibrosis trial are being paid £300 to participate? Or perhaps you would prefer me to couch it in the correct language, 'compensated for their time'.
Beatrice Hemming

❦

As I'd predicted, I didn't hear back from Professor Rosen. But I carried on searching on the net, still wearing my coat from when I'd got in from visiting Kasia, my bag just dumped at my feet. I hadn't switched the light on and now it was dark. I hardly noticed Todd coming in. I didn't even wonder, let alone ask, where he'd been all day, barely glancing up from the screen.

'Tess was paid to take part in the CF trial, so was Kasia, but there's no record of that anywhere.'

'Beatrice . . .'

He'd stopped using the word 'darling'.

'But that's not the important thing, though,' I continued. 'I hadn't thought to look at the financial aspect of the trial before, but several reputable sites, the *FT*, the *New York Times*, are saying that Chrom-Med are going to float on the stock market in just a few weeks' time.'

It would have been in the papers, but since you'd died I had stopped reading them. Chrom-Med's floatation was a crucial bit of news to me, but Todd didn't react at all.

'The directors of Chrom-Med stand to make a fortune,' I continued. 'The sites have different estimates, but the amount of money is enormous. And the employees are all share-holders so they're going to get their share of the bonanza.'

'The company will have invested millions if not billions in their research,' Todd said, his voice impatient. 'And now they're having a massively successful trial, which is payback time for their investment. Of course they're going to float on the stock market. It's a completely logical business decision.'

'But the payments to the women—'

'Stop. For God's sake, stop,' he shouted. For a moment both of us were taken aback. We'd spent four years being polite towards each other. Shouting was embarrassingly intimate. He struggled to sound more measured. 'First it was her married tutor, then an obsessed weirdo student and now you've added this trial to your list – which everyone, including the world's press and scientific community, have wholeheartedly endorsed.'

'Yes. I am suspicious of different people, even a trial. Because I don't know yet who killed her. Or why. Just that someone did. And I have to look at every possibility.'

'No. You don't. That's the police's job, and they've done it. There's nothing left for you to do.'

'My sister was murdered.'

'Please, darling, you have to face the truth at some point that—'

I interrupted him. 'She would never have killed herself.'

At this point in our argument, both of us awkward and a little embarrassed, I felt that we were going through the motions, actors struggling with a clunky script.

'Just because it's what you believe,' he said. 'What you *want* to believe, that doesn't make it true.'

'How can you possibly know what the truth is?' I snapped back. 'You had only met her a few times, and even then you barely bothered to talk to her. She wasn't the kind of person you wanted to get to know.'

I was rowing with apparent conviction, my voice raised and my words sharpened to hurt, but in truth I was still on our relationship ring road and inside I was uninvolved and unscathed. I continued my performance, marvelling slightly at how easy it was to get into my stride. I'd never had a row before.

'What did you call her? "Kooky"?' I asked, not waiting for a reply. 'I don't think you even bothered to listen to anything she said to you on the two occasions we actually all had a meal together. You judged her without even having a proper conversation with her.'

'You're right. I didn't know her well. And I admit that I didn't like her all that much either. She irritated me as a matter of fact. But this isn't about how well—'

I interrupted him. 'You dismissed her because she was an art student, because of the way she lived and the clothes she wore.'

'For God's sake.'

'You didn't see the person that she was at all.'

'You're going way off the point here. Look, I do understand that you want to blame someone for her death. I know you don't want to feel responsible for it.' The composure in his voice sounded forced and I was reminded of myself talking to the police. 'You're afraid of having to live with that guilt,' he continued. 'And I do understand that. But what I want you to try to understand is that once you accept what really happened then you'll realise that you weren't to blame at all. We all know that you weren't. She took her own life, for reasons that the police, the Coroner, your mother and her doctors are satisfied with, and no one else is to blame, including you. If you could just believe that then you can start to move forwards.' He awkwardly put his hand on my shoulder and left it there, like me he finds being tactile difficult. 'I've got tickets home for both of us. Our flight leaves the evening after her funeral.'

I was silent. How could I possibly leave?

'I know that you're worried your mother needs you here for support,' continued Todd. 'But she agrees that the sooner you get back home, back to your normal life, the better.' His hand slammed onto the table. I noticed the disturbance on my screen before his uncharacteristic physicality. 'I don't recognise you any more. And now, I'm laying my guts out here and you can't even be bothered to look up from the fucking internet.'

I turned to him, and only then saw his white face and his body huddled into itself in misery.

'I'm sorry. But I can't leave. Not till I know what happened to her.'

'We know what happened to her. And you need to accept that. Because life has to go on, Beatrice. Our life.'

'Todd . . .'

'I do know how hard it must be for you without her. I do understand that. But you do have me.' His eyes were blurred with tears. 'We're getting married in three months.'

I tried to work out what to say and in the silence he walked away from me into the kitchen. How could I explain to him that I couldn't get married any more, because marriage is a commitment to the future and a future without you was impossible to contemplate? And that it was for this reason, rather than my lack of passion for him, which meant I couldn't marry him.

I went into the kitchen. His back was towards me and I saw what he would look like as an old man.

'Todd, I'm sorry but—'

He turned and yelled at me, 'For fuck's sake I love you.' Shouting at a foreigner in your own language as if volume will make them understand; make me love him back.

'You don't really know me. You wouldn't love me if you did.'

It was true, he didn't know me. I'd never let him. If I had a song, I'd never tried singing it to him; never stayed in bed with him on a Sunday morning. It was always my idea to get up and go out. Maybe he had looked into my eyes but if he had I hadn't been looking back.

'You deserve more,' I said and tried to take his hand. But he pulled it away. 'I'm so sorry.'

He flinched from me. But I was sorry. I still am. Sorry that

I had neglected to notice that it was only me on the safe ring road while he was inside the relationship, alone and exposed. Once again I had been selfish and cruel towards someone I was meant to care for.

Before you died, I'd thought our relationship was grown-up and sensible. But on my part it was cowardly; a passive option motivated by my insecurity rather than what Todd deserved – an active choice inspired by love.

A few minutes later he left. He didn't tell me where he was going.

❧

Mr Wright had decided on a working lunch and has now got sandwiches from the deli. He leads me through empty corridors to a meeting room, which has a table. For some reason, the large office space, deserted apart from us two, feels intimate.

I haven't told Mr Wright that during my research I broke off my engagement, and that with no friends in London Todd must have walked through the snow to a hotel that night. I just tell him about Chrom-Med floating on the stock market.

'And you phoned DS Finborough at eleven thirty p.m.?' he asks, looking down at the police call log.

'Yes. I left a message for him asking him to phone me back. By nine thirty the next morning he still hadn't, so I went to St Anne's.'

'You'd already organised to go back there?'

'Yes. The Senior Midwife had said she should have found Tess's notes by then and had made an appointment for me to see her.'

❧

I arrived at St Anne's, the skin around my skull tight with nerves because I thought I would soon have to meet the person who was with you when you had Xavier. I knew I had to do this, but wasn't sure exactly why. Maybe as a penance; my guilt faced full on. I arrived fifteen minutes early and went to the hospital café. As I sat down with my coffee I saw I had a new email.

> To: Beatrice Hemming's iPhone
> From: Professor Rosen's office, Chrom-Med
> Dear Ms Hemming,
> I assure you that we offer no financial inducement
> *whatsoever* to the participants in our trial. Each
> participant volunteers without coercion or inducement. If
> you would like to check with the participating hospitals'
> ethics committees you will see that the highest ethical
> principles are strictly enforced.
> Kind regards
> Sarah Stonaker, media PA to Professor Rosen

I emailed straight back.

> From: Beatrice Hemming's iPhone
> To: professor.rosen@chrom-med.com
> One 'participant' was my sister. She was paid £300 to
> take part in the trial. Her name was Tess Hemming,
> (second name Annabel after her grandmother). She was
> 21. She was murdered after giving birth to her stillborn
> baby. Her funeral and that of her son is on Thursday. I
> miss her more than you can possibly imagine.

It felt a reasonable place to be writing such an email. Illness and death may be shut away in the wards above but I

206

imagined the fallout blowing invisibly into the atrium and landing in the hospital café's cappuccinos and herbal teas. I wouldn't have been the first to write an emotional email at this table. I wondered if the 'media PA' would pass it on to Professor Rosen. I doubted it.

I resolved to ask the hospital staff if they knew anything about the money.

Five minutes before my appointment time I took the lift up to the fourth floor, as instructed, and walked to the maternity wing.

The Senior Midwife seemed fraught when she saw me, although maybe her escaping frizzy red hair made her seem that way all the time. 'I'm afraid we still haven't found Tess's notes. And without them I haven't been able to find out who was with her when she gave birth.'

I felt relief but thought it cowardly to give in to.

'Doesn't anyone remember?'

'I'm afraid not. For the last three months we've been very short-staffed, so we've had a high percentage of agency midwives and locum doctors. I think it must have been one of them.'

A young punky nurse standing at the nurses' station, her nose pierced, joined in, 'We have the basic info on a central computer, like the time and date of admission and discharge, and sadly in your sister's case, that her baby died. But nothing more detailed. Nothing about their medical history or the medical staff looking after them. I did check with the psych department yesterday. Dr Nichols said her notes hadn't ever got to him. Told me our department should "pull our socks up", which is pretty angry coming from him.'

I remembered Dr Nichols commenting that he didn't have your 'psychiatric history'. I hadn't known it was because your notes had got lost.

207

'But aren't her notes also on computer somewhere? I mean the detailed information, as well as the basics?' I asked.

The Senior Midwife shook her head. 'We use paper notes for maternity patients, so the woman can carry them with her in case she goes into labour when she's not near her home hospital. We then attach the handwritten notes of the delivery and it's all meant to be safely stored.'

The phone rang but the Senior Midwife ignored it, focusing on me. 'I really am sorry. We do understand how important it must be to you.'

As she answered the phone, my initial relief that your notes were lost became weighted by suspicion. Did your medical notes hold some clue about your murder? Was that why they were 'lost'? I waited for the Senior Midwife to finish her phone call.

'Isn't it odd that a patient's notes just go missing?' I asked.

The Senior Midwife grimaced. 'Unfortunately it's not odd at all.'

A portly consultant in a chalk-striped suit was passing, he stopped and chipped in, 'An entire trolley of notes went missing from my diabetic clinic on Tuesday. The whole lot vanished into some administrative black hole.'

I noticed that Dr Saunders had arrived at the nurses' station and was checking a patient's notes. He didn't seem to notice me.

'Really?' I said, uninterested, to Chalk-striped Consultant. But he carried on warming to his theme. 'When they built St John's hospital last year no one remembered to build a morgue and when their first patient died there was nowhere to take him.'

The Senior Midwife was clearly embarrassed by him and I wondered why he was being so open with me about hospital errors.

'There's been relocation of teenage cancer patients and no one remembered to transport their frozen eggs,' continued Chalk-striped Consultant. 'And now their chances of a baby when they've recovered is zero.'

Dr Saunders noticed me and smiled reassuringly. 'But we're not totally incompetent all of the time, I promise.'

'Did you know that women were being paid to take part in the cystic fibrosis trial?' I asked.

Chalk-striped Consultant looked a little peeved by my abrupt change of subject. 'No I didn't know that.'

'Nor me,' said Dr Saunders. 'Do you know how much?'

'Three hundred pounds.'

'It could well have been a doctor or nurse being kind,' Dr Saunders said, his tone considerate. And again he reminded me of you, this time for thinking the best of people. 'There was that nurse in oncology last year, wasn't there?' he asked.

Chalk-striped Consultant nodded. 'Spent the department's entire transport fund on new clothes for an old man she felt sorry for.'

The young punky nurse joined in, 'And midwives sometimes try to help hard-up mums by giving them nappies and formula when they leave. Occasionally a steriliser or a baby bath finds its way out too.'

Chalk-striped Consultant grinned. 'You mean we've reverted to the days when nurses were caring?'

The punky nurse glowered at him and Chalk-striped Consultant laughed.

Two beeps went off and a phone rang on the nurses' station. Chalk-striped Consultant walked away to answer his bleep; the punky nurse answered the phone; the Senior Midwife was answering a patient's buzzer. I was left alone with Dr Saunders. I've always been intimidated by handsome men, let alone beautiful ones. I associate them not so much with inevitable rejection as with turning me completely invisible.

'Would you like to have a coffee?' he asked.

Probably blushing, I shook my head. I didn't want to be the recipient of emotional charity.

I have to admit, that despite still being with Todd, I entertained a fantasy about Dr Saunders, but knew that it wasn't one to pursue. Even if I could create a fantasy in which he was attracted to me, his wedding ring prevented it from stretching into something long term or secure or anything else I wanted in a relationship.

⁂

'I gave the Senior Midwife my contact details in case she found Tess's notes. But she warned me they might be permanently lost.'

'You said you found her notes going missing suspicious?' asks Mr Wright.

'To start with, yes. But the longer I was at the hospital the harder it was to imagine anything sinister happening. It just seemed too public, a cheek-by-jowl working environment with people literally looking over each other's shoulders. I couldn't see how anyone would get away with something. Not that I knew what that "something" was.'

'And the payments?'

'The people at St Anne's didn't seem even surprised by them, let alone suspicious.'

He looks down at the police log of our calls. 'DS Finborough didn't return your call and you didn't chase that?'

'No, because what could I tell him? That women had been paid, but no one I'd spoken to at the hospital thought that

210

sinister or even strange; that Chrom-Med was floating on the stock market, but even my own fiancé thought that was just a logical business decision. And Tess's notes had gone missing, but the medical staff thought that pretty routine. I had nothing to go to him with.'

My mouth has become dry. I drink some water, then continue, 'I thought that I'd been going down a dead end and should have kept going with my initial distrust of Emilio Codi and Simon. I knew most murders were domestic. I can't remember where I heard that.'

But I remember thinking that murder and domestic was an oxymoron. Doing the ironing on Sunday night and emptying the dishwasher is domestic, not murder.

'I thought Simon and Emilio were both capable of killing her. Emilio had an obvious motive and Simon was clearly obsessed by her, his photos were evidence of that. Both of them were connected to Tess through the college: Simon as a student there and Emilio as a tutor. So after I left the hospital I went to the college. I wanted to see if anyone there could tell me anything.'

Mr Wright must think I was keen and energetic. But it wasn't that. I was putting off going home. Partly because I didn't want to return home without being any further forwards, but also because I wanted to avoid Todd. He'd phoned and offered to come to your funeral but I'd told him there was no need. So he planned to fly back to the States as soon as possible and would be coming to the flat to pick up his things. I didn't want to be there.

❧

The snow hadn't been cleared from the paths up to the Art College and most of the windows were in darkness.

211

The secretary with the German accent told me it was the last of three inset days. She agreed to me putting up a couple of notices. The first was information about your funeral. And the second asked your friends to meet me in a café that I'd seen opposite the college in a couple of weeks' time. It was an impulsive note, the date of the meeting chosen randomly, and as I pinned it up next to flat shares and equipment for sale I thought it looked a ridiculous kind of notice and that nobody would come. But I left it anyway.

When I got home, I saw Todd waiting in the darkness, his hood pulled up against the sleet.

'I don't have a key.'

I'd thought he'd taken one with him. 'I'm sorry.'

I unlocked the door and he went into the bedroom.

I watched from the doorway as he packed his clothes, so meticulously. Suddenly he turned and it was as if he caught me off guard, for the first time we were properly looking at each other.

'Come back with me? Please.'

I faltered, looking at his immaculately packed clothes, remembering the order and neatness of our life in New York, a refuge from the maelstrom here. But my neatly contained life was in the past. I could never fly back to it.

'Beatrice?'

I shook my head and the small movement of denial made me vertiginous.

He offered to take the car back to the car hire people at the airport. After all, I clearly had no idea how long I'd be staying. And it was ludicrously expensive. The mundanity of our conversation, the attention to practical detail, was so soothingly familiar that I wanted to ask him to stay with me, plead with him to stay. But I couldn't ask that of him.

'You're sure that you don't want me to stay for the funeral?' he asked.

'Yes. Thank you though.'

I gave him the keys to the hire car and only when I heard the car start up realised I should have given him the engagement ring. Twisting it around my finger, I watched through the basement window as he drove away and continued watching long after his car had disappeared from sight, the sounds of cars now strangers' cars.

I felt caged in loneliness.

❦

I have told Mr Wright about my notice in the college but not about Todd.

'Shall I go and get us some cakes?' he asks.

I am completely taken aback. 'That would be nice.'

Nice – I should bring a thesaurus tomorrow. I wonder if he's being kind. Or hungry. Or maybe it's a romantic gesture – an old-fashioned tea together. I am surprised by how much I hope it's the latter.

When he's left, I dial Todd's number at work. His PA answers the phone but doesn't recognise my voice, it must be fully re-anglicised. She puts me through to Todd. It's still awkward between us but less so than it was. We've started the process of selling our apartment and discuss the sale. Then he abruptly changes the subject. 'I saw you on the news,' he says. 'Are you OK?'

'Yeah. Fine, thank you.'

'I've been meaning to apologise.'

'You have nothing to apologise for. Really, it's me that—'

213

'Of course I should apologise. You were right all along about your sister.' There's a silence between us, which I break. 'So are you moving in with Karen?'

There's a slight pause before he answers. 'Yes. I'll still pay my share of the mortgage of course, until it's sold.'

Karen is his new girlfriend. When he told me I felt guiltily relieved that he had found a relationship so quickly.

'I didn't think you'd mind,' says Todd and I think he wants me to mind. He sounds falsely cheerful. 'I expect it's a little like you and me, but the boot on the other foot.'

I have no idea what I can say to that.

'"If equal affections cannot be",' says Todd, his tone light, but I know not to misinterpret that now. I dread him adding 'let the more loving one be me'.

We say goodbye.

I reminded you I studied literature, didn't I? I've had an endless supply of quotations at my disposal, but they had always highlighted the inadequacy of my life rather than providing an uplifting literary score to it.

Mr Wright comes back with the cakes and cups of tea and we have five minutes time out from my statement and talk instead about small inconsequential things – the unseasonably warm weather, the bulbs in St James's Park, the emerging peony in your garden. Our tea together feels a little romantic, in a safe nineteenth-century kind of way, though I doubt Jane Austen's heroines took tea from Styrofoam cups and had cakes packed inside clear plastic boxes.

I hope he isn't slighted that I was too nauseous to finish my cake.

After our tea, we go back over a couple of pages in my statement, as he double-checks a few points, and then he suggests we end for the day. He has to stay and finish off

214

some paperwork but he still accompanies me to the lift. As we walk down the long corridor, past empty unlit offices, it feels as if he's escorting me to my front door. He waits for the lift doors to open and I am safely inside.

I leave the CPS offices and go to meet Kasia. I'm blowing two days' wages on tickets for the London Eye, which I had promised her. But I'm worn out, my limbs feel too heavy to belong to me, and I just want to go home and sleep. When I see the length of the queues I resent the Eye that's turned London into an urban Cyclops.

I spot Kasia waving at me from the front of a queue. She must have been waiting for hours. People are glancing at her, probably anxious that she's about to go into labour in one of the capsules.

I join her and ten minutes later we are 'boarding'.

As our capsule climbs higher, London unfurls beneath us and I no longer feel so ill or tired, but actually elated. And I think that, although I'm hardly robust, at least I didn't blackout today, which must be a good sign. So maybe I should allow myself to hope that I've survived this intact; that everything really might be OK.

I point out the sights to Kasia, asking people on the south side to move so I can show her Big Ben, Battersea Power Station, the House of Commons, Westminster Bridge. As I wave my arms around, showing off London to Kasia, I feel surprised – not just by the pride I feel for my city, but also by the word 'my'. I'd opted to live in New York, an Atlantic ocean away, but for no discernible reason I feel a sense of belonging here.

14

Monday

This morning I have woken up ludicrously early. Pudding is a furry, purring cushion on my legs (I never used to understand why you took in a stray). Mr Wright told me that that today we are going to 'cover' your funeral and at five thirty I give up on the idea of sleep and go out into your garden. I ought to go through it in my mind first, make sure I can remember what's important, but my thoughts flinch when I try to look backwards with any focus. Instead I look at the leaves and buds now flourishing along the lengths of the once-presumed-dead twigs. But there has been one fatality I'm afraid. The Constance Spry rose was killed by a fox urinating, so in her place I've planted a Cardinal Richelieu. No fox would dare to wee on him.

I feel a coat draped around my shoulders and then see Kasia sleepily stumbling back to bed. Your dressing gown doesn't meet over her bump any more. There's only three days to go now till her due date. She's asked me to be her birthing partner, her 'doula' (it sounds too posh for my rudimentary knowledge of what to do). You never told me about 'doulas' when you asked me to be with you when you had Xavier, you just asked me to be there. Perhaps you thought I'd find it all a little off-putting. (You'd have been right.) Or with you I didn't need a special name. I'm your sister. And Xavier's aunt. That's enough.

You might think Kasia is giving me a second chance after I failed you. But although that would be easy, it's not true. Nor is she a walking, talking Prozac course. But she has forced me to look into the future. Remember Todd telling me '*Life has to go on*'? But as my life couldn't rewind to a time you were still alive I'd wanted to pause it, moving forward was selfish. But Kasia's growing baby (a girl, she found out) is a visual reminder that life does go on – the opposite of a memento mori. I don't know if there's such a thing as a memento vitae.

Amias was right; the morning chorus is really noisy out here. The birds have been singing fit to burst for an hour already. I try to remember the order that he told me and think it must be the larks' turn now. As I listen to what I think is a woodlark playing notes similar to Bach's preludes, a little amazed and strangely comforted, I remember back to your funeral.

❀

The night before I stayed in Little Hadston in my old bedroom. I hadn't slept in a single bed for years and I found the narrowness of it and the tightly tucked in sheets and the heavy eiderdown securely comforting. I got up at 5.30 but when I went downstairs Mum was already in the kitchen. There were two mugs of coffee on the table. She gave me one. 'I would have brought your coffee up to your room for you, but I didn't want to wake you.' I knew before I took a sip that it would be cold. Outside it was dark with the sound of rain hammering down. Mum distractedly drew back the curtains as if you could see something outside but it was still dark and all she could see was her own reflection.

'When someone dies they can be any age you remember, can't they?' she asked. As I tried to think of a reply she continued, 'You probably think about the grown-up Tess, because you were still close to her. But when I woke up I thought of her when she was three wearing a fairy skirt I'd got her in Woolworth's and a policeman's helmet. Her wand was a wooden spoon. On the bus yesterday I imagined holding her when she was two days old. I felt the warmth of her. I remembered all her fingers clasped around my finger, so tiny they didn't even meet. I remembered the shape of her head, and stroking the nape of her neck till she slept. I remembered her smell. She smelled of innocence. Other times, she's thirteen and so pretty that I worry for her every time I see a man look at her. All of those Tesses is my daughter.'

At 10.55 a.m. we walked to the church, the wind blowing the driving cold rain against our faces and our legs, making Mum's black skirt stick coldly to her damp tights, my black boots were splattered in mud. But I was glad it was raining and windy, 'blow winds and crack your cheeks'; yes I know, this was hardly a blasted heath but Little Hadston on a Thursday morning with cars parked two deep along the road to the church.

There were over a hundred people standing outside the church in the slicing rain, some under umbrellas, some with just their hoods up. For a moment I thought that the church wasn't open yet, before realising that the church was too full for them to get inside. Among the crowd I glimpsed DS Finborough next to WPC Vernon, but most people were a blur through rain and emotion.

218

As I looked at the crowd outside the church and thought of the others packed inside I imagined each person carrying their own memories of you – your voice, your face, your laugh, what you did and what you said – and if all these fragments of you could be put together then somehow we could make a complete picture of you; together we could hold all of you.

Father Peter met us at the gate to the graveyard leading up to the church, holding an umbrella to shelter us. He told us that he'd put people into the choir stalls and got extra chairs but there wasn't even standing room left now. He escorted us through the graveyard towards the door of the church.

As I walked with Father Peter, I saw the back view of a man on his own in the graveyard. His head was bare and his clothes soaked through. He was hunched over by the gaping hole in the ground that was waiting for your coffin. I saw that it was Dad. After all those years of us waiting for him, when he never came, he was waiting for you.

The church bell began tolling. There is no more ghastly a sound. It has no beat of life, no human rhythm, only the mechanical striking of loss. We had to go into the church now. I found it as impossible and terrifying as stepping out of a window at the top of a skyscraper. I think Mum felt the same. That single footstep would inexorably end with your body in the sodden earth. I felt an arm around me and saw Dad. His other hand was holding on to Mum. He escorted us into the church. I felt Mum's judder through his body as she saw your coffin. Dad kept his arms around us as we walked up the seemingly endless aisle towards our places at the front. Then he sat between us holding our hands. I have never been so grateful for human touch before.

At one moment I turned, briefly, and looked at the packed

church and people spilling out beyond in the rain and wondered if the murderer was there, amongst us all.

Mum had asked for the full Monty funeral Mass and I was glad because it meant there was longer till we had to bury you. You've never liked sermons but I think you'd have been touched by Father Peter's. It had been Valentine's Day the day before and maybe for that reason he talked about unrequited love. I think I can remember his words, or just about:

'When I talk about unrequited love most of you probably think about romantic love, but there are many other kinds of love that are not adequately returned, if they are returned at all. An angry adolescent may not love her mother back as her mother loves her; an abusive father doesn't return the innocent open love of his young child. But grief is the ultimate unrequited love. However hard and however long we love someone who has died they can never love us back. At least that it is how it feels . . .'

After the Mass in the church we went outside to bury you.

The unrelenting rain had turned the snow-covered white earth of the churchyard to dirty mud.

Father Peter started the burial rite: 'We have entrusted our sister Tess and baby Xavier to God's mercy, and we now commit their bodies to the ground: earth to earth, ashes to ashes, dust to dust: in sure and certain hope of the resurrection to eternal life.'

I remembered back to Leo's burial and holding your hand. I was eleven and you were six, your hand soft and small in mine. As the vicar said 'in sure and certain hope of the resurrection to eternal life' you turned to me, *'I don't want sure and certain hope, I want sure and certain, Bee.'*

At your funeral I wanted sure and certain too. But even

the church can only hope, not promise, that the end of human life is happy ever after.

Your coffin was lowered into the deep gash that had been dug in the earth. I saw it brush past the exposed roots of grass, sliced through. Then further down. And I would have done anything to hold your hand again, anything at all, just once, just for a few seconds. Anything.

The rain hammered down onto your coffin, pitter-patter; *'Pitter-patter, pitter-patter, I hear raindrops'*; I was five and singing it to you, just born.

Your coffin reached the bottom of the monstrous hole. And a part of me went down into the muddy earth with you and lay down next to you and died with you.

Then Mum stepped forwards and took a wooden spoon from her coat pocket. She loosened her fingers and it fell on top of your coffin. Your magic wand.

And I threw the emails I had signed 'lol'. And the title of older sister. And the nickname Bee. Not grand or important to anyone else, I thought, this bond that we had. Small things. Tiny things. You knew that I didn't make words out of my alphabetti spaghetti but I gave you my vowels so you could make more words out of yours. I knew that your favourite colour used to be purple but then became bright yellow; (*'Ochre's the arty word, Bee'*) and you knew mine was orange, until I discovered that taupe was more sophisticated and you teased me for that. You knew that my first whimsy china animal was a cat (you lent me 50p of your pocket money to buy it) and that I once took all my clothes out of my school trunk and hurled them around the room and that was the only time I had something close to a tantrum. I knew that when you were five you climbed into bed with me every night for a year. I threw everything we had together – the strong roots and stems and leaves and beautiful soft blossoms of sisterhood – into the earth with you. And I was left standing on the edge, so diminished by the loss, that I thought I could no longer be there.

All I was allowed to keep for myself was missing you. Which is what? The tears that pricked the inside of my face, the emotion catching at the top of my throat, the cavity in my chest that was larger than I am. Was that all I had now? Nothing else from twenty-one years of loving you. Was the feeling that all is right with the world, my world, because you were its foundations, formed in childhood and with me grown into adulthood – was that to be replaced by nothing? The ghastliness of nothing. Because I was nobody's sister now.

I saw Dad had been given a handful of earth. But as he held out his hand above your coffin he couldn't unprise his fingers. Instead, he put his hand into his pocket, letting the earth fall there and not onto you. He watched as Father Peter threw the first clod of earth instead and broke apart, splintering with the pain of it. I went to him and took his earth-stained hand in mine, the earth gritty between our soft palms. He looked at me with love. A selfish person can still love someone else, can't they? Even when they've hurt them and let them down. I, of all people, should understand that.

Mum was silent as they put earth over your coffin.

An explosion in space makes no sound at all.

❧

Mum's silent screaming is in my head as I reach the CPS offices. It's Monday and crowded with people. When I get in the packed lift I start fretting, as I always do, that it will get stuck and my mobile doesn't get a signal, so Kasia will be unable to contact me if she goes into labour. As soon as I arrive at the third floor I check for messages: none. I also check my pager. Only Kasia has that number. Overkill, yes, but like a recent convert to Catholicism, my conversion to being thoughtful is going to be done *absolutely properly*, with rosary beads and incense sticks, a pager and a special ring tone on my phone reserved for her. I don't have the security of being born a considerate person. I've learned that at least. I can't treat it casually as part of my intrinsic make-up. And yes, maybe my anxiety about Kasia is a way of re-routing my thoughts for a while onto someone who is alive. I need the memento vitae.

I go into Mr Wright's office. He doesn't smile at me this morning, maybe because he knows that today we have to start with your funeral; or maybe the flicker of a romance I thought I felt at the weekend has been doused by what I am telling him. My witness statement, with its central topic of murder, is hardly a love sonnet. I bet Amias's birds don't sing to each other of such things.

He's closed the Venetian blinds against the bright spring sunshine and the sombre lighting seems appropriate for talking about your funeral. Today I will try not to mention my physical infirmities, as I said I have no right to complain, not when your body is broken, beyond repair, buried in the ground.

I tell Mr Wright about your funeral, sticking to facts not feelings.

'Although I wasn't aware of it at the time, her funeral gave me two important new leads,' I say, omitting the soul-suffocating torture of watching your coffin being covered with earth. 'The first was that I understood why Emilio Codi, if he had murdered Tess, would have waited until after Xavier was born.'

Mr Wright doesn't have a clue where I'm going with this, but I think you do.

'I'd always known Emilio had a motive,' I continue. 'His

affair with Tess jeopardised his marriage and his job. True, his wife hadn't left him when she found out, but he couldn't have known that. But if it was him, and he killed to protect his marriage and career, why not do it when Tess refused to have an abortion?'

Mr Wright nods, and I think he's intrigued.

'I'd also remembered that it was Emilio Codi who had phoned the police after the reconstruction and told them that Tess had already had her baby. It meant, I thought, that he must have either seen her or spoken to her afterwards. Emilio had already made a formal complaint about me to the police, so I had to be careful, make sure he couldn't tell them I was pestering him. I phoned him and asked if he still wanted his paintings of Tess. He was clearly angry with me, but wanted them all the same.'

⁂

Emilio seemed too large for your flat, his masculinity and rage swamping it. He had unwrapped each of the nude paintings – to check I hadn't damaged them? Applied fig leaves? Or simply to look at your body again? His voice was ugly with anger.

'There was no need for my wife to know about Tess, the cystic fibrosis, any of it. Now she's getting herself tested as a carrier of CF and so am I.'

'That's sensible of her. But you are clearly a carrier; otherwise Xavier couldn't have had it. Both parents need to be carriers for a baby to have it.'

'I know that. The genetic counsellors rammed it into us. But I may not be the father.'

I was stunned by him. He shrugged. 'She wasn't hung up about sex. She could easily have had other lovers.'

'She would have told you. And me. She wasn't a liar.'

He was silent because he knew it was true.

'It was you who phoned the police to say she'd had Xavier, wasn't it?' I asked.

'I thought it was the right thing to do.'

I wanted to challenge him. He had never done 'the right thing'. But that wasn't why I was questioning him. 'So she must have told you that Xavier had died?'

He was silent.

'Was it a phone call or face to face?'

He picked up his paintings of you and turned to leave. But I stood in front of the doorway.

'She wanted you to own up to Xavier, didn't she?'

'You need to get this straight. When she told me she was pregnant I made it *crystal clear* where I stood about the baby. I told her that I wouldn't help her or the baby in any way. I wasn't going to be a father to it. And she didn't make a fuss about that. She even said that the baby would be better off without me.'

'Yes. But what about when Xavier died?'

He put down the paintings. I thought for a moment he was going to push me out of the way so he could leave. But he made an absurdly theatrical gesture of surrender, ugly in its childishness.

'You're right. Hands up. She threatened to expose me.'

'You mean she wanted you to say that you were Xavier's father?'

'Same thing.'

'Her baby had died. She just wanted his father not to be ashamed of him.'

His hands were still held up, he tensed his fists, and for a moment I thought he was going to hit me. Then he let them drop to his side.

225

'It's that boy you should be questioning, always following her around with that bloody camera of his. He was obsessed with her. And jealous as hell.'

⁂

'I knew that Tess wouldn't have asked anything from Emilio if Xavier had lived,' I say. 'But when Xavier died it would have been intolerable to her for Emilio to deny him then.'

When I had watched Dad at your graveside he had redeemed himself. When it mattered – when your dead body was going into the muddy cold earth – he had stepped up as the man who is your father. You cannot disown a dead child.

Mr Wright waits a moment before asking his next question. 'Did you believe him about Simon?'

'I was suspicious of both him and Simon, but I had nothing tangible against either of them; nothing that would challenge the police's certainty that she committed suicide.'

I have told Mr Wright about my encounter with Emilio as if I were a detective, but the heart of it for me was as your sister. And I must tell him that too, in case it is relevant. It's embarrassingly exposing, but I can no longer be modest and shy. I must risk what he thinks of me. So I continue.

⁂

Emilio was standing at the open front door, anger sweating out of the pores in his face, holding the nude paintings of you.

'You just don't get it, do you? It was sex between me and Tess, great sex, but just sex. Tess knew that.'

'You don't think that someone as young as Tess may have been looking to you as a father figure?'

It's what I thought, however many times you denied it.

'No. I do not think that.'

'You don't think that as her own father had left and you were her tutor that she was looking to you for something more than "just sex"?'

'No. I don't.'

'I hope not. She'd have been so let down.'

I was glad I had finally said it to his face.

'Or maybe she got a kick out of breaking the rules,' he said. 'I was out of bounds and maybe she liked that.' His tone was almost flirtatious. 'Forbidden fruit is always more erotic, isn't it?'

I was silent and he moved a little closer. Too close.

'But you don't like sex, do you?'

I was silent and he watched me for a reaction, waiting. 'Tess said you only have sex to pay for the security of a relationship.'

I felt his eyes on mine, spying into me.

'She said you chose a job that was dull but secure and the same went for your fiancé.' He was trying to rip away the insulating layers of our sisterhood and still he continued, 'She said you'd rather be safe than happy.' He saw that he'd hit his mark and continued to hit it. 'That you were afraid of life'.

You were right. As you know. Other people may sail through lives of blue seas, with only the occasional squall, but for me life has always been a mountain – sheer-faced and perilous. And, as I think I told you, I had clung on with the footholds and crampons and safety ropes of a safe job and flat and secure relationship.

Emilio was still staring at my face, expecting me to feel betrayed by you and hurt. But instead I was deeply moved.

227

And I felt closer to you. Because you knew me so much better than I'd realised – and still loved me. You were kind enough not to tell me that you knew about my fearfulness, allowing me to keep my Big Sister self-respect. I wish now that I'd told you. And that I knew if I dared look away from my treacherous mountainside, I'd have seen you flying in the sky untrammelled by insecurities and anxieties, no safety ropes tethering you.

And no ropes keeping you safe.

I hope you think I have found a little courage.

15

Mr Wright has listened to my encounter with Emilio and I am trying to detect if he thinks less of me. Mrs Crush Secretary bustles in with coffee for Mr Wright in a china cup, Maryland cookies balanced on the saucer, the chocolate melting onto the white china. I have a polystyrene cup with no biscuits. Mr Wright is a little embarrassed by the favouritism. He waits for her to leave and puts one of his cookies next to my cup.

'You said the funeral gave you two new leads?'

Lead? Did I really use the word? Sometimes I hear my new vocabulary and for a moment the absurdity of all this threatens to turn my life into farce.

'It's Colonel Mustard in the kitchen with the candlestick.'

'Bee, you're so silly. It's Professor <u>Plum</u> in the <u>library</u> with the <u>rope</u>!'

Mr Wright is waiting.

'Yes. The other was Professor Rosen.'

ॐ

Although most people at your funeral were blurred by grief and rain, I noticed Professor Rosen, maybe because he was a known face from television. He was amongst the crowd who couldn't fit inside the church, holding an umbrella with vents, a scientist's umbrella, letting the wind through while other mourners had their umbrellas turned inside out. Afterwards he came up to me and awkwardly stretched out his hand, then let it fall to his side, as if too shy to continue with the gesture. 'Alfred Rosen. I wanted to apologise to you, for the email that the PR woman sent you. It was callous.' His glasses were misted up and he used a handkerchief to wipe them clean. 'I have emailed you my personal contact details, should you want to ask me anything further. I'd be happy to answer any questions that you have.' His language was starched and his posture tense, I noticed that much, but nothing else because my thoughts were with you.

᛭

'I phoned Professor Rosen on the number he'd given me, about a week after the funeral.'

I gloss over that week of emotional turmoil after your funeral, when I didn't think straight, couldn't eat and barely spoke. I continue briskly, trying to blot out the memory of that time.

'He said he was going away on a lecture tour, and suggested we meet before he left.'

'Were you suspicious of him?' asks Mr Wright.

'No. I had no reason to think either he or the trial were connected to Tess's death. By then I thought the payments to the women were probably innocent, as the people at the hospital had said, but I hadn't directly asked him, so I wanted to do that.'

230

I thought I had to question everything, be suspicious of everyone. I couldn't afford to go down just one avenue, but had to explore all of them until at the end of one, at the centre of the maze, I would find your killer.

'Our meeting was at ten o'clock, but Chrom-Med run information seminars starting at nine thirty, so I booked a place.'

Mr Wright looks surprised.

'It's a bit like the nuclear industry used to be,' I say. 'Wanting everything to look open and innocent. "*Visit Sellafield and bring a picnic!*" You know the kind of thing.'

Mr Wright smiles, but the strangest thing has happened. For a moment as I was speaking I heard myself talking like you.

༘

It was the morning rush hour and the tube was packed. As I stood squashed up against other commuters I remembered, appalled, the note I'd put up on the college notice board asking your friends to meet me. In the turmoil after your funeral I'd somehow forgotten. It was at twelve that day. I felt far more apprehensive about that than my meeting with Professor Rosen.

At just before 9.30 a.m. I arrived at the Chrom-Med building – ten storeys high in glass with transparent lifts going up the outside like bubbles in sparkling mineral water. Light tubes encircled the building with purple and blue bolts of light shooting around its circumference; 'science fiction becomes science fact' seemed to be the message.

The sparkling fantasy image was tarnished by a knot of around ten demonstrators holding placards, one saying 'NO TO DESIGNER BABIES!' Another 'LEAVE PLAYING GOD TO GOD!' There were no shouts to go with the placards, the demonstrators yawning and lacklustre, as if it was too early to be up and about. I wondered if they were there to get on the telly, although media coverage had tailed off in the last few weeks with the TV using library footage now. Maybe they'd turned out because it was the first day in weeks that wasn't snowing or sleeting or raining.

As I got nearer I heard one demonstrator, a multi-pierced woman with angrily spiky hair, talking to a journalist.

'. . . and only the rich will be able to afford the genes to make their children cleverer and more beautiful and more athletic. Only the rich will be able to afford the genes that will stop their children getting cancer or heart disease.'

The journalist was just holding the Dictaphone looking a little bored, but the spiky-haired protester was undaunted and furiously continued. 'They will eventually create a genetic super-class. And there won't be any chance of intermarrying. Who's going to marry someone uglier than they are, and weaker, more stupid and prone to illness? After a few generations they will have created two species of people. A gene-rich and a gene-poor.'

I went up to the spiky-haired demonstrator. 'Have you ever met someone with cystic fibrosis? Or muscular dystrophy? Or Huntington's disease?' I asked.

She glared at me, annoyed I'd interrupted her flow.

'You don't know what it's like living with cystic fibrosis, knowing that it's killing you, drowning in your own phlegm. You don't know anything about it all, do you?'

She moved away from me.

'You're lucky,' I called after her. 'Nature made you gene-rich.'

And then I walked into the building.

I gave my name into a security grill on the door and was buzzed in. I signed my name at reception and presented my passport as I'd been instructed. A camera behind the desk automatically took my photo to make an identity card and then I was allowed through. I'm not sure what they were scanning for, but the machines were far more sophisticated than anything I'd been through at airport security checks. Fifteen of us were then shown into a seminar room, dominated by a large screen, and were welcomed by a young woman called Nancy, our perky 'facilitator'.

After an elementary lesson in genetics, Perky Nancy showed us a short film of mice that had been injected as embryos with a jellyfish gene. In the film, the lights went off – and hey presto! – the mice glowed green. There were many oohs and aahs, and I noticed that only one other person, a middle-aged man with a grey ponytail, like me, wasn't entertained.

Perky Nancy played us the next film, which showed mice in a maze. 'And here's Einstein and his friends,' she enthused. 'These little fellows have an extra copy of a gene that codes for memory, making them much cleverer.'

In the film 'Einstein and his friends' were finding their way around a maze at dazzling speed compared with the meanderings of their dimmer, non-genetically engineered friends.

The man with the grey ponytail spoke up, his voice aggressive. 'Does this "IQ" gene get into the germ line?' he asked.

Nancy smiled at the rest of us. 'That means, is the gene passed on to their babies?' She turned, still smiling, to Ponytail Man. 'Yes. The original mice were given the genetic enhancement nearly ten years ago now. They were these little fellows' great, great, great – well I'm running out of greats – grandparents. Seriously, though, this IQ gene has been passed on through many generations.'

Ponytail Man's posture as well as his tone was belligerent. 'When will you be testing it on humans? You'll make a killing then, won't you?'

233

Perky Nancy's expression didn't flicker. 'The law doesn't allow genetic enhancement on people. Only the treating of disease.'

'But as soon as it's legal, you'll be ready and waiting, right?'

'Scientific endeavour can be purely to forward our knowledge, nothing more sinister or commercial than that,' responded Perky Nancy. Maybe she had flashcards for this kind of question.

'You're floating on the stock market, right?' he asked.

'It's not my job to talk about the financial aspect of the company.'

'But you have shares? Every employee has shares, right?'

'As I said—'

He interrupted. 'So you'd cover up anything that went wrong. Wouldn't want it to be public?'

Perky Nancy's tone was sweet but I sensed steel under her linen suit. 'I can assure you that we are totally open here. And nothing whatsoever has gone "wrong" as you put it.'

She pressed a button and played us the next film footage, which showed mice in a cage with a researcher helpfully putting a ruler in. It was then that you realised their size – not so much by measuring them against the ruler but against the size of the researcher's hand. They were enormous.

'We gave these mice a gene to boost muscle growth,' enthused Perky Nancy. 'But the gene for that had a surprising effect elsewhere. It made the mice not only much bigger but also meek. We thought we'd get Arnold Schwarzenegger and we ended up with a very muscular Bambi.'

Laughter from the group and again only me and Ponytail Man didn't join in. As if controlling her own mirth, Perky Nancy continued, 'There is a serious point to this experiment, though. It shows us that the same gene can code for two totally different and unrelated things.'

234

It's what I'd been worried about with you. I hadn't been such a fusspot after all.

As Perky Nancy led our group out of the seminar room, I saw a security guard talking to grey Ponytail Man. They were arguing but I couldn't hear what the argument was about; then Ponytail Man was led firmly away.

We walked in the other direction and were escorted into a large room which had been totally devoted to the CF trial. There were photographs of cured babies and newspaper headlines from all over the world. Perky Nancy galloped us through the beginners' guide to cystic fibrosis as a huge screen behind her showed a child with CF. I noticed the others in our little party gazing at it, but I looked at Perky Nancy, her cheeks pink, her voice trilling with enthusiasm.

'The story of the cure for cystic fibrosis started in 1989 when an international team of scientists found the defective gene that causes cystic fibrosis. That sounds easy, but remember that in every cell of every human body are forty-six chromosomes and on each chromosome are thirty thousand genes. Finding that one gene was a fantastic achievement. And the search for a cure was on!'

She made it sound like the opening to a *Star Wars* movie, and continued with gusto, 'Scientists discovered that the defective CF gene was making too much salt and too little water in the cells that line the lungs and the gut, causing sticky mucus to form.'

She turned to the screen, where the child was struggling to breathe, and her voice quavered a little. Maybe it did that every time she showed the film.

'The problem was how to get a healthy gene into a sufferer's body,' she continued. 'The existing method of using a virus was far from ideal. There were risks associated with it and often

235

it wore off too quickly. Then Professor Rosen, backed by Chrom-Med, created an artificial chromosome. It was a new and totally safe way of getting the healthy gene into the body.'

An anxious-faced young man in an Oxford university sweatshirt spoke up. 'You're saying you put an *extra chromosome* into every cell of the body?'

'Yes,' said Perky Nancy, starry-eyed. 'In treated patients each cell will have forty-seven, not forty-six, chromosomes. But it's only a micro-chromosome and—'

He interrupted her and the group tensed. Was he replacing grey Ponytail Man as the rude member of the group? 'Does this extra chromosome get into the germ line?' he asked.

'Yes, it'll be passed down to future generations.'

'Don't you find that worrying?'

'Not really, no,' said Perky Nancy, smiling. Her anodyne response seemed to mop up any hostility he might have had. Or maybe I just couldn't see it any more because Nancy had dimmed the lights.

On the huge screen a film began, showing the double helix of DNA blown up millions of times. I saw with thirteen other people the two faulty CF genes highlighted. And then, incredibly, I watched the faulty genes being replaced by healthy ones.

The wonder of scientific discovery, real frontiers being pushed back, is an astonishing thing to behold. Like looking through Hershel's telescope as he discovered a new planet or Columbus's as he saw the New World. You think I'm exaggerating? *I saw the cure for cystic fibrosis*, Tess, right there in front of me. I saw how Leo's death sentence could have been rewritten. He'd be alive now; that's what I kept thinking as she told us about telomeres and DNA chips and factory cells; he'd be alive now.

As the film moved on to footage of newborn babies, born free of cystic fibrosis, being kissed by grateful mothers and self-consciously emotional fathers, I thought about a boy who grew up; who no longer had Action Man cards for his birthday; who would be taller than me now.

The film ended and I realised that for a short while I'd forgotten my preoccupation for the last month, or at least temporarily parked it. Then I remembered, of course I remembered, and I was glad that there was no reason for this cure to be implicated with your death or Xavier's. I wanted the genetic cure for cystic fibrosis to be our New World with no cost or sacrifices or wickedness involved.

I thought the film had ended, but then on the screen Professor Rosen was shown giving a speech. I'd already heard it on the net and read it printed in the papers but now it resonated in a different way.

'Most people don't think scientists do their job with passion. If we played instruments or painted pictures or wrote poetry people would expect it, but scientists – we're cold, analytical, detached. To most people the word "clinical" means cold and unemotional, but its real meaning is to be involved in medical treatment – *to be doing something for good*. And we should do that, as artists and musicians and poets do, with energy, commitment and passion.'

Ten minutes later his secretary escorted me from reception, via a bubble lift, to the top floor, where Professor Rosen greeted me. He looked just as he had on the TV and at your funeral, the same caricature wire-rimmed glasses and narrow shoulders and gaucheness: a reassuring boffin. I thanked him for coming to your funeral and he nodded, a little curtly I thought. We walked down the corridor together and I broke the silence.

'My brother had cystic fibrosis. I wish you'd been around a few years earlier.'

He half-turned away from me and I remembered from the TV interviews how uncomfortable he had been when praised. He changed the subject and I liked him for his modesty.

'So did you find the seminar informative?' he asked.

'Yes. And extraordinary.' I was about to continue but he interrupted me without even being aware that he was doing it.

'I find the mice with high IQ the most disquieting. I was asked to participate in the original trial. A young research fellow at Imperial was looking for the difference between the super bright and the norm or some such nonsense. It was years ago now.'

'But the mice are on Chrom-Med's film?'

'Yes, the company bought the research, the gene for that matter, for all the good it's done them. Fortunately, genetic engineering, in humans anyhow, isn't allowed. Otherwise we'd no doubt have glow-in-the-dark people by now or giants who sing lullabies.'

I thought that the line was borrowed or at least rehearsed. He didn't seem a man who could attempt any type of witticism.

'But the cystic fibrosis cure is totally different,' I said.

He stopped walking and turned to me. 'Yes. There is no comparison between the genetic cure for cystic fibrosis, which treats a terrible disease, and tinkering with genes for the sake of some kind of genetic enhancement. Or freak show. No comparison whatsoever.'

The vigour of his words was startling and for the first time I realised that he had physicality.

We reached his office and went in.

It was a vast room, glass on three sides, with a panorama

across London, in keeping with the rest of the boastful building. His desk, however, was small and shabby and I imagined it being moved with him from student rooms to a variety of bigger offices until it ended up incongruously here. Professor Rosen closed the door behind us. 'You had some questions you wanted to ask?'

For a moment I'd forgotten any suspicions and when I remembered it seemed ridiculous to quiz him over the payments (as I said before, a paltry £300 when the investment in the trial must have been colossal) – and in the light of what I'd seen it also seemed churlish. But I was no longer constrained by what was appropriate or polite.

'Do you know why women on the trial were paid?' I asked.

He barely reacted. 'The PR woman's email was callously worded, but it is correct. I don't know who did pay your sister, or anyone else, but I can assure you it wasn't us or anyone else administering the trial. I have the names and reports of the participating hospitals' ethics committees for you. So you can see for yourself that no payments are offered or made. It would be totally improper.' He handed me a bundle of documents and continued, 'The reality is that if there was any money changing hands, it would be the mothers paying us rather than the other way around. We have parents begging for this treatment.'

There was an awkward silence. My question was answered and we'd barely been in his office three minutes.

'Do you still work for Imperial?' I asked, giving myself a little time to think of more important questions. But I struck a nerve, his body as well as his voice was on the defensive.

'No. I am a full-time employee here. They have better facilities here. They let me out to give lectures.' I heard the bitterness in his voice and wonder what caused it.

'You must be in demand?' I asked, still being polite.

'Yes, very much so. The interest has been quite over-whelming. All the most prestigious universities in Europe have asked me to speak and in America all eight of the Ivy League universities have invited me to give a keynote address and four of them have offered me honorary professorships. I start my lecture tour in the States tomorrow. It will be a relief to speak for hours at a time to people who understand at least a little of what I am saying rather than in sound bites.'

His words were a genie escaping, revealing I'd got him completely wrong. He *did* want the limelight, but he wanted it shining on him at lecterns in prestigious universities rather than on television. He did want accolades, but from his peers.

I was sitting a distance away from him but even so he leaned away from me as he spoke as if the room was cramped. 'In the email you sent back you seemed to imply that there may be a link between your sister's death and my trial.'

I noticed that he said '*my* trial' and remembered that on the TV he'd called it '*my* chromosome'. I hadn't grasped before how much he personally identified with the cystic fibrosis trial.

He turned, not looking at me, but at his own half-reflection in the glass wall of his office.

'It's been my life's work, finding a cure for cystic fibrosis. I've literally spent my life, spending everything I have that is precious – time, commitment, energy even love – on that one thing. I have not done that for anyone to get hurt.'

'What did make you do it?' I asked.

'I want to know that when I die I have made the world a better place.' He turned to face me and continued. 'I believe that my achievement will be seen as a watershed by future generations, leading the way to the time when we can produce a disease-free population – no cystic fibrosis, no Alzheimer's,

240

no motor-neurone disease, no cancer.' I was taken aback by the fervour in his voice, and he continued, 'We will not only wipe them out but ensure that these changes can carry on through the generations. Millions of years of evolution haven't even cured the common cold let alone the big diseases, but we can and in just a few generations we probably will.'

Why, when he was talking about curing disease, did I find him so disturbing? Maybe because any zealot, whatever his cause, makes us recoil. I remembered his speech when he likened a scientist to a painter or a musician or a writer. I found that correlation disquieting now – because instead of notes or words or paints, a genetic scientist has human genes at his disposal. He must have sensed my uneasiness, but misinterpreted the reason for it.

'You think I'm exaggerating, Miss Hemming? My chromosome is in our gene pool. I have achieved in under a lifetime a million years of human development.'

I handed in my temporary ID and left the building. The demonstrators were still there; more vocal now that they'd had some coffee out of their Thermoses. Ponytail Man was with them. I wondered how often he went on the seminar and provoked Perky Nancy. Presumably for PR and legal reasons they couldn't ban him.

He saw me and came after me.

'Do you know how they measure IQ in those mice?' he asked. 'It's not just the maze.'

I shook my head and started to walk away from him but he followed.

'They are put into a chamber and given electric shocks. When they're put in again the ones with genetically enhanced IQ know to be afraid. They measure IQ by fear.'

241

I walked faster but still he pursued me.

'Or the mice are dropped into a tank of water with a hidden platform. The high IQ mice learn to find the platform.'

I walked hurriedly towards the tube station, trying to find again my elation at the cystic fibrosis trial, but I was unsettled by Professor Rosen and by the mice. '*They measure IQ by fear*' becoming indelible in my head even as I tried to erase it.

༆

'I wanted to believe that the CF trial was totally legitimate. I didn't want it to be associated in any way with Tess's murder or Xavier's death. But I was disturbed by my visit.'

'Because of Professor Rosen?' asks Mr Wright.

'Partly, yes. I had thought he didn't like fame because he was so uncomfortable on TV. But he was boastful about the lecture tours he'd been asked to give, he made a point of saying they were at the "*most prestigious*" universities in the world. I knew that I'd completely misjudged him.'

'Were you suspicious of him?'

'I was wary. Before, I'd assumed he'd come to Tess's funeral, and offered to answer my questions, out of compassion, but I was no longer sure of his reason. And I thought that for most of his life he'd have been seen as the science geek, certainly through school and probably through university. But now he'd become the man of the moment – and, through his chromosome, the future too. I thought that if anything was wrong with his trial he wouldn't want to jeopardise his new-found status.'

༆

But it was the power of any genetic scientist, not just Professor Rosen, that disturbed me most. As I walked away from the Chrom-Med building I thought of the Fates – one spinning the thread of human life, one measuring it, one cutting it. I thought of the threads of our DNA, coiling on their double helix, two strands in every cell of our body with our fate coded in them. And I thought that science had never been so intimately connected to what makes us human – what makes us mortal.

16

Preoccupied after my visit to Chrom-Med, I walked much of the way to the café opposite the art college. So many of your friends had come to your funeral, but I was unsure if any of them would turn out for me.

When I went inside the café it was packed full of students, all of them waiting for me. I was completely at a loss, tongue-tied. I've never liked hosting anything, even a lunch party, let alone a group meeting with strangers. And I felt so staid compared to them with their arty clothes and attitude hair and piercings. One of them with Rasta hair and almond eyes introduced himself as Benjamin. He put his arm around me and led me to a table.

Thinking I wanted to hear more about your life, they told me stories illustrating your talent, your kindness, your humour. And as they told their lovely stories about you I looked at their faces and wondered if one of them could have killed you. Was Annette with her copper bright hair and slender arms strong enough and vicious enough to kill? When Benjamin's beautiful almond eyes shed tears were they real, or was he just aware of the attractive picture he made?

⚜

'Tess's friends all described her in different ways,' I tell Mr Wright. 'But there was one phrase that everyone used. Every single person spoke of her "joie de vivre".'

Joy and life together. It's such an ironically perfect description of you.

'She had a great many friends?' asks Mr Wright and I am touched by the question because he doesn't need to ask it.

'Yes. She valued friendships very highly.'

It's true, isn't it? You've always made friends easily, but you don't discard them easily. At your twenty-first birthday party you had friends from primary school. You move people from your past along with you into your present. Can you be green about friendships? They are too valuable to be junked when they stop being immediately convenient.

'Did you ask them about the drugs?' asks Mr Wright, bringing my thoughts back into focus.

'Yes. Like Simon, they were adamant that she never touched them. I asked them about Emilio Codi, but didn't find out anything useful. Just that he was an "arrogant shit", and too preoccupied with his own art to be a decent tutor. They all knew about the affair and the pregnancy. Then I asked them about Simon and his relationship with Tess.'

⚜

The feeling in the café changed, the atmosphere heavier, loaded with something I didn't understand.

'You all knew Simon wanted a relationship with her?' I asked.

People nodded, but no information was volunteered.

245

'Emilio Codi said he was jealous?' I asked, trying to provoke a conversation.

A girl with jet-black hair and ruby-red lips, like a story-book witch, spoke up. 'Simon was jealous of anyone Tess loved.'

I wondered briefly if that included me.

'But she didn't love Emilio Codi?' I said.

'No. With Emilio Codi it was a more like a competitive thing for Simon,' replied the pretty witch. 'It was Tess's baby he was jealous of. He couldn't bear it that she was going to love someone who hadn't even been born yet, when she didn't love him.'

I remembered his montage picture of a prison, made of babies' faces.

'Was he at their funeral?' I asked.

I saw hesitation on the Pretty Witch's face before she spoke. 'We waited for him at the station, but he never showed. I phoned him, asked him what the fuck he was playing at. He said he'd changed his mind and wasn't coming. Because he wouldn't have a "special place" and his feelings for Tess would be – let me get this right – "ignored" and he "couldn't tolerate that".'

Was that why I'd sensed the heavier atmosphere when I'd asked about Simon?

'Emilio Codi said he was obsessed by her . . . ?' I said.

'Yeah, he was,' said the Pretty Witch. 'When he had that project going, the *Female of the Species* or some such crap, he used to follow her around like her fucking shadow.'

I saw Benjamin give the Pretty Witch a warning look but she took no notice. 'For fuck's sake, he was practically stalking her.'

'With his camera as an excuse?' I asked, remembering the photos of you on his bedroom wall.

'Yeah,' said the Pretty Witch. 'He wasn't man enough to

246

look at her directly, had to do it through a lens. Some of them were really long, like he was a fucking paparazzi.'

'Do you know why she tolerated him?' I asked.

A shy-faced boy who'd been quiet up to now, spoke up. 'She was kind and I think she felt sorry for him. He didn't have other friends.'

I turned to the Pretty Witch. 'Did the project stop, you seemed to imply . . . ?'

'Yeah, Mrs Barden, his tutor, told him he had to stop. She knew it was just an excuse to follow Tess around. Told him he'd be expelled if he carried on.'

'When was this?' I asked.

'The beginning of the course year,' said Annette. 'So it must have been last September, the first week. Tess was relieved about it.'

But his photographs documented you through all of autumn and winter.

'He was still doing it,' I said. 'Did none of you know that?'

'He must have got more subtle about it,' said Benjamin.

'That wouldn't have been hard,' said the Pretty Witch. 'But we didn't see so much of Tess after she went on that "sabbatical".'

I remembered Emilio saying '*It's that boy you should be questioning, always following her around with that bloody camera of his.*'

'Emilio Codi knew it hadn't stopped,' I said. 'And he's a tutor at the college. So why didn't he get Simon expelled?'

'Because Simon knew about Emilio Codi's affair with Tess,' replied the Pretty Witch. 'They probably each kept the other one quiet.'

I couldn't put off my question any longer.

'Do you think either of them could have killed her?'

The group was silent, but I sensed embarrassment and

247

awkwardness more than shock. Even the Pretty Witch didn't meet my eye.

Finally Benjamin spoke up, to be kind to me I think. 'Simon told us that she had post-natal psychosis. And because of the post-natal psychosis she committed suicide. He said that's what the Coroner's verdict was and that the police are sure about it.'

'We didn't know if he was telling the truth,' said the shy-faced boy. 'But it was in the local paper too.'

'Simon said you weren't here at the time,' ventured Annette. 'But he said that he saw her and she was . . .' She trailed off, but I could imagine what Simon had told them about your mental state.

So the press and Simon had convinced them of your suicide. The girl they knew and had described to me would never have killed herself, but you'd been the victim of possession by the modern-day devil of puerperal psychosis – a devil that made a girl with joie de vivre hate life enough to end it. You had been killed by something that has a scientific name rather than a human face.

'Yes. The police do believe she committed suicide,' I said. 'Because they think she was suffering from puerperal psychosis. But I am certain that they are wrong.'

I saw compassion on some faces as they looked at me, and its poorer cousin pity on others. And then it was 'already past one thirty' and 'classes start in ten minutes' and they were leaving.

I thought that Simon must have manipulated them against me before they'd even met me. He'd no doubt told them about the unstable older sister with her loopy theories, which explained why they had been more embarrassed than shocked when I'd asked them about murder, and their awkwardness towards me. But I didn't blame them for wanting to believe

Simon rather than me; for wanting to choose a non-murderous death for you.

Benjamin and the Pretty Witch were the last to go. They asked me to come to the art show in a week's time, were touchingly insistent, and I said I would. It would give me another opportunity to question Simon and Emilio.

Alone in the café, I thought that Simon had not only lied to me about his 'project', he had even embellished it, *'They're for my final year portfolio . . . My tutor thinks it's the most original and exciting project of the year group.'* I wondered what else was lies. Had you really spoken to him on the phone the day you died and arranged to meet? Or had he followed you that day, as he so often followed you, and everything else was a construct so I wouldn't suspect him? He was clearly highly manipulative. Had there really been a man in the bushes that day, or had Simon invented him – or more cleverly your paranoia, which had conjured him up – to take the focus off himself? How many times did he sit on your doorstep with a huge bouquet hoping he'd be found and appear innocently waiting for you, even though you were dead?

Thinking about Simon and Emilio I wondered, as I still do now, if all very beautiful young women have men in their lives that appear sinister. If I had been found dead there would be no one suspicious in my life, so the focus would have had to go outside my circle of friends and former fiancé. I don't believe outstandingly beautiful and charismatic women create obsession in what would otherwise be normal men, but rather they attract the weirdos and the stalkers; a flame in the darkness that these disturbing people inhabit, unwittingly drawing them closer until they extinguish the very flame they were drawn to.

❧

'And then you went back to the flat?' asks Mr Wright.

'Yes.'

But I feel too tired to tell him about returning to the flat that day; to have to remember what I heard there. My words are slower, my body slumping.

Mr Wright looks at me, with concern. 'Let's end it there.'

He offers to get me a taxi but I say that a walk will do me good.

He accompanies me to the lift and I realise how much I appreciate his old-fashioned courteousness. I think Amias would have been a little like Mr Wright as a young man. He smiles goodbye and I think that maybe the little sparkles of romance haven't been doused after all. Romantic thoughts pep me up a little, more sweetly than caffeine, and I don't think there's any harm in entertaining them. So I shall think about Mr Wright, allow myself that small luxury, and walk across St James's Park rather than be squashed in a crowded tube.

The fresh spring air does make me feel better and inconsequential thoughts make me a little braver. When I reach the end of St James's Park I wonder if I should continue my walk across Hyde Park. Surely it's about time that I found the courage to confront my demons and finally lay to rest my ghosts.

Heart pumping faster, I go in through the Queen Elizabeth gates. But like its neighbour, Hyde Park too is a riot of colour and noise and smells. I can't find any demons at all in all this greenery; no whispering ghost amidst the ball games.

I walk through the rose garden and then past the bandstand, which looks like a pop-up from a children's storybook, with its pastel pink surround and sugar-white top held up by liquorish sticks. Then I remember the bomb exploding into a crowd, the nails packed around it, the carnage and I feel someone watching me.

I feel his breath behind me, cold in the warm air. I walk quickly, not turning round. He tracks me, his breath coming faster, lifting the hairs on the nape of my neck. My muscles tense to a spasm. In the distance I can see the lido with people. I run towards it, adrenaline and fear making my legs shake.

I reach the lido and sit down, legs still jittery and my chest hurting every time I take a breath. I watch children splashing in the paddling pool and two middle-aged executives paddling with their suit trousers rolled up. Only now do I dare turn around. I think I see a shadow, amongst the trees. I wait until the shadow is no more than the dappled shade of branches.

I skirt round the copse of trees, making sure I keep close to people and noise. I reach the other side and see a stretch of bright-green new grass with polka-dot crocuses. A girl walks barefoot across it, her shoes in her hand, enjoying sun-warmed grass, and I think of you. I watch her till she's at the end of the polka-dotted grass and only then see the toilets building, a hard dark wound amidst the soft bright colours of spring.

I hurry after the girl and reach the toilets building. She's the far side now, with a boy's arm around her. Laughing together, they're leaving the park. I leave too, my legs still a little wobbly, my breathing still laboured. I try to make myself feel ridiculous. There is nothing to be scared of, Beatrice; it's what comes of having an overly active imagination; your mind can play all sorts of tricks – reassurances pilfered from a childhood world of certainty. There's no monster in the wardrobe. But you and I know he's real.

17

At the CPS I squeeze into a lift, which smells of burned rubber sweat; bodies unwillingly pressed against each other. Surrounded by people, in the bright light of morning, I know that I will not say anything about the man in the park. Because Mr Wright would just tell me, correctly, that he's in prison, refused bail, and that after the trial he'll be sentenced to life imprisonment, without parole. Rationally, I should know that he can never hurt me again. As the lift reaches the third floor I tell myself sternly that he is not here and never will be, that he is an absence, not a presence, and I must not allow him to become one, even in my imaginings.

So this morning is one of new resolutions. I will not be intimidated by a spectre of imagined evil. I will not allow him any power over my mind as he once had over my body. Instead I will be reassured by Mr Wright and Mrs Crush Secretary and all the other people who surround me in this building. I know that my blackouts are still happening and

252

more frequently, and that my body is getting weaker, but I will not give way to irrational terror nor to my physical frailty. Instead of imagining the frightening and the ugly, I will try to find the beautiful in the everyday things, as you did. But most of all, I will think about what you went through – and know, again, that in comparison I have no right to indulge myself in a phantom menace and self-pity.

I decide that today it will be me who is the coffee maker. It is nonsense to think that my arms are trembling. Look. I've managed to make two cups of coffee – and carry them into Mr Wright's office – no problem.

Mr Wright, a little surprised, thanks me for the coffee. He puts a new cassette into the recorder and we resume.

'We'd got to you talking to Tess's friends about Simon Greenly and Emilio Codi?' he asks.

'Yes. Then I went back to our flat. Tess had an ancient answerphone that she'd got in a car-boot sale I think. But she thought it was fine.'

I'm skirting round the issue, but must get to the point.

'When I came in I saw a light flashing, indicating the tape was full.'

Still in my coat, I played the message, which was just something from a gas company, unimportant. I'd already listened to all the other messages, other people's one-way conversations with you.

I took off my coat and was about to rewind the tape, when I saw it had an A side and a B side. I'd never listened to the B side so I turned it over. Each message was preceded by a time and date in an electronic voice.

The last message on the B side was on Tuesday, 21 January at 8.20 p.m. Just a few hours after you'd had Xavier.

The sound of a lullaby filled the room. Sweetly vicious.

༜

I try to sound brisk, and a little too loud, wanting my words to drown out the vocal memory in my head.

'It was a professional recording, and I thought whoever had played it must have put the telephone receiver against a CD player.'

Mr Wright nods; he has already heard the recording, though, unlike me, he probably doesn't know it by heart.

'I knew from Amias that she felt threatened by the calls,' I continue. 'That she was afraid of whoever was doing this, so I knew he must have done it many times, but only one was recorded.'

No wonder your phone was unplugged when I arrived at your flat. You couldn't bear to listen to any more.

'You phoned the police straight away?' asks Mr Wright.

'Yes. I left a message on DS Finborough's voicemail. I told him about Simon's fake project and that I'd also discovered a reason why Emilio would have waited till after the baby was born to kill Tess. I said I thought there might be something wrong with the CF trial because the women were paid and Tess's medical notes had gone missing, although I thought it unlikely there was a link. I said I thought the lullabies were the key to it. That if they could find out who had played her the lullabies they'd find her killer. It wasn't the most moderate or calm of messages. But I'd just listened to the lullaby. I didn't feel moderate or calm.'

༜

After I'd left my message for DS Finborough I went to St Anne's. My anger and upset were visceral, needing physical release. I went to the psychiatric department where Dr Nichols was having an outpatient clinic. I found his name written on a card pinned to a door and pushed past a patient who was about to go in. Behind me, I heard the receptionist remonstrating but took no notice.

Dr Nichols looked at me, startled.

'There was a lullaby on her answerphone,' I said. Then I started singing the lullaby, 'Sleep, baby, sleep/Your father tends the sheep/Your mother shakes the dreamland tree/And from it fall sweet dreams for thee/Sleep, baby, sleep.'

'Beatrice, please—'

I interrupted. 'She heard it the evening she got back from the hospital. Only a few hours after her baby had died. God knows how many more times he played her lullabies. The phone calls weren't "auditory hallucinations". Someone was mentally torturing her.'

Dr Nichols, looking at me shocked, was silent.

'She wasn't mad but someone was trying to drive her mad or make everyone think she was mad.'

His voice sounded shaken. 'Poor girl, the lullabies must have been appalling for her. But are you sure they were intentionally cruel? Do you think they may have just been a terrible blunder by one of her friends who didn't know her baby had died?'

I thought how convenient that would be for him.

'No, I don't think that.'

He turned away from me. He was wearing a white coat this time, but it was crumpled and a little stained, and he seemed even more scruffily hopeless.

'Why didn't you just listen to her? Ask her more?'

'The only occasion I met her my clinic was overbooked

as usual, with emergencies just added with no more time allocated, and I had to get through them, keep down waiting times.' I looked at him but he didn't meet my eye. 'I should have taken longer with her. I'm sorry.'

'You knew about the PCP?'

'Yes. The police told me. But not until after our last meeting. I told them it would cause hallucinations, probably terrifying hallucinations. And it would be especially potent given Tess's grief. The literature says that users frequently harm themselves. The lullabies must have been the final straw.'

There was no dog in his NHS consulting room but I could sense how much he wanted to reach out and stroke a reassuring silky ear.

'It would account for why she changed that morning from when I saw her to being suicidal,' he continued. 'She must have heard one of the lullabies, maybe taken some PCP too, and the combination—' He stopped as he saw the expression on my face. 'You think I'm trying to make excuses for myself?'

I was surprised at his first intuitive remark.

'But there aren't any excuses,' he continued. 'She was clearly having visual hallucinations. And whether that was from psychosis or PCP isn't the point. I missed it. Whatever the cause – psychosis or a drug – she was a danger to herself and I didn't protect her as I should have done.'

As in our first meeting I heard shame seeping out of his words.

I'd come to vent my rage but there seemed little point now. He seemed to be already punishing himself. And he wasn't going to change his opinion. The door swung open and a receptionist with a male nurse bustled in and seemed surprised by the silence in the room.

I closed the door behind me. There was nothing left to say to him.

I walked hurriedly down a corridor, as if I could outpace the thoughts that were stalking me because now I had no purpose to distract me, I could only think about you listening to the lullaby.

'Beatrice?'

I'd virtually stumbled into Dr Saunders. Only then did I realise that I was crying, my eyes streaming, nose running, a sodden handkerchief in my hand.

'She was mentally tortured before she was murdered. She was framed for her own suicide.'

Without asking questions, he gave me a hug. His arms around me felt strong but not safe. I'd always found physical intimacy unsettling, even with family let alone a near stranger, so I was more anxious than reassured. But he seemed quite used to holding distressed women, totally at ease with it.

'Can I ask you for coffee again?'

I agreed, because I wanted to ask him about Dr Nichols. I wanted to get proof that he was incompetent and that the police should rethink everything he'd told them. And partly too, because when I'd spilled out about you being mentally tortured, he'd taken it in his stride, not showing any sign of incredulity, and had joined Amias and Christina in the very small band of people that didn't dismiss me out of hand.

We sat at a table in the middle of the bustling café. He looked directly at me, giving me his full attention. I remembered our staring competitions.

'Just look into the pupils, Bee, that's the trick.'

But I still couldn't. Not when the eyes belonged to a beautiful man. Not even in these circumstances.

'Dr Saunders, do you—'

257

He interrupted. 'William, please. I've never been good at formalities. I blame my parents for sending me to a progressive school. The first time I ever put on a uniform is when I got a white coat for this job.' He smiled. 'Also, I have a habit of volunteering more information than I was asked for. I interrupted, you wanted to ask me something?'

'Yes, do you know Dr Nichols?'

'I used to. We were on an SHO rotation together many years ago and we've stayed friends, although I don't see much of him nowadays. Can I ask why?'

'He was Tess's psychiatrist. I want to know if he's incompetent.'

'No, is the short answer to that. Although you think otherwise?'

He waited for me to answer, but I wanted to get information not give it and he seemed to understand that.

'I know Hugo comes across as a little shambolic,' William continued. 'Those tweedy clothes and that ancient dog of his, but he *is* good at his job. If something went wrong with your sister's care then it's far more likely to be down to the pitiful state of mental health funding in the NHS rather than Hugo.'

Again, he reminded me of you, looking at the best in people, and as so often with you, I must have looked sceptical.

'He was a research fellow before becoming a hands-on doctor,' William continued. 'The rising star of the university, apparently. Rumour had it that he was brilliant – destined for greatness and all of that.'

I was taken aback by this description of Dr Nichols; it didn't tally with the man I'd met at all; nothing about Dr Nichols had suggested this.

William went to get milk from the counter and I wondered if Dr Nichols had played me. Had the dog and the scruffy clothes at our first meeting been carefully constructed to present a certain image, which I had unwittingly bought? But why would he go to that much trouble? Be that deceitful? Manipulative? Used now to suspecting everyone I encountered, distrust felt familiar. But I couldn't sustain my suspicion of him. He was just too decent and scruffily hopeless to be connected to violence. The rumour of his brilliance was surely wrong. In any case, he only met you after you had Xavier, and then only once, so unless he was a psychopath what possible reason could he have for murdering you?

William came back with the milk. I wanted to confide in him, it would have been a relief to share what I knew, but instead I stirred my coffee, and saw my ring. I should have given it back to Todd.

William must have noticed it too. 'Quite a rock.'

'Yes. Actually I'm not engaged any more.'

'So why are you wearing it?'

'I forgot to take it off.'

He burst out laughing, reminding me of the way you laugh at me, with kindness. No one but you ever teases me that way.

His bleep went off and he grimaced. 'Usually I have twenty minutes to get to the emergency. But the juniors on today need more hand-holding.'

As he got up his gold wedding ring, hanging on a chain around his neck, swung out from beneath his scrubs top. Maybe I signalled more than I intended.

'My wife's in Portsmouth, a radiologist,' he said. 'It's not easy finding jobs in the same city let alone the same hospital.' He tucked the ring on its chain back inside his top. 'We're not allowed to wear a ring on a finger – too many germs can fester underneath. Rather symbolic, don't you think?'

259

I nodded, surprised. I felt that he was treating me differently than I'd been treated before. And I was suddenly conscious that my clothes were a little crumpled, my hair not blow-dried, my face bare of make-up. No one from my life in New York would have recognised me as I furiously sang the lullaby in Dr Nichols' consulting room. I wasn't the slickly presented, self-controlled person I'd been in the States and I wondered if that encouraged other people to let the untidy aspects of themselves and their lives show in return.

As I watched William leave the café, I wondered, as I still do now, if I'd been wanting to meet someone who reminded me of you, even a little bit. And I wondered if it was hope that made me see a likeness to you, or if it was really there.

꙰

I have told Mr Wright about my visit to Dr Nichols, followed by my conversation with William.

'Who did you think had played her the lullabies?' Mr Wright asks.

'I didn't know. I thought that Simon was capable of it. And Emilio. I couldn't imagine Professor Rosen knowing enough about a young woman to torture her like that. But I'd got him wrong before.'

'And Dr Nichols?'

'He'd know how to mentally torture someone. His job guaranteed that. But he didn't seem in the least cruel or sadistic. And he had no reason to.'

'You questioned your opinion of Professor Rosen but not Dr Nichols?'

'Yes.'

Mr Wright looks as if he's about to ask me another question, then decides against it. Instead he makes a note.

'And later that day Detective Inspector Haines phoned you back?' he asks.

'Yes. He introduced himself as DS Finborough's boss. I thought, to start with, it was a good thing that someone more senior was calling me back.'

⚜

DI Haines's voice boomed down the telephone; a man used to making a noisy room listen to him.

'I have sympathy for you, Miss Hemming, but you can't simply go around indiscriminately blaming people. I gave you the benefit of the doubt when Mr Codi lodged his complaint, out of sympathy for your loss, but you have used up your quota of my patience. And I have to make this clear – you cannot continue crying wolf.'

'I'm not crying wolf, I—'

'No,' he interrupted. 'You're crying several wolves all at once, not sure if any of them are actually wolves at all.' He almost chortled at his own witticism. 'But the Coroner has reached a verdict about your sister's death based on the facts. However unpalatable the truth is for you – and I do understand that it is hard for you – the truth is she committed suicide and no one else is responsible for her death.'

I don't suppose the police service recruit people like DI Haines any more: superior; patriarchal; patronising towards other people and unquestioning of himself.

I struggled to sound self-possessed, not to be the irrational woman he thought me. 'But surely with the lullabies you can see that someone was trying to—'

He interrupted. 'We already knew about the lullaby, Miss Hemming.'

261

I was completely thrown. DI Haines continued, 'When your sister went missing, her upstairs neighbour, an elderly gentlemen, let us into her flat. One of my officers checked to see if there was anything that might help us find her whereabouts. He listened to all the messages on her answerphone tape. We didn't think the lullaby was sinister in any way.'

'But there must have been more than one lullaby, even though only one was recorded. That's why she was scared of the phone calls. That's why she unplugged the phone. And Amias said there were calls, plural.'

'He is an elderly gentleman who readily admits that his memory is no longer perfect.'

I was still trying to seem composed. 'But didn't you find even *one* strange?'

'No more strange than having than a wardrobe in the sitting room or having expensive oil paints but no kettle.'

'Is that why you didn't tell me before? Because you didn't think the lullaby was sinister or even strange?'

'Exactly.'

I turned the phone on to speaker and put it down, so he wouldn't realise that my hands were shaking.

'But surely together with the PCP found in her body, the lullabies show that someone was mentally torturing her?'

His booming voice on speakerphone filled the flat. 'Don't you think it far more likely that it was a friend who didn't realise that she'd already had the baby and was unintentionally tactless?'

'Did Dr Nichols tell you that?'

'He didn't need to. It's the logical conclusion. Especially as the baby wasn't due for another three weeks.'

I couldn't stop the shake in my voice.

'So why did you phone me? If you already knew about the lullabies but had dismissed them?'

'*You* phoned us, Miss Hemming. As a courtesy I am returning your call.'

'The light is better in her bedroom. That's why she moved the wardrobe out, so she could use it as a studio.'

But he had already hung up.

Since living there, I understand.

❦

'And a week after you heard the lullaby it was the college's art show?' asks Mr Wright.

'Yes. Tess's friends had invited me. Simon and Emilio were bound to be there, so I knew I had to go.'

And I think it's appropriate that it was at the college's art show – with your wonderful paintings on display; your spirit and love of life visible to everyone – that I finally found the avenue that would lead me to your murderer.

263

18

The morning of the art show your friend Benjamin came round looking businesslike, his Rasta hair tied back, with a young man I didn't recognise and a beaten-up white van to take your paintings to the college. He said it wasn't the end of year one, which was a big formal affair, but it was important. Potential buyers could come and everyone had family attending. They were solicitous towards me, as if I was fragile and could be broken by loud noise or laughter.

As they left your flat with the pictures I saw that both of them were near tears. Something had prompted it, but it was a part of your life I didn't know; maybe they were simply remembering the last time they were at the flat and the contrast – me here and not you – was painful.

I had packed up your paintings myself, but when I walked into the exhibition I think I literally gasped. I hadn't seen them on a wall before, just stacked on the floor, and put together they were an explosion of living colour, their painted vibrancy arresting. Friends of yours who I'd met at the café came to talk to me, one after another, as if they had a rota of looking after me.

I couldn't see any sign of Simon, but through the crowded room, I saw Emilio on the far side of the exhibition hall. Near to him was the Pretty Witch and by her expression I knew something was wrong. As I went towards him I saw he had the nude paintings of you on display.

I went up to him, livid, but I kept my voice quiet, not wanting anyone to hear, not wanting him to have an audience.

'Does your affair with her carry no penalties for you now she's dead?' I asked.

He gestured to the nudes, looking as if he was enjoying this spat with me. 'They don't mean we had an affair.'

I must have looked incredulous.

'You think artists always sleep with their models, Beatrice?'

Actually, yes, that's what I did think. And using my first name was inappropriately intimate, just as displaying the nudes of you were inappropriately intimate.

'You don't have to be a woman's lover to paint a nude of her.'

'But you were her lover. And you'd like everyone to know about it now, wouldn't you? After all, it reflects pretty well on you that a beautiful girl twenty years your junior was prepared to have sex with you. The fact that you were her tutor and you're married probably doesn't count for much against your macho posturing.'

I saw the Pretty Witch nod at me, approving and a little surprised, I think. Emilio glared at her and she shrugged and moved away.

'So you think my paintings are "macho posturing"?'

'Using Tess's body. Yes.'

I started walking back towards the display of your paintings, but he followed me.

'Beatrice . . .'

I didn't turn.

'There's a piece of news you may find interesting. We've had the results of the cystic fibrosis tests back. My wife isn't a carrier of the CF gene.'

'I'm glad.'

But Emilio hadn't finished. 'I'm not a carrier of the cystic fibrosis gene either.'

But he had to be. It didn't make sense. Xavier had cystic fibrosis so his father had to be a carrier.

I grabbed at an explanation. 'You can't always tell by a simple test. There are thousands of mutations of the cystic fibrosis gene and—'

He interrupted. 'We've had all the tests there are, the whole works – you name it, we've had it and we have been told, categorically, that neither of us are carriers of cystic fibrosis.'

'Sometimes a baby can spontaneously have CF even when one of the parents isn't a carrier.'

'And what are the chances of that? A million to one? Xavier was nothing to do with me.'

It was the first time I'd heard him say Xavier's name – in the same expelled breath to say the words to disown him.

The obvious explanation was that Emilio wasn't Xavier's father. But you'd told me he was and you don't lie.

༈

I sense an increase in Mr Wright's concentration as he listens closely to what I am saying.

'I knew that Xavier had never had cystic fibrosis.'

266

'Because both parents need to be carriers of the cystic fibrosis gene?' asks Mr Wright.

'Exactly.'

'So what did you think was going on?'

I pause a moment, remembering the emotion that accompanied the realisation. 'I thought Chrom-Med had used gene therapy on a perfectly healthy baby.'

'What did you think their reason was?'

'I thought it must be fraud.'

'Can you elaborate?'

'It was hardly surprising Chrom-Med's "cure" for cystic fibrosis was so successful if the babies had never had it in the first place. And it was because of Chrom-Med's supposed miraculous cure that their value had skyrocketed. They were weeks away from floating on the stock market.'

'What about the regulatory bodies who'd monitored the trial?'

'I couldn't understand how they'd been so misled. But I thought somehow they must have been. And I knew that the patients, like Tess, would never have questioned the diagnosis. If you've had someone in the family with cystic fibrosis you always know that you might be a carrier.'

'Did you think Professor Rosen was involved?'

'I thought he had to be. Even if it hadn't been his idea he must have sanctioned it. And he was a director of Chrom-Med, which meant he stood to make a fortune when the company floated.'

When I'd met Professor Rosen at Chrom-Med I'd thought he was a zealous scientist who craved admiration by his peers. I found it hard to replace that image with a money-grabbing fraudster; that instead of being driven by that age-old motive of glory he was driven by the even older one of avarice. It was difficult to believe he was that good an actor; that his

267

speech about eradicating disease and a watershed in history was no more than hot wind designed to throw me, and everyone else, off course. But if it really was the case, he'd been disturbingly convincing.

'Did you contact him at this stage?'

'I tried to. He was in the States giving a lecture tour and wouldn't be back until the sixteenth of March, twelve days away. I left a message on his phone but he didn't reply.'

'Did you tell DS Finborough?' asks Mr Wright.

'Yes. I phoned and said I needed to meet him. He set up an appointment early that afternoon.'

Mr Wright glances down at his notes. 'And at your meeting with DS Finborough, Detective Inspector Haines was there too?'

'Very much so.'

A man who infringed the subtle boundaries of personal space, as if it was his right to invade.

'Before we move on, I just want to get one thing clear,' says Mr Wright. 'How did you think the fraud was linked to Tess's death?'

'I thought she must have found out.'

※

DI Haines's jowly face loomed across the table at me, his physique matching his overbearing voice. Next to him was DS Finborough.

'Which do you think more likely, Miss Hemming,' DI Haines boomed, 'an established company with an international reputation, complying with a myriad of regulations, tests out a gene therapy on perfectly well babies or a student is mistaken about the father of her baby?'

268

'Tess wouldn't have lied about the father.'

'When I last spoke to you on the phone I asked you, courteously, to stop indiscriminately apportioning blame.'

'Yes, but—'

'On your phone message just a week ago, you put Mr Codi and Simon Greenly at the top of your list of suspects.'

I cursed the message I'd left on DS Finborough's phone. It showed me as emotional and unreliable, damaging any credibility I might have had.

'But now you've changed your mind?' he asked.

'Yes.'

'But we haven't, Miss Hemming. There is nothing new that brings into question the Coroner's verdict of suicide. I'll state the bald facts for you. You may not want to hear them but that does not mean they don't exist.'

Not just a double but a triple negative. His oratory wasn't as impressive as he believed it to be.

'An *unmarried* young woman,' he continued, enjoying his emphasised words, 'who is an *art student* in London, has an *illegitimate* baby with cystic fibrosis. The baby is successfully treated by a new genetic therapy in utero,' (I thought how proud he was of this little bit of knowledge, this smidgen of Latin thrown into his monologue) 'but unfortunately it dies when it is born of an unrelated condition.' (Yes, I know – 'it'.) 'One of her friends, of whom she apparently had many, leaves her a tactless message on her answerphone which drives her further down her path towards suicide.' I tried to say something but he continued, barely pausing for the breath needed to patronise me. 'Suffering hallucinations from the *illegal drugs* she was taking she takes a kitchen knife with her into the park.'

I noticed a look between DS Finborough and DI Haines.

'Maybe she bought the knife specially for the purpose,' snapped Haines. 'Maybe she wanted it to be expensive and

269

special. Or just sharp. I am not a psychiatrist, I cannot read a suicidal young woman's mind.'

DS Finborough seemed to flinch away from DI Haines, his distaste for him clear.

'She went into a deserted toilets building,' continued Haines. 'Either so she wouldn't be found or because she wanted to be out of the snow, again I cannot accurately tell you her reason. Either outside in the park or in the toilets building, she took an overdose of sedatives.' (I was surprised he managed to hold back 'a belt and braces suicide' because that was the kind of thing he was itching to say.) 'She then cuts the arteries in her arms with her kitchen knife. Afterwards it transpires that the father of her illegitimate baby isn't her tutor as she'd thought but someone else, who must carry the cystic fibrosis gene.'

I did try to argue with him, but I might as well have been playing the triangle on the hard shoulder of the M4. I know, one of your sayings, but remembering it comforted me a little as he shouted me down. And as he patronised me, not listening to me, I saw how scruffy my clothes were and that my hair needed cutting and I was no longer polite, or respectful of his authority, and it was no wonder he didn't pay attention to me. I didn't used to pay attention to people like me.

As DS Finborough escorted me out of the police station, I turned to him. 'He didn't listen to a word I said.'

DS Finborough was clearly embarrassed, 'It's the accusation you made about Emilio Codi. And Simon Greenly.'

'So it's because I've cried wolf too often?'

He smiled. 'And with such conviction. It doesn't help that Emilio Codi made a formal complaint against you and Simon Greenly is the son of a cabinet minister.'

'But surely he must be able to see that something's wrong?'

'Once he has arrived at a conclusion, backed up by facts

and logic, it's hard to dissuade him. Unless there are heavier counterbalancing facts.'

I thought DS Finborough was too decent and professional to publicly criticise his boss.

'And you?'

He paused a moment, as if unsure whether to tell me. 'We've had the forensic results back on the Sabatier knife. It was brand new. And it had never been used before.'

'She couldn't have afforded Sabatier.'

'I agree, it doesn't fit when she didn't even own a kettle or a toaster.'

So the last time he'd been in the flat, when he'd come to talk about the post-mortem results, he'd noticed. It hadn't just been, as I'd thought at the time, a compassionate visit. I was grateful to him for being first a policeman. I worked up the courage to ask my question.

'So do you now believe that she was murdered?'

There was a moment while my question was static in the silence between us.

'I think there's a query.'

'Are you going to answer your "query"?'

'I'll try. That's the best I can offer.'

❦

Mr Wright is concentrating intently on what I am telling him, his body bent towards mine, his eyes responding; not a passive but an active participant in the tale and I realise how seldom people are fully listened to.

'When I left the police station I went straight to Kasia's flat. I needed her and Mitch to be tested for the CF gene. If either of them tested negative, then the police would have to act.'

❦

Kasia's dingy sitting room had become damper since my last visit. A one-bar electric fire didn't stand a chance against the coldly seeping concrete walls. The thin fabric of the Indian throw at the closed window flapped in the draught around the window frame. Three weeks had passed since I'd last seen her, and she was nearly eight months pregnant now. She looked bewildered.

'But I don't understand, Beatrice.'

Again I wished someone wouldn't use the intimacy of my name this time because, coward that I was, I didn't want to be close to her as I distressed her. I put on my corporate distancing voice as I spelt it out, 'Both parents have to carry the cystic fibrosis gene for the baby to be born with cystic fibrosis.'

'Yes. They tell me in clinic.'

'Xavier's father doesn't carry the gene. So Xavier couldn't have had cystic fibrosis.'

'Xavier not ill?'

'No.'

Mitch came in from the bathroom. He must have been eavesdropping. 'For fuck's sake, she just lied about who she had sex with.'

Without the plaster dust his face was handsome, but the contrast between his finely sculpted face and muscular tattooed body was oddly menacing.

'She had no embarrassment about having sex,' I said. 'If she'd been having sex with someone else as well she would have told me. There was no reason for her to lie. I really think you should get tested, Mitch.'

Using his name was a mistake. Instead of sounding friendly I sounded like a primary school teacher. Kasia was still looking bemused. 'I have cystic fibrosis gene. I test plus for that.'

'Yes. But maybe Mitch is negative, maybe he isn't a carrier and—'

'Yeah right,' he interrupted, sarcasm biting. 'The doctors are wrong and you know best?' He looked at me like he hated me, perhaps he did. 'Your sister lied about who the father was,' he said. 'And who'd blame her? With you looking down your nose at her. Patronising bitch.'

I hoped he was being verbally aggressive for Kasia's sake; that he was trying to prove that your baby did have cystic fibrosis, like their baby had had cystic fibrosis, that the treatment wasn't a con. And the only way for that to be true was for you to be a liar and me an uptight, patronising bitch. But he was enjoying his verbal attack too much for it to be for a kinder reason.

'Truth is, she probably fucked so many men she had no idea who the father was.'

Kasia's voice was quiet but clear. 'No. Tess not like that.'

I remembered how she'd said you were her friend, the simplicity of her loyalty. The glance he gave her was spiked with anger but she continued, 'Beatrice is right.' As she spoke, she stood up and I knew as I watched that reflexive movement that he had hit her in the past, that she'd instinctively stood up to avoid him.

The silence in the room met the damp coldness in the walls and as it continued I wanted the heat of a row, for words to be fighting, rather than the fear that it would be fought later with physical brutality. Kasia motioned me to the door and I went with her.

We walked down the stained sharp-edged concrete steps. Neither of us said anything. As she turned to go back I took hold of her arm. 'Come and stay with me.'

Her hand moved to her bump, she didn't meet my eye. 'I can't.'

'Please, Kasia.'

I startled myself. The most I'd ever given of myself before

273

was my signature on a cheque to a worthy cause, but now I was asking her to stay and really hoping that she would. It was the hope that startled me. She turned away from me and walked back up the stained concrete steps towards the cold damp flat and whatever waited for her there.

As I walked home, I wondered if she'd told you why she once loved Mitch. I was sure that she must have done, that she wasn't the kind of person who had sex without love. I thought how William's wedding ring was a sign that he was taken, spoken for, but that the small gold crucifix Kasia wore around her neck wasn't about ownership or promises; it was a 'no trespassing' sign unless you have love and kindness for the wearer. And I was furious that Mitch was ignoring it. Because he did ignore it, violently.

At just after midnight, the doorbell rang and I hurried to answer it, hoping that it would be Kasia. When I saw her standing on the doorstep I didn't see her tarty clothes and cheap hair colour only the bruises on her face and the welts on her arms.

That first night we shared the bed. She snored like a steam train and I remembered you telling me that pregnancy could make you snore. I liked the sound. I had spent night after night awake, listening to my grief, my sobbing the only sound in the room, my heart screaming as it rhythmically thumped into the mattress, and her snoring was an everyday sound, innocent and annoyingly soothing. That night I slept deeply for the first time since you'd died.

❧

Mr Wright has had to go off to a meeting, so I am coming home early today. It's pouring with rain when I leave the tube station and I get drenched as I walk home. I see Kasia looking for me out of the window. Seconds later she greets me, smiling, at the front door. 'Beata!' (It's Polish for Beatrice.) As I think I told you, she has the bed to herself now and I have a futon in the sitting room and it feels absurdly cramped; my feet touching the wardrobe and my head the door.

As I change into dry clothes, I think that today has been a good day. I've managed to keep my morning resolutions of not being afraid or intimidated. And when I felt faint and shivery and sick, I tried to ignore it and not let my body dominate my mind, and I think I succeeded pretty well. I didn't get as far as finding something beautiful in the everyday, but maybe that's just a step too far.

Now changed, I give Kasia her English lesson, which I do every day. I have a textbook for teaching Polish people English. The book groups words together and she learns a group before our 'lesson'.

'*Piękn,*' I say, following the pronunciation instructions.

'Beautiful, lovely, gorgeous,' she replies.

'Brilliant.'

'Thank you, Beata,' she says, mock solemn. I try to hide how much I like her using her Polish name for me. '*Ukochanie?*' I continue.

'Love, adore, fond of, passionate.'

'Well done. *Nienawiść?*'

She's silent. I am on the other side of the page now and the antonyms. I gave her the Polish word for hate. She shrugs. I try another, the Polish for unhappy, but she looks at me blankly.

At the beginning I got frustrated at the holes in her vocabulary, thinking it was childish that she refused to learn the negative words, a linguistic head-in-the-sand policy. But on the positive ones she's forging ahead, even learning colloquialisms.

'How are you, Kasia?'

'Tip-top, Beata.' (She likes 50s musicals.)

I've asked her to stay on with me after her baby's born. Both Kasia and Amias are delighted. He's offered us the flat rent free, till we 'get on our feet again' and somehow I'll just have to look after her and her baby. Because I will get through this. It will all be OK.

After our lesson, I glance out of the window and only now notice the pots down the steps to your flat. They are all in flower, a host (a smallish host but a host nonetheless) of golden daffodils.

I ring on Amias's bell. He looks genuinely delighted to see me. I kiss him on the cheek. 'The daffodils you planted, they're flowering.'

Eight weeks before I'd watched him planting the bulbs in snow-covered earth and even with my lack of gardening knowledge knew they couldn't survive. Amias smiles at me, enjoying my confusion. 'You don't need to sound quite so surprised.'

Like you, I see Amias regularly, sometimes for supper, sometimes just for a whisky. I used to think you went out of charity.

'Did you pop some in ready potted when I wasn't looking?' I ask.

He roars with laughter, he's got a very loud laugh for an old person doesn't he? Robust and strong.

'I poured some hot water in first, mixed it with the earth, then planted the bulbs. Things always grow better if you warm their soil up.'

I find the image comforting.

19

When I arrive at the CPS offices this morning, I discover other people also have diminutive hosts of daffodils growing because Mr Wright's secretary is taking a bunch out of damp paper. Like Proust's tea-soaked *petites madeleines*, the soggy kitchen roll around their stems pulls me sensuously backwards to a sunny classroom and my bunch of home-picked daffodils on Mrs Potter's desk. For a moment I hold a thread to the past back to when Leo was alive and Dad was with us and boarding school hadn't cast its shadow over Mum's goodnight kiss. But the thread frays to nothing as I hold it and is replaced by a hardier, harsher memory five years later – when you brought a bunch of daffodils to Mrs Potter, and I was upset because I didn't have a teacher I wanted to bring flowers to any more, and because I was off to boarding school where I suspected even if they had flowers they wouldn't let me pick them. And because everything had changed.

Mr Wright comes in, his eyes red and streaming.

277

'Don't worry. Hay fever. Not infectious.'

As we go into his office I feel sorry for his secretary who even now must be binning the happy beauty of her daffodils out of loving consideration for her boss.

He goes to the window. 'Would you mind if I close it?'

'No, that's fine.'

He's clearly in a great deal of discomfort, and I'm glad I can focus on someone else's maladies rather than my own, it makes me feel a little less self-centred.

'We'd got to Kasia coming to stay with you?' he asks.

'Yes.'

He smiles at me. 'And I see that she's still staying with you.'

He must have seen it in the paper. I was right about that photo of me, my arm around Kasia, being in all the newspapers.

'Yes. The next morning I played her the lullaby on the answerphone. But she just assumed it was a friend who'd been unknowingly horribly tactless.'

'Did you tell her what you thought?'

'No, I didn't want to upset her for no reason. She'd already told me, when I first met her, that she didn't even know Tess was frightened, let alone who may have been frightening her. It was stupid of me to play her the lullaby.'

But if I'd seen her as fully my equal would I have told her what I thought? Would I have wanted company in this, someone to share it with? But by the time I'd spent that night listening to her snore, by the time I'd woken her with a cup of tea and cooked her a decent breakfast, I'd decided my role was to look after her. Protect her.

'And then the answerphone tape ran on,' I continue. 'There was a message from a woman called Hattie, who I didn't know, and hadn't thought important. But Kasia

278

recognised her, and told me she was at the "Mummies with disasters" clinic with her and Tess. She assumed that Hattie had had her baby but didn't expect her to call. She's never been close to Hattie; it was Tess who always organised their get-togethers. She didn't have a phone number for Hattie but she did have her address.'

𝕔

I went to the address that Kasia had given me, which makes it sound easy but without a car and a rudimentary know-ledge of public transport, I found getting anywhere stressful and time-consuming. Kasia had stayed behind, too self-conscious about her bruised face to go out. She thought I was going to see one of your old friends out of sentiment and I didn't correct her.

I arrived at a pretty house in Chiswick and felt a little awkward as I rang the bell. I hadn't been able to phone ahead and wasn't even sure if Hattie would be there. A Filipino nanny, with a blond toddler in her arms, answered the door. She seemed very shy, not meeting my eye.

'Beatrice?' she asked.

I was perplexed about how she could know who I was.

She must have seen my confusion. 'I'm Hattie, a friend of Tess's. We met at her funeral, very briefly, shook hands.'

There had been a long line of people queuing to see me and Mum, a cruel parody of a wedding reception receiving line, all waiting their turn to say sorry – so many sorries as if it was all their faults that you had died. I had just wanted it to be over with, not to be the cause of the queue, and didn't have the emotional capacity to take in new names or faces.

Kasia hadn't told me that Hattie was Filipino; there was

279

no reason why she should I suppose. But it wasn't just Hattie's nationality that surprised me, it was also her age. While you and Kasia are young, one foot still in girlhood, Hattie is a woman nearing forty. And she was wearing a wedding ring.

Hattie held the door open for me. Her manner demure, deferential even. 'Please, come in.'

I followed her into the house and strained to hear the sound of a baby, but could only hear a children's TV programme from the sitting room. I watched her as she settled the blond toddler in front of *Thomas the Tank Engine*, and remembered that you had told me about a Filipino friend of yours who worked as a nanny, but I hadn't listened to her name, irritated by another of your trendy liberal friendships (a Filipino nanny for heaven's sake!).

'I've got a few questions I'd like to ask you, is that OK?'

'Yes, but I have to pick up his brother at twelve. Do you mind if I . . .' She gestured to the ironing board and laundry basket in the kitchen.

'Of course not.'

She seemed so passively accepting of me just appearing on her doorstep and asking her questions. I followed her into the kitchen and noticed her flimsy cheap dress. It was cold out but her shoes were old plastic flip-flops.

'Kasia Lewski told me that your baby was on the cystic fibrosis trial?' I asked.

'Yes.'

'Do you and your husband both carry the gene for cystic fibrosis?'

'Clearly.'

The tone was sharp edged from behind her meek façade. She didn't meet my eye and I thought I must have misheard.

280

'Have you been tested for the cystic fibrosis gene in the past?' I asked.

'I have a child with CF.'

'I'm sorry.'

'He lives with his grandmother and father. My daughter is also with them. But she doesn't have cystic fibrosis.'

Both Hattie and her husband were clearly CF carriers so my theory about Chrom-Med treating healthy babies wasn't going to be backed up by her. Unless,

'Your husband, he's still in the Philippines?'

'Yes.'

I started to imagine various scenarios as to how a very poor, very shy Filipino woman may become pregnant when her husband is back in the Philippines.

'Are you a live-in nanny?' I asked and I still don't know if it was a crass attempt at small talk or if I was hinting that the dad of the house was the father of her baby.

'Yes. I live here. Georgina likes having me here when Mr Bevan is away.'

I noticed that the mum was 'Georgina' but the father 'Mr Bevan'.

'It would be nicer for you to live out?' I asked, back on my Mr Bevan-as-dad scenario. I'm not quite sure what I imagined, a sudden confession along the lines of 'Oh yes, and then the master of the house won't be able to have his wicked way with me at nights.'

'I am happy here. Georgina's a very kind-hearted person. She's my friend.'

I instantly discounted that; friendship means some kind of parity between two people.

'And Mr Bevan?'

'I don't know him very well. He's away a lot on business.'

No further info from going down that track. I watched

281

her as she carried on ironing, meticulous and perfect, and thought how Georgina's friends must envy her.

'You're *sure* that the father of your baby carries the cystic fibrosis gene?'

'I told you. My son has cystic fibrosis.' The sharp tone I'd heard earlier was back and unmistakable. 'I see you because you are Tess's sister,' she continued. 'A courtesy. Not for you to question me like this. What business is it of yours?'

I realised my impression of her had been completely false. I'd thought her eyes didn't meet mine out of shyness, but she had been carefully guarding the territory of herself. She wasn't passively shy but fiercely private.

'I'm sorry. But the thing is, I'm not sure if the cystic fibrosis trial is legitimate, which is why I want to know if both you and your baby's father carry the CF gene.'

'You think I can understand a long English word like "legitimate"?'

'Yes. I think I've patronised you enough, actually.'

She turned, almost smiling, and it was like looking at a completely different woman. I could imagine now that Georgina, whoever she was, really was friends with her.

'The trial is legitimate. It cured the baby. But my child in the Philippines cannot be cured. It's too late for him.'

She still wasn't telling me who the dad was. I'd have to revisit it, when hopefully she'd trust me with the answer.

'Can I ask you another question?' She nodded. 'Were you paid to take part in the trial?'

'Yes. Three hundred pounds. I need to collect Barnaby from nursery school now.'

There were so many questions I still hadn't asked and I felt panicked that I wouldn't have another opportunity. She went into the sitting room and coaxed the toddler away from the television.

'Can I see you again?' I asked.

'I'm babysitting next Tuesday. They'll be out from eight. You can come then if you like.'

'Thank you, I—'

She motioned at me to be quiet, the toddler in her arms, protecting him from a possibly unsuitable conversation.

☙

'When I first met Hattie I thought she wasn't anything like Tess or Kasia,' I say. 'She was a different age, different nationality, had a different occupation. But her clothes were cheap, like Tess's and Kasia's, and I realised that one thing they had in common, as well as being on the cystic fibrosis trial at St Anne's, was that they were all poor.'

'You found that significant?' asks Mr Wright.

'I thought they were more likely to be seen as financially persuadable or open to bribery. I also realised that with Hattie's husband in the Philippines all three were effectively single.'

'What about Kasia's boyfriend, Michael Flanagan?'

'At the time Kasia was put on the trial he had already left her. When he did come back they were only together for a few weeks. I thought that whoever was behind this was deliberately choosing women on their own because there would be no one who would look too hard, care too much. He was exploiting what he thought was an isolated vulnerability.'

Mr Wright is about to say something kind, but I don't want to go off on a guilt/reassurance tangent so I briskly keep going.

'I'd seen footage on TV and at Chrom-Med of babies who had been on the trial, and there were fathers as well as mothers very much in the picture. I wondered if it was only

283

at St Anne's Hospital that the women were single. If it was only at St Anne's that something terrible was happening.'

❧

Hattie had carefully settled the blond toddler into the pushchair with drink and teddy. She set the alarm and picked up her keys. I had been looking for signs of a young baby but there had been nothing – no sound of crying, no baby monitor, no basket of nappies. She herself had said nothing. Now she was leaving the house and it was clear that there could be no baby upstairs somewhere. I was on the doorstep, halfway out, before I could muster the nerve or the callousness to ask the question, 'Your baby . . . ?'

Her voice was quiet so that the toddler couldn't hear.
'He died.'

❧

Mr Wright has had to go to a lunch meeting, so I've come outside. The park is rain-washed after yesterday, the grass shiny green and the crocuses jewel-coloured. I'd rather talk to you out here, where colours can be bright even without sunshine. Hattie told you that her baby had died, after an emergency caesarean. But did she also tell you that she had to have a hysterectomy, her womb taken out? I'm not sure what the people out here think of my weeping, probably that I'm a little mad. But when she told me I didn't even pause for a thought about her baby, let alone weep, totally focused instead on the implications.

I get back to the CPS offices and continue with my statement to Mr Wright, giving bald facts stripped of their emotional resonance.

'Hattie told me her baby died of a heart condition. Xavier had died of some type of kidney failure. I was sure that the deaths of the two babies were linked and that they must be related to the trial at St Anne's.'

'Did you have any idea what the link may be?'

'No. I didn't understand what was going on. Previously, I'd had a neat theory that well babies were being put on a fake trial; that it was a huge fraud for profit. But now two of the babies had died, it didn't make any sense.'

Mr Wright's secretary interrupts with antihistamine tablets for Mr Wright. She asks me if I'd like one too, misinterpreting the reason for my red-rimmed eyes. I realise that I've misjudged her, not so much for her attempted thoughtfulness towards me but for her initiative at trying to reprieve her daffodils. She leaves the room and we continue.

'I phoned Professor Rosen, who was still on his lecture tour in the States. I left a message on his mobile asking him what the hell was going on.'

I wondered if his pride in being invited to all those Ivy League universities was to distract from his real purpose. Was he running away, worried that something would be unearthed?

'You didn't talk to the police again?' asks Mr Wright. The log he has of my calls with the police clearly shows a gap at this point.

'No. DI Haines already thought me irrational and ridiculous, which had been pretty much my own fault. I needed to get some "heavier counter-balancing facts" before I went back to the police.'

⁂

Poor Christina, I don't suppose that when she ended her condolence letter with the statutory 'if there's anything I can do please don't hesitate to ask' that I would take her up on it, *twice*. I phoned her on her mobile and told her about Hattie's baby. She was at work and sounded briskly efficient.

'Was there a post-mortem?' she asked.

'No. Hattie told me that she didn't want one.'

I heard the sound of a bleep in the background and Christina talking to someone. Sounding harassed, she said she'd have to call me back that evening, when she wasn't on duty.

In the meantime I decided to go and see Mum. It was the twelfth of March and I knew it would be hard for her.

20

I'd always sent flowers to Mum on Leo's birthday and phoned her; thoughtfulness at a distance. And I'd always made sure there would be an end to the phone call – a meeting I had to get to, a conference call that had to be taken – creating a barrier against any potential emotional outpouring. But there had never been any outpouring, just a little awkwardness as emotions were bitten back and passed off as the judder of a transatlantic phone call.

I'd already bought Leo a card, but at Liverpool Street Station I bought a bunch of cornflowers for you, wild and vividly blue. As the florist wrapped them, I remembered Kasia telling me that I should lay flowers at the toilets building for you, which she'd done weeks before. She was uncharacteristically insistent, and thought that Mum would find it 'healing' too. But I knew Mum found this modern expression of grief – all those floral shrines by zebra crossings and up lamp-posts and on roadside verges – unsettling and bizarre. Flowers should be laid where you were buried, not where you died. Besides I would do my damnedest to make sure Mum never saw the toilets building. Me too for that matter. I never wanted to go near that building again. So I'd told Kasia that I'd rather plant something beautiful in your garden; look after it; watch it as it grew and flourished. And, like Mum, lay flowers on your grave.

I walked the half-mile from Little Hadston station to the church, and saw Mum in the graveyard. I told you about my lunch with her just a few days ago, jumping ahead in the chronology of the story so I could reassure you and be fair to her. So you already know how she changed after you died; how she became again the mum of babyhood in the rustling dressing gown, smelling of face cream and reassurance in the dark. Warm and loving, she's also become worryingly vulnerable. It was at your funeral that she changed. It wasn't a gradual process but horrifyingly fast, her silent scream as you were lowered into the wet mud shattering all of her character artifices, leaving the core of her exposed. And in that shattering moment, her fiction around your death disintegrated. She knew, as I did, that you would never have killed yourself. And that violent knowledge leached the strength from her spine and stripped the colour from her hair.

But every time I saw her, so old and grey now, it was newly shocking.

'Mum?'

She turned and I saw tears on her face. She hugged me tightly and pressed her face against my shoulder. I felt her tears through my shirt. She pulled away, trying to laugh. 'Shouldn't use you as a hanky, should I?'

'That's fine, any time.'

She stroked my hair. 'All that hair. It needs a cut.'

'I know.'

I put my arm around her.

288

Dad had gone back to France, with no promises of phone calls or visits; honest enough now not to make promises he couldn't keep. I know that I am loved by him but that he won't be present in my everyday life. So, practically, Mum and I only have each other now. It makes the other one more precious and also not enough. We have to try to fill not only our own boots but other people's too – yours, Leo's, Dad's. We have to expand at the moment we feel the most shrunk.

I put my cornflowers on your grave, which I hadn't seen since the day of your burial. And as I looked at the earth heaped above you and Xavier, I thought that this is what it all meant – the visits to the police, the hospital, the internet searches, the questioning and querying and suspicions and accusations – this is what it came down to: you covered with suffocating mud away from light, air, life, love.

I turned to Leo's grave, and put down my card, an Action Man one, that I think an eight-year-old would like. I've never added years to him. Mum had already put on a wrapped-up present, which she'd told me was a remote-control helicopter.

'How did you know he had cystic fibrosis?' I asked.

She told me once that she knew he had it before he showed any signs of illness, but neither she nor Dad knew they were carriers, so how did she know to get him tested? My mind had become accustomed to asking questions, even at Leo's graveside, even on what should have been his birthday.

'He was still a baby and he was crying,' said Mum. 'I kissed his face and his tears tasted salty. I told the GP, just a by-the-by comment, not thinking anything of it. Salty tears are a symptom of cystic fibrosis.'

Remember how even when we were children she hardly ever kissed us when we cried? But I remember a time when she did; before she tasted the salt in Leo's tears.

We were silent for a few moments and my eyes went from Leo's established grave back to your raw one, and I saw how the contrast visualised my state of mourning for each of you.

'I've decided on a headstone,' Mum said. 'I want an angel, one of those big stone ones with the enveloping wings.'

'I think she'd like an angel.'

'She'd find it ludicrously funny.'

We both half-smile, imagining your reaction to a stone angel.

'But I think Xavier would like it,' Mum said. 'I mean for a baby an angel's lovely, isn't it? Not too sentimental.'

'Not at all.'

She'd got sentimental, though, bringing a teddy each week, and replacing it when it gets wet and dirty. She was a little apologetic about it, but not very. The old Mum would have been horrified by the poor taste.

I remembered again our conversation when I told you that you must tell Mum you were pregnant including the ending that I had forgotten, deliberately, I think.

'Do you still have knickers with days of the week embroidered on them?' you asked.

'You're changing the subject. And I was given those when I was nine.'

'Did you really wear them on the right day?'

'She's going to be so hurt, if you don't tell her.'

Your voice became uncharacteristically serious. 'She'll say things she'll regret. And she'll never be able to un-say them.'

You were being kind. You were putting love before truth. But I hadn't seen that before, thinking you were just making up an excuse – 'Avoiding the issue.'

'I'll tell her when he's born, Bee. When she'll love him.'

You always knew she would.

Mum started to plant a Madame Carriere rose in a ceramic pot next to your grave. 'It's just temporary, till the angel arrives. It looks too bare without anything.' I filled a watering can so we could water it in and remembered you as a small child trundling after Mum with your mini-sized gardening tools, your fingers clutched around seeds that you'd collected from other plants, aquilegias I think, but I never really took much notice.

'She used to love gardening, didn't she?' I asked.

'From the time she was tiny,' said Mum. 'It wasn't till I was in my thirties that I started liking it.'

'So what started you off?'

I was just making conversation, a safe conversation, that I hoped Mum would find soothing. She's always liked talking about plants.

'When I planted something it became more and more beautiful, which at thirty-six was the opposite of what was happening to me,' Mum said, testing the soil around the rose with her bare fingers. I saw her nails were filled with earth. 'I shouldn't have minded losing my looks,' she continued. 'But I did then, before Leo died. I think I missed being treated with kindness, with leeway, because I was a pretty girl. The man who came to do our rewiring, a taxi driver once – were unnecessarily unpleasant; men who would normally have done a little extra job for free were aggressive, as if they could tell I had once been pretty, beautiful even, and they didn't want to know that prettiness fades and ages. It was as if they blamed me for it.'

I was a little taken aback by her, but only a little. Shooting

291

from the hip as a style of conversation was getting almost familiar now. Mum wiped her face with her grimy fingers leaving a streak of dirt across her cheek. 'And then there was Tess growing up, so pretty, and unaware of how generous people were to her because of it.'

'She never played on it though.'

'She didn't need to. The world held its door open for her and she walked through smiling, thinking it would always be that way.'

'Were you jealous?'

Mum hesitated a moment, then shook her head. 'It wasn't jealousy, but looking at her made me see what I had become.' She breaks off. 'I'm a little drunk. I allow myself to get a little plastered actually, on Leo's birthday. The anniversary of his death, too. And now there'll be Tess and Xavier's anniversaries, won't there? I'll become a drunkard if I don't watch out.'

I held her hand tightly in mine.

'Tess always came down to be with me on his birthday,' she said.

When we said goodbye at the station, I suggested an outing together on the following Sunday, to the nursery at Petersham Meadows, that you used to love but couldn't afford. We agreed we'd choose a new plant that you'd like for your garden.

I got the train back to London. You'd never told me that you visited Mum on Leo's birthday. Presumably to spare me the guilt. I wondered how many other times you visited her, until the bump started to show. I already knew from the phone bill that I'd been cruelly neglectful of you, and I realised it applied to Mum too. It was you who was the caring daughter, not me, as I'd always self-righteously assumed.

I ran away, didn't I? My job in New York wasn't a 'career opportunity'; it was an opportunity to leave Mum and responsibility behind as I pursued an uncluttered life in another continent. No different to Dad. But you didn't leave. You may have needed me to remind you when birthdays were coming up, but you didn't run away.

I wondered why Dr Wong didn't show me my flaws. Surely a good therapist should produce a Dorian Gray-style portrait from under the couch so the patient can see the person that they really are. But that's unfair on her. I didn't ask the right questions about myself; I didn't question myself at all.

My phone ringing jolted me out of my self-analysis. It was Christina. She made small talk for a while, which I suspected was because she was putting off the reason for her phone call, and then came to the point.

'I don't think Xavier's death and this other baby's death can be linked, Hemms.'

'But they must be. Both Tess and Hattie were on the same trial at the same hospital—'

'Yes, but medically there isn't a connection. You can't get something that causes a heart condition serious enough to kill one baby, and kidney problems – most likely total renal failure – which kills another baby.'

I interrupted, feeling panicky. 'In genetics, one gene can code for completely different things, can't it? So maybe—'

Again she interrupted, or maybe it was the bad connection in the train. 'I checked with my professor, just in case I was missing something. I didn't tell him what this was about, just gave him a hypothetical scenario. And he said there's no way two such disparate and fatal conditions could have the same cause.'

I knew that she was dumbing down the scientific language so that I would understand it. And I knew in its more complex version, it would be exactly the same. The trial at St Anne's couldn't be responsible for both babies' deaths.

'But it's strange, isn't it, that two babies have died at St Anne's?' I asked.

'There's a perinatal mortality rate in every hospital and St Anne's delivers five thousand babies a year, so it's sad but unfortunately a blip that wouldn't be seen as remarkable.'

I tried to question her further, find some flaw, but she was silent. I felt jolted by the train, my physical discomfort mirroring my emotional state, and the discomfort also made me worry about Kasia. I'd been planning a trip for her, but that might be irresponsible, so I checked with Christina. Clearly glad to be able to help, she gave me an unnecessarily detailed reply.

⁂

I finish telling Mr Wright about my phone call with Christina. 'I thought that someone must have lied to the women about what their babies really died from. Neither baby had had a post-mortem.'

'You never thought you might be wrong?'

'No.'

He looks at me with admiration I think, but I should be truthful.

'I didn't have the energy to think I might be wrong,' I continue. 'I just couldn't face going back to the beginning and starting again.'

'So what did you do?' he asks and I feel tired as he asks the question, tired and daunted as I did then.

'I went back to see Hattie. I didn't think she'd have anything to say that would help, but I had to try something.'

⁂

I was grasping at straws, and I knew that, but I had to keep grasping. The only thing that might help was the identity of the father of Hattie's baby, but I didn't hold out much hope.

When I rang on Hattie's doorbell a pretty woman in her thirties, who I guessed to be Georgina, answered the door, holding a child's book in one hand, lipstick in the other.

'You must be Beatrice, come in. I'm a little behind, promised Hattie I'd be out of here by eight at the latest.'

Hattie came into the hallway behind her. Georgina turned to her. 'Would you mind reading the children the cow story? I'll get Beatrice a drink.'

Hattie left us to go upstairs. I sensed that this had been engineered by Georgina, though she seemed genuinely friendly. '*Percy and the Cow* is the shortest, start to finish in six minutes, including engine noises and animal sounds, so she should be down soon.' She opened a bottle of wine and handed me a glass. 'Don't upset her, will you? She's been through so much. Has hardly eaten since it happened. Try and . . . be kind to her.'

I nodded, liking her for her concern. A car hooted outside and Georgina called up the stairs before she left. 'There's an open Pinot Grigio, Hatts, so dig in.' Hattie called down her thanks. They seemed more like flatmates than a boss and a nanny both in their thirties.

Hattie came down from settling the children and we went into the sitting room. She sat on the sofa, tucking her legs under her, glass of wine in her hand, treating the place as home, rather than as a 'live-in' domestic helper.

'Georgina seems very nice . . . ?' I asked.

'Yes, she is. When I told her about the baby she offered to pay my airfare home and to give me two months' wages on top. They can't afford that, they both work full time and they can only just about manage my wages as it is.'

So Georgina wasn't the stereotypical Filipino-nanny employer, just as Hattie didn't live in the broom cupboard. I ran through my, by now, standard questions. Did she know if you were afraid of anyone? Did she know anyone who may have given you drugs? Any reason why you may have been killed (bracing myself for the look that I usually got at this point)? Hattie could give me no answers. Like your other friends she hadn't seen you after you'd had Xavier. I was now scraping the bottom of my barrel of questions, not really thinking that I'd get very far.

'Why didn't you tell anyone the name of your baby's father?'

She hesitated and I thought she looked ashamed.

'Who is he, Hattie?'

'My husband.'

She was silent, letting me have a stab at working it out. 'You took the job pregnant?'

'I thought no one would employ me if they knew. When it became clear I pretended that the baby was due later than it was. I'd rather Georgina thought I had loose sexual morals than that I lied to her.' I must have looked bemused. 'She trusted me to be her friend.'

For a moment I felt excluded from threads of friendships that bind women together and which I've never felt I needed, because I'd always had you.

'Did you tell Tess about your baby?' I asked.

'Yes. Hers wasn't due for another few weeks. She cried when I told her, on my behalf, and I was angry with her. She gave me emotions I didn't have.'

Did you realise that she was angry with you? She was the only person I'd spoken to who'd had any criticism of you; who you had misunderstood.

'The truth is, I was relieved,' she said. Her tone was one of challenge, daring me to be shocked.

296

'I understand that,' I replied. 'You have other children at home that you need to look after. A baby would mean losing your job, however understanding your employers are, and you wouldn't be able to send money home to them.' I looked at her and saw I was still off-track. 'Or couldn't you bear to leave another child behind while you came to the UK to work?' She met my eye, a tacit confirmation.

Why could I understand Hattie when you could not? Because I understand shame, and you've never experienced it. Hattie stood up. 'Is there anything else you'd like to know?' She wanted me gone.

'Yes, do you know who gave you the injection? The one with the gene?'

'No.'

'What about the doctor who delivered your baby?'

'It was a caesarean.'

'But surely you still saw him or her?'

'No. He wore a mask. When I had the injection. When I had the operation. All the time in a mask. In the Philippines there's nothing like that. No one's bothered that much about hygiene, but over here . . .'

As she spoke I saw those four nightmarish canvasses you painted, the woman screaming and the masked figure over her. They weren't a record of a drug-induced hallucination but what actually happened to you.

'Do you have your hospital notes, Hattie?'

'No.'

'They got lost?'

She seemed surprised that I would know.

☙

I drain my cup of coffee and don't know if it's the caffeine hit or the memory of those paintings that makes a shudder run through me, spilling some of the coffee on the table. Mr Wright looks at me, with concern. 'Shall we end it there?' he asks.

'Yes, if that's OK.'

We go out into reception together. Mr Wright sees the bunch of daffodils on his secretary's desk and stops. I see her tensing. He turns to me, eyes reddening.

'I really like what Tess told you about the gene for yellow in a daffodil saving children's sight.'

'Me too.'

Detective Sergeant Finborough is waiting for me in Carluccio's near the CPS building. He phoned me yesterday and asked if we could meet. I'm not sure if it's allowed but I agreed. I know he won't be here for his own sake, no pleas to buff up the truth of what happened so he reflects better in it.

I go up to him and we hesitate a moment, as if we may kiss on the cheek as friends rather than as – what? What are we to one another? He was the person who told me it was you they'd found; you in the toilets building. He was the man who'd taken my hand and looked me in the eye and destroyed who I was up until that moment. Our relationship isn't cocktail-style pecking on the cheek but nor is it simply that of policeman to relative of a victim. I take his hand and hold it as he once held mine; this time it's my hand that's the warmer.

'I wanted to say sorry, Beatrice.'

I am about to reply when a waitress pushes between us, tray held aloft, a pencil stuck businesslike into her ponytail. I think that we should be somewhere like a church – a quiet, serious place – where the big things are talked about in whispers not shouted above the clatter of crockery and chit-chat.

We sit down at a table and I think we both find it awkwardly intimate. I break the silence. 'How is WPC Vernon?'

'She's been promoted,' he replies. 'She's working for the domestic violence unit now.'

'Good for her.'

He smiles at me and, ice broken now, he takes the plunge into a deeper conversation. 'You were right all along. I should have listened to you and believed you.'

I used to fantasise about hearing exactly that kind of a sentence and wish I could whisper to my earlier self that one day a policeman would be telling me that.

'At least you had a query,' I say. 'And acted on it.'

'Much too late. You should never have been put in jeopardy like that.'

The sounds of the restaurant suddenly mute, the lights are dimming into darkness. I can just hear DS Finborough talking to me, reassuring me that I'm OK, but then his voice is silenced and everything is dark and I want to scream but my mouth can't make any sound.

When I come round, I'm in the café's clean and warm Ladies'. DS Finborough is with me. He tells me I was 'out' for about five minutes. Not so long then. But it's the first time I've lost sound too. The staff at Carluccio's have been solicitous and call me a taxi to get home. I ask DS Finborough if he'll accompany me and he willingly agrees.

I'm now in a black cab with a policeman sitting next to me, but I still feel afraid. I know that he's following me; I can feel his malevolent presence, murderous, getting closer.

I want to tell DS Finborough. But, like Mr Wright, he'd tell me that he's locked up on remand in prison; that he can't hurt me again; that there's nothing to fear. But I wouldn't be able to believe him.

DS Finborough waits till I'm safely inside the flat, and then takes the taxi on to wherever he is going. As I close the door, Pudding bends her warm furry body around my legs, purring. I call out Kasia's name. No reply. I dampen down flaring sparks of anxiety then see a note on the table saying she's at her antenatal group. She should be home any minute.

I go to the window to check, pulling back the curtains. Two hands pummel the glass from the other side, trying to smash it. I scream. He vanishes into the darkness.

21

Thursday

It's a beautiful spring day, but I take the tube to the CPS offices, rather than crossing the park, so that I'm always in a crowd.

When I get there I am glad for the crush in the lift but anxious, as usual, that my pager and mobile don't get reception and it'll get stuck and Kasia won't be able to get hold of me.

As soon as I'm spat out onto the third floor I check that they're both working. I didn't tell her about the man at the window last night, I didn't want to frighten her. Or to admit the other possibility – that it's not just my body that is deteriorating but my mind too. I know that I am physically unwell, but never thought I might be mentally unwell too. Is he simply a delusion, a product of a diseased mind? Maybe you need physical strength, which I no longer have, to keep a grip on sanity. Going mad is the thing I fear the most, even more than him, because it destroys who you are inside a body that somehow, grotesquely, survives you. I know you must have been afraid too. And I wish that you'd known it was PCP – not some weakness or disease in your own mind – that threatened your sanity.

Maybe I've been given PCP too. Has that thought crossed your mind before it has mine? Perhaps a hallucinogenic is responsible for creating the evil that stalks me. But no one could have given it to me. I've only been at the CPS offices, the Coyote and the flat, where no one wishes me harm.

I won't tell Mr Wright about the murderer at the window, not yet; nor my fear of going mad. If I don't tell him, then he'll treat me normally, and I will behave that way in return. He has expectations of me to be completely sane and I will rise to meet them. Besides, at least for the hours I'm with him, I know that I am safe. So I'll wait till the end of the day and tell him then.

This morning, Mr Wright's office is no longer bright; there's darkness around the edges, which I try to blink away. As I start talking to him I hear my words slur a little and it's an effort to remember. But Mr Wright has said we may be able to finish my statement today so I will just have to push myself on.

Mr Wright doesn't seem to notice anything wrong. Maybe I've become adept at hiding it or he's just totally focused on getting through the last part of my statement. He recaps the last part of our interview.

'Hattie Sim told you that the man who gave her the injection and delivered her baby wore a mask?'

'Yes. I asked her if it was the same person and she said it was. But she couldn't remember any more – voice or hair colour or height. She was trying to blank out the whole experience and I couldn't blame her.'

'Did you think that the man who delivered her baby also delivered Tess's?'

'Yes. And I was sure he was the man who murdered her. But I needed more before going to the police.'

'Heavy counterbalancing facts?' asks Mr Wright.

'Yes. I needed to prove that he wore a mask to hide his identity. I hadn't been able to find out who had delivered Tess's baby – deliberately, I realised. But maybe I could find out who had given Tess and Hattie the injections.'

⁂

By the time I got to St Anne's Hospital from Hattie's house in Chiswick, it was late, past midnight. But I had to find out *straight away*. When I arrived the wards were in darkness and I realised this wasn't the most sensible time to start asking questions. But I'd already pressed the buzzer on the maternity ward door, and a nurse I didn't recognise was opening it. She looked at me suspiciously and I remembered the security was to stop babies being stolen.

'Can I speak to the Senior Midwife? I think her name is Cressida.'

'She's at home. Her shift finished six hours ago. She'll be back tomorrow.'

But I couldn't wait till then.

'Is William Saunders here?' I asked.

'You're a patient?'

'No.' I hesitated a moment. 'A friend.'

I heard the sound of a baby crying, then more joining in. A buzzer went. The young nurse grimaced and I saw how stressed she looked.

'OK. He's in the on-call room. Third door on the right.'

I knocked on the door, the nurse watching me, and then I went in. The room was in semi-darkness, just lit by the open doorway. William woke up instantly, fully alert, presumably because he was on call and was expected to be functioning at a hundred per cent immediately.

'What are you doing here, Bee?'

No one but you has ever called me that and it was as if you'd lent him some of our closeness. He got out of bed and I saw that he was fully dressed in blue scrubs. His hair was tangled from where it had been on the pillow. I was conscious of the smallness of the room, the single bed.

'Do you know who gives the women on the CF trial their injection?' I asked.

'No. Do you want me to try to find out?'

That simple. 'Yes.'

'OK.' He was looking businesslike, totally focused, and I was grateful to him for taking me seriously. 'Are there any other patients, apart from your sister, that you know about?'

'Kasia Lewski and Hattie Sim. Tess met them at the CF clinic.'

'Can you write them down?'

He waited while I fumbled in my bag and wrote down their names, then gently took the piece of paper from me. 'Now can I ask why you want to know?'

'Because whoever he is wore a mask. When he gave the injections, when he delivered the babies.'

There was a pause and I sensed that any urgency he'd shared with me was dissipated.

'It's not that unusual for medical staff to wear masks, especially in obstetrics,' he said. 'Childbirth is a messy business, lots of body fluids around, medical staff wear protective gear as a matter of course.'

He must have seen the disbelief on my face, or my disappointment.

'It really is pretty routine, at least in this hospital,' he continued. 'We have the highest percentage of patients with HIV outside Johannesburg. We're tested regularly to avoid infecting our patients, but the same isn't true the other way

304

around. So we simply don't know when a woman comes through our doors whether or not she's ill or a carrier.'

'But what about giving the gene? Giving the injections?' I asked. 'That doesn't have fluids around does it? So why wear a mask then?'

'Maybe whoever it was has just got into the habit of being cautious.'

I had once found his ability to see the best in people endearing, reminding me of you, but now that same trait made me furious.

'You'd rather find an innocent explanation than think that someone murdered my sister and hid his identity with a mask?'

'Bee—'

'But I don't have the luxury of choosing. The ugly violent option is the only one open to me.' I took a step away from him. 'Do you wear a mask?'

'Often I do, yes. It might seem overly cautious but—'

I interrupted. 'Was it you?'

'What?'

He was staring at me and I couldn't meet his eye. 'You think I killed her?' he asked. He sounded appalled and hurt.

I was wrong about conflict with words being trivial.

'I'm sorry.' I made myself meet his eye. 'Someone murdered her. I don't know who it is. Just that it *is* someone. And I have probably met that person by now, talked to them, and not known. But I don't have a shred of proof.'

He took hold of my hand and I realised I was shaking.

His fingers stroked my palm, gently; too softly at first for me to believe that this was really a gesture of attraction. But as he continued I knew, hardly believing it, that there was no mistake.

I took my hand away from his. His face looked disappointed but his voice sounded kind. 'I'm not a very good bet, am I?'

Still astonished, and more than flattered, I went to the door.

Why did I leave that room with its possibilities? Because even if I could ignore the morality of him being married – not insurmountable I realised – I knew it wouldn't be long term or secure or anything else I wanted and needed. It would be a moment of passion, nothing more, and afterwards a heavy emotional debt would be exacted from me. Or maybe it was simply him calling me Bee. A name that only you used. A name that made me remember who I had been for so many years. A name that didn't do this.

So I closed the door behind me and stayed wobbling but still upright on my narrow moral tightrope. Not because I was highly principled. But because I again chose safety rather than risk short-term happiness.

On the road a little way from the hospital I waited for a night bus. I remembered how strong his arms had felt when he'd hugged me that time, and the gentleness of his fingers as he'd stroked my palm. I imagined his arms around me now and the warmth of him – but I was alone in the dark and the cold, regretting now my decision to leave, regretting that I was a person who would always, predictably, leave.

I turned to go back, even started walking a few steps, when I thought I heard someone, just a few feet away. There were two unlit alleys leading off the road, or maybe he was crouching behind a parked car. Preoccupied before, I hadn't noticed that there were virtually no cars on the road, and no one on the pavements. I was alone with whoever was watching me.

I saw a black cab, without a light on, and stuck out my hand praying he would stop for me, which he did, chastising me for being on my own in the middle of the night. I spent money I no longer had on him driving me all the way home. He waited until I was safely inside the flat before driving off.

☙

Mr Wright looks at me with concern, and I'm aware of how ill I feel. My mouth is as dry as parchment. I drain the glass of water his secretary has left for me. He asks if I'm OK to carry on, and I say yes; because I find it reassuring to be with him and because I don't want to be on my own in the flat.

'Did you think about the man following Tess?' asks Mr Wright.

'Yes. But it was a sense of someone watching me, and a sound I think, because something alerted me, but I didn't actually see anyone.'

He suggests we get a sandwich and go into the park for a working picnic. I think it's because I'm becoming groggy and inarticulate and he hopes that a spell outside will wake me up. He picks up the tape recorder. It never occurred to me that it might be portable.

We get to St James's Park, which looks like that scene from *Mary Poppins*, all blossom and buds and blue sky with white meringue clouds. Office workers are splayed over the grass, turning the park into a beach without a sea. We walk side by side, closely, along a path looking for somewhere less crowded. His kind face is looking at mine, and I wonder if he can feel my warmth as I feel his.

A woman with a double buggy comes towards us and we have to go single file. On my own for a few moments I feel a sudden sense of loss, as if the warmth has gone from the left-hand side of my body now that he isn't there. It makes me think of lying on a cold concrete floor, on my left side, feeling the chill of it go into me, hearing my heart beat too fast, unable to move. I'm panicking, fast-forwarding the story, but then he's beside me again and we get back in step and I'll return to the correct sequence.

We find a quiet spot and Mr Wright spreads out a rug for us to sit on. I am touched that when he saw blue sky this morning he thought ahead to a picnic in the park with me.

He switches on the tape recorder. I pause a moment while a group of teenagers walks past then I begin.

'Kasia woke up when I got in, or maybe she'd been waiting up for me. I asked her if she could remember the doctor who'd given her the injection.'

⁂

She pulled your dressing gown around herself.

'I don't know name,' she said. 'Is there problem?'

'Was he wearing a mask, is that why you don't know?'

'Yes, a mask. Something bad? Beata?'

Her hand moved unconsciously to her bump. I just couldn't frighten her.

'Everything's fine. Really.'

But she's too astute to be fobbed off so easily. 'You said Tess baby not ill. Not have CF. When you came to flat. When you ask Mitch to get tested.'

I hadn't realised that she'd really understood. She'd probably been brooding about it ever since but hadn't questioned me, presumably trusting me to tell her if there was something she needed to know.

'Yes, that's true. And I'm trying to find out more. But it's nothing to do with you. You and your baby are going to be fine, right as rain.'

She smiled at 'right as rain', an expression that she'd recently learned; a smile that seemed forced, on cue for me.

I gave her a hug. 'You really will be all right. Both of you. I promise.'

I couldn't help you and Xavier, but I would help her. No one was going to hurt her or her baby.

⁂

A little way away the teenagers are playing a game of soft-ball and I wonder for a moment what the person who listens to these tapes will make of the background noises of the park, the laughter and chatter around us.

'And the next day you got an email from Professor Rosen?' Mr Wright asks.

'Yes. On Saturday morning at around ten fifteen.'

I was on my way to work a shift for 'weekend brunch', a new idea of Bettina's.

'I noticed it was sent from his personal email,' I continue, 'rather than the Chrom-Med one he'd used before.'

Mr Wright looks down at a copy of the email.

To: Beatrice Hemming's iPhone
From: alfredrosen@mac.com
I have just come back from my American lecture tour to your message. As is my custom on these trips, I do not take my mobile with me. (My close family members have the number of the hotel should I need to be contacted urgently.) It is *ludicrous* to say that my trial is in any way dangerous to the babies. The whole point of my trial is that it's a safe way of getting the healthy gene into the body. It is to affect a cure in the safest possible way. Alfred Rosen. Professor. MA Cantab. MPhil. Ph.D.

From: Beatrice Hemming's iPhone
To: alfredrosen@mac.com
Can you explain why the doctor at St Anne's wore a mask, both when he delivered the babies and when he gave the injections of the gene?

From: alfredrosen@mac.com

309

Clearly medical staff wear appropriate protection when they deliver babies but it is not my area of expertise so if you are concerned I suggest you ask someone in obstetrics.

In terms of the injections, whoever it was must have completely missed the point of my chromosome. Unlike a virus, it carries no infection risk whatsoever. There is no need for such precautions. Perhaps, they are just in the habit of being cautious? However, at your sister's funeral I said I would answer your questions so I will look into it. I very much doubt there will be anything to find.

I didn't know whether to trust him or not. I certainly didn't know why he was helping me.

❧

Bettina's brunch initiative was a success and by twelve the Coyote was packed. I saw William pushing his way through, trying to get my attention. He smiled at my evident astonishment.

'Cressida, our Senior Midwife, told me you worked here; I hope that's OK.'

I remember I'd given her my contact details at the flat and the Coyote when she was looking for your notes.

Bettina grinned at me and took over the drinks order I was doing, so that I could talk to William. I was perplexed that she wasn't more surprised at a beautiful man coming to see me. I went down to the end of the bar and he followed me.

'I couldn't find out who gave Tess the injection, or the other women, their notes have seemingly just disappeared without trace. I'm sorry. I shouldn't have offered to do it.'

But I'd already realised it would be impossible for him. If no one could find out who was with you when you gave birth to Xavier, an event covering at least a few hours, it would be impossible for him, without notes, to find out who gave you an injection, which presumably was quick and uneventful.

'I knew I'd let you down,' continued William. 'So I did a bit of asking around at the genetic clinic. Pulled in a few favours. I've got you these.'

He handed me a packet of hospital notes as if giving me flowers. 'Your shreds of proof, Bee.'

I saw the notes were Mitch's.

'Michael Flanagan is Kasia Lewski's partner,' William said and I realised how little I'd told him about my friendship with Kasia. 'He isn't a carrier of the cystic fibrosis gene.'

So Mitch had got himself tested – and clearly hadn't told Kasia the results. I presumed that like Emilio he had assumed – or chosen to assume – that he wasn't the father of her baby. I imagined his relief at the result, his get-out clause, turning Kasia into the trollop who'd tricked him. I wondered if he could really believe that.

From my silence and lack of excitement, William thought I hadn't understood. '*Both* parents need to be carriers of the cystic fibrosis gene for their baby to have it. This dad doesn't carry the CF gene so there's no way the baby could have had it. I don't know what's going on with the CF trial but something's clearly very wrong and these notes prove it.'

Again he misinterpreted my silence. 'I'm sorry. I should have listened to you properly, supported you from the beginning. But you can take these to the police, can't you? Or would you like me to?'

'It won't do any good.'

He looked at me, perplexed.

'Kasia, his former partner, she's the type of person people make mistakes about. The police will think that she was wrong about Michael Flanagan being the father, or lied about it. Just like they did with my sister.'

'You don't know that for sure.'

But I did, because I myself had once been prejudiced against Kasia. I knew DI Haines would see her, as I once had, as a girl who most probably slept around; a girl who could easily be mistaken, or lie, about the father of her baby.

William's bleep went off, a strange sound amongst the conversations and clinking drinks at the bar. 'I'm sorry, I have to go.'

I remembered he only had twenty minutes to get back to the hospital.

'Will you make it?'

'Absolutely. I brought the bike.'

As he left, I saw Bettina grinning at me again. I returned her smile. Because despite the fact that his shreds of proof were worthless I was buoyed up. For the first time someone was on my side.

Bettina sent me home early, as if giving me a present for my smile.

When I got home, I found Kasia on her knees scrubbing the kitchen floor.

'What on earth are you doing?'

She looked up at me, face sweating. 'They said it be good for baby; get in right position.' Your flat had quickly come to resemble hers, everything gleaming around the chips and the rust and the stains. 'Anyway, I said. I like cleaning.'

She told me that when she was a child her mother worked

312

long shifts at a factory. After school, Kasia would scrub and polish so that when her mother got home the apartment would sparkle for her. It's a gift, Kasia's cleaning.

I didn't tell her that Mitch wasn't a carrier of the CF gene. I hadn't yet told her that Hattie's baby had died. Last night I'd thought I was protecting her, but now I wondered if I was betraying her trust in me. I honestly didn't know which was true.

'Here,' I said, handing her tickets. 'I have something for you.'

She took the tickets from me, a little bemused.

'I couldn't afford the air fare to Poland, so these are just coach tickets, six weeks after your baby is due. There's one for each of us, the baby will travel free.'

I thought that she should take her baby to Poland to meet his grandparents, all four of them, and her uncles and aunts and cousins. She has a cat's cradle of relations for this baby to be supported by. Mum and Dad both being only children meant we had no web of relations to fall back on. Our family was pre-shrunk before we were born.

Kasia was just staring at the tickets, uncharacteristically quiet.

'And I've got you support stockings, because my friend who's a doctor says you must be careful not to get a thrombosis, *zakrzepica*,' I said, translating the last word into Polish, which I'd looked up before. I couldn't read her expression, and was worried I was imposing.

'I don't have to stay with your family. But I really don't think you should go that far with a new baby on your own.'

She kissed me. I realised that, despite everything, this was the first time I'd seen her cry.

✿

I have told Mr Wright about Mitch's notes.

'I thought that was another reason poor single girls were being chosen – they were less likely to be believed.'

The sunshine has made me feel sleepier rather than waking me up. I finish telling Mr Wright about Mitch's notes.

It's now an effort to be coherent.

'Then I gave Kasia tickets to Poland and she cried.'

My intellect is too unfocused now to decide what is relevant.

'That night I realised, properly, how brave she'd been. I'd thought her naive and immature, but she's actually really courageous and I should have seen that when she stood up for me with Mitch, knowing that she'd be hit for it.'

The bruises on her face and the welts on her arms were clear enough badges of courage. But so too was her smiling and dancing in the face of whatever was thrown at her. Like you, she has the gift of finding happiness in small things. She pans life for gold and finds it daily.

And so what if, like you, she loses things? It's no more a sign of immaturity than my knowledge of where my possessions are is a sign of my adulthood. And imagine acquiring a new language and only learning the words to describe a wonderful world, refusing to know the words for a bleak one and in doing so linguistically shaping the world that you inhabit. I don't think that's naive, but fantastically optimistic.

The next morning I knew that I had to tell her what was going on. Who was I to think that after what happened to you, I could look after another person?

'I was going to tell her, but she was already on her mobile phoning half of Poland to tell them about bringing the baby to see them. And then I got another email from Professor

314

Rosen, asking to meet me. Kasia was still chatting to her family when I left the flat.'

⁂

I met Professor Rosen, at his suggestion, at the entrance to the Chrom-Med building, which was bustling despite it being Sunday. I was expecting him to escort me to his office but instead he led me to his car. We got in and he locked the doors. The demonstrators were still there – a distance away – and I couldn't hear their chants.

Professor Rosen was trying to sound calm but there was a shake in his voice that he couldn't control. 'An active virus vector has been ordered under my cystic fibrosis trial number at St Anne's.'

'What does that mean?' I asked.

'Either there's been a monumental cock-up,' he said and I thought that he never used words like 'cock-up', that this was as extreme as his language would get. 'Or a different gene is being tested out at St Anne's, one that needs an active virus vector, and my cystic fibrosis trial is being used as a cover.'

'The cystic fibrosis trial has been hijacked?'

'Maybe, yes. If you want to be melodramatic about it.'

He was trying to belittle what was happening, but couldn't quite pull it off.

'For what?' I asked.

'My guess is that, *if* an illegal trial is happening, it is for genetic enhancement, which in the UK is illegal to test on humans.'

'What kind of enhancement?'

'I don't know. Blue eyes, high IQ, big muscles. The list of absurdity goes on. But whatever gene it is, it needs an active virus vector to transport it.'

He was talking as a scientist, in facts, but beneath the words his emotion was clear. He was livid.

'Do you know who is giving the injection of the CF gene therapy at St Anne's?' I asked.

'I don't have access to that type of information. They keep us very much inside our own pigeonholes at Chrom-Med. It's not like a university, no cross-pollination of ideas or information. So no, I don't know the doctor's name. But if I were him or her I would administer the genetic treatment for cystic fibrosis on foetuses who genuinely had CF and at the same time test the illicit gene. But maybe whoever it is became careless, or there just weren't enough patients.' He broke off and I saw the anger and hurt in him. 'Someone is trying to make babies even more perfect in some way. But healthy is already perfect. *Healthy is already perfect.*' I saw that he was shaking.

I wondered then if you'd found out about the hijacked trial – and the hijacker's identity. Was that why you'd been murdered?

'You must tell the police.'

He shook his head, not meeting my eye.

'But you *have* to tell them.'

'It's still just conjecture.'

'My sister and her baby are dead.'

He stared through the windscreen as if driving the car rather than hiding in it. 'I need to get proof first that it's a rogue trial that's to blame. Once I have that proof I can save my cystic fibrosis trial. Otherwise my trial will be stopped in all hospitals until they've found out what's going on and that could be months away, or years away. It may never be resumed.'

'But the cystic fibrosis trial shouldn't be affected at all. Surely—'

He interrupted. 'When the press get hold of this, with their subtlety and intelligence, it won't be a maverick trial that's to blame for babies dying and God knows what else, it will be my cystic fibrosis trial.'

'I don't believe that's true.'

'Really? Most people are so poorly informed and poorly educated that they don't see a difference between genetic enhancement and genetic therapy.'

'But that's absurd—'

Again he interrupted. 'Mobs of imbeciles have hounded paediatricians, even attacked them, because they think *paedi*atrician is the same thing as *paedo*phile, so yes they will target the cystic fibrosis trial as wicked too because they won't understand there's a difference.'

'So why did you investigate in the first place?' I asked. 'If you're going to do nothing with the findings?'

'I investigated because I'd told you I'd answer your questions.' He looked at me, anger sparking in his face, furious with me for putting him in this position. 'I thought there'd be nothing to find.'

'So I'll have to go to the police without your support?' I asked.

He looked physically intensely uncomfortable, trying to smooth out the sharp creases of his pressed grey trouser legs, which wouldn't lie flat.

'The order of the virus vector could well be a mistake; computer glitches occur. Administrative errors happen worryingly frequently.'

'And that's what you'll tell the police?'

'It's the most credible explanation. So yes, that's what I'll tell them.'

'And I won't be believed.'

Silence hung between us like glass.

I broke it. 'What's this really about, curing babies or your own reputation?'

317

He unlocked the car doors, then turned to me. 'If your brother were an unborn baby now what would you have me do?'

I did hesitate, but only for a moment. 'I'd want you to go to the police and tell them the truth and then work like hell at saving your trial.'

He walked away from the car, not bothering to wait for me, not bothering to lock it again.

The woman with the spiky hair recognised him and yelled at him, 'Leave playing God to God!'

'If God had done his job properly in the first place we wouldn't need to,' he snapped at her. She spat at him.

The demonstrator with the grey ponytail shouted, 'Say no to designer babies!'

He pushed his way through them and went back into the building.

I didn't think Professor Rosen was wicked, but weak and selfish. He simply couldn't bear to give up his new-found status. But he had a mental alibi for his lack of action; exonerating circumstances that he could plead to himself – the cystic fibrosis cure *is* very important. You and I both know that.

I reached the tube station and only then realised that Professor Rosen had given me a crucial piece of information. When I'd asked him if he knew who was giving the injection on the CF trial at St Anne's, he'd said that he didn't know; that he didn't have access to that information. But he had talked about that person choosing patients, '*who genuinely had* CF and at the same time testing the illicit gene'. In other words the person giving the injection was the same person who was running the CF trial at St Anne's. It had to be, if that person was responsible for choosing who was on it. And finding out who was in charge of the CF trial at St Anne's was light years easier than finding the identity of someone giving a single injection.

֍

It's lovely out here, the sky a pure Wedgwood blue. As office workers straggle back to work, I remember at St Mary's how we had lessons outside when it was hot, the children and the teacher all pretending to be interested in a book while soaking up summer and for a moment I forget how cold I am.

'Do you think Professor Rosen meant to tell you?' Mr Wright asks.

'Yes. He's far too clever and too pedantic to be careless. I think that he salved his conscience by hiding this titbit of information and it was up to me to have the intelligence to find it. Or maybe his better self won out at this one point of our conversation. But whatever it was, I now just had to find out who was administering the trial at St Anne's.'

My legs are almost completely numb now. I'm not sure that when I try and stand up I'm going to be able to.

'I phoned William and he said that he would find out who was in charge of the CF trial and get back to me, hopefully by the end of the day. Then I phoned Kasia on her mobile but she was engaged, presumably still chatting to her family – although by now her phone credit would have run out and it must be them phoning her. I knew that she was going to meet some Polish friends from church, so I thought I'd tell her when she got back. When we'd know who was behind it all and she'd be safe.'

֍

In the meantime I went to meet Mum at Petersham Nursery to choose a plant for your garden, as we'd arranged. I was glad of the distraction; I needed to do something rather than pace the flat waiting for William to ring me.

Kasia had been on at me again to lay flowers at the toilets building for you.

She'd told me I'd be putting my '*odcisk palca*' of love onto something evil. (*Odcisk palca* is fingerprint, the nearest translation we could find, and a rather lovely one.) But that was for other people to do, not me. I had to find that evil and confront him head on, not with flowers.

After weeks of cold and wet, it was the first warm dry day of early spring and at the nursery camellias and primroses and tulips were unfolding into colour. I kissed Mum and she hugged me tightly back. As we walked, under the canopy of old greenhouses, it was as if we'd stepped back in time and into a stately home's garden.

Mum checked plants for frost-hardiness and repeat flowering while I was preoccupied – after searching for almost two months, by the end of the day I should know who killed you.

For the first time since I'd arrived in London, I felt too warm and took off my expensive thick coat, revealing the outfit underneath.

'Those clothes, they're awful, Beatrice.'

'They're Tess's.'

'I thought they must be. You have no money at all now?'

'Not really, no. Well some, but it's tied up in the flat until it's sold.'

I have to own up that I had been wearing your clothes for quite a while. My New York outfits seemed ludicrous outside that lifestyle, besides which I'd discovered how much more comfortable yours are. It should have felt odd, and definitely serious, to be wearing your dead sister's clothes but all I could imagine was your amusement at seeing me in your hand-me-downs of hand-me-downs; me who had to have the latest designer fashion, who had outfits dry-cleaned after one wearing.

'Do you know what happened yet?' asked Mum. It was the first time she'd asked me.

'No. But I think I will. Soon.'

Mum reached out her fingers and stroked a petal of an early flowering clematis. 'She'd have liked this one.'

And suddenly she was mute, a paroxysm of grief passing through her body that looked unbearable. I put my arm around her but she was unreachable. For a while I just held her, then she turned to me.

'She must have been so frightened. And I wasn't there.'

'She was an adult, you couldn't have been with her all the time.'

Her tears were a wept scream. 'I should have been with her.'

I remembered being afraid as a child, and the sound of her dressing gown rustling in the dark and the smell of her face cream, and how just the sound of her and the smell of her banished my fears and I wished she'd been with you too.

I hugged her tightly, trying to make myself sound believable.

'She wouldn't have known anything about it, I promise, nothing at all. He put a sedative into her drink so she'd have fallen asleep. She wouldn't have been afraid. She died peacefully.'

I had learned finally, like you, to put love before truth.

We carried on through the greenhouse, looking at plants, and Mum seemed a little soothed by them.

'So you won't be staying much longer then,' she said. 'As you'll know soon.'

I was hurt that she could think I could leave her again, after this.

'No. I'm going to stay, for good. Amias has said I can stay in the flat, pretty much rent free I think.'

My decision wasn't entirely selfless. I'd decided to train as an architect. Actually, I needn't put that in the past tense, it's what I still want to do when the trial is over. I'm not sure if they'll take me, or how I'll fund it and look after Kasia and her baby at the same time, but I want to try. I know my mathematical brain, obsessed with detail, will do the structural side well. And I'll search myself for something of your creative ability. Who knows? Maybe it's lying dormant somewhere, an unread code for artistic talent wrapped tightly in a coiled chromosome waiting for the right conditions to spring into life.

My phone went and I saw a text from William wanting to meet, urgently. I texted back the address of the flat. I felt sick with anticipation.

'You have to go?' asked Mum.

'In a little while, yes. I'm sorry.'

She stroked my hair. 'You still haven't had a haircut.'

'I know.'

She smiled at me, still stroking my hair. 'You look so like her.'

22

When I arrived home William was waiting for me at the bottom of the steps. He looked up at me, his face was white, his usual open expression pinched hard with anxiety.

'I've found out who's in charge of the cystic fibrosis trial at St Anne's. Can I come in? I don't think we should be . . .'

His normally measured voice was rushed and uneven. I opened the door and he followed me inside.

There was a moment before he spoke. I heard Granny's clock tick twice into the silence.

'It's Hugo Nichols.'

Before I could ask any questions William turned to me, his voice still quick, pacing now.

'I don't understand. Why on earth has he been putting babies without cystic fibrosis on the trial? What the hell's he been doing? I just don't understand.'

'The CF trial at St Anne's has been hijacked,' I replied. 'To test out another gene.'

'My God. How did you find that out?'

'Professor Rosen.'

'And he's going to the police?'

'No.'

There was a moment before he spoke. 'So it'll be up to me then. To tell them about Hugo. I'd hoped it would be someone else.'

'It's hardly telling tales, is it?'

'No. It's not. I'm sorry.'

But I still couldn't make sense of it. 'But why would a psychiatrist run a genetic therapy trial?'

'He was a research fellow at Imperial. Before he became a hospital doctor. I told you that, didn't I?'

I nodded.

'His research was in genetics,' continued William.

'You never said.'

'I never thought – my God – I just never thought it was relevant.'

'That was unfair of me. I'm sorry.'

I remembered William telling me that Dr Nichols was rumoured to have been brilliant and 'destined for greatness', but I'd thought the rumour must be wrong, believing instead my own opinion that he was scruffily hopeless. Remembering my view of Dr Nichols, I realised that I'd dismissed him as a suspect not only because I'd thought him too hopeless to be violent, nor even because I'd thought he had no motive, but because of my entrenched belief that he was fundamentally decent.

William sat down, his face strained, his hands drumming the arms of the sofa. 'I spoke to him about his research once, years ago now. He told me about a gene he'd discovered and that a company had bought it from him.'

'Do you know which company?'

'No. I'm not sure he even said. It was a long time ago. But I do remember some of what he said because he was so passionate, so different to how he usually is.' He was pacing again now, his movements jerky and angry. 'He told me it had been his life's ambition, actually no, he said it was his life's *purpose*, to get his gene into humans. He said he wanted to leave his fingerprint on the future.'

'Fingerprint on the future?' I echoed, repelled, thinking of your future being cut from you.

William thought I didn't understand. 'It meant he wanted to get his gene into the germ cells so it would be passed to future generations. He said he wanted to "improve what it is to be human". But although the animal tests went well he wasn't allowed to test his gene on humans. He was told it was genetic enhancement and it's illegal to use that in people.'

'What was "his" gene?' I asked.

'He said it increases IQ.'

William said that he hadn't believed him because it would have been such an extraordinary and astonishing achievement, and he was so young, and something else but I wasn't really listening. Instead I remembered my visit to Chrom-Med.

I remembered that IQ was measured by fear.

'I thought he had to have been making most of it up,' continued William. 'Or at least embellishing it a hell of a lot. I mean, if his research really was that glittering, why on earth leave it to go into humdrum hospital medicine? But he must have become a hospital doctor deliberately – waiting all this time for the opportunity to test out his gene in humans.'

I went into the garden as if I needed more literal space to accommodate the hugeness of these facts. I didn't want to be alone with them and was glad when William joined me.

'He must have destroyed Tess's notes,' William said. 'And then fabricated the real reason why the babies died, so that their deaths couldn't be connected to the trial. And somehow he managed to get away with it. Christ, it makes you talk like, I don't know, somebody else, somebody off the telly or something. This is Hugo I'm talking about for God's sake. A man I thought I knew. Liked.'

I'd been talking in that alien language since your body was found. I understood the realisation that your previous vocabulary can't describe what is happening to you now.

I looked at the little patch of earth where Mum and I had decided to plant the winter-flowering clematis for you.

'But someone else must have been part of this?' I said. 'He can't have been with Tess when she had her baby.'

'All doctors do six months obstetrics as part of their training, Hugo would know how to deliver a baby.'

'But surely someone would have noticed? A psychiatrist delivering a baby, surely someone . . . ?'

'The labour ward is heaving with people and we're desperately understaffed. If you see a white coat in a room you're just grateful and move on to the next potential calamity. Many of the doctors are locums and sixty per cent of our midwives are agency so they don't know who's who.' He turned to me, his expression harsh with anxiety. 'And he was wearing a mask, Bee, remember?'

'But surely someone . . .'

William took my hand. 'We're all so bloody busy. And we trust each other because it's just too exhausting and too much hassle to do anything else and we're naive enough to think our colleagues are there for the same purpose as we are – to be treating people and trying to make them well.'

His body was taut and his hands were clenched tightly around mine. 'He had me fooled too. I thought he was a friend.'

༈

Despite the warm sun and the woollen picnic rug, I am shivering.

'I realised that he'd been perfectly positioned all along,' I say. 'Who better than a psychiatrist to drive someone mad? To force someone into suicide? And I only had his word about what really happened at their session.'

'You thought he actually tried to force Tess into taking her life?'

'Yes. And then when she didn't – even though she was being mentally tortured to a sadistic degree – then he murdered her.'

I thought it no wonder Dr Nichols had been so adamant about his failure to diagnose puerperal psychosis – loss of professional face was a small price to pay next to murder.

Mr Wright glances at a note I remember him making much earlier. 'You said that Dr Nichols wasn't among the people you suspected of playing Tess the lullabies?'

'No. As I said, I didn't think he had a motive.' I pause a moment. 'And because I'd thought he was a hopeless but decent man who had owned up to a terrible mistake.'

I am still shivering. Mr Wright takes off his jacket and puts it around my shoulders.

'I thought Tess must have found out about him hijacking the CF trial and that's why he murdered her. Everything fitted into place.'

'Fitted into place' sounds so neat, a piece completing the jigsaw picture and proving satisfying rather than metal grinding into metal, blood spilling rust-coloured onto the ground.

❧

We stood in silence in your tiny back garden and I saw the green shoots had grown a good few centimetres along

327

the once-dead twigs, and that there were now tiny buds, everything alive and growing, the tight tiny buds containing the open-petalled flowers of summer.

'We'd better phone the police,' said William. 'Shall I do it or you?'

'You're probably more credible. No history of crying wolf or getting hysterical.'

'OK. What's the policeman's name?'

'Detective Inspector Haines. If you can't get him, ask for Detective Sergeant Finborough.'

He picked up his mobile. 'This is going to be bloody hard.' Then he dialled the number as I gave it to him, and asked for DI Haines.

As William spoke to DI Haines, telling him everything he had told me, I wanted to yell at Dr Nichols. I want to hit him, blow after blow; I wanted to kill him actually, and the sensation was oddly liberating. At last my rage had a target and it was a release to give way to it – finally throwing the grenade you've been holding for so long, pin out, that's been threatening to destroy you, and you're freed of the burden and tension as you hurl it.

William hung up. 'He's asked us to go down to the police station but wants us to give him an hour to get the top brass in.'

'You mean he's asked you to go.'

'I'm sorry, Bee, coming in at the last minute, the Americans at the end of the war and all that.'

'But if we're being honest, they're the reason we won.'

'I think both of us should go. And I'm glad we have a little time to ourselves first.'

He reached over to my face and stroked a strand of hair away from my eyes.

He kissed me.

I hesitated. Could I step off my mountainside – or that moral tightrope you had me on?

I turned and walked into the flat.

He followed me and I turned and kissed him back. And I was grabbing the moment as hard as I could and living it to the full because who knew when it would be taken away. If all your death has taught me it is that the present is too precious to waste. I finally understood the sacrament of the present moment, because it's all we have.

He undressed me and I shed my old self. All of me exposed. The wedding ring was no longer hanging around his neck, his chest bare. And as my cool skin felt the warmth of him on me, my safety ropes fell away.

❧

Mr Wright produces a bottle of wine from a carrier bag, with two plastic cups from the water dispenser at the CPS offices, and I think how like him it is to be so thoughtful and organised. He pours me a cup and I drink it straight down, which is probably not sensible. He doesn't comment on this, just as he didn't comment on me having sex with William and I like him so much for not being judgemental.

❧

We lay in your bed together, the low rays of early spring sunshine coming in through the basement window. I leaned against him and drank the tea he'd made for me, trying to make it last as long as possible, still feeling the warmth of his skin against mine, knowing that we would have to get out of bed, re-enter the world again; and I thought of Donne chastising the busy old fool of a sun for making him leave his lover and marvelled that his poetry now applied to me.

❧

329

For a moment the wine has boosted me a little, I can feel it warming my body.

'William went to the bathroom, and looked in the cupboard. He found a bottle of pills with a hospital label on them. It was the PCP. It had been there all the time. He said many drugs are illegal on the street but are legally prescribed by doctors for therapeutic reasons.'

'Did the label give the name of the prescribing doctor?'

'No, but he said the police could easily track it down to Dr Nichols through the hospital pharmacy records. I felt so stupid. I'd thought that an illegal drug would be hidden, not openly on show. It had been there all the time.'

I'm sorry; I'm starting to repeat myself. My mind is losing focus.

'And then . . . ?' he asks.

But we're nearly at the end, so I summon what remains of my mental energy and continue.

'We left the flat together. William had left his bike chained to the railings on the other side of the road, but it had been stolen, though they'd left the chain. He took that with us, and joked that we could report the theft of his bike at the same time.

⁂

We decided to walk through Hyde Park to the police station, rather than take the ugly road route. At the gates of the park there was a flower stall. William suggested we lay flowers where you'd died and went to buy some.

As he spoke to the stall-holder, I texted Kasia two words: 'odcisk palca' – and knew she'd understand that I was finally putting on my own fingerprint of love.

William turned to me, holding two bunches of daffodils.

330

'You told me they were Tess's favourite flower. Because of the yellow in a daffodil saving children's sight.'

I was pleased and surprised that he had remembered.

He put his arm around me and as we walked into the park together I thought I heard you teasing me, and I admitted to you that I was a big fat hypocrite. The truth is, I knew that the affair wouldn't last, that he'd stay married. But I also knew that I wouldn't be broken by it. I wasn't proud of myself but I did feel liberated from a person I no longer was or wanted to be. And as we walked together I felt small green shoots of hope and decided I would allow them to grow. Because now I had found out what had happened to you I could look forwards and dare to imagine a future without you. I remembered being here almost two months before, when I sat in the snow and wept for you amongst the lifeless, leafless trees. But now there were ball games and laughter and picnics and bright new foliage. It was the same place but the landscape was entirely changed.

We reached the toilet building and I took the cellophane off the daffodils, wanting them to look home-picked. As I laid them at the door a memory – or lack of one – tugged its way through, unbidden.

'But I never told you that she liked daffodils, or the reason.'

'Of course you did. That's why I chose them.'

'No. I talked about it with Amias. And Mum. Not you.'

I had actually told him very little about you, or me for that matter.

'Tess must have told you herself.'

Carrying his bunch of daffodils for you, he came towards me. 'Bee—'

'Stop calling me that.' I backed away from him.

He came closer then pushed me hard inside.

☙

'He shut the door behind us and put a knife against my throat.'

I break off, shaking from the adrenaline. Yes, his call to DI Haines had been faked. He probably got the idea from a daytime TV soap, they're on the whole time in the wards – I remember that from Leo. Maybe it was sheer desperation. And maybe I was too distracted to notice anything very much. Mr Wright is considerate enough not to point out my ludicrous gullibility.

The teenagers have abandoned their loud game of soft-ball for raucous music. The office workers picnicking have been replaced by mothers with pre-school children; their high barely formed voices quickly turning from shrieks of happiness into tears and back again, a mercurial quicksilver sound. And I want the children to be louder, the laughter more raucous, the music turned up full volume. And I want the park to be crowded with barely a place to sit. And I want the sunshine to be blinding.

He closed the door of the toilets building and used the bicycle chain to fasten it shut. There had never been a bicycle, had there? Light seeped through the filthy cracked windows and was turned dirty by them, casting the gloom of a nightmare. The sounds of the park outside – children laughing and crying, music from a CD player – were muffled by the damp bricks. Yes, it's uncanny how similar that day was to today in the park with Mr Wright, but maybe the sounds of a park remain the same, day to day, give or take. And in that cold, cruel building I also wanted the children to be louder, the laughter more raucous, the music turned up to full volume. Maybe because if I could hear them then there was a chance they could hear my screams; but no, it couldn't have been that because I knew if I screamed he would silence me with a knife. So it must have been simply that I wanted the comfort of hearing life as I died.

'You killed her, didn't you?' I asked.

If I'd been sensible maybe I should have given him a let-out, made out that I thought he had pushed me in there for some weird sort of sadistic sex, because once I'd accused him was he ever going to let me go? But he was never going to. Whatever I did or said. I had wild thoughts racing through my head about how you're meant to make friends with your kidnapper. (Where on earth did that nugget of information come from? And why did anyone think the general population would need to know such a thing?) Remarkably, I did, but I couldn't make friends with him because he'd been my lover and there was nowhere for us to go.

'I'm not responsible for Tess's death.'

For a moment I thought that he wasn't; that I'd read him all wrong; that everything would play out the way I'd been so sure of, with us going to the police and Dr Nichols being arrested. But self-deception isn't possible with a knife and a chain on the other side of the equation.

'I didn't want it to happen. I didn't *plan* it. I'm a doctor, for God's sake. I wasn't meant to kill anyone. Have you any idea what it feels like? It's a living hell.'

'So stop now with me. Please.'

He was silent. Fear pricked my skin into a hundred thousand goosebumps, a hundred thousand tiny hairs standing to upright attention as they offered their useless protection.

'You were her doctor?'

I had to keep him talking – not because I thought anyone was on their way to rescue me, but because a little longer to live, even in this building with this man, was precious.

And because I needed to know.

'Yes. I looked after her all through her pregnancy.'

You'd never mentioned his name, just said 'the doctor', and I hadn't asked, too busy multitasking with something else.

'We had a good rapport, liked each other. I was always kind to her.'

'You delivered Xavier?' I asked.

'Yes.'

I thought of the masked man in your nightmarish paintings, dark with menace in the shadows.

'She was relieved to see me in the park that day,' William continued. 'Smiled at me. I—'

I interrupted. 'But she was terrified of you.'

'The man who delivered the baby, not me.'

'But she must have known it was you, surely? Even with a mask, she must have recognised your voice at least. If you'd looked after her for all her pregnancy, surely . . .'

Still he was silent. I hadn't realised that it was possible to be more appalled by him.

'You didn't speak to her. While she was in labour. When she gave birth. Even when her baby was dead. You didn't speak to her.'

'I came back and comforted her, twenty minutes or so later. I've told you. I was always kind to her.'

So he'd taken off the mask, switching personas back into the caring man you thought he was; who I'd thought he was.

'I suggested I phoned someone for her,' he continued. 'And she gave me your number.'

You thought I knew. All that time, you thought I knew.

Mr Wright looks at me with concern. 'You look pale.'

'Yes.'

I feel pale, inside and out. I think of that expression 'paling into insignificance' and think how well it fits me, a pale person in a bright world that turns me invisible.

🙢

Outside I could hear people in the bright afternoon sunshine, but in the toilets building I was invisible to them. He'd taken off his tie and used it to bind my hands behind my back.

'You called her Tess, the first time I met you.'

Still keeping him talking – the only way to stay alive. And still needing to know.

'Yes, it was a stupid blunder,' he replied. 'And it shows I'm not good at this, doesn't it? I'm useless at subterfuge and lies.'

But he had been good at it. He'd manipulated me from the start, guiding conversations and subtly deflecting questions. From my wanting your notes to asking who was in charge of the CF trial at St Anne's he'd made sure I had no real information. He'd even given an excuse, in case his acting wasn't convincing.

'*Christ, it makes you talk like, I don't know, somebody else, somebody off the telly or something.*'

Because that was what he was imitating.

'I didn't *plan* this. A vandal threw a stone through her window not me; she just thought it was targeted at her.'

He was using twine to tie my legs together.

'The lullabies?' I asked.

'I was panicking, just doing whatever came into my head. The CD was in the post-natal ward. I took it home, not really knowing what I was doing. Not thinking anything

335

through. I never stopped to think she'd record the lullabies onto a tape. Who has an answerphone nowadays with a tape? Everyone's got an answer service with their telephone provider.'

He was lurching between the minutiae of the everyday and the large horror of murder. The enormity of what he had done ensnared in small domestic details.

'You knew Mitch's notes would be useless, because Kasia would never be believed.'

'The worst-case scenario was that you took her boyfriend's notes to the police. And made a fool of yourself.'

'But you needed me to trust you.'

'It was you who kept on going with this. Making me do this. You left me no other choice.'

But I'd trusted him before he produced Mitch's notes, long before. And it had been my insecurity that had helped him. I'd thought my suspicion of him was because of my customary anxiety around handsome men, rather than seriously suspecting him of your murder, and so had dismissed it. He was the one person in all this who'd been about me – not about you.

But I'd been thinking too long; I couldn't allow a silence to grow between us.

'It was you not Dr Nichols who was the researcher who found the gene?'

'Yes. Hugo's a sweet man. But hardly brilliant.'

His tale about Dr Nichols had been a boast as much as a deceit. I realised that he had been framing Dr Nichols from early on, carefully casting the shadow of guilt onto him so that it wouldn't fall on himself. The long-term planning was viciously calculated.

'Imperial College and their absurd ethics committee wouldn't allow a human trial,' continued William. 'They didn't have the vision. Or the guts to go for it. Imagine it, a gene that increases IQ, think of what that means. Then Chrom-Med approached me. My only requirement was that they ran human trials.'

'Which they did.'

'No. They lied; let me down. I—'

'You really believe that? The directors of Chrom-Med are pretty bright. I've read their biographies. They're certainly clever enough to want someone else to do their work for them. To take the rap in case it went wrong.'

He shook his head, but I could see I'd got to him. An avenue was opening up and I ran hell for leather down it. 'Genetic enhancement, that's where the real money lies, isn't it? As soon as it becomes legal it'll be huge. And Chrom-Med want to be ahead of the game, ready for it.'

'But they can't know.'

'They've been playing you, William.'

But I'd done it wrong, too scared to be as slick as I'd needed to be; I'd simply dented his ego and released new anger. He'd been holding the knife almost casually, now his fingers tightened around it.

'Tell me about the human trial, what happened?'

His fingers were still gripping the knife, but the knuckles no longer showed white, so he wasn't gripping as hard. In his other hand he held a torch. He had come equipped for this: knife and torch and bicycle chain, a grotesque parody of a Boy Scout trip. I wondered what else he'd thought to bring.

꘏

Mr Wright holds my hand and I'm again overwhelmingly grateful, not brushing away kindness any more.

337

'He told me that in humans his IQ gene codes for two totally different things. It affects not only memory capacity but also lung function. It meant that the babies couldn't breathe when they were born.'

I'm so sorry, Tess.

'He told me that if the babies are intubated immediately after they're born, if they're helped to breathe for a while, they'd be fine. They'd live.'

�֍

He had made me lie on the floor, on my left side, the damp cold of the concrete was seeping into my body. I tried to move but my limbs were too heavy. He must have drugged me when he gave me the tea. I could only use words to stay alive.

'But you didn't help them to breathe, did you? Xavier. Hattie's baby.'

'It wasn't my fault. It's a rare lung disorder and someone would ask questions. I just need to be left alone. Then there would be no problems. It's other people, crowding around me, not giving me space.'

'So you lied to them about what really killed their babies?'

'I couldn't risk people asking questions.'

'And me? Surely you're not going to stage my suicide, like you staged Tess's? Frame me for my own murder like you did my sister? Because if it happens twice the police are bound to be suspicious.'

'Staged? You make it sound so thought out. I didn't plan it, I told you that. You can see that because of my mistakes,

338

can't you? My research and my trial I planned in meticulous detail, but not this. I was forced into doing this. I even paid them, for God's sake, not stopping to think that it might look suspicious. And I never thought they might talk to each other.'

'So why did you pay them?'

'It was just kindness, that's all. I just wanted to make sure they had a decent diet, so the developing foetuses had the optimum conditions. It was meant to be spent on food, not bloody clothes.'

I didn't dare ask him if there were others or how many. I didn't want to die with that knowledge. But there were some things I needed to know.

'What made you choose Tess? Because she was single? Poor?'

'And Catholic. Catholic women are far less likely to terminate when they know there's a problem with their baby.'

'Hattie is Catholic?'

'Millions of Filipinos are Catholic. Hattie Sim put it on her form, no father's name mind you, but her religion.'

'Did her baby have cystic fibrosis?'

'Yes. Whenever I could I treated the cystic fibrosis and tested my gene out too. But there weren't enough babies who fitted all the criteria.'

'Like Xavier?'

He was silent.

'Did Tess find out about your trial? Is that why you killed her?'

He hesitated a moment. His tone was close to self-pitying; I think that he genuinely hoped I would understand.

'There was another consequence that I hadn't foreseen. My gene got into the mother's ovaries. It means there is the same genetic change in every egg and if the women have more

339

babies they will have the same problem with their lungs.

Logistically I couldn't expect to be there for the next baby, or the next. People move house, move away. Eventually someone would discover what was going on. That's why Hattie had to have a hysterectomy. But Tess's labour was too quick. She arrived at the hospital with the baby's head already engaged. There wasn't time to do a caesarean, let alone an emergency hysterectomy.'

You hadn't found out anything at all.

He killed you because your body was living evidence against him.

⁂

Around us people are starting to leave the park, the grass turning from green to grey, the air cooling into evening. My bones ache with cold and I focus on the warmth of Mr Wright's hand, holding mine.

'I asked him what made him do it; suggested it was money. He was furious, told me his motives weren't avaricious. Impure. He said he wouldn't be able to sell a gene, which hadn't been legally trialled. Fame wasn't motivating him either. He couldn't publish his results.'

'So did he tell you the reason?'

'Yes.'

I'll tell you what he said out here, in this grey-green park in the cool fresh air. Neither of us need to return to that building to hear him.

'He said that science has the power that religion once claimed, but it's real and provable, not superstition and cant. He said that miracles don't happen in fifteenth-century churches but in research labs and hospitals. He said the dead are brought back to life in ITU units; the lame walk again after hip replacements; the blind see again because of laser surgery. He told me that in the new millennium there are new deities with real, provable powers and that the deities are scientists who are improving what it is to be human. He said that his gene would one day safely get into the gene pool and that would mean who we are as humans would be irrevocably changed for the better.'

His overweening hubris was huge and naked and shocking.

⁂

He was shining his torch in my face and I couldn't see him. I was still trying to move but my body had been too drugged by the spiked tea to respond to my brain's screamed commands for action.

'You followed her into the park that day?'

I dreaded hearing it, but I needed to know how you died.

'When the boy left, she sat on a bench and started writing a letter, in the snow. Extraordinary thing to do, don't you think?'

He looked at me, waiting for my response, as if this were a regular conversation and I realised I would be the first and last person to whom he'd tell his story. Our story.

'I waited a while, to make sure the boy wasn't coming back. Ten minutes maybe. She was relieved when she saw me, I told you that, didn't I? She smiled. We had a good rapport. I'd brought a Thermos of hot chocolate and gave her a cup.'

⁂

The grey park is darkening now into soft pansy purples and blacks.

341

'He told me that the hot chocolate was full of dissolved sedative. After he'd drugged her, he pulled her into the toilets building.'

I feel overwhelmed by exhaustion and my words are sluggish. I imagine them inching along, slow, ugly words.

'Then he cut her.'

I'll tell you what he said; you have the right to know, although it will be painful for you. No, painful is the wrong word entirely. Even the memory of his voice makes me so afraid that I am five years old alone in the dark with a murderer bashing down the door and no one to help me.

'It's easy for a doctor to cut. Not at first. The first time a doctor cuts into skin, it feels a violation. The skin, the largest human organ, covering the entire body unbroken and you deliberately harm it. But after the first time it no longer feels an abuse, because you know that it's to enable a surgical procedure. Cutting is no longer violent or violating but the necessary step to healing.'

Mr Wright tightens his warm fingers around mine.

My legs are turning numb now.

꽃

I could hear my heart beating fast and hard against the concrete; the only part of my body that was alert as I looked at him. And then, astonishingly, I saw him put the knife into the inside pocket of his jacket.

Optimism heated my numbed body.

He helped me sit up.

He told me that he wasn't going to cut me because an overdose is less suspicious than a knife.

342

I can't use his actual words. I just can't.

He said he had already given me enough sedative in the tea to make it impossible for me to struggle or escape. And that now he was going to give me a fatal dose. He assured me that it would be peaceful and painless and it was the false kindness of his words that made them so unbearable, because it was himself he was comforting.

He said he'd brought his own sedatives but didn't need to use them.

He took a bottle out of his pocket, the sleeping pills Todd had brought with him from the States, prescribed for me by my doctor. He must have found them in the bathroom cupboard. Like the bicycle chain and the torch and the knife, the bottle of sleeping pills showed his detailed planning and I understood why premeditated murder is so much worse than spontaneous killing; he had been evil for far longer than the time it would actually take to kill me.

❧

The dusk has brought the chill of darkness. They're shutting the gates now, the last of the teenagers are packing up to go. The children will already be at home for baths and bedtime but Mr Wright and I remain, not finished yet. For some reason they haven't made us leave. Maybe they didn't notice us here. And I'm grateful because I need to keep going. I need to reach the end.

My legs have lost all feeling and I'm worried Mr Wright will have to carry me, fireman style, out of the park. Or maybe he will get an ambulance to drive all the way in.

But I will finish this first.

❧

I pleaded with him. Did you do that too? I think that you did. I think that like me you were desperate to stay alive. But of course it didn't work, it just irritated him. As he twisted the cap off the bottle of sleeping pills, I summoned the residue of my physical energy and tried logical argument.

'If I'm found here, in the same place as Tess, it's bound to make the police suspicious. And it'll make them question Tess's death too. It's madness to do it here – isn't it?'

For a moment the irritation left his face and he stopped twisting the cap and I'd won a reprieve in this perverted balloon debate.

Then he smiled, as if reassuring me as much as himself that I needn't have such worries. 'I did think about that. But the police know how you've been since Tess died; they already see you as a little unhinged, don't they? And even if they don't get it themselves, any psychiatrist will tell them that you *chose* this place to kill yourself. You wanted to kill yourself where your little sister had died.'

He took the cap off the bottle of sleeping pills.

'After all, if we're being logical, who in their right mind would choose to end the life of two people in the same building?'

'End the life.' He was turning brutal killing into something passive; as if it was assisted euthanasia not murder.

As he poured the pills into his cupped hand I wondered who would question my suicide or vouch for my sane state of my mind. Dr Nichols, at whom I had furiously sung the lullaby? Even if he thought I wasn't suicidal at our last meeting he would probably doubt that diagnosis, as he did with you, and blame himself for not seeing the signs. And DI Haines? He already thought I was overly emotional and irrational, and I doubted DS Finborough, even if he wanted to try, could convince him otherwise. Todd thought I was 'unable to accept

344

the facts', and many others agreed, even if they were too kind to say so to my face. They'd think that, in emotional turmoil after your death, irrational and depressed, I could easily have become suicidal. The sensible, conventional person I'd been a few months ago would never have been found dead from an overdose in this place. They would have asked questions for her but not for the person I had become.

And Mum? I'd told her I was about to find out what happened to you and I knew she would tell the police that. But I knew too that they wouldn't believe her, or rather what I'd said to her. And I thought that after a while Mum wouldn't believe it either, because she'd choose to bear the guilt of my suicide rather than think that I had felt a moment of this fear. And I found it unbearable to imagine her anguish when she'd have to mourn me too, with no one to comfort her.

He put the empty bottle in my coat pocket. Then he told me that the post-mortem must show I swallowed the pills whole because that would make it look voluntary. I am trying to shut out his voice but it breaks in, refusing to be silenced.

'Who can make another person swallow pills against their will?'

He held a knife to my throat; in the darkness I could feel the cold edge of metal against the warmth of my skin.

'This isn't what I am. It's like a nightmare and I've turned into a stranger.'

I think he expected my pity.

He put his hand with the pills in it up to my mouth. The bottle had been full which meant at least twelve pills. The dose was one in twenty-four hours. Any more was dangerous. I remembered reading that on the label. I knew that twelve would be more than enough to kill me. I remembered Todd telling me I should take one, but refusing because I had to stay alert; because I wasn't allowed a few

345

hours of drugged oblivion, however much I craved it; because I knew taking a sedative would be a cowardly reprieve which I'd want to repeat over and over again. This is what I was thinking as he pushed the pills into my mouth, my tongue uselessly trying to stop him.

Then he tipped water from a mineral water bottle into my mouth and told me to swallow.

⚜

It's dark now, countryside black. I think of all the nocturnal creatures, which are out here now the humans have gone home. I think of that storybook we had about the teddy bears coming out at night to play in the park. '*There goes the bear at number three, sliding down the slide.*'

'Beatrice . . . ?'

Mr Wright is helping me along, prompting and coaxing so I can finish this statement. His hand still holds mine but I can hardly see his face any more.

'Somehow I managed to wedge the pills behind my teeth and inside my cheeks, and the water went down my throat with just one, maybe two, I think. But I knew it wouldn't be long before they all dissolved in my own saliva. I wanted to spit them out, but his torch was still full on my face.'

'And then?'

'He took a letter out of the inside pocket of his jacket. It was from Tess to me. It must have been the one she was writing on the park bench just before she died.'

I pause, my tears falling onto the grass, or maybe onto Mr Wright, in the dark I can't tell.

'He shone his torch on her letter so he could read it out to me. It meant that the torch was no longer shining on me. I had a brief opportunity and I hung my head down towards

346

my knees, and spat out the sleeping pills onto my lap. They fell into the folds of my coat and made no sound.'

You know what you wrote to me, but it was William's voice not yours that I heard; William's voice telling me of your fear, your desperation, your grief. It was your murderer's voice telling me that you walked the streets and through parks, too afraid to be in the flat, that you yelled up at the dark winter sky at a God you no longer believed in, yelling at him to give your baby back. And that you thought this was also a sign of your madness. It was your killer who told me that you couldn't understand why I hadn't come over, hadn't phoned, hadn't answered your calls. It was the man who killed you who told me that you were sure there was a good reason; and his voice as he spoke your written words violated their faith in me. But at the end of your letter your soft voice whispered to me beneath his:

'I need you, right now, right this moment, please Bee.'

Then, as now, your words pricked my face with tears.

'He put the letter back in his pocket, presumably to destroy it later. I'm not sure why he kept it or why he read it to me.'

But I think it's because, like me with Mr Wright earlier, his guilt was desperate for some company.

'I need you. Right now, right this moment, please Bee.'

He wanted to make me as culpable in some way as he was.

'And then?' asks Mr Wright, needing to prompt me now to make sure I remember all of it. But we're nearly finished.

'He switched off my phone and put it near the door where I couldn't reach it. Then he took a scarf of mine out of his pocket, he must have taken it from the flat. He tied it around my mouth, gagging me.'

As he gagged me, panicking thoughts filled my head, one bashing into the other, a six-lane highway of thoughts, all happening simultaneously, backing up, bumper to bumper, unable to get out and I thought that some would be released simply by screaming, others by crying, others if I was held. Most of my thoughts had become primal and physical. I hadn't known before that it's our bodies that think most powerfully, and that was why it was so cruel to be gagged. It wasn't because I couldn't shout for help – who'd hear me in an empty building in the middle of a deserted park? It was because I couldn't scream or sob or moan.

'Then his bleep went off. He phoned the hospital on his mobile and said that he'd be on his way. I suppose it would have looked too suspicious not to go.'

I hear myself catch my breath in the darkness.

'Beatrice?'

'I worried that Kasia was in labour and that was why he was leaving.'

Mr Wright's hand feels solid in the darkness. I am reassured by the definition of his knuckles in my soft palm.

'He checked the gag and the ties around my wrists and legs. He told me that he'd come back and remove them later, so that nothing would look suspicious when I was found. He still didn't know I'd spat out so many of the pills. But I knew if I was still alive when he came back he'd use the knife, as he did on Tess.'

'*If* you were still alive?'

'I wasn't sure how many pills I'd swallowed, or how much sedative had dissolved in my saliva, if it was enough to kill me.'

I try to just focus on Mr Wright's hand holding mine.

'He left. Minutes later, my pager went off. He'd turned off my phone but he didn't know about the pager. I tried

to persuade myself that Kasia was paging me for something
trivial. After all, her baby wasn't due for another three
weeks.'

Yes, like you.

Mr Wright strokes my fingers, and the gentleness of it
makes me want to cry.

'And then?' he asks.

'He'd taken the torch with him. I'd never been in such
total darkness.'

I was alone in the black. Pitch black. Pitch that is made
from tar.

The blackness smelled rotten, putrid with fear. It smothered my face going into my mouth and nose, and I was
drowning and I thought of you on holiday in Skye, coming
out of the sea, spluttering and pink-cheeked – *'I'm OK! Just
seawater going up the wrong way!'* – and I took a breath. The
blackness choked my lungs.

I saw the darkness move – a monstrous, living thing, filling
the building and out into the night beyond, no skin of sky
to contain it. I felt it dragging me with it into a void of infi-
nite fear – away from light, life, love, hope.

I thought of Mum in her rustling silk dressing gown,
smelling of face cream, coming towards our beds, but the
memory of her was padlocked into childhood and couldn't
lighten the darkness.

I wait for Mr Wright to prompt me further. But there is no
further to go. We have finally arrived at the end.

It's finished now.

I try to move my hands but they are bound tightly together
with a tie. The fingers of my right hand are tightly clasped

around my left. I wonder if it's because I am right-handed that my right hand has taken the role of comforter.

I am alone in the pitch black, lying on a concrete floor.

My mouth is as dry as parchment. The harsh cold concrete has seeped into my body numbing me through to the bone.

I begin a letter to you, my beloved younger sister. I pretend it's Sunday evening, my most safe time, and that I'm surrounded by press all wanting to tell our story.

Dearest Tess,

I'd do anything to be with you, right now, right this moment, so I could hold your hand, look at your face, listen to your voice. How can touching and seeing and hearing – all those sensory receptors and optic nerves and vibrating eardrums – be substituted by a letter? But we've managed to use words as go-betweens before, haven't we?

I think back to boarding school and the first letter you ever sent me, the one with invisible ink and that ever since kindness has smelled of lemons.

And as I think of you and talk to you I can breathe again.

23

Hours must have passed so he will surely be back soon. I don't know how much sedative I swallowed, but all through this night I have felt a torpor of exhaustion sucking the warmth from my body and the clarity from my brain. I think I have slipped in and out of consciousness, in total darkness how could I tell? But if so, in my unnatural forced sleep I was still talking to you and maybe that was when my imaginings became peculiarly vivid.

Now I feel wide awake, all senses tense, buzzing and jittery; it must be adrenaline – a fight or flight hormone that's powerful enough to restart a heart after a cardiac arrest; so powerful enough to startle me into consciousness.

I try to move, but my body is still too doped and numb and the bindings too tight. The darkness feels almost solid now – not velvety like storybooks, not smooth and soft, but with spikes of fear and if you prodded it you'd find hard jagged evil crouching behind it. I can hear something inches away from my face as I lie on the concrete, a mouse? An insect? I have lost sense of auditory perspective. My cheek feels sore, it must be pressed into a little unevenness in the concrete.

What if it isn't adrenaline that's keeping me awake, but I am properly conscious now? Perhaps I swallowed less sedative than I feared – or have somehow come through the other side of the overdose and survived it.

But it makes no difference. Even if my body isn't fatally drugged, I am tied up and gagged and William will be back. And then he'll discover that I'm alive. And he'll use the knife.

So, before he returns I need to make things clear to you. Everything happened as I told you, beginning with Mum's phone call telling me you'd gone missing, to the moment William left me here to die. But my ending will be the same as yours, here in this building, untold. I didn't have the courage to face that, or maybe I just love life too much to let it go so quietly. I couldn't fantasise a happy ever after but I did imagine an ending that was just. And I made it as real as I could, my safe fantasy future, all details in place.

I worry that you've been waiting for DS Finborough to save me, but I think you felt a judder in the story when I told you about our lunch in Carluccio's. It was only a comforting rug of a daydream to lie on instead of cold concrete, and it wasn't admirable or courageous of me, but I know you understand.

And I think you'd already guessed, a little while ago, that there was no Mr Wright. I invented a lawyer not only so I could play my part in a just ending – a trial and guilty verdict – but because he would make me keep to verifiable facts and a strict chronology. I needed someone who would help me understand what happened and why – and who would stop me going mad. I'm not sure why being sane as I die is so important to me, just that it is, overwhelmingly. I do know that without him, my letter to you would have been a

352

stream-of-consciousness scream, raging despair, and I would have drowned in it.

I made him kind and endlessly patient as I told him our story; and bereaved so he would understand. Maybe I'm more Catholic than I realised and also made him my confessor but one who, even when he knew everything about me, may in some fantasy future have loved me. And during the long hours he became more real to me than the darkness around me; more than just a figment of a desperate imagination; acquiring his own personality and whims which I had to go along with; because he didn't always do my bidding or serve the purpose I asked of him. Instead of helping me paint a pointillist painting of what happened, I made a mirror and saw myself properly for the first time.

And around him I put a secretary with a crush and painted fingernails and daffodils and a coffee machine and inconsequential details which braided together made a rope of normality – because as I fell over the precipice of terror and my body became incontinent and retched and shook with fear, I needed to grab hold of something.

And I made his office overly bright, the electric light permanently on, and it was always warm.

My pager sounds. I try to shut my ears to it, but with my hands tied behind my back it's impossible. It has sounded all through the night, every twenty minutes or so I think, although I can't be certain how long I was fully conscious. I find it unbearable that I can't help her.

I hear the sound of trees outside, leaves rustling, boughs creaking; I never knew trees made so much noise. But no footsteps, yet.

Why isn't he back? It must be because Kasia is having her baby and he's been with her all this time, and is still with her now. But I will end up mad if I think this so instead I try to persuade myself that there could be any number of reasons why William was called to the hospital. He's a doctor; he gets bleeped all the time. His hospital delivers five thousand babies a year. It's for someone else that he's been called away.

And maybe DS Finborough investigated that 'query' he had about your death, as he said he would, and has arrested William and even now is on his way to find me. It isn't just wishful thinking; he *is* a diligent policeman and a decent man.

Or perhaps Professor Rosen has decided to do the right thing in the present and risked his mark on the future. Maybe he chanced his CF trial and academic glory and went to the police. He does want to do something for good, to cure, and his ambitions – fame, glory, even money – are so human against William's hubristic lust for unadulterated power. And he did come to your funeral and he did try to find out what was happening even if, initially, he did nothing with his findings. So I choose to believe that Professor Rosen is, at his core, a good man as much as he is a vainglorious one. I choose to think the best of him.

So maybe one of these two men have set in motion the wheels that have led to William's arrest and my rescue. And if I strain hard enough can I hear a siren on the very edge of the night's stillness?

I hear the trees' leafy whispers and timber groans, and know that there are no sirens for me.

But I will allow myself a final daydream and hope. That Kasia isn't in labour after all. Instead, she returned home as usual for her English lesson, pages of optimistic vocabulary learned and ready to tell me. William doesn't know that she's living with me now; nor that after you died, my conversion to being thoughtful was done *absolutely properly*. So when I wasn't there and she couldn't reach me on my mobile or pager she knew something was very wrong. My castle in the sky looks selfish, but I have to tell her that her baby needs help to breathe. So I imagine that she went to the police and demanded that they search for me. She stood up for me once before, even though she knew she'd be hit for it, so she'd square up to DI Haines.

My pager goes again and my fantasy splinters into razor-edged shards.

I can hear birds. For a moment I think it must be the dawn chorus and morning already. But it's still dark so the birds must have got it wrong. Or more probably I'm imagining them, some drug-induced kind of bird tinnitus. I remember the sequence Amias told me: blackbirds–robins–wrens–tawny owls–chaffinches–warblers then song thrushes. I remember you telling me about urban birds losing their ability to sing to each other and linking that to me and Todd, and I hope that I put that in my letter to you. Did I tell you I researched more about birdsong? I found out that when a bird sings it doesn't matter if it's dark or there's thick vegetation because birdsong can penetrate through or around objects and even over great distances can always be heard.

I know I can never fly like you, Tess. The first time I tried it, or thought I was, I have ended up here, tied up, lying on a concrete floor. So if that was flying, I crash-landed pretty spectacularly. But, astonishingly, I'm not broken. I'm not destroyed. Terrified witless, shaking, retching with fear, yes. But no longer insecure. Because during my search for how you died I somehow found myself to be a different person. And if by a miracle I was freed and my fantasy played out, with William arrested and Kasia and her baby on a coach to Poland with me next to them, then that mountain I've been clinging on to would tilt right over until it was lying flat on the ground and I wouldn't need footholds and safety ropes because I'd be walking, running, dancing even. Living my life. And it wouldn't be my grief for you that toppled the mountain, but love.

I think I can hear my name being called, high and light, a girl's voice. I must be imagining it, an auditory hallucination born of thinking about you.

Did you know that there's a dawn chorus far out in space? It's made by high-energy electrons getting caught in the Earth's radiation belts then falling to Earth as radio waves that sound like birds singing. Do you think that is what seventeenth-century poets heard and called the music of the spheres? Can you hear it now where you are?

I can hear my name again, on the periphery of the bird-song, barely audibly legible.

I think the darkness is turning to dark grey.

The birds are still singing, more clearly now.

I hear men's voices, a group of them, shouting out my name. I think they must be imagined too. But if they aren't, then I must call back to them. But the gag is still tight around my mouth, and even if it wasn't my mouth is incapable of making a sound. To start with I tried to spit out any saliva, fearful that sedative would have dissolved in it, but then my mouth became salt dry and in my imagination Mr Wright's secretary brought me endless cups of water.

'Beata!'

Her voice is clear amongst the men's as she screams out my name. Kasia. Unmistakable and real. She isn't having her baby. William isn't with her. I want to laugh out loud with relief. Unable to laugh through the gag I feel tears, warm on my cold cheeks.

William must have been right when he said the police think me capable of suicide and so would have taken Kasia reporting me missing seriously. Maybe, as he also predicted, they guessed that this would be the place I'd choose. Or was it just the two words '*odcisk palca*' that I texted to Kasia, which brought them all here?

I can just make out a stain on the concrete. It really is getting lighter. It must be dawn.

'Beata!' Her voice is much closer now.

The pager sounds again. I don't need to call back, because I realise it's become a homing beacon and they'll follow the sound to me. So Kasia has been paging me all through the night, not because she needed me with her while she had her baby, but because she's been worried about me. It is the final fragment of the mirror. Because all this time it's really been her looking after me, hasn't it? She came to the flat that night because she needed shelter, but she stayed because I was grieving and lonely and needy. It was her arms, with red welts on them, that comforted me that night – the first night I'd slept properly since you'd died. And when she made me dance when I didn't want to and smile when I didn't want to, she was forcing me to feel, for a little while, something other than grief and rage.

And the same is true of you. The smell of lemons alone should have been enough to remind me that you look after me too. I held your hand at Leo's funeral, but you held mine tightly back. And it's you who's got me through the night, Tess, thinking about you and talking to you; you who helped me to breathe.

I can hear a siren, wailing in the distance and getting closer. You're right, it is the sound of a civilised society taking care of its citizens.

As I wait to be rescued I know that I am bereaved but not diminished by your death. Because you are my sister in every fibre of my being. And that fibre is visible – two strands of DNA twisted in a double helix in every cell of my body – proving, visibly, that we are sisters. But there are other strands that link us, that wouldn't be seen by even the strongest of electron microscopes. I think of how we are connected by Leo dying and Dad leaving and lost home-work five minutes after we should have left for school; by holidays to Skye and Christmas rituals (ten past five you're allowed to open one present at the top of your stocking, ten to five you're allowed to feel but before that only looking and before midnight not even peeking). We are conjoined by hundreds of thousands of memories that silt down into you and stop being memories and become a part of what you are. And inside me is the girl with caramel hair flying along on a bicycle, burying her rabbit, painting canvasses with explosions of colour and loving her friends and phoning me at awkward times and teasing me and fulfilling completely the sacrament of the present moment and showing me the joy in life and because you are my sister all those things are part of me too and I would do anything for it to be two months ago and for it to be me out there shouting your name, Tess.

It must have been so much colder for you. Did the snow muffle the sound of the trees? Was it freezing and silent? Did my coat help keep you warm? I hope that as you died you felt me loving you.

There are footsteps outside and the door is opening.

It's taken hours of dark terror and countless thousand words, but in the end it reduces down to so little.

I'm sorry.

I love you.

I always will.

Bee

Acknowledgements

I'm not sure if anyone reads the acknowledgements, but I hope so because without the following people, this novel would never have been written or published.

Firstly, I want to thank my editor, the wonderful Emma Beswetherick, for her creativity, support and for not only having the courage of her convictions but inspiring other people to share them. I have been equally fortunate to have a dream agent, Felicity Blunt at Curtis Brown – creative, intelligent and takes the phone calls!

I would also like to thank Kate Cooper and Nick Marston also at Curtis Brown and the rest of the team at Piatkus and Little, Brown.

I want to thank, hugely, Michele Matthews, Kelly Martin, Sandra Leonard, Trixie Rawlinson, Alison Clements, Amanda Jobbins and Livia Giuggioli, who helped in so many practical ways.

Thank you Cosmo and Joe for understanding when I needed to write and for being proud.

Lastly, but most of all, my thanks go to my younger sister Tora Orde-Powlett – the inspiration for the book and a continued blessing.

Sister
Reading Guide

READING GROUP
DISCUSSION POINTS

* How would you compare and contrast Beatrice and Tess?

* Do you think that Beatrice changes throughout the course of the story and, if so, how?

* What are your thoughts on the structure of *Sister* and how do you think the different tenses and narrative techniques add to the overall effect of the story?

* In what ways does *Sister* explore fundamental human relationships? For example: the relationship between two sisters, a mother and a daughter, two lovers, doctor and patient etc.

* What is the central theme of the book and how did it resonate with you?

* Who is your favourite/least favourite character and how true did each of them feel?

* Did you agree with Beatrice in her determination to discover the truth, despite it driving those she loved away from her?

* There is much imagery in this story, such as the colour yellow, the sea etc. Can you explain why imagery is so important in the story and how effective it is?

* There are a number of significant male characters in this story. In what ways did each of them aid or abet Beatrice and how suspicious of each of them were you?

* The ending of the story throws up a shocking twist. Did the ending work for you? How else do you feel the story could have ended?

AUTHOR EXTENDED BIOGRAPHY

Rosamund Lupton read English Literature at Cambridge University. After a variety of jobs in London, including copywriting and reviewing for the *Literary Review*, she was a winner of Carlton Television's new writers' competition and was selected by the BBC for a place on their new writers' course. She was also invited to join the Royal Court Theatre's writers group. She was a script writer for television and film, writing original screenplays, until her two children were born. She is now a full-time novelist with a second book to be published in 2011.

AUTHOR Q&A

Q. Have you always wanted to be a writer?

Yes, ever since I can remember. As a child, my best friend's mother was Anthea Joseph (Hastings), a renowned publisher and a lovely woman, who inspired me at six to want to be 'an author' and made it seem achievable. I am sad that I can't thank her for that now.

Q. What is your writing day?

I began writing *Sister* after my youngest child started at school full time. I drop my two boys at school then race back to the house and write as much as I can by three o'clock. I'm lucky that my children ask 'how many words today, Mum?' rather than 'what's for supper?', as writing has led to domestic chaos. During the holidays family and friends rally round and I write in the evenings, sometimes into the night.

Q. What does it feel like to have your debut novel in print?

Astonishing. I walked around on cloud ten for quite a while. It's also a relief. So much work goes into writing a novel – this book took years off and on – and I was anxious that it might all have been in vain. I also find it, unexpectedly, a little daunting – the book is a one-way window, with readers able to see how I think and feel, but not the other way around!

That said, it is a privilege and a joy to know that people will read my story.

Q. What advice would you give to aspiring novelists?

Go for it! And if you meet rejection, keep on going for it. I could have wallpapered a small room with rejection letters before I 'broke into' script writing, so I was prepared for that with my novel. There seems to be quite an industry in telling writers how fruitless their endeavours are bound to be. I think you have to know what's important to you about your book, but also take on the chin what has to be re-written, however drastically, as long as it doesn't compromise your vision of your book. There's no doubt that luck is involved – mine was meeting Emma Beswetherick, my editor, early in the submission process.

Q. Where do your characters come from and how do they evolve?

In *Sister* I began with a central relationship, rather than the characters themselves – clearly in this book the central relationship is between sisters. I then find a small detail, or turn of phrase, that suddenly lights up a character for me. With Beatrice it was her obsessively neat and anxious pictures that she did as a child. Although she is not based on anyone I know, and is completely imagined, I couldn't have written her relationship with Tess without being close to my own younger sister. The emotional truth is one that I know well. The minor characters start as simply puppets of the plot but after a while they snip the strings and acquire a life of their own; just as Beatrice and Tess became more than vehicles to show a relationship. At some point the characters take over and that is when writing becomes a magical thing for me. Before the last draft, I changed the central characters' names and then read it again, as if meeting them for the first time to see if they seemed real.

Q. Did *Sister* throw up any surprises for you?

Yes, many. In the story itself I was surprised by how the characters developed, often changing a great deal from my original character sketches. For example, Kasia had a very small role initially, but seemed to demand more story time and to contribute in unforeseen ways. Other surprises were simply logistical. I hadn't appreciated how LONG a novel is, compared to the scripts I'd been used to writing, and how hard that middle section of a thriller can be. At one time I felt like a chess player needing to think twelve moves ahead and wondering if my brain was up to it! The ultimate surprise was how hugely satisfying it is to finish a hundred thousand words and have that bulk of paper sitting on my desk.

Q. A lot of medical research must have gone into writing *Sister*? How did you go about your research and was it difficult?

I read all I could on genetics – text books, newspaper articles, and the internet. The plot is entirely fictional, but I wanted it to be credible. I would take a documented case, for example the real story of a teenager dying because of a virus vector and the creation of a new micro-chromosome, and marry them together for a fictional genetics story. Fortunately, in terms of how hospitals and doctors work, my husband is a consultant obstetrician, so that was extremely easy!

Q. Your debut novel deals with some very dark and emotional issues. How did you go about handling such touching subjects?

I went with the characters and story, rather than consciously dealing with issues. I was wary of being prurient or voyeuristic, so closed the door early on a scene rather than dwell too long, trusting the reader to extrapolate for themselves. I didn't want this book to be dark but hopefully, finally, a celebration of sisterly love.

Q. In part this is a novel about the bonds that bind two sisters, but you also blend in elements of crime and thriller. How did this come about?

I tried to make the elements of crime and thriller reveal more about the two sisters and their relationship. For example, Tess going missing is the start of a crime story, but as Beatrice flies in to the rescue it also dramatically shows her protectiveness towards her younger sister. Her subsequent determination to find out what really happened to Tess sets the pace

369

for the thriller/crime story but also continually demonstrates the strength of their relationship. There are also subtler interactions. For example, the police reconstruction early in the book, when Beatrice plays the part of Tess, is part of the crime plot but also foreshadows Beatrice's gradual transformation throughout the rest of the novel into someone more like her sister.

Using genetics for the thriller part of the novel seemed apt as I wanted to explore what it means to be sisters – although at the end I discount the idea that their love for each other is based on shared genetics.

Q. There is a huge twist at the end of this story. Can you explain why you chose to end *Sister* the way you did?

I wanted to create a moment when a backward light is shone on Beatrice throughout the story, so that we understand her in a deeper way. For me, the fiction she has created for herself reveals more about her than any amount of character description. I also wanted the twist to help the reader empathise dramatically with her vulnerability. One of the most interesting aspects of the story to me is how would you spend the night you thought you were going to die, all alone? I find her need for human comfort and promised justice as she faced death human and moving.

Q. Is Beatrice really rescued at the end, or is it another fiction she's imagined?

That is up to each reader to decide. But for me, she is saved.

Q. What are you writing next?

Again I have chosen to write about a relationship, this time about a mother and her children. It begins with a school on fire, but is a detective story/thriller so I can't tell you too much yet . . .

ROSAMUND LUPTON'S
TOP-TEN READS

1. *Life of Pi* – Yann Martel
I think a part of me is still on that lifeboat with that tiger. And the twist at the end makes what went before even more beautiful.

2. *My Secret History* – Donna Tartt
A stunning book that made me realise what crime writing could become.

3 & 4. *Patchwork Planet* and *Breathing lessons* – Anne Tyler
If I could choose one writer to emulate it would be Anne Tyler, whose characters become so rounded that it seems you know them.

5. *Song of Myself* – Walt Whitman
Strange exciting poetry that is ever-inspiring.

6. *Behind the Scenes at the Museum* – Kate Atkinson
I love the zest, wit and originality of Kate Atkinson's books and in this one especially.

7. *Perfume* – Patrick Suskind
Proof that words can do anything!

8. *The Baby Who Wouldn't Go to Bed* – Helen Cooper
The perfect read for over-active toddlers and frazzled

mothers at the end of the day and now instantly evokes that time for me.

9. The Millennium Trilogy – Stieg Larsson
A great holiday read on the beach and issues to mull over during dinner later.

10. *War and Peace* – Tolstoy
The only book I've ever read where I am jealous of people who are yet to read it, that they have that experience in front of them still.

A sneak preview of Rosamund Lupton's new novel

Afterwards

Coming soon from Piatkus

I check my watch, it's almost three.

Still no sign of either Jenny or Adam.

The PE teacher blows his whistle for the last race – the relay – bellowing through his loud speaker for teams to get in position.

I look back towards the school – surely I'll see them coming towards me any moment.

Smoke is coming from the school building. Thick black smoke like a bonfire.

For a moment I am calm. A juggernaut of panic a little distance away, but getting closer.

It hits me in the chest, full on.

There is a fire and they are in there.

They are in there.

And I'm running at the velocity of a scream. Running so hard that I don't have time to breathe.

A running scream that can't stop until I hold them both.

Darting across the road, I hear sirens blaring on the bridge. But the fire engines aren't moving. There are abandoned cars by the traffic lights on the bridge blocking their path; and women are getting out of other cars, just left in the middle of the road, and are running across the bridge towards the school. But all the mothers are at the sports day. What are these women doing, kicking off their high-wedged shoes and tripping over flip-flops and screaming, as they run, like me? I recognise one, the mother of a reception child. They're the mothers of the four-year-olds coming to do their usual pick up. One has left a toddler in her abandoned SUV and the toddler is hitting the window, as he watches his mother in this ghastly mother's race.

And then I'm there first, before the other mothers because they still have to cross the road and run down the drive.

And the four-year-olds are lined up on the gravel with their teacher, a neat little crocodile; and Maisie is with the teacher, with her arm around her, and I see how shaken the teacher looked. Behind them black smoke pours out of the school like a factory chimney stack, staining the summer-blue sky.

And Adam is outside – *outside!*

I allow myself a second, maybe two, to feel gut-wrenching relief for Adam and then I look for Jenny. Bobbed blonde hair, slender. No one like Jenny outside. From the bridge the sirens wail.

And the four-year-olds are starting to cry as they see their mothers, running full tilt towards them down the drive, tears streaming down their faces, arms outstretched, waiting for that moment to hold their child.

I turn towards the burning building, black smoke billowing out of the class rooms on the second and third floors.

Jenny.